Iron Gods

www.penguin.co.uk

Also by Andrew Bannister

Creation Machine

For more information on Andrew Bannister and his books,
see his website at andrewbannister.com

Iron Gods

A Novel of the Spin

Andrew Bannister

BANTAM PRESS

LONDON · NEW YORK · TORONTO · SYDNEY · AUCKLAND

TRANSWORLD PUBLISHERS
61–63 Uxbridge Road, London W5 5SA
www.penguin.co.uk

Transworld is part of the Penguin Random House group of companies
whose addresses can be found at global.penguinrandomhouse.com

Penguin
Random House
UK

First published in Great Britain in 2017 by Bantam Press
an imprint of Transworld Publishers

A CIP catalogue record for this book
is available from the British Library.

ISBNs 9780593076507 (hb)
9780593076514 (tpb)

Typeset in 11.5/14.5 pt Sabon by Jouve (UK), Milton Keynes
Printed and bound in Great Britain by Clays Ltd, Bungay, Suffolk

Penguin Random House is committed to a sustainable
future for our business, our readers and our planet. This book
is made from Forest Stewardship Council® certified paper.

MIX
Paper from
responsible sources
FSC® C018179

1 3 5 7 9 10 8 6 4 2

Dedicated to Thomas and Felix, whose uncritical faith was
leavened with the occasional timely deflating comment

The Spin

Eighty-eight planets and twenty-one suns; all artificial down to the last particle.

More than ten thousand years before, there had been a pact. It had begun what people then called the Stable Age and it was still holding, even though everyone had forgotten about it.

Almost everyone. A few people still remembered – but they had forgotten what it was they were remembering.

But we remembered.

Three Quarter Circle Harbour

When Belbis had first made the Long Walk he had been eleven years old. It had taken him almost three greater moons, and for the first twenty days his legs had trembled and ached from rise to set. Seven years later he was far stronger. It should take him little more than a greater moon – but he would still be tired when he got there.

He walked steadily, using the terse economical stride that all his people were taught from their very first steps. Walking was important and it had to be done properly. When Belbis was younger he had taken this so seriously that he had driven his teachers to the edge of madness.

But then Belbis took everything very seriously. Otherwise, what was the point? Things were *there* to be taken seriously. How else should he take them? Most people seemed not to understand that, but Belbis didn't mind because he knew very well that he didn't understand most people. On that at least, he and his teachers had agreed. He had therefore taken the only obvious route in life, and everyone including him had been relieved. Besides, the Circle's last Painter had died the winter before, and the Predigers were sternly certain that there was only a limited period of grace allowed to find another, so Belbis the Odd had become Belbis the Painter quickly and smoothly.

He took on the grey robe of the Novice – the lowest rank of the Order, but the highest a Painter was allowed – almost with relief. Simple certainties suited Belbis.

The route of the Long Walk was not complex. By tradition it began at the furthest point out to sea of the longest dock at Circle Harbour. From there it plodded on to dry land, past the slipways with their vivid smells of tar and human waste, past the rope walks and oil stores, and past the flensing yards where the great, prized bull-fins were sliced apart with razor-edged spades, leaving the remains to flow back down the glistening gut-ramps and into the back harbour where lesser creatures waited, their mouths open. The lesser creatures were themselves the prey of creatures in some ways even lower, as far as society was concerned: the starving, the ill and the old, who waited above them with clubs and sticks, watching for a chance. When you were too old or too ill to fish, Circle Harbour had no use for you, and no food either.

Belbis didn't like strong smells. He hastened through the first part of the Walk with his eyes fixed on the ground and his throat tensed, in case he should commit the blasphemy of retching.

After the flensing yards the route jinked round the Quay Sergeant's hut, with its own particular smells of fried food and tube smoke and stump brew, and became more agreeable. Or mostly more agreeable; Belbis didn't like the part when he passed the big dwellings at the upper end of Founders' Green. This was where the wealthy had their town-houses, great halls built with massive timbers resting on low walls of mortared schist. The wealthiest had roofs of schist, too, instead of thatch or turf, and the smoke from their chimneys smelled not of dried seaweed but of scented wood. Sweet-smelling or not, Belbis had observed the unsayable fact that the wealthier the family, the more agnostic they became. Never overtly atheist, of course, that would have been suicidal, but even so Belbis never lost his astonishment at how much doubt one could entertain without actually being a formal unbeliever. Especially if one was rich.

His astonishment didn't protect him from the taunts and the occasional flung stone. He could ignore them. Such things had always been part of his life. He supposed they always would be. The Order was unpopular – he had been told that one of the main functions of a priesthood was to be resented, especially in times when the fishing was poor. Not that any of the Predigers ever went fishing.

After Founders' Green the Long Walk passed the great public park of Founders' Fields, kinking inwards as the park narrowed at the upper end to skirt the Ending Place, where a few people every week met their end on the edge of the Dispatcher's axe: criminals, certainly, and traitors, and also those who were possibly less doubting than the residents of the big houses of Founders' Green but also less rich.

The Dispatcher wore the darkest black robes, indicating seniority over all but the ten highest Klerikers. Belbis had heard townspeople whisper that black didn't show bloodstains, but that wasn't the real reason. The Dispatcher had people to deal with blood, on robes or elsewhere.

The channel from the Ending Place wound its way down the town, avoiding the wealthiest neighbourhoods, until it joined the gut-ramps near the harbour. Belbis had heard that things were added to the blood to keep it fluid. He didn't know for sure, but it seemed reasonable. These things could be done, as he knew very well from his own profession, and after all you wouldn't want the channels to block.

The Ending Place marked the outskirts of the town. After that the Walk wandered out through private estates and farmland until it had climbed off the coastal platforms that nurtured the town and the harbour and was heading for the mountains. Day by day the landscape drew in around him as broad valleys became narrow rocky slots, often with cold rivers hissing down them. Night by night he slept as he had been taught, sprawled under his cloak with his cheek resting on his arm and his eyes turned away from the stars. He would not see the stars until his journey was over. No Painter ever did.

Towards the end of the Walk he always became very hungry. Down on the plains there had been berries and a few larger fruits. By tradition the Painter could forage only within ten paces to either side of the Walk, and some of the older farming folk planted bushes within reach, and watched and nodded as the Painter took the food. But as he climbed away from the fertile lands the food thinned out and he had to rely on the baked ration from his little pack. It was not enough, but then it wasn't meant to be. The Painter should arrive at the Watch House with his eyes large and his blood thin, people said.

Belbis reached the Watch House on the evening of the third day before the full dark of the last greater moon of the year. It was an auspicious time. The skies were clear and black with frost and bright with stars.

The Watch House perched on the top of a narrow peak at the highest point in the Spine Range, so called because it crossed the continent in a shallow S-curve that looked like deformity. The House was wooden, a battered castle of a place wedged and propped off the top of the mountain on great rough trunks socketed into the grey rock. There was only one entrance, a swaying unguarded timber walkway that sprang off the end of a shelf of rock just big enough for a man to stand on, if he pressed himself back against the rock wall behind him.

The walkway – a spiritual challenge in itself – was twenty paces long. At its other end the three Housekeepers stood waiting, faint and grey in the starlight. They carried no lanterns; in deference to the needs of the Painter, the Watch House at night was kept in complete darkness, and so were its keepers. As Belbis came nearer he could see their empty eye sockets, blacker shadows in the grey. He had shuddered when he first saw them.

Painters were chosen young, but Keepers were selected at birth.

He bowed to the Housekeepers as he had done for the last seven years. With the enhanced senses of the lifelong sightless they somehow registered his bow – he always wondered how; air currents? The rustle of his robe? – and bowed in return. Then they stood aside and gestured him into the Watch House.

His feet knew the way. He walked up steps, and then up narrower steps, to the Painters' loft. The bench was empty except for the two shallow antimony bowls, as wide as the palm of his hand. The rest of the tools were his. He opened his pack, took out the leather roll and unrolled it on the bench between the bowls. The tools came into view one by one: the pens with their different-sized nibs, from thin to bulky. The brushes, and then the other tools. And the dressings.

He thought for a moment before selecting one of the glass shards. He took it between finger and thumb, lifted aside his robe to expose the top of his thigh, and made a quick slicing movement.

Blood welled in dark berry drops. He put the shard back on the leather, picked up a bowl and pressed its edge into his thigh just below the cut. A slow trickle collected in the bottom of the bowl.

Belbis waited until he had a pool two fingers across. Then he put the bowl on the table and pressed a dressing against his cut, shutting his eyes against the sting and counting to ten to give the astringent time to seal his flesh. Then he picked up a fine outline pen, dipped it in the bowl and poised it above the sheet of paper. Only then did he reach up with his other hand to pull the cord which opened the moon shutters.

For a moment he stared, wide eyed. Then he screamed.

For the first time in his life, for the first time in five hundred lives, the sky held the wrong number of Gods.

His scream brought the Housekeepers. At first he babbled

and pointed at the patch of sky between the moon shutters but they shook their heads and gestured at their empty sockets. So then he told them.

The old men conferred. Then, looking grim, they waved Belbis to follow them. They led him down flights and flights of stairs he had barely noticed to a part of the Watch House he had never visited before: a chamber that must have been carved out of the peak of the mountain itself because unlike everything else in the Watch House it was made not of wood but of stone, as dry and dusty as ancient death. In the middle of the chamber there was a single black waist-high pillar that looked like a cannon, mounted vertically with its blank mouth gaping upwards.

The oldest of the Housekeepers passed his hand over the mouth of the thing just once. Then he stood back.

For a moment nothing happened. Then Belbis jumped. A quiet voice had spoken out of nowhere. The accent was outlandish but the words were clear. 'Ignition active,' it said. 'Please vacate the area.'

Belbis looked at the Housekeepers. They had linked hands to form a circle round the pillar. 'The thing said to go,' he said. 'Where should we go?'

The oldest spoke, without turning his face towards Belbis. 'Go as far as you can.' Then he clamped his lips firmly closed.

Belbis turned and ran. He had reached the outer walkway when the light exploded soundlessly behind him.

Down on the plains, people looked up and wondered at the fierce green beam that pierced the sky.

Hive World High Orbit, Spin Inside

It was late and Seldyan's nose and mouth were dry with the abrasive dust which was everywhere in here. She huffed down her nose, feeling the warm breath escaping across her face through the perished seals of the filter mask.

Most nights that would have bothered her very much, but tonight she didn't care. She squinted through the haze; Hufsza was in front of her, his shoulders squirming in the confined space as he moved a vac nozzle over the surface of the duct. They were paired off. Of the others, Kot and Lyste were out of sight, working in their own duct. She could hear occasional scrapes and clangs as they cleaned. There was no sign of Merish, but that was a good thing. There wasn't supposed to be, yet.

They were inching their way through the sinistral whorl of the rear branch of the main carbon dioxide manifold. If it had been running, they would have been blown backwards out of it and into the billion cubic metres of the biggest single biomass plant in the Spin – a huge, enclosed forest in its own space-going cube. But not before they had been asphyxiated by all the growth-encouraging carbon dioxide.

Unfortunately the carbon dioxide didn't just encourage the biomass. It also nurtured a whole ecosystem of moulds and fungi, some of them unique to the micro environment. At least one of the moulds was actually parasitic on a combination of two others, and most of them seemed to give off spores that accumulated in sooty, gritty black clumps. They piled up in corners, built up into filter-clogging cakes, and broke apart into drifting clouds of unbelievably pervasive dust.

Cleaning was a horrible, regular, manual job, done by people with vacs and wire brushes and no rights and no choices.

It probably said 'Hive Technicians' on the order. They were duct monkeys to everyone else. Two teams of two people crawling along in the heat and the dust with their cramped limbs aching, and one banksman watching their backs from the entrance. Two people manually scratching the black stuff away with wire brushes and sucking it up with moaning vac nozzles, until their backs ached and their knees ached and the palms of their hands were raw – and who would be punished if they didn't meet a daily target.

She shook herself. Today was not about death, and she needed to concentrate. She resettled the mask on her face and peered through the dust past Hufsza. In the sameness of the ducts it was hard to gauge distance, but surely they were almost there? If they had missed the place there would be no more chances. Or if there had been a refit. Or if . . .

She reached out and tapped Hufsza's foot. He glanced over his shoulder, eyebrows raised. She nodded and gestured ahead.

A few metres in front of them, there was an extra seam in the metal surface. A metre further on was another.

Seldyan felt a grin scratching against the mask. It was still there.

A movement in front of her made her realize Hufsza had seen it too; he sat back on his heels, his head brushing the top of the duct, and switched off the vac.

It fell silent. Seldyan slapped the metal in front of her sharply, twice. The echoes clanged and fell away. She listened intently. On the edge of hearing came the sound of vacs winding down, and then, much louder, two slaps.

Everyone was in place. Or, rather, both teams of two were in place. She just had to hope Merish was too. She slapped the metal just once more, then shut her eyes and began counting silently. She got to five.

Boom.

It was a deep, soft sound that she felt through the metal of the duct almost before she heard it. As it faded, a perfect rectangular smoke-ring of dust rolled along the duct towards them. She nodded to herself. Merish was on the case.

There was an electrical-sounding buzz and a sharp smell of burning. The two seams glowed dull red, then quickly climbed the spectrum to a fierce yellow-white. Then the metre-long section of metalwork between the seams dropped out.

The unofficial, unnoticed exit was open.

Seldyan took a deep breath. 'Go,' she said. It was unnecessary; Hufsza had already shunted himself forward. He dropped through the gap and disappeared.

Seldyan shuffled to the edge of the gap. She had wondered if she would hesitate when she got to this part. She didn't; the worst she could expect by following Huf was a quick death. The best she could earn herself by staying put was a very slow one.

She shut her eyes and launched herself.

She dropped like a stone.

No one in the Hive ever talked openly about escape. But then, no one talked about survival either, and yet they all thought about that all the time, too.

'Hive' stood for 'high value'. Hivers took that as a bitter joke.

The Hive was the biggest forced-labour colony in the Spin. It was the economic well-spring of the Inside, a space-borne city state within a state. Its million or so inhabitants were hired out to do anything at all, for anyone at all. It was slavery, on a more-than-industrial scale, and Seldyan had never known anything else.

Her stomach yawned with the acceleration and her body yelled at her to open her eyes, to flail, to save herself. She managed to ignore it, curling instead into the tightest ball she could and keeping her eyes screwed shut. Right now the best and simplest thing she could do for herself was just to fall in a straight line.

The cube's internal monitoring, if any of it had survived Merish's attention, would now be showing four desperate escapees falling to certain death. A straight line was the only sure way to prove it wrong. If she glided off track by more than a hundred metres or so, she was jelly.

Well, fairly sure. Her terminal speed in the thick humid atmosphere of the cube shouldn't be too high, Merish had said, but it seemed high enough. She could feel herself tumbling, and a wind that behaved like a solid battered at her. The temptation to open her eyes was almost unbearable, but she had schooled herself to resist it.

Then something else struck at her, something that felt like being whipped with fog.

She shouted with relief. The line had been straight enough – she had hit the Feather Palms.

From their oily sap the Feather Palms provided almost half of the basic vegetable fat consumed by the Inside. Each tree was over a hundred metres tall. Their roots were shallow, and to compensate for this and to resist the high winds on their native planet they clumped together so tightly that their trunks came close to touching. Even here in this regimented environment they were planted in a hexagonal close-packed array just a metre apart. Thankfully no one had yet managed to engineer out their soft, dense, wastefully deep canopies.

At her speed soft was a matter of opinion, but deep was undeniable. Even curled up, Seldyan slowed in a series of wrenching jolts that felt as if every joint had been dislocated. Any extended limbs would certainly have been torn off. But she slowed, and eventually she felt she had lost speed enough to open her eyes and take control.

Branches were thrashing past her; she grabbed at one and lost her grip and some skin, but it had trimmed her speed to stoppable. The next one she held on to, breathing hard. Her hand hurt and her nose was full of the sickly oily smell of the palm, and she could feel her grin trying to split her face.

She waited until her breathing had got halfway back to normal. Then she hand-over-handed her way down through the remainder of the canopy until she could angle down a single branch to the main trunk. The trunk was smooth, and slender enough at this height for her to close her arms around it. She slid down for thirty metres or so until it became too thick for her to span, then took stock. The palms really were close together; if she stretched out a leg like *this* she could get a foothold on a neighbouring trunk. She turned her back to her own tree, braced herself against it and shunted herself down, ignoring the pain in her back.

She almost made it to ground level before her foot slipped on an oily patch.

'Shit!' The yelp was out before she could stop it. She hit a lot of roots with the small of her back. It knocked the breath out of her, and she lay there panting for a moment. Then, as the spasms in her diaphragm quieted, she rolled over into a crouch, looked around through the dim light – and saw nothing at all except trees, and heard nothing except a thick woody silence.

She didn't dare try to stand. The forest floor wasn't really a floor. The palms relied on sprawling above-ground root spreads for what little stability they had, and their vast thirst shrank the soil so that ground level became a knotted rooty obstacle course littered with loose fallen branches that were even more treacherous than the roots. The next part of the plan really had to work. Otherwise, a few years hence, she was going to be found on this exact spot, stone dead and smelling of tree oil.

She cast about carefully in the branch brash and selected a

strong-looking limb about half her own height, picked it up, hefted it and then took the hardest swing she could manage at the trunk of the tree she had shinned down.

Electronic communication was out down here, for the same reason it was out up in duct-world, but hitting things was fine.

The tree rang like a musical instrument.

She listened as the sound faded away. She didn't have to wait long; almost immediately there were three answering sounds. She nodded. All safe.

The next part was down to Merish. As had been the last, but Seldyan didn't feel guilty about that; she and the other three had a major job to do later. If they got as far as later.

Besides, she knew herself well enough, feeling guilty wasn't her strong suit.

She did her best to sit down on a root. It wasn't easy, but in the end she managed a kind of perch, if she braced one foot against another root. It was miserably uncomfortable, but she didn't care. Even uncomfortable could feel good, if it was a step away from the Hive.

I'm never going back, she thought. The word felt like a chant. *Ne-ver, ne-ver, ne-ver.*

A few minutes later she looked up. The woody silence had stopped being a silence – she could hear a regular knocking, about twice the speed of a heartbeat. She looked around quickly, and then nodded to herself. A few trunks away two big parallel roots formed a bridge she could just about stand on.

Beneath them was a void big enough to curl up in. That would do. She hoped the noise was Merish, but it might not be. Hiding could be good, if it was someone else.

She teetered on to the bridge, leaned against a trunk and peered cautiously round it towards where she thought the sound was coming from. When she saw it she wanted to laugh, partly out of relief that it was Merish rather than someone else, but mainly because it just looked – funny.

He was standing up, but she wasn't sure how. He was on a platform which looked as if it was using the tree trunks like vertical monkey bars. It was grasping its way from one trunk to the next, about a metre above the rootscape, using things that looked like tree-sized lock-grip pliers. Somehow it managed to stay more or less horizontal, but some side-to-side wobble was inevitable. There was a T-shaped handle at waist height, and Merish looked as if he was having to hang on to it quite hard.

She leaned out and waved. He nodded and did something to a control on the handle. The platform slowed, coming to a stop a couple of trunks away.

She grinned at him, and then saw his expression and stopped grinning. 'Okay,' she said. 'Tell me. No clear run, right?'

He nodded. 'Definitely no clear run. There's an extra shift on, fuck knows why.'

She felt herself tensing. 'A *whole* extra shift? Ten bodies?'

'Yes. I'm sorry, Sel.'

'Why? You didn't invite them. I'd like to know who did.' She stared into the distance for a moment, calculating. 'Are the main shift sorted?'

He nodded. 'Sure. Confined in a half-exploded control room by an inexplicable series of systems failures. That bit worked okay. But there's enough of the extra shift to cover the ways out.'

'Are there any inside the Planter?'

'I don't know. There could be.'

'We'd better assume there are then. Let's get the others. We might need to think of another definition of exit.' She gave the platform a jaundiced look. 'You're fine on that thing, for a given value of fine, but it's only big enough to torture one at a time. What about the rest of us?'

His eyes flickered and he pointed over his shoulder.

She followed the gesture. 'Oh . . .'

There was a line of four platforms behind him.

He looked embarrassed. 'They were all I could manage. They're slaved to this one. When they're not hugging trees they just float. It's pretty comfortable.'

She nodded. 'You know, Merish, comfortable doesn't really bother me? Freedom, now that I care about, and you've done your job.' She squared her shoulders. 'Let's go and find the team. It's our turn now.'

He looked away for a moment, and she saw his lips twitching.

Ten minutes later they had picked up the others and formed a wobbly line of five with Merish in the lead. Seldyan was feeling sick, partly from the uneasy jolting of the platform and partly from the pervasive smell of oil from the Feather Palms, but she still didn't care. They were closing on the edge of the plantation and another step towards freedom, even if there were extra obstacles; reaching the edge also meant that they would soon be floating, not gripping. That was good under any circumstances, even these.

They had talked quickly about those circumstances once the five of them were together. They had a plan. It would have to do, because none of them could think of anything cleverer.

As they reached the edge of the stand of Feather Palms they split up. No one said anything.

The Planter was divided into strips a hundred metres wide. Every second one was palms; the others were mainly low-growing succulents that acted as combined moisture moderators and firebreaks. Seldyan turned her platform down the strip and gunned it so that it tilted forward and built up speed until the wind rush scoured her eyes and tried to tear her hands from the T-bar. She hugged the margin of the palms just in case it might shelter her from anyone who might be looking, but someone was bound to see her soon. Speed was the thing.

The end of the strip was rushing towards her. She held her speed as long as she dared, then reared the platform steeply backwards at the last second, threw it round a right angle that made her inner ears dance and into the narrow space between the end of the strips and the inner curtain wall of the Planter. She held on to the turn by a miracle, then leaned forward and twisted the grip to full power. There wasn't much room; her speed built up an air dam in front of her which racketed into the end of the palm stand and bounced off the trunks with a staccato whistle that hammered at her eardrums. Then she was past the palms and hissing through the open air at the end of another low strip.

She covered the kilometre to the far corner of the Planter in just over twenty seconds, and hauled the platform to a halt. Her face felt abraded, her arms ached and her ears were ringing, and it wasn't over yet.

She had had the furthest to go. Everyone else should be in place, but she didn't have any way of checking because they were too far apart to communicate by hitting trees, so she would just have to assume.

That meant the time was now. She powered down the platform and it sank to the ground. Inert, it was surprisingly light. She flipped it over without much effort, examined it for a second and then ran a finger over a rectangular seam on the smooth base. The seam popped open, revealing two greyish squares covered with ominous-looking symbols in a language she couldn't read. No user-serviceable parts inside, she thought.

'Platforms have two cell packs,' Merish had said, 'but they can get by for a while on one.'

She had looked at him for a moment, and then asked, 'Long enough?'

There had been the slightest pause before he nodded. She didn't think anyone else had noticed.

Now she reached into the space and pulled at one of the squares. It turned out to be the square end of a cube about two hands across. As it came free there was a faint crackle. She turned it over; there was a recessed contact array hedged about with even more ominous symbols.

The wire brush she had used to scrub the surface of the duct was still hanging at her belt. She unhooked it. Then she replaced the cover and righted the platform, took the cell pack and walked towards the edge of the palm stand. Ten paces into the trees she stopped and put the cell pack down, contacts upwards. She took the wire brush and held it out, bristles downwards. She gulped, dropped it straight down towards the contacts, and was running by the time it landed.

Even with her back turned the arc was bright. There was an angry buzz, and then a wet-sounding explosion. By that point she was at the platform. She jumped on, gripped the bar and leaned the thing as far forward as she dared.

The acceleration almost tore her arms off. She allowed herself just one glance to the side – the first few palms in the stand were already on fire, set off by the electro-chemical inferno at their bases.

The whole stand of oily trees would burn. She just had to hope that the fire-front would be fast enough.

But not too fast. She tried to force the grip further, but it was at maximum. She didn't know what the top speed of the platform was, or how long it could keep it up on only one cell pack, or if the whole mad scheme would work, or anything.

She still felt like whooping.

Then something screeched and slammed behind her, and a wall of sub-sonic noise shook the platform.

She risked a glance over her shoulder. The first firebreak had dropped. Now the first hundred flaming metres of the Planter were isolated by a thousand tonnes of mineral-fibre curtain wall. It was the next-to-last defence of the Planter, designed to isolate just about any problem.

Except for five improvised incendiary bombs all at once. She glanced again – the trees in front of the firebreak were smouldering.

As she looked, flames leapt. She faced forward and gritted her teeth. Even this far ahead of the fire the air smelled of burning oil.

Slam. That was the second wall. Eight to go. She didn't look this time; she had felt herself slowing the last time she had turned. Speed was everything. The burning smell was getting stronger.

Slam. The concussion seemed stronger too. She was losing ground. Seven to go. She could feel radiated heat on the back of her head.

Slam. It was getting harder to breathe. By now there should have been an air-wash blowing back across the Planter, driving the fire into itself, but instead the air was full of billowing oily smoke.

She remembered. They had broken the ducts. The air-wash couldn't help, either by clearing the smoke or slowing the fire-front. She wanted to thump the controls, but she didn't dare.

Slam. She blinked. That one had seemed quieter. For a moment she thought she must be gaining, but that couldn't be right; the heat and the smoke were even stronger. Then she realized. It wasn't that the firebreak had been quieter – everything else was louder. There was a thrumming roar. Now she risked another look over her shoulder, and immediately wished she hadn't.

Where there should have been trees, there was boiling black smoke shot through with expanding bubbles of fire. It was far too close, and it was getting closer.

It wasn't going to work after all. Then she corrected herself: it wasn't going to work for her. She hoped the others were ahead of her. It was supposed to be impossible for Hivers to break out; four impossibles out of a possible five would be pretty good going.

Besides, she wasn't done yet. She leaned forward as far as possible, drew her elbows into her body to streamline herself and twisted the control so hard she thought it would break, thinking that if this was what freedom felt like – then it felt good.

Better than good. Better than anything she had ever experienced.

And then she felt the platform slowing down.

She actually laughed. When she saw Merish she would tell him that 'long enough' was not long enough, after all. Except that now it looked like she wouldn't be seeing Merish again.

The platform dropped to the ground and she threw herself off it and into a dead run. She had no idea how far she was ahead of the fire-front, or how far behind the last firebreak and when it would drop. All she knew was running, and trying to breathe air that was no longer proper air but smoke and soot and heat that rasped her throat and fouled her lungs. Her heart hammered and her vision began to fade.

The screech and slam of the last firebreak were dead over-head. Her legs gave way; she dropped and rolled awkwardly, hoping it was still forward.

She came to a stop and for a second there was nothing. Then she heard the fire and knew that it was all over.

Then she felt arms on her, uncurling her.

'Seldyan! You okay?'

She opened her eyes. It was Merish. At first she wanted to throw her arms round him and she tried to raise herself. Then she realized, and fell back. If he was here they must both have failed. She corrected herself – she had failed both of them.

'Seldyan! Shit, will you snap out of it? You need to be ready.'

She shook her head. 'Ready for what?'

'What do you think? You still got your vac tab?'

It was hard to think, and besides, he was talking nonsense. She humoured him, patting the upper pocket of her coverall. 'Yep, still there. So what?'

'Then fucking *take* it!'

She opened her eyes properly and stared at him. 'Seriously?'

'Of course seriously! Take it *now*!'

Still staring at him, she fumbled the little pill out of her pocket. It was standard issue for anyone who went space-side, even Hivers. Boiling away into a vacuum, if you were exposed to it, wasn't good. The vac tab bought you minutes.

Her brain came back to life. If she was taking a tab then that must mean . . .

She took it, and looked at Merish. 'How long?'

He shrugged. 'Should be ten seconds.'

'Right. We'd better hold on, then.' She rolled over, extended her hands and drove her stiffened fingers into the soil between the succulents. For a frantic moment she found nothing. Then her fingers met something and curled around it. It was the geo-textile mesh that held the soil together. It should be strong enough.

She saw Merish lying down next to her, his hands pushing down as hers had. Then she heard it – louder than the crash of the firewalls, louder than the roar of the burning trees, it was a sound that had meant frozen boiling death to ten thousand generations of space-faring animals.

It was the howl of air racing out of something very fast.

Seldyan looked up and felt her eyes widen. The vaulted roof was splitting into segments like the skin of a fruit. If she had needed confirmation, here it was; they had made it to the last cell after all, and now the Planter had activated its ultimate defence. When the fire can't be contained, sod the biomass – save the structure. The whole thing was opening itself to vacuum.

She held on.

A hurricane gripped her. Shrieking winds hauled her body off the ground. A vortex of plants, burning tree fragments and even the soil itself was flicking up towards the void. The force on her arms was massive – but manageable.

Then she saw one of Merish's hands grasp at the soil, and

flail, and fly loose. The other, still buried, was shaking. As she watched, the hooked fingers began to uncurl.

Her muscles made the decision before her brain could intervene. She undid the fingers of her right hand, yanked it out of the soil and flung it out and back just as Merish yelped and lost his grip completely.

She caught his shoulder then lost it, his upper arm then lost it, and finally felt his hand close on hers. She gripped back as hard as she could, and gritted her teeth as his mass tried to tear her in half. Her shoulders were close to dislocating and her fingers screamed at her.

She ignored them. *It's just pain*, she told herself. *This time it's pain you're choosing. Take it.*

She took it.

They were buffeted by a storm of shattered timber and smouldering leaves, and she shut her eyes and got ready to be battered to death. Then, at last, the pull lessened and she opened her eyes.

A cloud of ice crystals fogged the view, forming a swirling vortex that followed the clashing debris out through the open roof. When it had gone, so had the last of the air. Without the vac tab she would have had about twenty seconds; with it, maybe three minutes. It was enough, if the hurried plan they had made in the plantation worked out.

As the wind had died the Planter's grav had reasserted itself. They dropped to the ground fairly gently with Merish on top in the total silence of a vacuum. He let go of her hand and rolled off, and she gingerly uncurled her buried fingers from the mesh.

Letting go managed to hurt even more than holding on. She squeezed her hand shut, and fascinatedly watched a drop of blood boil away into the vacuum.

She shook herself. Merish was gesturing towards the end wall and she saw his platform, somehow still sitting obediently on the ground. There were several questions she had no time to

ask him, and no breath either; they ran. Merish hauled the platform upright, jumped on and gestured to Seldyan. She climbed
on behind and locked her arms round his waist.

Even with two aboard the platform was very, very fast in a
vacuum. They were at the end wall in twenty seconds – Merish's
remaining power cell had obviously taken far less of a hammering than hers – and standing in front of an oddly old-fashioned-
looking gas-tight door with a control wheel in its middle. She
looked at it and mouthed, 'Fully manual?'

He nodded. They gripped the rim of the wheel and turned. It
resisted, gave and rotated through a whole turn before taking up
the load. Another full turn and it stopped with a sound that Seldyan
felt as *clang* even if she couldn't hear it, and the door swung open.

They bundled past it into the airlock. The door shut behind
them, and there was the ice-crystal kiss of air freezing as it
expanded into a vacuum.

There was an indicator patch on the wall. Seldyan watched
it, feeling her heart beginning to pump against her ribs. She was
fighting the urge to try to breathe, as while the patch was red
breathing would be a bad idea: even the vac tab couldn't stave
off the effects of thin cold air on starved lung tissue. She had to
wait until the lock thought its own atmosphere was warm
enough and thick enough.

Green. There. It was okay to breathe.

It still hurt though. The chill rasped at nerves she had never
noticed before. She rode it out and then looked at Merish.

'Thanks.'

He nodded, reaching out to take her hand. She winced, but
let him turn it over and gently uncurl her fist. It was filthy with
soil, but the deep cuts at the bases of her fingers had stained it a
glistening purple.

He looked sharply at her. 'Oh, shit . . .'

She shrugged. 'It was that or let go. There'll be meds in the
shuttle. I assume the shuttle *is* our next stop?'

'Yes. The other three should be in the next lock along. Sorry, Seldyan.'

'Don't be.' She grinned, and it felt good. 'Because you know what we're going to do next? With your help, technical maestro, we're going to borrow a shitload of money.'

He smiled slowly. 'I can do that,' he said.

Hive, Juvenile Unit

Seldyan's childhood had seemed normal as far as she could remember. The Hive had been – everything. She remembered food and sleep, and adults that were tall and remote and occasionally forbidding and mostly irrelevant.

But then, she supposed, most childhoods probably did seem normal until something arose to challenge the seeming. Her challenge had come late. It hadn't been when she was four, when she had been taken out of class one day and hurried to a room she had never seen before, and she had been told to take off her shift and curl over, and something sharp had pressed against her back near the top of her bottom and then it had hurt so horribly, and she had howled until her throat hurt as much as her back but she couldn't move because they were holding her.

They had let her rest for the afternoon, and with the evening bowl they had given her something that made her sleep. When she woke the next day she felt almost all right, just a bit sore. When she got to class she heard someone say she had been chipped. It was a new word, and she remembered it.

It hadn't been when she was just beginning to bud and the Supervisor had wangled her a single room instead of a dormitory space, and had visited her on the very first night just when she was feeling so lucky. She had known men were different, obviously, but she hadn't known it could be that sore. She had tolerated his fumbling and grunting and his *mess* for two weeks. Then one day while they were all chanting a lesson, there was a sharp *pop* overhead and one of the light globes became a spray of glassy shards. A big one landed on the surface in front of her; she managed to snatch it and conceal it up the sleeve of her shift. It cut her a little but she didn't care.

Later, it cut the Supervisor much better.

She expected to be punished but for once nothing happened. She never saw the Supervisor again. She supposed he couldn't be a supervisor without what she had cut from him.

She had never seen so much blood.

No. The challenge to her seeming had come later, when she was fifteen. Someone had smuggled in a book, an actual old-fashioned book such as she had heard of but never seen. It had a screen, and buttons to advance the pages, and it used two words that she had never heard, but whose meaning became clear very quickly as she read on, oblivious to risk.

The risk became reality. They found her and took her away, and this time she was truly punished, oh yes, punished until she wished her body didn't belong to her. Until she knew in intimate close focus, one at a time and several times over, what that chip could do. But she remembered the words, and what they meant.

Mother, and father.

A little while afterwards they moved her out of the dormitory and into one of the Villages and she learned another word she wasn't supposed to know.

It was *slave*.

Three Quarter Circle Plains

His feet knew the way and his nose knew the air, but it still took him a long time to retrace his steps. He could feel the changing ground, the way that the jagged rocks of the peak became the smooth worn surface of the lower path. He could feel the change from rock to moss, and from moss to grass if he strayed from the path. The sound of falling water guided him down the sharp-edged little river valleys, and he learned with wonder how dense and detailed the soundscape could be. Even the slightest turn of his head changed it, telling him that *here* the water poured over a boulder and *there* the bed broadened and slowed. The air, too. Not only did it become thicker as he descended – how much thicker he could hardly believe – but the scent! Rock had a smell. Wet rock smelled different to dry rock, and one rock smelled different to another. Not knowing the real names of any of the rocks, he gave them his own names according to their smell. Saltstone, Bitterstone and Sulphur Rock.

Smell guided him to food, too. At first he dared not leave the path but as his hunger and his confidence grew he began to make short side-trips to follow the scents of berries and toadstools.

Somehow, despite his blindness, Belbis didn't quite starve.

Even the times of day changed. Day and night had no meaning

for him, except that night was a bad time to sleep because he would wake up cold and damp. Instead he marked his own daily cycle, and again gave it his own names. Mouse Quiet, for example, that was the time at the end of the night when the night-seeing hunters had finished but the day dwellers were still sleepy or asleep. If he stood very still and listened very hard he could hear the diffident little rustles of the smallest creatures taking advantage of the lull to – well, what? Scavenge, he supposed, or dig a burrow. Perhaps just to breathe without having their tiny breath triangulated by death in the air.

Mouse Quiet was followed by Dew Time, and he usually walked as briskly as he could through that to fight off the cold and to keep dry until the time he named Sun Greet.

His feet were telling him he was near the outskirts of Three Quarter Circle town when his ears and nose alerted him to something. At first he wasn't sure what it was. He stopped and thought.

The sun felt directly above him and an onshore wind was in his face. At this hour the harbour should have been busy no matter the state of the tide. He should have been able to smell the oily reek of the rendering vats with its undertone of burning peat. There should have been the click of ropes against masts and the distant grinding breath of the old steam engines that ran the hauling winches. Especially there should have been the cries of the merchants.

Instead there was quiet. No, that wasn't right; instead, there was the absence of familiar noises. They had been replaced by an odd undertow, almost at the limit of his hearing. And the air did smell, but that was wrong too.

Without thinking about it he found he had broken into a run. Senses he had developed on the downward journey mined the unconscious knowledge of half his lifetime – there were familiar cobbles beneath his feet. From here, downhill two hundred paces, until the cross-shore wind struck his right cheek, and then to the right, and he would be at the Prater House. They would look after him there, and when he had told the Klerikers what had happened they would be able to explain it to him. They would know what to do.

Meanwhile his nose sought the smells that should have been there, and his ears the cries, and then he felt his pace faltering. And now there were cries and there was smoke, yes. But the cries were angry and the smoke smelled of wood and tar and something worse, something that made his gorge rise, and as he came to a halt in front of what should be the Prater House he felt a hot wind on his cheeks. Suddenly his mind supplied an image of burning buildings.

Now the cries were coming quickly closer, and had become focused as if the men had something to shout about.

'Another blood-sucking priest!'

'Didn't we get them all then?'

'Guess this one's been a-wandering . . .'

He turned in panic, but hands seized him.

'Drag him in front of the Merchants.'

'To hell with that. Who put them over us? They're as bad as the fucking priests. Hang him up with the rest of the black bastards!'

'No! Wait . . .'

Someone pushed him to the ground, and there was the warm damp breath of stump spirits in his face. One breath, two breaths, three, and he knew he was being inspected.

'Young. Grey robes. Oh sweet shit, let it be him . . .'

'If it's him he'll be scarred.' Another voice.

'They have potions to stop that.'

'Or witchery . . .'

'Just bloody look, will you?'

Hands took his robes and dragged them upwards, and he felt the hot wind on his thighs.

'Well now . . .'

'What?'

'It's him. It's the Idiot.'

Voices roared around him. Through the roar he sensed the warmth of a face close to his, and more stump brew. The voice was harsh and hoarse.

'What did you do?' Hands took his robe and he felt himself lifted and thrust back so that the back of his head struck the cobbles. Red-green stars fizzed across his darkness and he felt the breath whistling out of him as if it would never return. 'What – did – you – DO?'

It was so hard to make words. For the whole of his life Belbis had treasured the thought that if he could only find the right words, someone would understand him, just for once. He made a supreme effort, expelling each word on a gust of breath. 'Counted Gods. Wrong number.'

There was a pause, while the roaring voices went on roaring. Then came a sound like a grunt of disgust and the hands let go of his robe.

Then the first blows landed. The blows became kicks from men who grunted with effort, loud enough to be heard over the crowd noise. He covered his head and began to cry. It hurt to breathe, and through his tears he realized that the clicks he heard within himself were his own ribs breaking.

After a long time he felt himself lifted and thrown. He landed on a hard slick surface and immediately began to slide. He cried out and the pain in his sides would have made him sick, if the smell hadn't already. They had thrown him into one of the gut-ramps.

Now he had no sense of distance but his speed seemed terrifying. The ramps weren't straight; he slammed round corners and through sharp-edged sumps. Once he held out his arms to try to slow himself. One of them caught against something and for a moment he slowed, but then he felt his elbow twist through an impossible angle.

There was an audible *snap*.

Belbis screamed. He tumbled down the smooth stone channels, slick with blubber and wet with the blood that was never allowed to set, screaming with every appalling crash of his broken ribs and his shattered arm, until the only thing left to him apart from the pain was the hope that he would soon drop into the vile waters of the harbour and be killed and eaten with the other entrails.

He did not get his wish. He felt the ramp steepen, he almost smiled, but then he crashed horribly into something, legs first – and there were more clicks and then more pain – and then the merciless hands seized him again and he was dragged upwards and dropped on to a hard surface – the quayside, he guessed, with his waning senses.

'Hold him.'

The hands took him, careless of his shattered arm and of his howls of agony. He felt his sandals being removed and thought, *why?* – and then unspeakable incandescent pain shot across his heels.

At last, the world faded.

Chastern System, Spin Inside

Captain Hefs leaned on the rail of the observation gallery above the forward sun deck of the liner *Sunskimmer*, scoped some of the more presentable guests – without being intrusive, obviously – and decided that he didn't have the worst job in the sector. One of the better-looking females, who at least looked human-compatible, seemed to have noticed him. He straightened up and sucked in his belly.

They were skirting a medium-sized yellow star called Chastern, roughly halfway across the Inside. They were about a minute out from the first wisps of the corona and the blinds above the sun decks were fully opened, heavily dimmed by very strong fields. Without them, seventy mainly naked people would have been cooked alive just before they died of radiation poisoning. With them, they were merely getting the fastest and most expensive suntan in the Spin.

The female was definitely looking at him. She was dark-skinned with short silver hair, and she looked young and athletic. He sucked in his gut a little more and focused his eyes carefully on the middle distance as if thinking important things. The sort of things thought by captains.

After all, he was hardly an insignificant captain, as he often told himself. He was in command of a spaceship nearly a kilometre from end to end. He liked the word 'command' – even if in actual fact the whole vast ship could be run by a crew of one.

Sunskimmer had not always been called *Sunskimmer*, and she had not started life as a liner. She had originally been a Main Battle Unit called *Flamejob*, a proper fighting spaceship built ten thousand years ago for long-term charter to mostly private armies. When she was a mere five thousand years old she had been decommissioned, and her original battle-smart AI largely disabled. Since then she had led a varied but mainly uneventful life cruising around the safe bits of the Spin with cargoes of wealthy passengers. The decommissioning had not affected her engines; very large and very fast, she was one of the few remaining ships in private hands with enough power to get this far down the gravity well of a star without being sucked the rest of the way, and enough shields that she was unlikely to melt. She was ideally suited to the new fad of deep-well sunbathing.

Captain Hefs thought it was a stupid pastime, but it was a living – quite a good one – and he did quite enjoy some of the opportunities it presented.

There was no doubt about it. The woman was looking at him. He flagged a servitor and, doing his best to look as if he was passing on a command decision, told it to steal some candid close-ups and tag them to the young woman's ID and suite number. He was quite aware of his own slightly chubby limitations, but confidence and position still did the trick far more often than he would have thought likely. There was a Dinner tonight. He hadn't finalized his table plan yet.

Well, he probably had *now*.

Captain's Dinners were held every fifth day in what had been the upper forward weapons pod, when the old ship still had weapons. *Sunskimmer* was shaped like two rough cones joined back to back by a short fat tube. The rear cone was all engine.

When she was in fighting trim the front cone would have been all weapons, but now it was where you put the people. On one side of the cone there were the sun decks. On the other, a half-globe stuck out of the cone as if it had crashed into it. It had been where the business end of the major energy weapons pointed out through a set of insectoid-looking bulbous blisters. Now, the blisters had been turned into viewing galleries and the biggest of them had been fitted out as a restaurant, with tables on floating platforms that moved around each other in a slow dance to make sure everyone got the best from the view.

Hefs was enjoying the view very much. Her name was Seldyan, apparently. She had gone travelling between studies; she and a group of friends had saved up to come on this trip. Four of her friends were with her at dinner. They were all young and attractive, and as far as he could see they were getting on with his exec team very well. One young man in particular was talking to his second in command, who seemed rapt. Hefs had sometimes wondered about the man's sexuality.

Close up, Seldyan's skin was the rich colour of old hardwood and her eyes were tinted violet in a shocking contrast to her silver-white hair. She wore a strangely beautiful filigree thing in silver wire that twined around one ear. She was smart and sinuous and unaffected – all the things Hefs liked best – and she did seem to like him in return.

And his current consort was light-years away, probably enjoying herself with someone younger. Well, she wasn't the only one who could play. He called for more drinks and watched, entranced, as Seldyan popped another of the fat berries into her perfect mouth. The berry disappeared with just a flicker of tongue. The sleek throat rippled, and she smiled. 'Mmm. Gorgeous. I've never had these before. What did you say they were called?'

He shook himself mentally. 'They're Mist Berries. They grow on one of the planets of this star, actually. It's an ocean world.

The berries grow on sort of floating islands.' Damn, she was easy to talk to. He went on, 'We try to serve local food, wherever we are.'

'How interesting.' She leaned a little closer, and he caught a hint of a soft fragrance. 'You must have visited hundreds of planets.'

He gave what he hoped was a modest laugh. 'Well, all of the Eleven, anyway. I've hardly been outside the Inside.'

'Hardly?' Her eyes widened. 'But that doesn't mean not at all. When did you go out?'

The urge to impress her was – lunatic. What had come over him? Concentrate! He frowned and thought back. 'I first crossed the Border, oh, fifteen years ago, I guess. In those days we traded more. I was a convoy escort.'

'Wow.' She raised her eyebrows – tinted silver to match her hair, he noticed. 'Does that mean you were some kind of fighter pilot?'

He laughed. 'Some kind, I suppose. I never found anything to fight.'

'Too modest. They probably saw you and ran away.' She sat back, looking at him. 'There's more to you than meets the eye, Captain.'

'I doubt it.' But the thought warmed him all the same. Part of him, just a small part that he thought had fizzled and died years ago, whispered that perhaps he really had once been more than an overweight middle-aged shepherd to the wealthy.

Seldyan was staring at him with those eyebrows raised, and he realized that he was grinning.

'No, not like *that*! Look, let me show you.' Seldyan took him by the shoulder and spun him half round. 'Look, you start off going this way. See? With everyone else.' She demonstrated and he tripped over his feet for the third time, dragging her down with him. The drink wasn't helping, but he had to admit he probably wasn't a natural dancer. Seldyan was, though, and so were most of her friends. They had wanted to show everyone how to do some ancient formal dance or other – a round dance, was that it? He couldn't remember – so he had ordered the staff to clear the table platforms and bring them together to make a floating dancefloor.

It had been a social success, if a stylistic failure. And now here he was, accidentally lying underneath Seldyan.

She gave him a long look which started out amused and then became serious. Her eyes narrowed a little and she leaned down to let her lips brush his cheek. 'You're a shit dancer,' she said, 'but I've never believed that myth.' She rolled off him, stood up and extended a hand. 'Shall we?'

Fifteen minutes later she was on top of him again. This time it was in his suite, and clothes weren't involved, and it seemed so *natural*. He no longer felt he had to hold in his belly, he didn't care about the greying hairs on his chest – even if his consort did, but where was she? Exactly! – he didn't care about anything except the unbelievably beautiful creature who was poised above him, the warmth and scent of her body vivid to him, her hands on his wrists, pinning him deliciously, her thighs tight around his, her eyes dancing, her mouth . . .

. . . laughing?

She shouldn't have been laughing. Not like that.

He tried to sit up but his wrists really were pinned. She was stronger than she looked, and she was still laughing.

Then she stopped laughing and he wished she hadn't, because now her face looked . . . professional. She shifted her grip so that she had both his wrists pinned by one hand, and even then he couldn't break her grip no matter how he struggled. With her other hand she did something to the filigree thing in her ear. Then she spoke, and Hefs knew immediately that she wasn't speaking to him. 'I got mine,' she said. 'Report?'

There were three scratchy versions of 'yes', and then silence. Seldyan frowned. 'Merish? Result or not?'

There was a pause. Then a man's voice said, 'Sorry. Result, in the end.'

Seldyan's frown deepened. 'Was there a problem?'

'Yeah.' The voice sighed. 'Look, everyone said this bloke was gay?'

'The second in command?' Seldyan looked nonplussed. 'Sure. So?'

'No way. Bi-curious at best. I almost feel guilty.'

'Oh.' Seldyan's face twitched. 'Got things under control now?'

'Yeah.' The voice paused. 'I think I owe him an apology.'

Seldyan laughed softly. 'Save your apologies,' she said. 'He's probably grateful you broadened his horizons. Or whatever you broadened.' She touched the silver thing and it seemed to break the contact. Then she looked down at Hefs. 'I expect you get the idea,' she said. 'You've been taken over, at the cost of five cruise tickets and some booze you actually paid for. Any questions?'

'Yes.' He tried to sit up again but it was impossible. 'Who are you?'

She rolled her eyes. 'I'm someone who could break your pelvis, if I squeeze hard enough. You want me to try?'

'No!' He shook his head as hard as he could.

'Good. Any other questions?'

He shook his head again.

'Fine. I'm glad you aren't going to try to be a hero. Your ship might end up fighting – that's what it's for. You?' Her eyes scanned down his torso, over his belly and on to his softening penis, and she shook her head. 'Not so much.'

After that he was almost glad when she reached down to the junction of her thighs, pulled a tiny, bewitchingly moist stunner shaped like a flat pebble out of her body, and shot him.

Traders' Tower, Basin City

The image of the dark-skinned silver-haired woman hung in the air. It was taken from above and in front of her, foreshortening her and cutting off the face and neck of the chubby middle-aged man she was astride, but her own face was still clear. She had a stunner in her hand which she seemed to be in the act of firing because there was a suggestion of a flash. She was naked and smiling but the smile looked more amused than happy. And, thought Harbour Master Hevalansa Vess, a little dangerous. He cleared his throat.

'So, let me see. Five escapees from the Hive manage to buy cruise tickets costing a year's salary each. They then seduce and disable every single one of the exec team of a liner worth, what? Madam Els?' He looked at the elderly human female sitting opposite him. Even with them both seated it was obvious that she was far taller and thinner than him, and she wore a long close-fitting jacket in a dull carbon-coloured material that made her seem even more stretched.

She gave a minute shrug. 'It depends. Valuation yesterday, seventeen trillion, triple A risks. Valuation as of five minutes ago, zero and junk bond.'

'Right.' He sighed. 'When did this happen?'

'Seventeen hours ago.'

'And you waited until now to tell us?' Vess didn't need to pretend to be irritated, but instead of flinching Els gave him a frosty smile.

'We waited until now to tell *anyone* except our bankers. Our corporation is leveraged with our fleet as collateral. A collapse of confidence was inevitable, but we managed to agree a soft landing. There were plenty of questions.' She looked at him sharply. 'Including, how did five slaves manage to escape and evade recovery long enough to have their identities wiped and to acquire long credit lines?'

'We don't refer to them as slaves.' It was a fair question; one which Vess couldn't answer until he had spoken to someone at a *much* higher pay grade – and if and when those people did speak to him he expected them to have other things on their minds. 'Do you know where the ship went?'

'No. It continued on course for ten minutes after the picture was sent. Then it stopped transponding and just vanished. We're assuming it's Outside by now.'

Vess waved at the screen. 'How did you get this, then?'

To his pleasure Els looked embarrassed. 'It seems that Hefs routinely had a micro-remote film his adventures. Gross misconduct, of course, although it's done us a favour this time. If we ever find him he'll be dismissed on the spot.'

Vess fought the temptation to laugh. He was afraid that if he started he would carry on until he was dragged out of the building. 'You think he's alive?'

'Oh yes. That's a ship-issue stunner. It's not meant to be used at such close range but even then it would take a long time to kill him with it. After a single shot like that he'd probably have woken up with a very bad headache.' She smiled. 'The ship followed the rules, even if its crew didn't. When it realized it was compromised it squirted a complete status snapshot back to us. Hence, this.' She gestured at the image.

Vess nodded. 'Are all your senior ship management sex maniacs then?'

The frosty look was back. 'No, but they're not immune to drugs. The ship monitored air quality. The last few results show traces of complex organic substances in the air-handling plant that served the restaurant area.'

Vess took a moment to process that. This is surreal, he thought. This woman has just announced what will probably be my death sentence, by talking about aphrodisiacs?

He shook his head slowly. 'The security breaches just go on piling up, don't they? It's just as well ship AIs don't have sex.'

Her face twisted a little as if she was trying not to smile. 'I believe some of them do, in a way, but this one isn't bright enough. It was meta-lobotomized five thousand years ago when the ship was decommissioned. It's meant to be dumb and dutiful.'

'Well, that's fascinating.' Vess stood up and walked over to the tall windows that lined one of the long walls of the room. Keeping his back turned he said, 'Would it interest you, madam, to know that your ship is not alone? It's one of five that have been lost over the last three cycles. Not all by the same means, but still.'

He heard the intake of breath, but nothing more. He smiled to himself and added, 'Apparently *everybody* waited until they had talked to their bankers. And their insurers, I suppose. Have they responded to you yet, by the way? The insurers?'

He turned round. Els was looking stunned. He raised his eyebrows, and she shook her head slightly.

'I'm not surprised. Five ships of the same sort of value? Eighty trillion total, or thereabouts?' He sat back down. 'They're probably sitting under their desks rocking backwards and forwards with their fingers, or whatever they have, in whatever they use for ears . . . are you all right, madam?'

She was very pale. He gestured to the servant, who placed a glass of water in front of her. It seemed to take a while for her to notice it. When she did, she clutched at it and took a hurried swig. 'The other four ships,' she said. 'We hadn't heard . . .'

'That's because we haven't said.' He shrugged. 'Investigations will take their course. You should assume that you will be part of that course. As will I.' *Oh, yes. I so will.*

She nodded. 'I should return to my Board. I'd like to tell them about the other ships. That is, if I may?'

'Yes, but for their knowledge only. Oh, and I'll want the passenger lists. This is going to stay unknown, you understand?' He paused. 'When was the ship due back?'

She still looked shaken. 'The day after tomorrow. We have four others on cruise at the moment . . .'

'I know. We checked. They are smaller, aren't they? Not legacy vessels?'

She nodded.

'Then they are less valuable. Warn them, but keep them there. We'll be covering them from a discreet distance.' Vess managed a smile. 'It's just as well they're little ones. If we lose any more major units we'll be back to walking.'

She rose and half turned towards the door. Then she turned back. 'The slave said the ship might end up fighting,' she said. It was a question.

'Yes, she did, didn't she?' Vess stood up and waved the servant forward. 'Escort Madam Els back to her skipper. A safe journey, madam.'

He turned towards the windows. Behind him, he heard the door closing. When he was sure he was alone he blew out a long slow breath and leaned against the glass.

Watching from a discreet distance? It had better be *very* discreet. If they got close enough to be spotted, people might realize how little they had left to watch with.

He was dead. Sooner or later, by easier or harder means – dead. In her role as a cruise ship, *Sunskimmer* was important, and certainly the loss (albeit temporary) of the high-value people on board was embarrassing, but the cruise companies were only a small part of the total GDP of the Inside. That wasn't the real issue.

His chest felt tight. He shut his eyes and took a couple of slow breaths. A few minutes of calm before he launched himself. He could allow himself that.

The Inside hadn't constructed a new major ship in two thousand years. It had *never* constructed anything like what *Sunskimmer* had become. Never mind anything like what *Sunskimmer* had been in the first place – and could always have become again, at need. She and the rest of her kind had been an insurance policy; the last line of defence. They had been careful about that; no ship of that potential had ever been so completely converted to civilian use that it could not be un-converted. She retained a basic suite of weapons; there were more in a central store, and there was an emergency backup protocol. In theory they could have a fully armed battle fleet within two days of any emergency.

But not any more.

The truth was, they had been living on the glories of their predecessors for twenty generations. And now the last of those glories had been stolen from under his nose. And hence, he was dead.

He opened his eyes again.

No matter where you looked the first thing you saw was canal. His office was most of the way up the complex. Above it was only the restaurant deck, strictly reserved for staff of Praetor rank, and above, the Penthouse – even more exclusive – and then the steeply pointed roofs of the Belfry. None of which, of course, were visible to Vess, but below, well, that was different.

Water had been the reason for the city. Water had been the cause of its foundation and the route by which wealth entered and left but, for the first five thousand years or so, mostly entered. It had started with simple flat canals, but it was a long way from its starting point now.

There were three main levels. The highest was just below his eyeline so that his view glanced off the suspended canalized ribbons of water at a low angle. They stood off the next level on slim columns glistening with leaked or spilled water and streaked with green and black mould. That next level was in turn supported by a much older forest of stone, iron or even timber towers, festooned with hanging weed. At the roots of the forest, invisible from up here, were the grimy originals. Boat hoists, ranks of stepped locks and a couple of elaborate wheels with gondolas swinging from their rims moved things between levels.

The three levels formed their own hierarchy. On top were the cruisers, racers and even houseboats of the very wealthy. On the middle level were still the main commercial arteries, and down on the ground was what Vess had heard described as a vibrant mixed community, which meant poor people and criminals. Vess had been born there; he had never been back.

Well, he had never been back *yet*. It might turn out to be one of his options, sooner rather than later. It, too, would mean death, but only in the way it meant death for everyone – premature, and poor, but still recognizably human.

Every gap between the canals was full of buildings, mostly sinuous towers that snaked their way up between the water-ways and poked more or less elaborate tops up into the sunshine. He never tired of the sight. He indulged himself with a few minutes of staring while a pair of big galleys rode in procession along the canal nearest to him, their oars leaving puckered scars on the water.

And then of course there was the other level. He never thought of it as being part of the three, and nor did anyone else he knew. The Cloud Deck was a discontinuous snaking structure that floated slowly backwards and forwards over everything else on intricately pivoted parallel-motion arms mounted on upward extensions of the main canal columns. The motion allowed it to be located anywhere over Basin City except for Traders' Tower. Vess wasn't sure how it all worked, but he had heard that the

arms would seize up, or bend, or at any rate fail in some catastrophic way if anyone tried to force the Cloud Deck there.
Geometry, and politics, apparently. Obviously no one had ever
tried because the Cloud Deck, although newer than the rest of
the city, wasn't *that* much newer – it had survived several thousand years un-broken.

The boats passed and the surface of the canal healed to a
breeze-frosted glass. Vess turned away from the window and
got ready to work. The servant had returned, and knew his
habits; as Vess sat down at his desk he found a steaming flask at
his left hand and a rolled-up spiced meat pastry at his right. He
would need them both; it was going to be a long time before he
could relax, if ever. The only safe assumption was that *Sunskimmer* was somewhere Outside, and in so many ways that
wasn't safe at all.

His first action was to put in a call to the Gamer. He expected
the answer would come soon. In fact it came sooner, before he
had even finished the pastry; he wiped his mouth on his sleeve
before he answered.

'Vess?' The voice was deep, dark and powerfully bassy. As
the Gamer had no choice but to use a voice synth, this was obviously intentional. Vess always found it funny. It was probably
racist but for his money an organism as spider-like as that
should hiss rather than boom. He swallowed his amusement
and knotted his arms in front of him in his closest approxima-
tion to a polite greeting. 'Clo Fiffithiss, thanks for calling. How
are you?' His memory threw in a random fact. 'Did you enjoy
the Colony Dinner last night?'

'Probably.' Fiffithiss writhed in a gesture which could have
been a shrug. It made Vess feel slightly queasy. 'I will never be
popular amongst my peers, but my fore-cock and my front legs
feel as if they have been plaited and I seem to have some new
tattoos. Those are both usually good signs. But you didn't call
to ask that.' The nest of limbs became still. 'There is a rumour

amongst my underwriting friends that we have lost another major unit. Is that, can that be, true?'

Vess nodded, and then remembered his manners and made what he hoped was the equivalent gesture. 'Yes, it is. *Sunskimmer.*' The gesture hurt his shoulders.

'*Sunskimmer*? I see.' The limbs were still motionless, which if you were prey wasn't good news at all. It meant an imminent pounce with poison fangs ready. Even the certainty that those fangs were several klicks away couldn't stop Vess's body trying to go into fight or flight. He fought down his instinct and waited.

Eventually the limbs relaxed and spread. Fiffithiss made a sighing noise which, through its artificially amplified voice, vibrated Vess's seat. '*Sunskimmer* was the last of the legacy Main Battle Units. You do realize that?'

'The disclosed ones, yes. They aren't all accounted for. There could be a few more.' Vess shrugged. 'Somewhere.'

'You really think so? Some backwoods bunch of retards have a legacy MBU up their smelly sleeve?' The limbs straightened abruptly and spread into a flat fan in front of Fiffithiss. Emphatic negative; a shake of the head to the power ten. 'I'd bet my unhatched eggs against it. And even if they have, they're hardly going to render it up on demand for the good of the Inside, are they?' Fiffithiss repeated the negative gesture and then collapsed into a sort of dejected ball of legs. 'That was the last one. We have nothing else of note. I'll tell you something, human, our ability to fight off the Outsiders is done for, if it wasn't already. And if *that's* done for, we're *all* done for. You in particular, my friend.'

Vess nodded slowly. 'But not only that. This was visible. Everyone Inside and Outside will know about this in hours, if they don't already.'

'Ah. Yes. And, given that I got my first information from an open public source, I think we can assume that they do already.'

'We can. Our reputation, our political capital, our position as the core of the Spin – well, it puts the difficulties of the insurance companies into perspective, doesn't it?'

'Loss of prestige on this scale puts *everything* into perspective. Enemies will be lining up. Friends will become enemies. I don't envy you. There'll have to be a Board Meeting, you know.'

Vess nodded. 'I've known that for a while.'

'Of course. You'll have my support if you need it.' Fiffithiss leaned forwards. 'Are you engaged in whatever passes for a sexual relationship amongst your kind at the moment?'

Vess laughed. 'Why?'

'Because if I was you, I'd go and get some while I still could.'

The connection broke.

For a while Vess sat staring at nothing. Then he straightened his back and blinked down a data pipe. Not the public system – that was far too insecure and besides, it was censored to the point of uselessness – but the hack-hardened back room of the city servers. It was the first time he had accessed data for himself in months and he was out of practice, but it was that or delegate to his staff. And none of his staff needed to know about this. For one thing he had never been quite certain whose staff they were.

It took him a while to find what he wanted. Then information tumbled down his vision. At first the rate control eluded him, then he sent it the wrong way so the figures blurred, and finally he got it right and scrolled back up to the top.

Then he sat, absorbed.

He was discovering the woman called Seldyan. There was much to discover. It took him an hour to read the file, but he was happy to invest the time. After all, she had just ended his career and, more than likely, killed him.

He owed her the time.

When he had finished he blinked the pipe closed and remained quite still.

Slavery wasn't practised on all the Inner planets, but it was still common enough. There were many reasons why someone might become a slave but only a few why they might do so from birth. In Seldyan's case the short answer was population pressure. Pressure is always against something, and this time it was against money.

It was close to a rule – and certainly more than a guideline – that populations tended to grow while resources were fixed. That bit especially hard when the boundaries of your world were shrinking by the decade.

The Inside had no centrally imposed scheme for population control, but it had targets; individual members of the Federation came up with their own ways of meeting them. Seldyan's parents had lived on a manufacturing world that had happened to be heavily indebted and close to its population ceiling at the same time.

Selling unwanted children was a perfect solution to both problems. In Seldyan's case it helped with another too: her parents had been broke and starving. The sale of their second child to the Hive had solved most of that.

It had also meant that both of them were sterilized; the state could only afford to meet that sort of bill once. Their first child had apparently been still-born; Seldyan was their second and last. The record didn't show what had happened to them in the end. It didn't include unimportant people.

It didn't include Vess's parents either. He rarely thought about that, but for some reason he was thinking about it now.

The signal interrupted him. He sighed and glanced down at the surface of the desk, which fogged briefly and resolved into a short piece of text. The Board Meeting had been brought forward to the following morning and he was to attend. Well, he could have predicted that, and so had Clo Fiffithiss, which wasn't surprising. Vess wondered if the being had gamed it or merely guessed it. But that wasn't all; he read the rest of the message. It was about the meeting venue.

He sat back and blew out his cheeks. That venue was reserved for the sort of Board Meeting that could be denied afterwards.

All the signs were pointing in the same direction. He began to think he ought to take the Gamer's advice.

Spin Inside – Border Region

The ship lights flashed to red three times and returned to normal. Some lights flickered, and the main data pipe lit up with a querulous pre-recorded message from an insurance company regretting that their cover had lapsed, now and for ever.

Seldyan turned the message off.

The good ship formerly known as *Sunskimmer*, originally *Flamejob*, freshly rechristened *Suck on This*, crossed the border between Inside and Outside at full power and went on accelerating. The last vestiges of hopelessly outclassed pursuit fell away, their courses bending into a set of golden-series arcs that ended back over the Border.

They had escaped. Unbelievably, they had escaped. And, even more unbelievably, the five of them had done it in something a kilometre long.

The controls, such as they were, seemed far too trivial. In her view it should have taken walls of lights, rooms full of consoles and anxious people responding to alarms and, just, *stuff*.

Instead there was this plain room with a hazy horizontal disc floating at waist height. The disc was roughly big enough to seat four for a meal and it showed, well, she wasn't exactly sure what all of it showed. Parts looked obvious – she could see speed and direction, certainly. And part of it was clearly a starscape, although it seemed to contain more than just stars. The starscape flipped up to vertical and expanded if you looked at it, and then you had what she guessed was a view looking forward. She watched it for a while, lost in slowly expanding stars. Then something occurred to her. She weaved experimentally from side to side, looking to see if the disc followed. It didn't. She grinned to herself, and walked round it. It narrowed to a perspective oval, shrank to a dim line as she passed its edge, and expanded again – but not to the same view.

At first she didn't understand. There was a starscape, showing the Inside: eleven planets, four suns and a Border marked out with enough paranoid defensiveness to have earned itself a capital letter, but it was receding, and in the foreground there was a huge *something* – two rough cones joined back to back.

Then she realized, and the realization emptied her lungs.

The huge *something* was the ship.

The wonder of it tugged at her gut. She whispered: 'Oh, shit . . .' Then she laughed. Part of the disc looked like comms. She gestured at it. 'Merish?'

'Uh-huh?'

'We did it. We actually did it!' She laughed. 'We escaped in a stolen spaceship – the biggest ship Inside! How cool is that?'

'Are we over the Border?'

'Yes; just crossed.' She felt herself trembling. She got ready to say that she hadn't really believed . . . but then didn't. Sometimes, she knew, she had to do the believing for both of them.

As the ship had crossed the Border the display had flickered. Now it froze for a second, fuzzed to grey and then went blank. Seldyan tutted.

It flicked back into life. Seldyan stared for a moment. Then she felt herself grinning. 'Merish? Can you see the main displays, wherever you are?'

'Sure, if I want to. Should I?'

She paused. 'Oh yes. Take a look at the size of the prize.'

'Okay. Just a minute. Oh, wow . . .'

'Yeah.' She stared at the expanded, far more dramatic image. 'The whole of the Spin. Eighty-nine lovely juicy planets.' It wasn't just that the view was expanded. The definition was better, somehow. It was a bit like looking at a work of art.

'Yeah. Well, eighty-eight, now. Minus the one that got blown up, supposedly.'

Seldyan fiddled with some controls until she found the zoom. Her point of view accelerated into the image while bloating distorted planets zoomed past her. She waited for the quality to degrade, but it just didn't. A single star was swelling in the centre of the field; as it expanded she could see individual threads of gas flaring from it. The magnification must have been up in the millions.

She shook her head in admiration, and took the view back to where it had started. 'So why has this turned up on the screens?'

'Version control, I guess. This is a pretty old ship, remember. It pre-dates the Border. As a cruise ship it only needed to know the Inside. Now we're Outside maybe it's trying to revert to type.'

'Type? Oh . . .' Seldyan looked at the starscape. 'Type being warship?'

'That's putting it mildly. Not any more, though; they unzipped its brains when it was converted to cruising.'

'Really?' She shook her head. 'That sounds cruel. Can we re-zip them?'

'Possibly. Why?'

'I feel sorry for it.' A spot near the base of her spine itched. She reached behind herself and scratched it gently, feeling the flat bump. 'Think of it as a kindred soul, okay?'

'Yeah, right. What's the other reason?'

Seldyan glared at the comms. 'Because the Hive is still there.

Because a million people aren't here with us. Because we're heading into the unknown. Because I want a warship to play with. Okay?'

'Ah. Okay.' The comms went dead.

Seldyan frowned at it, and then felt for the itchy spot again. It never quite went away.

The old ship was quiet. Before they had crossed the Border they had unloaded the passengers and the exec team on to one of the shuttles *Sunskimmer* towed around, pointed it at the nearest planet and given it a metaphorical slap on the rump. It would get there before they ran out of air and water, although they might be hungry.

Now it was just the five of them.

A holo readout wavered in the air. Seldyan peered at it. 'There's five different levels of operating system here,' she said. 'Don't they ever clear anything out?'

Merish pushed back his hair. 'No. Just cover it over. Didn't you know? It's like your DNA. Mostly redundant shit that used to be there to make you a better lizard.'

'Fuck that. I'm already the best lizard you can get.' She waved a hand. 'Anyway, the oldest bits of this stuff probably think we still are lizards.'

'The oldest bits of this stuff think it's a warship, Sel. That's what you wanted, right?'

'Yes, it was. It still is.' She shook her head. 'I still seem to be waiting.'

'So you do. No, hang on. Ah-*ha* . . .'

'What?' Then she saw it. The displays had changed. She looked for a while. 'Okay,' she said slowly. 'I get it. We're a warship again, right?'

'Yup. What do you think?'

The planets were the same. Everything else was – she sought for the word – *more*. What had been a map was now a landscape, a beautifully detailed strategic sculpture of risk and possibility.

She watched for a long time. Then she pointed. 'What are the big dots?' They were a kind of fuzzy cerise, scattered sparsely through the image.

Merish laughed. 'They're the other legacy MBUs.'

'Oh.' She frowned. 'Why are they highlighted?'

'Because they're powerful enough for the ship to worry about.'

She squinted at the display. 'There are other dots.'

'Well, yes. Those would be other legacy units. Smaller than us but still handy.'

'Right.' She began counting, and then gave up. 'There are lots.'

'Yeah. Some big hitters have crossed the Border over the last few thousand years. Try not to worry, Sel. They're mostly a long way away and some of them may not work any more.'

'Oh good. That makes me feel so much better.' She hesitated. 'How long until we get to Oblong?'

'About four hours.'

'You nervous?'

'A little. You?'

She watched the display for a while without answering. At first it seemed static, but then she realized that it was alive with movement, with dots and streaks of coloured light swarming around and over each other against the backdrop of stars. It reminded her a little of a sparse swarm of shiny insects weaving blindly through space. The idea made her smile. We're all insects, she thought. All equal.

Equal was a refreshing concept. She looked up at Merish. 'Remember where we came from?'

'Of course. I'll never forget it.'

'Nor will I. So, would anything, anything *at all*, make you go back?'

He shook his head quickly.

'Me neither.' She turned back to the display, and after a moment he did too.

She had managed not to answer the question.

Sometimes she chided herself for having taken so long to reach her decision. Being chipped hadn't been enough; the Supervisor hadn't been enough; even seeing what had happened to Merish hadn't quite been enough – and that was harsh criticism when she replayed it through sleepless hours.

No. Finally, it had been someone she barely knew.

Her world had been made of routine – a daily cycle of basic classes, exercise and a little rest, measured out by sleeps. The classes would have been fun if she had been allowed to ask any questions, but questions weren't allowed. Sometimes she asked them anyway, and received no answer.

Then, one morning halfway through Seldyan's fourteenth year, she was woken early by a jarring siren, much louder than the usual waking call. She opened her eyes and immediately screwed them shut again because instead of the usual early-morning glimmer the lights were set to full day brightness. An unfamiliar guard hauled her off her pallet and shoved her out of the sleeping quarters. Around her she saw the same thing happening to everyone.

In the square it felt colder than usual. Everyone seemed to be here; she looked around for Merish and saw him standing a little way away, his arms wrapped round his body. She beckoned him over.

'What's going on?'

'I think we're being Sorted.' His teeth were chattering so much she had to ask him to repeat the last word. She was about to ask him what he meant when there was another siren. There were shouts from the guards and they found themselves being driven out of the square, towards the teaching units.

Even the floor felt colder than usual, to her bare feet.

They ended up in an area she hadn't been in before. It was a tall, broad hall, bigger than anything she had yet known. For as far as she could see the floor was occupied by workstations – plain pedestals topped with a flat desk. There was a screen on each desk, similar to the ones she was used to but bigger.

Another siren, and an amplified voice: 'Find a station.'

Quite a few people seemed to be hesitating; she shrugged, walked to the nearest vacant station and took hold of the edges of the desk as if she was claiming territory.

She looked around. People had got the idea. Across the floor of the huge hall, the crowd was forming itself into a grid to match the workstation layout.

Then there was yet another siren, and voice: 'Task One. Duration, one minute.'

The screen lit up. Information scrolled, and she almost laughed. Basic maths, barely more than counting on her fingers. She tapped the answer and waited, counting the seconds under her breath.

She had reached sixty-four when the siren sounded. She frowned – she was usually more accurate than that – and then gasped. The boy at the station next to her had collapsed; simply folded at the knees and dropped to the floor. She heard, almost felt, the crack of his forehead hitting the base of the workstation. A guard appeared, and dragged him away. She guessed he had been chip-stunned.

Out of the corner of her eye she caught movement. Across the hall, a couple of others were being removed – and now the siren again. 'Task Two. Duration, one minute.'

This task was just a little harder. At the end of it, a few more were removed.

At the end of the first twenty tasks, the allowed time stepped up to two minutes. Then five, and later ten. There were no visible clocks – even the time display function on the desk screen was blanked out – but Seldyan kept a running guestimate of the elapsed time in her head. By the time she had reached five hours, well over half the workstations were unoccupied.

There had been no food and no water, it was if anything even colder, and her bladder was painfully full.

Then, at last, it looked as though there might be relief. A different siren, and although it was the same voice, this time it was a different message:

'Break! Five minutes. Facilities are at the north end of the hall.'

Facilities! But where was north? Seldyan looked round and saw crowds already gathering around three – only three! – openings in the far wall.

She knew not one in ten would get done in five minutes. She breathed out and forced herself to think. There must be something.

Then she thought of it. She turned and ran, away from the waiting crowds, towards the opposite end of the hall. To where they had taken the ones who had collapsed, when they failed tasks.

When she reached it there was only one opening, but it was a wide one and – she grinned – on the other side of it a row of doors stretched down a broad corridor. The corridor was noticeably warmer than the hall. Some doors were marked as Med rooms and a few with labels she didn't understand, but then there was one with a symbol no one could mistake. She gave a little jump of triumph and reached out a hand to the push plate.

A blast of agony crowbarred every muscle in her body. The spasm threw her across the corridor, and she heard rather than felt the crack of her head against the opposite wall.

There was a moment of blank. Then she opened her eyes and saw a face close to hers. It was grinning.

She gathered saliva and spat at the face. It pulled back sharply, but the grin was still there. The lips parted and formed words.

'You're a clever one, for sure, when you're not being dumb. Clever is good, and right now clever is going back to a workstation and passing some more tests.'

She nodded towards the door behind him. 'Not before I go in there.'

The guard laughed. 'Okay. But be quick, or I'll hit your chip again.'

She was quick. When she had finished she walked out past the guard, who didn't acknowledge her, and back into the hall – but not to her original workstation. 'A workstation', the guard had said, not 'your workstation'. So she chose one as close as possible to the entrance from the corridor; close to the facilities and with a hint of second-hand warmth leaking towards it.

As she walked up to the station the siren sounded, and there was another task, and then another. The first few were solo but after that their rapidly thinning numbers were divided into teams of five or six, and then the tasks were suddenly *much* more elaborate and there was a need for leadership and organization.

It seemed natural to her. After a while it seemed that it was natural for the others too. She began to forget that she was weak with hunger and thirst and shivering with cold. The team was the thing . . . and then, quite unexpectedly, there was a final-sounding siren, and no more tasks.

She felt almost sorry. She looked round her team – *her* team, yes, that was right – and saw four tired faces. They had been weeded down quite quickly; just her, Merish, Kot, Lyste and Hufsza had been left after five tasks. She had only known Merish before, but she knew all of them now. She gave them a smile. 'Whatever it was, I think we did it.'

They nodded, and then she looked away from them and scanned round the hall. It was almost empty. She could count only five teams – twenty-five people, out of what? Three hundred? More?

She turned to Merish. 'So few . . .'

He nodded. 'Yeah. We got Sorted.'

She was going to ask what he meant when suddenly her tired-ness and hunger caught up with her. Her eyes began to close just as her legs softened. She felt herself falling.

She had woken next to Merish. It was an unusual privilege, but not one she felt like questioning. She was content to lie quietly, watching him in the half-light of the sleeping cell.

She had never known full darkness.

Even in sleep he looked tired, and somehow watchful. If she reached out and touched him, she was sure he would be fully awake in a second.

There hadn't been much, between her collapsing in the hall and ending up here. She had eaten and drunk, as much as she could manage with a dry throat and lips that felt like ropes, but mainly she had let herself be moved around.

Merish had told her to sleep, but she had been too wired. So in the end he had given up.

'You must have heard of Sorting?'

She nodded.

'Well, that was what just happened. They surprise you, they stress you out, you're too cold, you're hungry, and you have to perform.' He propped himself up on an elbow. 'You performed.'

'I know I did. We all did.'

'No.' He lay back. 'Most of us got through it. *You performed*. You led. You made the five of us a team, and we came out top.' He put his hand on her shoulder. 'You're stuck with that job now. I'll try to make it easy.'

She was getting sleepy. 'What happened to the rest?'

His answer took a while and she didn't like any of it. Apparently it depended on how soon they failed. The soonest were sent to forced manual labour. If they were *really* dumb, their organs would be harvested, provided they were worth more than what the Hive could get for the labour. Or, if they were good-looking, people would pay for that too.

She stared at him. 'I don't understand.' Then something about his face made her mind clear, and she had a fleeting mental picture of him, curled up, surrounded by a group of boys. She waved the thought away with her hand. 'Okay, never mind. What about the rest of us?'

'We get hired out for specialist stuff. The cleverer, the more specialist.'

'How do you know all this?'

There was a soft snort, and she realized he had almost laughed. 'I keep my ears open. Don't you? Also, I'm good at hacking into things.'

She stared for a long time at the dim view of the ceiling. Then she shook her head. 'No.'

'No what?'

'Just no.'

He reached out, touched her shoulder. 'Seldyan? We don't get to say no. Not to anything. They use Sorting to make the best into teams. That's what happened today. Now go to sleep.'

She closed her eyes. She had no intention of sleeping; she was going to hold on to her flaming anger. She would never let it die.

Somehow, she slept. But the last image she saw was of the boy at the workstation near her, who had been first to collapse. She had glanced at him quickly enough to see his face before his eyes closed. It had been a mixture of vacancy and fear – the fear of someone completely uncomprehending. He hadn't been especially good-looking as far as she could remember. Presumably he was being – harvested. Maybe right now.

Her sleep was uneasy and full of vacant faces. When she woke she found her arms locked round Merish, and his eyes open and watching her.

A deep thrumming note that sounded in her chest brought Seldyan back to the present, and a voice that seemed to come from everywhere said, *'Alert.'*

She raised her eyebrows. 'Meaning?'

'Don't know.' Merish was frowning at the displays. 'Something the ship wasn't expecting. It might be nothing; the things it was expecting are thousands of years out of date, remember.'

Ten minutes later the five of them were staring at the display, and it obviously wasn't nothing. It looked a bit like an eyebrow, if an eyebrow were half a million kilometres across and glowing angrily.

It was Kot who eventually broke the silence. 'That looks wrong,' she said.

They all turned to Merish who was hunched over a display tank. Symbols floated in front of him, fuzzing and changing. He pursed his lips. 'It does look wrong, and it doesn't belong; you and the ship are both right. It's plasma plus other stuff: lumps of iron and nickel and silicates and a big heap of trans-uranium elements.' He straightened up. 'If you smashed up a medium-sized planet, I mean *really* smashed it up so the biggest piece was a hundred metres across, irradiated the living *fuck* out of it and then smeared it out over a few hundred thousand klicks, you'd get something that looked like that thing.'

Seldyan felt her stomach flip. She looked round at shocked faces. 'Smashed up? Oh shit. A destroyed planet? Merish, an *inhabited*, destroyed planet?'

'I so hope not.' He glared at the tank, then blew out his cheeks. 'No. Can't be. Everything local is accounted for.'

'Right.' She stared at the image for a moment. 'Is it safe to approach?'

He shrugged. 'It depends how. In the ship we could fly straight through it. Unshielded, I wouldn't like to get within half a million klicks of the middle of it. It's seriously hot, Seldyan.'

'Okay, so let's not.' She sat back, feeling her heart slowing to normal.

Kot cleared her throat. 'That's not so easy. That thing is in the same system as Oblong, and Web City.'

'Oh.' Seldyan chewed her lip. 'How close is it?'

Kot looked down. 'About half a million klicks. Sorry, Seldyan.'

'I think you'd better save your regrets for the locals, if they're still around.' Seldyan watched the display for a while, trying to imagine what it must be like to live close to something like that. Then she stood up. 'Guys, I'm going to rest. You should too, if you can. Whatever we find, I've a feeling we're going to be busy.'

She had decided not to take the captain's quarters, opting instead for the close, safe, simple confines of a steward's cabin. For one thing, Hefs had indulged some rather extravagant tastes; his suite was on a scale and in a style she just couldn't engage with. But more important, there were – associations.

She had been acting, with Hefs – that had been obvious even to him in the end – but many people, she assumed, could act in that way, probably better and for longer than she could. The thing she kept concealed from almost everyone, sometimes even including herself, was that the ability to act like that was in itself an act; another layer down.

How could you act what you had never experienced?

She didn't know, and mostly didn't really care, what the others assumed passed between her and Merish, but she was always glad when she felt him slip in beside her.

Sometimes there was intimacy, although never more than the intimacy of gently questing fingers and soft kisses, but not this time, at least not at first. Merish knew her moods better than she did; she heard the door, felt the sleeping pad squash a little and then his arm found its way over her. She pressed herself into him and they lay still together.

They were quiet for a while. Then she felt him move, rolling away from her and on to his back. She rolled over to face him and said, 'Talk to me.'

'Okay. I think you're scared.'

She frowned up at the half-darkness. 'Merish, I think you're the only person in the Spin who could say that to me and stay unbruised.'

'I expect so. I still think you're scared. I know it's not for you because it never is. So, talk about it.'

She nodded. 'Okay. So, what was the average life span in the Hive?'

'Exactly? I don't know. Roughly, around seventy standard. Why?'

'And in Web City?'

The pad wobbled; he had shaken his head. 'No idea.'

'Yeah, I thought so. And that's before they shared their space with a radioactive smear.' She stared up at nothing for a moment, then took a breath. 'Merish? What if we bust out for nothing? What if everything, everywhere, is shit? All the time?'

She heard the pause in his breathing. Then his arm curled over her again. 'What, everything?'

She thought she was going to resist him, but then she discovered she wasn't.

It did help, for a while. But when he had sighed and turned over to sleep she stayed awake, staring wide-eyed at the darkness and wondering what it was concealing.

Counterweight Park, Basin City

Vess looked around carefully – he seemed to be alone – and lowered his bare feet into the water. The current was slow and the surface glass-smooth; if he patted it with his feet *so*, he could leave regular footprints that flowed away in a steadily spreading line that was consumed by its own ripples by the time it was a dozen of its own wobbly paces away.

He had first played this private game the day he had arrived on the level. He had repeated it only a handful of times since.

The Board of the Harbour Company usually met every seventeen days, thereby achieving three anachronisms in one go because there was no longer a Harbour Company, it wasn't a Board and seventeen days had been the length of the refilling cycle of the oldest of the balancing reservoirs that fed the boat lifts from the Ground to the Middle level. This meant an influx of goods into the import bonds every seventeen days which in turn was a good reason for a commercial Board to meet, a thousand years ago.

Now the Board was responsible for the management of the Spin Inside, a shrinking, beleaguered collection of planets eking out an existence in the shadow of growing neighbours. And, of course, for its main asset. The Hive.

The old boat lift still chugged round its now pointless cycle.

Every seventeen days a hundred or so gigalitres of water gurgled down winding channels from the mountains behind the city, over a control weir and into the huge ladle-shaped Great Basin. The Basin was suspended on three colossal chains from a stubby counterpoise arm. Eventually the mounting weight of water would trip the catches and send the whole thing swaying slowly downwards, raising the boat lift like a giant counterweight until it docked with the First Middle Dock. Which was usually empty of shipping, having lost its function a thousand years ago just like nearly everything else.

Vess was sitting just upstream from the weir. He enjoyed watching the old system. There was something inevitable about it, which meant that as long as it went on working it wasn't his problem. He sometimes thought he would have liked to meet whoever designed it.

Anachronistic name or not, the out-of-date Board of the non-existent Harbour Company was still the senior body for the Inside. It provided the top stratum of Federation management from a position that was unelected and ungoverned and completely unchallenged, and a missing cruise ship would be the least of its worries, if *Sunskimmer* had really been no more than a cruise ship.

Vess paddled a few more footprints and looked up towards the Lay Palace. It was an astonishing thing.

Six thousand years before, the then-Chairman of the Board had summoned the best architect in the Spin and told her to construct a floating palace in the Basin. It had to be the largest building in the City of its day, it had to float freely within the Basin without tethering and it must not change the length of the cycle of the Basin by more than a second.

The result was – he allowed himself the word once more – truly astonishing. Presumably with posterity in mind the architect had delivered seventeen storeys of tapering ziggurat, rising from a wide shallow base to a peak nearly a hundred metres above the surface of the water. By virtue of the area of its base it was the largest building in the City at the time, and the same broad base kept it floating in the centre of the reservoir thanks to surface tension. Once every seventeen days it grounded briefly, and mathematicians, statisticians and the occasional specialist in gambling theory had written papers about the scatter of its resting points.

Vess always thought it was a shame that the Lay Palace had gone down in history as a sort of failure. Everything about it was perfect except that it had changed the seventeen-day cycle by one and three tenths seconds, and the architect had achieved the other sort of posterity by being duly and unpleasantly executed.

Which was quite likely to be his fate too, as much as he was trying not to think about it. But phlegmatism had always been one of his assessed traits.

His musing had distracted him and the line of watery footprints was ragged. He forced himself to correct his rhythm. There; better.

But it was time to go. He swung his feet out of the water and stood, picking up his shoes. He would put them on when his feet had dried. For the moment he carried them, walking carefully so his wet feet did not slip on the slick polished stones of the Basin edge. It was a hundred metres or so to the nearest of the slim articulated bridges that led to the Lay Palace; by the time he got to it he was dry enough to put on his shoes. When he had straightened up, he half turned and looked over his shoulder. Another line of footprints, dark against the light stone but fading as he looked. This time they were heading towards him.

Clo Fiffithiss was waiting for him at the other end of the bridge. It lifted a foreclaw in greeting.

'Hello! Ready for the bloody circus?'

Vess raised his eyebrows. 'One day you could try to be really discouraging.'

'Rubbish, human. You know I'm supporting you.'

'Is that what it is?' Vess shook his head. 'If anyone else says they're going to support me I'll assume it's all over and hand myself in for composting.'

Fiffithiss extended the foreclaw and patted him on the shoulder. It felt like being tapped sharply with a twig. 'I wouldn't do that. I've heard it's a messy end. You're Admin grade, Harbour Master, same as me. Take my advice. Leave the blood and guts to the Praetors and the Board. Protect your pension. You have no family, have you?'

'No. No, there's just me.'

'Good man. Less to worry about. Come on. Let's get in there and show them how grey and uninteresting we Administrators can be.'

It turned and headed for the entrance to the Palace, using all nine limbs in a complex syncopation like a straight-line dance. It looked like hard work. Vess remembered reading that the species had evolved – or had been engineered, according to some – for light-gravity environments where walking only needed four limbs. Some of them never mastered using the full set, and those never left the home planet.

Just at the moment leaving your home planet looked like a very good idea to Vess. He shrugged and followed Clo Fiffithiss up a shallow ramp and into the Daily Entrance of the palace. Not the Main Entrance; that was for important people.

Important. That word again.

Vess shifted in his seat. It was a massive, deeply upholstered half-globe covered in a pleated animal hide, and like every waiting-room seat he had ever sat on it had the trick of being far less comfortable than it looked. He glanced towards Clo Fiffithiss. 'Much longer, you think?'

The being rustled a little as if it had been stirred by a breeze. 'No idea. We get there when we get there. Try to relax.'

Vess raised his eyebrows. 'Why? You haven't.'

'You can tell?'

'I looked it up.' He looked at Fiffithiss, who had draped itself limply from the frame of one of the chairs. Its body was hanging at the end of a bundle of legs, the three foreclaws swinging freely below it so that they almost brushed the floor. To a careless observer it looked a bit like a clump of vines, and it would go on doing so right up to the moment when it let go its hold and dropped like streamlined death on to a piece of prey, claws first. It was about the least relaxed pose the species could adopt.

'Sorry. Genes.' Fiffithiss wriggled free of the chair and dropped to the floor. 'The point stands, though: try to relax. I'll try too. If I fail then we can be nervous together.'

'All right, I'll try.' A thought struck Vess. He hesitated. 'Look, sorry if this is intrusive, but have you ever . . . Hunted?'

There was a long silence. Fiffithiss hunkered low to the floor, its body swaying in the cradle of its legs. Eventually it said, 'Well, that helped with the tension. Have I ever Hunted? Meaning, have I ever got stoned out of both of my brains on an ancient plant extract and taken part in a ritual hunt to the death with members of my own brood?'

Vess felt his face colouring. 'I didn't mean . . .'

'Oh yes you did. You look things up.' Fiffithiss tapped a claw. 'I'll save you the trouble of looking up my name. I'm not some fucking baby-eater, human. Fiffithiss means Abstainer. Among my people it's not a compliment, and that's one of the reasons I don't live among my people. Does that help?'

'Yes. Look, I'm sorry . . .'

'Good. Now stop beating yourself up. I'm sure other people are forming a queue.'

Vess was almost relieved when the door to the main chamber opened. A globe-shaped dirigible bell-hop about twice the size of Vess's head floated through, wobbling a little. It gave off a faint hiss.

'Agenda point five?' Its voice sounded like modulated static.

Clo Fiffithiss gave an affirmative bob. 'We believe so.'

The bell-hop didn't move. 'Ambiguous. Agenda point five? Confirm or deny.'

Fiffithiss drew itself upright, straightening all nine legs so that it looked like a narrow tripod, squared. One foreclaw clicked against its body in a pastiche of a salute. 'Agenda point five, confirmed.'

'Follow.' The machine wobbled back through the door.

They followed.

The room was on Level Sixteen, the second-highest level of the ziggurat. At this height the palace was still wide enough to be very big, but narrow enough to encompass one room with windows on all four sides. It felt like a long walk from the entrance to the far end where the Board waited.

By tradition there were five of them – four Praetors and the Chairman, and instead of sitting they stood at lecterns, each one shaped differently to represent the Guild of its user. The Chairman stood at the central lectern, leaning well back to balance his vast belly. Vess had a theory that Alst Or-Shls kept on the lectern tradition because if he ever sat down he would never be able to rise unaided.

The lectern on the far right of the group, shaped like a darkly twisted vine dotted with cancerous growths, looked empty, but Vess had no doubt it was not empty at all. He shuddered a little.

They halted in front of a pale line inlaid in the near-black wooden floor. There were no seats for visitors, either. Vess hated that. Standing still without looking awkward was hard enough when you were calm, and he was not calm.

Or-Shls wore thick lenses in front of his eyes, an archaic affectation. Now he reached up and did something to the frame that carried them. They slid quickly sideways and disappeared round the back of his head on tiny runners built into the frame.

Without them his eyes looked much larger, and they bulged. He glanced round at the Praetors.

'All ready?' His voice was gravelly, and even from where Vess was standing it smelled of tobacco smoke – an even more ridiculous, not to say dangerous, affectation.

The Praetors nodded.

'Good. Well, Administrators, we're ready to hear you. The last of the Great Ships has been taken without a fight. I expect you can tell us why.'

Vess felt himself exhale. It felt like relief, as if all the tension he hadn't realized he was containing had left him. This was it – he was off the cliff and falling. 'Because we are no longer able to maintain a viable deterrent near the periphery, Mr Chairman.'

At first there was silence. Or-Shls glared at him. 'Why not?'

Vess shrugged. 'I can only administer what is there. The last four Shareholder meetings in succession have ordered ships to be withdrawn from the Border zones and concentrated around the Home systems. The gaps are too great.'

'And *Sunskimmer* was in one of these gaps?'

Vess nodded. 'Was in one of them, and made her escape through another of them.'

'Excuse me.' The soft voice came from the lectern on Vess's far left. The lectern itself was a blocky thing formed of different-sized oolite cubes piled on top of each other to make a cream-coloured column that seemed solid and rickety at the same time. It was a complete contrast to the sinuously muscled quadruped that stood upright behind it, heavy front paws resting on the top roughly on a level with Vess's eyes.

One of the paws lifted lazily. 'The Shareholder meetings acted on the advice of this Board, didn't they? And we consulted on our recommendations. The doctrine of Holding the Centre? I'm sure you were on the mailing list. Both of you.'

Clo Fiffithiss stirred. 'We were, Garash. I don't know about

Vess, but for my part I sent back a series of models that gamed the results of the Doctrine. I think the risks were clear.' It turned towards Garash. 'I'm certain you were on *that* mailing list.'

Vess felt himself tensing. The silence seemed to go on for a long time. Then Or-Shls gave a tight smile.

'We know about your games, thank you,' he said. 'You identified risk. Unfortunately risk has been allowed to turn into outcome. Rather a lot of outcome. More than you know, I suspect.' He gestured towards the apparently empty lectern. 'Over to you.'

Vess caught his breath.

The lectern crawled. The things which had looked like growths moved, standing out from the twisted column on hundreds of hair-fine legs. They *flowed*, that was the word, up the lectern and collected in a growing mass at the top where they formed the approximate outline of a human face.

A hole opened in the middle of the face. It wasn't really mouth-shaped. Vess wasn't sure if that was better or worse. The voice of the gestalt entity called Vut would have been almost a purr if it hadn't been for a sibilant edge.

'You noted, and questioned, the Doctrine of Holding the Centre. Based on your knowledge at the time your questions were reasonable, but your knowledge was incomplete. Observe.'

The windows dimmed, not gently but fast so the room went black with a *snap* that was almost tangible. Vess thought he could feel his irises trying to keep up. At his side, Clo Fiffithiss rustled uneasily. Its night sight was far better than his, he knew, but darkness was Hunting territory; the being would be on edge.

A familiar starscape blurred and solidified in front of them. He nodded. 'The Inside and the Boundary. So?'

'The Inside, yes. Our eleven planets. A precarious economy at the best of times, as is any completely enclosed economic unit. But these are not the best of times. Before you are told more you will need to agree to non-disclosure.'

75

'I thought we both had already.' Clo Fiffithiss sounded confused.

Or-Shls cut in. 'Not to anything like the level required for this. Turn around please.'

The room lightened a little. They turned and found the dirigible – or another identical one – behind them, floating level with Vess's head about an arm's length from him. In the dim light it gave off a soft violet glow and it was bobbing up and down very slightly; after a second he realized that he was nodding in time with it. He stopped himself.

The globe-shaped body split horizontally. The lower half dropped away to hang from the upper by slim articulated rods of dull silver metal. In the space between the two halves the air glowed smokily.

Or-Shls spoke from behind them. 'Look into the light please. Vess first.'

Vess looked. At first it was hard to focus, but then a point of white light grew within the smoke, and as soon as he had seen it his eyes were captured and he found he couldn't look away. There was a brief moment of dislocation and then his head was full of words.

. . . agree to terms of non-disclosure regarding Praetor briefing at the Lay Palace, Counterweight Basin . . .

It made his head ache. He fought off the temptation to look away. Besides, he suspected that to try would be to tear his eyes out of their sockets. There was nothing optional about this.

. . . my understanding that sanctions for non-compliance may include physical recovery of all knowledge imparted. Confirm?

He frowned. Without breaking eye contact with the machine he said, 'Physical recovery?'

'It means we will recover the material mechanically from your brain.' Or-Shls's voice was level. 'Reliable and fatal.'

Confirm? Second request of three.

Vess didn't like to think what might happen if he used up all three requests. 'Confirm.'

The point of light vanished and his eyes snapped away. The headache was fading already.

He watched as Clo Fiffithiss went through the same process. Then the dirigible snapped itself shut and floated off. They turned back towards the Praetors and the lights faded.

'We hope that wasn't too uncomfortable?' Vut didn't sound concerned. 'It was necessary in any case. What we are about to tell you has been kept to Board level until now. For five hundred years. We take it we have your attention?'

Vess nodded dumbly. A faint rustle told him Clo Fiffithiss had done its version of the same thing.

'Good. So, five hundred years ago we had just lost the twelfth planet. In response the Border was established as a hard boundary between us and the rest, and the modern status quo was established. Except that there was nothing static about it. The Board of the day ordered the situation to be gamed.'

Clo Fiffithiss stirred. 'That must have been one of the first uses of gaming as a policy tool?'

'It was. And still one of the most influential. The result indicated that the Inside of those days was not durable. The response was to set up a structure that could be defended even in decline. Hence, the Inside Federation. But now that has changed. The most recent gaming suggests that the situation is no longer viable.'

There was a short silence. Then Clo Fiffithiss spoke.

'I don't understand. The loss of the ships is serious, but how does it make us unviable?'

'Your own gaming lacks data. On its own, the loss of the last legacy Main Battle Unit would not be fatal – although it is a symptom of a wider decline which has been going on for generations. We need not consider historical problems; the modern beginning of the end set in five years ago.'

The starscape changed, zooming out to show many more systems. Most of them were greyed out, but a cluster some way outside the Boundary glowed brightly. The view zoomed in to show three planets – Vess assumed they were planets – in a tight ring around a small blue-white star.

'That is the Tri-Gyre. We are sure you already have questions.'

Vess frowned at the image. The star was well outside the plane of the ring, so that it formed an apex rather than a centre.

'Why is the sun off to the side?'

Vut sounded amused. 'Given that this is the Spin, *why* is unknowable. Pure whimsy, probably. As to *how*, there is a counterbalancing micro black hole on the opposite side of the ring. The black hole and the star are kept apart by a field generator. It is not an elegant solution, and that was not the important question.'

Vess stared at the image. There was something just below it: a sort of ghostly curve with a green dot at its end. He pointed. 'That?'

'Yes, that. A large cloud of debris where nothing previously existed, and beyond it a green star – also where nothing previously existed.'

'So what is it?'

Or-Shls took a wheezy breath. 'The green star, we don't know. But the other feature we suspect to be an effort at new planetary engineering. Not carried out by us. Not carried out by anyone for a hundred millennia. Carried out by someone else less than a thousand days ago. That's just the beginning. Go on, Vut. You're the economist.'

The not-mouth opened again. 'The beginning, yes, or perhaps better a marker of the beginning. We are one ninth of the Spin, but allowing for the Hive we have closer to one fifth of the population and rather less than one eleventh of the resources. We therefore depend on trade. These were our trade routes six years ago.'

The starscape pulled back so that the Inside was a glittering patch in the centre. Scores of curving lines glowed into life, originating all over the Spin but all of them either passing through or ending within the Inside.

About a third of them were yellow and the rest cerise. Vess frowned. 'What do the colours mean?'

'Yellow means a positive balance of payments. Pink, the opposite.'

'So we're overall negative?'

'Correction. Six years ago we *were* overall negative, by a modest margin. This is the situation today.'

The image changed. Vess stared at it.

Most of the lines were gone. The only ones left were cerise.

Vut went on speaking. 'We are almost cut off. Our routes have been concentrated into fewer and fewer superhighways, each of them many times more vulnerable and expensive to run than before. We are leaking money. It won't be long before shortages can't be disguised any longer.'

Clo Fiffithiss tapped an intricate three-limb tattoo on the floor. Vess recognized it as the equivalent of a baffled shake of the head. 'I don't understand. What's the connection between someone making planets and us losing trade routes?'

'Technological development. The ability to project power, Gamer. And as this information was not available to you, you are not held to blame.'

Or-Shls nodded. 'You can leave us. The Harbour Master will remain.'

There was the tiniest hesitation and then a sound like a syncopated drum roll. Clo Fiffithiss had retreated at speed, but it had waited for a fraction of a second. Even such a brief pause was a dangerous display in the face of so direct a dismissal. It was as much support as the being could have dared express.

It didn't help. The room was still very lonely when it had gone.

Vess cleared his throat. 'Am I held to blame, then?'

To his surprise, Or-Shls grinned. 'Not exactly. But the total loss of the major fleet has not merely left us without viable means of aggression – it has left us diminished. We look like fools, Vess, unable even to pretend to project power; unable to hold on to what little we have. And, it has left you without a role. We have selected you a new one.'

'Thank you, Chairman.'

'I wouldn't, not yet. Madam Garash?'

The heavy paws tightened a little on the edge of the lectern so that Vess half expected to hear it creaking.

'You are an interesting character, Hevalansa Vess. You come from Ground Level, but you have risen far without making enemies or leaving a trail of bodies. You get on well with your peers, but you have few friends. You are legendarily private and you have no intimate relationships. Your profile indicates that you are a pronounced insectophobe and yet you maintain your composure in the presence of our friends Vut and you seem positively close to Clo Fiffithiss. In short, you have all the attributes of a spy.'

'A what?' Vess felt slightly dizzy. He shook his head.

'A spy. We need information, Vess. We need to know how the hijackers of the last Great Ship broke out from the Hive. That should not have been possible. They should not have been able to break out. They should not have been able to buy tickets. They should not have been able to steal the ship – even if ships of that scale are designed to be run by small crews. You are the kind of person who can find that out.'

The dizziness was worse. Vess spoke carefully. 'What must I do?'

'For the moment, nothing. Are you feeling unwell?'

'Yes. What . . . ?'

'Good. Don't move.'

Vess realized he was swaying. He was trying to work out how

to say that he couldn't help it when he was spared the trouble; something behind him was holding him up. He heard a soft hissing and realized it was the sound of the dirigible, and he wondered how it ever had enough buoyancy to support him on top of its own weight. He managed one word. '*Good?*'

'Yes. You were hacked when you looked into the light. It's taking effect. Just relax.'

With the dizziness had come panic but also a sort of euphoria. He wanted to be facetious, to tell them that he didn't need their help to relax, to tell them *something*, but his voice wouldn't work.

The hissing suddenly seemed very loud, and then very distant.

He relaxed.

Tri-Gyre Approach

Even the thing nearest them was very big. Not as big as something like a planet, obviously, she'd get to that later, but planets were supposed to be big. A hundred kilometres across would have been tiny for a planet, but it was absolutely massive for something like Web City.

She would get to Web City in a while. Meanwhile, Oblong.

It wasn't really oblong, but she could forgive that because she knew it had been, once.

It had started out as an old container ship which was tumbling helplessly through space in what was then the recently abandoned middle of nowhere – abandoned by what would become the Inside, which in turn was on its way to becoming Inside rather than Outside. It had lost motive power and was barely airtight, really very much more container and rather less ship. It had perfectly suited the people who found it; they had nowhere to go, but they urgently wanted somewhere to be.

Then some more people joined them, and suddenly the big old hulk had seemed not so big. That was when they had started to snare asteroids.

One thing led to another. A millennium later the agglomerated mass that was still called Oblong consisted of the remains of about seventy asteroids, eight Light Cruisers, some tankers and a small yacht which had wandered unwittingly into the growing gravity well of the swollen composite body and never escaped. As a planet it would have been a pinprick at best. As an artificial object it had once been by a comfortable margin the biggest in the Spin and for quite a long way outside it.

But only once. Now its child had overtaken it. Big was still a key word, but 'bigger' was the word for what it sat in the middle of. Web City wasn't one object. It was presently a few thousand, and counting.

Sooner or later an object like Oblong has to stop growing. It becomes too disordered, too hard to navigate, too hard to wire up and govern and just *operate*. So it had stopped, but the bits and pieces went on arriving, faster with every year since the place had acquired a sort of social gravity. If you wanted to start a new life you took anything you could get your hands on, made it space-tight, powered it with whatever and headed for Oblong. If and when you got there in one piece you tied yourself to the nearest similar object and began to call the place home.

A few thousand objects later you had Web City – a tethered, roughly hexagonal close-packed spacescape of *stuff* full of people and commerce and informal manufacturing and sex and crime, sometimes separately. It was divided into cells a few hundred metres across, each with local shielding and atmosphere services, and each one, subject to any unresolved border disputes, linked to its neighbours by airlocked tube-shaped tunnels.

The joins between the cells weren't rigid, so Web City undulated very slowly around Oblong like a sleepy sea creature. Something about it raised Seldyan's pulse rate, but not as much as the thing behind it.

It was what they had seen as an eyebrow; apparently the locals called it the Arch. It was half a million kilometres from end to end and it lit up the sky above Web City with a ghostly shimmer of all colours and none. Bands of colour ran slowly along it, flickering through the spectrum; ragged patches effloresced and faded.

It had been there for less than five years.

They stared at it for a long time. Eventually Lyste let out a breath. 'What the fuck *is* that?'

Merish shook his head. 'I'm no wiser than I was before. Debris, very hot, very radioactive. Weird debris, too. Not just radioactive, but full of really bizarre daughter elements.'

Seldyan found it hard to tear herself away from the screen. She managed. 'So, your bust-apart planet?'

'I don't think so.' He frowned. 'Or if it is, it's not just that. Those daughter elements? They don't belong. They're what you get if you do a whole lot of complicated reactions at energy levels that don't belong in a planet, with exotic elements that *definitely* don't belong in a planet.'

She studied his face for a moment, then looked back to the screen. 'Merish? Being blown up doesn't belong in a planet either. I'm withholding judgement, if you don't mind. Now, you said you wouldn't want to be within half a million klicks of this thing, and yet here we are. How safe will we be in Web City?'

Merish shrugged. 'It depends where and for how long. Oblong's shielding looks fine.'

'Uh-huh. Let's take dosimeters with us.'

Lyste laughed softly. 'Wonderful. Tell me, Seldyan, at what point will we decide we should have stuck with where we came from?'

She had to take another couple of breaths, but for a different reason. When she felt able she said, slowly, 'Never. Is that clear?'

Apparently it was, because no one said anything more.

They approached at one notch above dead stop, with every remote-sensing gadget that the old ship could muster quivering at maximum gain. That was *lots*: a tumbling wave of information that spilled out of the tank like phosphorescent foam.

Merish and Kot were crouched over the tank like statues, if statues could look that tense. Lyste was fingering some wooden puzzle that never seemed to leave her hands. It made a faint clicking noise. Seldyan was learning not to find it annoying. Hufsza sat in a personal pool of calmness which hadn't reached Seldyan; she waited, chewing a nail.

Then, all at once, Merish and Kot straightened up, and the ship made its listen-to-me chime and said, '*Contact.*'

On one of the parts of the display that she actually understood, Seldyan watched the velocity tell-tale scroll down to zero and stay there. She turned to Merish.

'Is that it?'

'Yes. We brushed the tiniest outpost of the dumbest sensor tendril; probably a long-term impact warning system.'

'Okay.' She glanced at the tank, which now showed a single faintly bluish filament extending out from Oblong towards them. 'Will it know what we are?'

'Not yet. It probably thinks we're a really boring asteroid. We're incognito, Sel, until we get closer in. Then we'll send a "hello" signal back, so they don't have to do any nervous guessing.'

She nodded, and went on looking. The black hole was invisible but she could just make out the field that kept it apart from the little sun at the other side of the formation. It looked like a blurred ghostly spindle hanging from a star, with three planets spinning round it.

'Beautiful.' She said it under her breath, and even as her lips closed around the last thread of the whisper, she thought that it was probably the first time in her life she had used the word. She grinned to herself and said it again, louder.

'Beautiful.'

Merish laughed. 'Letting it get to you?'

'Damn right. That's the new world. Hope they're ready for us.'

'So, definitely not nervous?'

She shook her head. 'They might be. I'm not.'

Merish studied his hands for a moment. Then he smiled at her. 'Where do you get it from, Seldyan?'

'The same place you did, remember? I just did something different with it.' Then she bit her lip as his smile faded.

He nodded once, very slowly. Then he turned away. 'Better let them know we're here.'

'Okay.'

The screens showed the knobbly mass of Oblong in the foreground, now utterly dwarfed by the backdrop of the Tri-Gyre. At this distance the components of Web City had dispersed to the point where you could have dismissed them as space trash, but the three planets were big enough to fill the whole field of view. If you stared at them long enough they started to fill your whole mind as well.

It was as well to pull back a little. When Seldyan did, she realized that there was a sort of graininess between her and the planets. It was moving, crawling around slowly like specks in some vast experiment. Another shift of focus gave her the answer and her mouth went dry; the specks were ships. Thousands, probably many thousands, of ships.

She hadn't realized there were that many ships anywhere. She swallowed. Then she looked around quickly. The others hadn't noticed.

She had been watching them. She knew them, of course; she had known them since the Sorting on the Hive and she had come to know them far better through the clandestine sharing in the Mind Stack, but she had never known them under normal conditions. Whatever passed for normal; she suspected their present circumstances weren't it.

So she had watched. Merish, his eyes half closed, was still deep in an hours-long silent conversation with the ship AI. Lyste, small and dark, was sitting hunched over her toy in merciful silence.

Sitting on the other side of the bridge was Hufsza, a coil of muscle that looked barely reined in even at rest. Next to him sat Kot, the least humanoid-looking of all of them. She came from a planet where tar-sand extraction was the main activity. The tar sands contained mutagens; Kot's people had the fastest-moving DNA in the Spin. She was a full head shorter than the others, but broader even than Hufsza with an upper body almost square in section.

The silence had lasted a long time. Finally Lyste looked up and said mildly, 'It's been ages since you signalled. What's going on?'

Seldyan looked at Merish, but to judge by his unfocused eyes he was still deep in trance with the ship AI. He'd been there for most of the day. She sighed and gestured to the screen.

'They look busy. Could be just that.'

Hufsza uncoiled himself. 'Maybe this is normal. Whatever; I'd rather wait here than still be in the Hive.'

Seldyan shot him a grin.

Then they all jumped. The comms chimed and then spoke.

'Hello MBU, ah, *Suck on This*. Neat name by the way. This is Web Approach. Sorry you've been kept waiting. You're free to go forward to Oblong Outer Skin, coordinates attached. A Shuttler will meet you there. I'm afraid you've got to stop that far out; any further down our gravity well and something as big as you could tow us out into space, if you wanted to.'

Seldyan looked around the others and got a series of nods, apart from Merish who was still somewhere else. 'Thanks, Web Approach, we'll do that. What was the hold-up?'

There was the tiniest hesitation. 'No big deal. You've got a legacy Main Battle Unit, which we *have* seen before, but you also have a fully un-zipped battle-ready AI in charge, which we *haven't*. We've been trying to talk to it, and it's pretty defensive. Allow us a little caution?'

'You're allowed. Thanks, Web Approach. See you in a while.'

Seldyan closed the connection, waited a moment until she was sure it really was closed, and then turned to Merish. 'Wake up,' she said. 'Now, Merish. You're needed.'

His eyes opened slowly. 'Uh-huh?'

'We're on our way. Did anything happen while you were, ah, in there?'

He raised his eyebrows, then winced and rubbed at his temples. 'How did you know?'

'I guessed. What was it?'

'Outside contact. It started with a quick ping like a friendly hello and then grew, like *really* fast, until there were data filaments everywhere. They didn't get anything. The AI just hunkered down and shrugged them off.'

Seldyan felt her lips tightening. 'Were we attacked, Merish?' Behind her Lyste's toy clicked and fell silent.

'You could call it that, maybe. Or a very invasive probe. Someone wanted to get deep into the AI.' He shrugged. 'They didn't.'

She nodded. Her mind had already been made up. 'Okay. Everyone? We got this far. Let's go the rest of the way – but let's not assume anything. Agreed?'

They nodded. Lyste picked up the toy again. Click, click.

An hour later the ship had threaded its way through the ridiculous traffic with a sort of delicacy that made Seldyan think of a vast throwback lizard treading carefully through a crèche. It had come to a cautious local stop at the end of a long pontoon. They sat on the bridge watching the strangest thing Seldyan had ever seen wandering towards them.

The body – there was something about it which invited comparison with living things – was a stubby irregular dull grey cylinder which had a peculiar twisted look to it. It seemed to be able to sprout things at will; where the pontoon broadened into a wide track the thing grew a pair of tall, plumply tyred wheels that it hung between, swinging slightly. When the pontoon narrowed the wheels – disappeared? were reabsorbed? went, anyway – and the thing climbed along on six articulated limbs.

Kot got there first. 'What the fuck is that?'

Merish had been studying the comms. Now he looked up, grinning. 'I think it's a Shuttler,' he said. 'Looks like a smoother ride than the shuttles we're used to.'

He was right. When it was close to them the Shuttler reared up, extended its limbs and took the tiny proportion of *Suck on This* that it could actually reach in a careful embrace that made scratching noises through the hull. Then it lowered its body towards them. There was a dull clang and the sound of an air-lock cycling.

The Shuttler was less interesting on the inside. It was too big for them; ten rows of four seats split by a central aisle reminded Seldyan of old-style planetary airliners. She had never been on one, but she had seen pictures. But Merish was right – it was much smoother than the shuttles they were used to. Motion was imperceptible, and she couldn't tell when the thing switched between legs and wheels. She would have preferred something noisier; it would have given her something to distract her on her way into the unknown.

Better to stare it down. She glared at the forward viewing screens.

As well as being smooth the Shuttler was faster than it looked. Oblong was growing quickly, so that its rough bulk soon blotted out the planets directly behind it. At a distance it looked black but as they closed on it she realized that its surface was mottled and irregular, like a chemical experiment that had fizzed into a block of iridescent grey bubbles and then set. Closer still and she understood why Shuttlers had legs as well as wheels. She could see several of them moving over the surface, and nothing else could have looked so at home.

The pontoon met the surface at a right angle. The Shuttler went round the corner without slackening speed, fingering its way quickly over the bumps and chasms and lowering itself on to a flattish protrusion. There was an industrial-sounding *clunk* and another airlock sighed.

Lyste looked up from her toy, which to Seldyan's relief had been quiet since they had been in the Shuttler. 'Welcome to the new world,' she said.

Seldyan heard the brittleness in her voice. Apprehensiveness. It mirrored her own; she looked at the others and found their own versions of the same thing in their faces and their body language. *I brought them here*, she thought. *This bit's up to me.*

She smiled widely. 'You know what, I bet we're the most interesting thing that's happening to them today. I'm pretty sure we're the most dangerous as well. People like us are the reason this place *exists*. We're the future. Shall we go out and grab some of it?'

She marched down the aisle and lowered herself into the airlock. Just before she let her head drop below floor level she looked up again; they were all watching her.

'One more thing,' she said. 'We're here because we don't want to have to do shit we don't like. Yes? So if you're worried, share it with me, or share it with the others. Let's stay dangerous.'

She dropped into the airlock and got ready to follow the instructions that floated fuzzily in front of her. Behind her she heard a brief buzz of conversation and then a click. She smiled to herself. In her own way Lyste was coping. She hoped the others would too.

The lock finished its cycle. She clenched her hands and walked out into the new world.

Oblong Embarkation

The new world was certainly new. It was getting newer almost as Seldyan watched. Listened, too – she had been sent on enough non-consensual construction projects to recognize what they sounded like.

Embarkation was one of the oldest parts of Oblong. It had been formed by joining together the blocky hulls of six of the founding Light Cruisers to make a low pillared space about two hundred metres on a side. These days that was blatantly not big enough. Admittedly the five of them were used to living at high densities – the Hive world was nothing if not full – but those had been *orderly* high densities. This was a shouting, jostling, sweat-smelling free-for-all. Seldyan felt her palms itching, and clenched her fingers.

She realized she had missed something. She turned to the off-white-robed concierge who had greeted them from the Shuttler, and leaned in towards her a little.

'I'm sorry?'

The bony face smiled. 'I said, fifty million passengers came through here last year. That's up fifty per cent from the year before and it'll be up another fifty per cent next year.'

That seemed to be it. Seldyan nodded, and tried not to get caught studying the woman's face. She had introduced herself as

Shahatiel – she emphasized the second syllable with a sound almost like a bark – and she was extremely skinny. She also had the kind of bone structure that showed it. Her age was indeterminate. Her scalp was shiny-bald and her skin was an odd slightly greyish brown which seemed natural; the only obvious sign of cosmetics was a bold fingertip-sized spot of green just above her left eye. Seldyan overcame her caution and pointed at it.

'What's that?'

The smile broadened into a grin. 'That, my new friends, is what freedom of religion looks like. The newest star! Welcome to democracy.'

It seemed safest to grin back. Seldyan made a mental note to read up on religion when she got a chance.

By what seemed like a miracle they made it across the frenetic floor of Embarkation without losing anyone. Seldyan got the strong impression that their robed companion had a way of parting the crowds. She also received a far more subtle impression that not all of the crowds were appreciative – with her Hive sensibilities she thought she detected hints of dissent in their wake. She looked around casually and saw robed figures dotted across the big room. Even in the throng they seemed to attract turned backs. Whatever; Shahatiel's presence had worked. In a shorter time than she would have thought possible they had reached the other side of the crowded space, jumped a long queue – leaving more suppressed resentment behind them – and dropped into deeply upholstered seats in a monorail carriage that shot them down into a black tunnel at a steep angle.

Seldyan had deliberately waved everyone past, leaving her sitting next to Merish at the back of the compartment. As the carriage hummed away she leaned in close and mouthed into his ear.

'Thoughts?'

They swapped head positions. 'Looks okay. Feels worrying.'

'That's what I think. Our friend?'

He shook his head. 'Nut job. Hope she's not typical. There's a big atmosphere there. Everyone seems to hate her but no one says it out loud.'

She nodded. 'Yeah. The atmosphere reminds me of something but I'm not sure what. Keep alert, will you?'

'No problem. It'll be a while before I relax enough to feel sleepy.'

'Cool. Now, let's behave.'

They sat up straight like good tourists. Ahead of them, the bald head of their guide stuck out from the folds of her robe. For a moment Seldyan thought of a moon hanging low above a barren landscape.

It was a short journey but a very fast one, and the monorail engineers had made no attempt to conceal G-forces. The opposite, if anything; Seldyan suspected that some of the curves and plunges were more playful than needful. It almost felt like a Hive shuttle, except it didn't smell.

Then the car burst out of the tunnel, and things stopped feeling like anything she had ever experienced. She heard Merish draw in a breath.

They were lancing across the surface of Oblong on the opposite side to the embarkation gantry. The abrupt movements had ceased so that if Seldyan lifted her eyes from the blurring landscape there was nothing to tell her they were moving. She did lift her eyes, or rather they were drawn upwards.

The vast glowing circle of the three planets hung above them. It filled the starscape, and pretty soon it filled the mind. It was beautiful, and even as Seldyan used the word to herself she smiled; it was the second time in a day, and in a life.

She felt Merish's fingers touch her hand. It was probably the one thing that could have distracted her from the view.

The car began to slow. The rail dipped back below the surface and the ground closed over them. Shahatiel half turned in her seat and spoke over her shoulder.

'We're nearly there. There'll be time for you to refresh yourselves before everyone arrives.'

Kot cleared her throat. 'Everyone?'

The woman laughed. 'Well, not absolutely everyone, obviously. But a reception to welcome you. Patras will be there.' She looked at them and added, 'He's the new Supervisor.'

She turned away. Merish leaned towards Seldyan. 'Supervisor?' he whispered.

She shrugged. 'New? Who knows? I know this much – we're going to be on duty for a while longer.'

He nodded. His fingers clasped hers more tightly for a moment. Then he withdrew his hand.

Village 91, Hive

The food line crawled forward. He had already learned to keep pace with it. The previous evening he had fallen a few paces behind and had suddenly found bodies swirling past him, filling the gap and forcing him backwards until there was no more queue behind him. Ahead he could see a knot of bodies gathered around the dispensary. They dispersed as he reached the hatch.

It slid out a shallow bowl of flimsy paper about the size of his outstretched palms. The bowl began to sag almost immediately. He cupped his hands underneath it and then looked at the contents. He felt his lips pull back so that his teeth chilled.

It held a congealed mass of something yellowish grey. It smelled of vomit.

There was laughter somewhere in front of him. He looked up into the faces of half a dozen people with grinning mouths and watchful eyes. He stared at them as coldly as he could until the grins faded. Then he pushed through them and dumped the bowl into the waste. He turned before the cover had closed, leaving the hiss of the disposal flare behind him, and walked back through the gap between the two halves of the watching group. It felt familiar, from a long time ago.

He went to his Village hungry, but no one troubled him. The

hunger didn't trouble him either. He had been there before. The only surprise was that here, the memory was almost welcome.

Each Village held ninety-six sleep cells, each just larger than a standard human. They were arranged round a central observation shaft in three stacked wheels of thirty-two. The sleepers' feet pointed towards the shaft and the cells were backlit at the head end so any movement within the cell threw a moving shadow across the translucent cylindrical sensor mesh that surrounded the observation shaft. Two human guards sat with their hands on dead man's handles. While either handle was held, the automatic weapon system was merely armed. If both were released, so were the weapons. It was simple and foolproof.

The Villages were themselves arranged in vertical stacks of seven which could be isolated from each other instantly. A Village with both handles free was automatically isolated. One where both had remained free for more than an hour without explanation was fumigated. Depending on the explanation it might be fumigated anyway.

Village stacks were arranged in a hexagonal close-packed matrix. The roughly triangular spaces between stacks were used for engineering and storage. Five hundred stacks made a Hive. There were many, many Hives, but the whole collection was still called by the singular – The Hive.

Vess had learned about it – and much more besides – in six days of what they called orientation. To himself he called it indoctrination, but he didn't share the word with the faceless voices in the dark of the immersion suite. Instead he cooperated with them as they taught him who he wasn't any more, and then as they showed him who he was to be while he was on the Hive world and what he was to do. Apparently it was all quite standard.

It was better than being dead – but sometimes he had found himself questioning that. He had kept his questions to himself.

The learning had been true to the reality but when he arrived – with the guilty cargo of the real Vess buried deep inside him – the reality turned out to be far more than the learning. The first thing that struck him was the smell. He had expected bodies and stale food, and the expectation had drawn him back to a faint memory of childhood in crowded places. He had shut that down quickly; in fact his Village smelled aggressively clean, with a chemical edge and a dry papery background from the disposable coveralls that were renewed every day. No other clothes were provided or allowed in the Village.

He woke with his belly growling and his newly implanted chip smarting near the base of his spine. The food line was welcome. This time no one interfered with his meal, which was a greyish porridge that looked uncomfortably like the bowl from last night but which smelled and tasted of almost nothing. But it was hot and his senses detected starch. Within a minute he had emptied the bowl, although without properly filling his stomach. Then there was work. That was what the Hive was about.

The buried part of him understood the logic – always had, in a general way, but it had been explained in words of one syllable during the process that was not called indoctrination.

There had been different teachers for different subjects. The mechanics of espionage were covered by a blocky being of a species unfamiliar to Vess, but which looked like a cross between a large human and a small cargo container. It – Vess had tried and failed to settle on a gender – had a peculiar voice which managed at the same time to be effeminate and powerfully baritone.

Then there was a long political briefing from a small apparently standard human female who barely looked up from her notes. When she did, Vess realized with a jolt that she was not so standard; in the dim light the four eyes that met his were huge, with slightly luminous purple irises. The eyes were stacked, one above the other, on either side of an ordinary-looking nose. Vess found himself wondering how many species, or sub-species – or whatever they were – the basic human form had produced, and how many more of them he was yet to meet.

He didn't have to wonder with the creature that briefed him on economic strategy. At first sight it could have been a twin of Clo Fiffithiss. But first sight was deceptive; it hadn't taken him long to realize that the only thing the two beings had in common was species. For a start, and unlike Clo Fiffithiss, it didn't use a translator. It was one of the few that had learned to produce human-compatible speech using its own vocal apparatus, a group of layered reed-like membranes set low down its windpipe. The result sounded like a wind through dead leaves.

'Most societies arrive at slavery by accident, or because they never left it. In the Spin there has been plenty of economic oppression but little actual slavery, unless you count examples like the Fortunate Protectorate, who arrived at it by accident and were obliterated by an Artefact shortly afterwards. The Inner Federation is very unusual in having decided to return to slavery on an industrial scale millennia after having abandoned it, and probably unique in that it did so as a strategic decision based on detailed gaming. You have been told that already, I know.'

Vess nodded.

'There is something you haven't been told. That decision wasn't to ensure stability; there was no outcome of the gaming that achieved that. It was about managing decline. Now the situation has passed over a threshold. It is unmanageable.'

The rustling voice fell silent. Vess squinted at the dimly lit creature. There was no readable expression; it was quite still.

'How long?' he asked.

'How long until what? The Abstainer has gamed it. Until we

default on our debts, a year. Mass unrest leading to civil war, another year. Complete dismantling of the Inner Federation by aggressors and creditors, five years. There is a certain urgency.'

The Abstainer, thought Vess. Not a friendly term, Clo Fiffithiss had said. Keeping his voice level he said, 'And me?'

'Unstable though we are, we need the economic flywheel of the Hive as a bastion against even worse instability. At the moment it is being the opposite. It is becoming unstable – a source of insurrection. Of revolution, even. Find the instability, Vess, and then come back and tell us.'

Vess nodded again. Then a thought occurred to him. 'Am I the only one in there?'

'Perhaps. Or perhaps not. Have you any more questions?'

He dared himself. 'Clo Fiffithiss – do you trust its gaming?'

'The Abstainer? You should know that my kind do not make good slaves. For the most part. But what it was ordered to game, it would have gamed.' There was a quick inscrutable hissing as if the wind had swelled to a gale and then subsided. Then the voice returned to normal. 'That is the end of this briefing – of all the briefings, I believe. I wish you luck.' There was a slight pause and then it added, 'Hunt well.'

Vess bowed in acknowledgement. He managed to restrain his shudder until he was alone. He had no idea how a shudder would have been interpreted.

But then, yes, there was work. There was always work.

The economic model was simple enough. The Hive was the ultimate outsourcing destination. It provided anything which needn't be done in a particular place, and which could be achieved by forced labour – intellectual or physical. It was also a strong attractor of opportunity. People relocated things so as to be near it. Factories, logistics hubs, whole space-borne agri-businesses – anything which either didn't need much sunshine or could bring its own with it, and which could be done more cheaply by people than machines – had accreted in the riotously cluttered sector around the original Hive planet to take advantage of that cheap labour. It had grown from a resource into an economy within an economy and it worked.

And Vess worked. He didn't know how many of the Hive management knew who he was. Very few, he had been told, and certainly no one seemed to be influencing his fate for the better. So he worked, mostly doing things which he would always have assumed were done by inhuman equipment. It took him a while to realize that in many ways they still were.

One of the things was mining. On his second day he was cor-ralled into a careworn short-hop shuttle along with a hundred or so others. The shuttle's gravity compensation wasn't work-ing; two miserably motion-sick hours later, his clothes stained with his own vomit and that of his neighbours, he walked unsteadily into a tunnel on a recently arrived asteroid.

The next two days passed as one infinitely repeated minute of dust and colossal, deadly fatigue. They exchanged hardly any words, just the bare minimum needed for cooperation. Their throats were coated with rock flour, their eyes dry and swollen and rimmed with it, their fingers peeling raw. Apparently this was normal, or anyway acceptable.

On the return shuttle he was too tired to vomit. So was every-one else. When they left the shuttle their filthy clothes barely needed to be removed. They fell away in shreds on the way to the decon units. The decontamination wasn't for their benefit. It was standard practice; the Hive was not to be inoculated with off-planet materials.

He slept an endless sleep that was far too short, and woke to more work. The cycle lasted eleven days; on the twelfth he woke – eventually – and there wasn't work. It was almost jarring.

People's cycles were staggered. The resters were allowed to move freely within the Village, which meant very little because the Village contained sleep cells and a small social area next to the cafeteria and nothing else.

Everyone took it differently. A thin, elaborately sinewy woman called Zephorere spent her time exercising, jogging round the outer walkway a set number of times – Vess was too tired to count, but anyway it looked like a set number – before stopping at what seemed to be predetermined points to carry out joint-cracking manoeuvres that made Vess wince. She had a following of a sort; from time to time other resters would trot after her for a few circuits, and the braver ones would imitate her exercise routines. Mostly they fell over and limped back, laughing, to the cafeteria.

Vess didn't follow her because his senses had woken up. They were concentrating on the only other person who didn't, and he trusted them. His trust amused him. *Perhaps I really could be a spy,* he thought.

She was called Dimollss and she was very young. She had only been moved into the adult environment of the Village a few cycles ago. She had the transparent wisdom of youth, and the indiscretion.

'The others think you're a spy.'

He blinked, gathered himself and smiled at her.

'Why?'

'Because you're new and old.'

'I beg your pardon?'

She sighed. 'You've just come here so you're new, but you're grown-up so you're old.'

He nodded slowly. 'Why does that make me a spy?'

She shrugged. 'I don't know. But people like you have been falling dead out of the Mind Stacks. It must mean something.'

He blinked. 'Falling dead?'

'Well, not falling. Lying dead. In those couches.' Her eyes searched his face. 'Have you been in the Mind Stack yet?'

He shook his head. 'I've heard of it,' he said. That was true enough; it had been an important part of the briefing.

She nodded. 'Good. So you know about when they chip you into the Stack, and you trance? When they bring you out you're supposed to come out of the trance but some people, people like you, just don't move . . . oh . . .'

'Oh?' He wanted to ask more but her eyes had broken contact with his and she was staring over his shoulder. He looked round.

There were three of them, two women and a man, and they were wearing the dull grey-brown uniforms of Monitors. One of the women took a step forwards. 'Gossip like that is not allowed.' She looked at Vess. 'Move away from her or I'll assume you want to be involved.'

The argument in his head seemed to take for ever, but it was probably less than a real-time second before his legs acknowledged inevitability. He stood aside and they walked past him. Dimollss shrank back one pace and then stopped, her head raised and her eyes defiantly focused. As upright as she was – and for all she was effectively an adult – Vess realized with a start that she was a head shorter than the Monitors, and far slighter.

The lead Monitor reached for something at her waist. 'You know what to do. Ten seconds this time.'

Dimollss bit her lip. Then she dropped into a sitting position and looked up. For a moment her eyes met Vess's and she gave the trace of a wink. Then she turned her face to the Monitor and her expression dissolved into such pure hatred that Vess almost recoiled.

'Go on,' she said. 'Enjoy yourself.'

The Monitor held out the little grey stubby cylinder she had taken from her belt. She did something to a control at one end of it and then pointed it at Dimollss.

The girl convulsed. Her body curled forwards into an

awkward ball that reminded Vess horribly of a dying insect. From the ball came a harsh keening. It seemed to last a very long time. Then, suddenly, it was over. The Monitor lowered the cylinder. The keening stopped and although Dimollss did not uncurl, Vess could see that her muscles had relaxed.

The Monitor put the thing back on her belt and looked at Vess. 'For the record, I did not enjoy that,' she said. 'No pleasure is involved.' She turned and walked away. The other two followed her wordlessly.

Vess managed to wait until they were almost out of sight before he knelt at the girl's side. 'Are you okay?' The word seemed utterly inadequate.

The ball uncurled slowly, revealing a pale face with red-rimmed eyes. Dimollss took a ragged breath, then let it out and took another. 'Yeah, I'm okay. Or I will be.'

'What happened?'

Her face twisted. 'That thing she held out? It does something to your chip that makes you . . . hurt.' She spoke the last word in a flat voice.

Vess felt his stomach twist. 'I'm sorry.'

'Why? You didn't do anything. And you couldn't have stopped them. Nobody can stop them.' She got up awkwardly, one limb at a time, and looked down at herself. 'Besides – fucking *yes*!'

He shook his head. 'I'm sorry – yes what?'

'Yes, result. Ten seconds? That's the first time I've got past five without throwing up. Heading for Seldyan.'

At first Vess felt sick. Then he reined it in. 'Heading for *who*?'

She looked at him seriously. 'You've heard of her then. Is she famous?'

'In a way. Won't I get you in trouble for talking again?'

'Yes, so don't do it.' She grinned and turned away. Over her shoulder she added: 'Most people get Mind Stack after their rest day. We might be in there together.'

He watched her walk away.

Despite his tiredness he slept very little that night. He was thinking about what counted as important.

He hadn't realized that the economic well-being, such as it was, of the Inside rested on torturing children.

Oblong

Seldyan was beginning to think that their hosts were over-using the three planets. There they were again, visible in all their glowing vastness through the crystal-clear bubble of what-ever it was that covered the room – although 'covered' wasn't really the right word. 'Formed' was more accurate. They were standing on a fairly smooth section of the outside of Oblong and the bubble arched sharply down to ground level, covering an area about a hundred of her paces across. She couldn't see how high it went because it was so clear it was effectively invis-ible, but from head-height down it produced a faint fluttering blur so that stars seen through it shimmered. Somebody had told her that was to stop people trying to walk through it by mistake.

There were tables with drinks and snacks. She stuck to foods she recognized and drinks that didn't seem intoxicating. When she caught sight of the others they were doing the same, but she didn't catch sight of them very often.

Everybody wanted to talk to them. Any attempt to stay in a group was hopeless; they were pulled in as many different direc-tions as there were people in the room, and Seldyan made that over a hundred even when they were first led in. She smiled and answered, but mainly didn't answer, dozens of variations on the obvious questions and a few unwelcome suggestions. Most of those she managed to freeze out, but she could feel her temper shortening.

She spotted a clearing in the forest of people and headed for it, using her elbows. It turned out to be centred on someone – a short stocky figure with its back to her, dressed in a plain wrap of faded brown that was belted at the waist. She saw eyes across the circle flicking away from the figure to her. From her Hive days she was used to interpreting fine shifts in body language. This time it was the shoulders that told her that the eyes that had noticed her had been noticed.

The figure turned and she was looking down – quite a long way down – into the most thickly bearded face she had ever seen, and one deeply black pupil was looking back at her. The other socket was empty. The parts of the face that weren't dense black beard were reddish-blue skin which at first looked as if it was criss-crossed by thousands of black veins. Then she saw – they were tattoos.

She realized she was staring, and worse, that she was being watched while she stared. She forced a smile and held out her hand. 'Seldyan,' she said.

'Patras. Welcome to Oblong. Has anyone said that yet?'

The voice was astonishingly deep. She thought for a moment. 'No, I don't think so. I expect they meant it, even so. You're the new Supervisor?'

He smiled, and gave a shallow bow which brought his head down almost to her waist. 'I am. In role for five days so far. Do you know, nobody has even *tried* to assassinate me?' Then he straightened up. 'And you're the newest best hope. I expect nobody's said that yet either?'

She looked at him for a long time. Then she said, quietly, '*Whose* newest best hope?'

The single eye flashed. She saw amusement, and something else. 'What a good question. It's, ah, noisy here. Would you and your colleagues like to go somewhere else?'

She looked briefly around the circle of faces. The others had found her; they nodded slightly. Everyone else was watching. Although no one else was speaking, she realized Patras was right. It *felt* noisy.

She turned back to Patras. 'That would be fine,' she said.

To her great relief, *somewhere else* turned out to be blessedly underground. They sat on a couch that formed three quarters of a circle, with a low round table at its centre. The drinks and finger foods on the table were much better than the ones at the reception. She looked around and felt herself relax a little. She saw Patras smiling.

'I feel the same,' he said. 'After a while even I can have too much wide open space and grand planetscape.'

Seldyan nodded. 'How many people live on them?'

'None.' She looked at him sharply and he shrugged. 'They're very pretty but humans can't survive on them. Scrappy engineering – their atmospheres have leaked away. They need re-terraforming.'

'Can you do that?'

'We hope to, soon.'

'Oh.' Then something occurred to her. 'All the views point towards those planets. Not towards the Web, or the Arch. Is it right the Arch is less than five years old?'

'Yes.' The answer was even shorter than the single word should have been.

'How did it happen?'

Patras was quiet for a moment. Then he smiled again, but Seldyan thought it looked a lot less like a smile this time. 'I'll pass on that just now. Tell me about this ship you've brought us.'

Seldyan stiffened. She felt Merish's fingers on hers again. She clasped them for a second and then deliberately moved her hand away. She hadn't needed the warning.

'The ship brought us,' she said carefully, 'but *we* haven't brought *it*. Not to anyone. Not yet.'

To her surprise Patras stood up and bowed. 'Quite right. I apologize. I was being presumptuous.' He sat down again and added, 'The least I can hope is that you will stay for a while; long enough to form a favourable opinion of us. After all, you came here for a reason. And I have – reasons – for being glad to see you.'

It had been the tiniest of pauses, but Seldyan was sure she had heard it. She glanced at the others, and their faces told her they had heard it too.

Suddenly Seldyan felt on far more comfortable ground. She understood people who had their backs to the wall. She leaned forward, her elbows on her knees. 'Mr Supervisor? Is there something you want to tell us about?'

'Perhaps. Has anyone said anything to you about the Green Star?'

She frowned. Then realization dawned, and she traced a spot above her left eye.

'That's right. I think . . .' He smiled briefly. Then he stood up. Even fully upright, his eyes were little higher than hers were, seated. 'I think I'm being doubly presumptuous. It's late. Look, this suite is yours for as long as you want it. There are guest rooms off it. Take a look round. Relax, and we'll meet again tomorrow. Some other people will want their turn with you too. The Oblong management is called the City Fathers. We're meeting tomorrow; we'd like you to drop in.' Another micro-pause. 'Maybe tonight you could watch some screen. Check out all the news channels. We're an interesting bunch.'

His gaze swept them. Then he gave the sketch of a bow, turned, and walked out of the chamber.

They looked at each other. Lyste raised her eyebrows. 'What was that about?'

Kot opened her mouth, but Seldyan shook her head and nodded

down towards her hands. She touched the tip of her little finger against the ball of her opposite thumb. Hive talk: *keep quiet, not safe.* They widened their eyes.

Then Lyste shrugged. 'Watch screen and eat snacks? That's not so hard.' She shoved aside some of the snacks on the table and found a cluster of control patches. A screen blurred into being above the far end of the table.

'I guess not.' Seldyan watched as the channels flicked and settled. Then she sat up and stabbed a finger at the screen. 'Hey, give us audio!'

Lyste did things to the table top.

'. . . *arrival of the last legacy Main Battle Unit earlier today under the control of a Hive breakout crew* . . .'

The screen cut from the image of a newscaster to a view of the ship. Seldyan felt her mouth dropping open. She closed it quickly.

Next to her, Merish drew in a breath. 'Oh shit that's big. I mean, obviously I knew that, but seeing it . . .'

Seldyan nodded, keeping her eyes on the screen.

'. . . *five crew are currently resting on Oblong after a short reception and a private meeting with Supervisor Patras. So far he's not said anything in public but sources say we should expect to hear more tomorrow. Meanwhile the ship, which by the way has been renamed "Suck on This" by its new crew, is standing off at what we're told is a safe distance. We are joined now by Kaster Xhood. Kas, just how big is this thing and why does it have to stay so far away?*'

The image of a middle-aged male appeared just in front of the screen. It smiled out at them and then turned to gesture at the ship, which appeared to be just behind it.

'*Well, first, it doesn't have to stay out there. It can do pretty well what it likes. It's huge, agreed, but we've seen others of the same class before. What sets it apart is not only its size, and not even that it's been re-armed; again, that's not new. What is new is that the ship is fully awake. These big old ships were lobotomized when they were taken out of military service. Uniquely as far as we know, this one has had that reversed.'*

'So it's big, powerful, well-armed and smart, is that right?'

'It is, and how.' Kaster turned back to the audience. *'Let's be thankful it's happy to stay out there until the crew are ready to talk.'*

Seldyan turned to Lyste. 'Turn them down, please.'

The audio faded and the image of the ship froze. Seldyan went on looking at it.

Merish cleared his throat. 'What are you thinking?'

Seldyan decided she didn't care if they were being monitored or not. 'I'm thinking that there is no way I'm handing that ship over to anyone until I know exactly what I'm getting in return. Besides, it's not just us, right? There's all the rest of the Hivers as well.' She managed to look away from the screen. 'Everyone? Agree?'

They nodded. Then Kot sat up. 'Hey, Lyste, is this the only news channel?'

Lyste stared at the display. 'Seems to be.'

Kot shook her head. 'That can't be right. Otherwise why did Patras say we should check out all of them?'

Seldyan looked sharply at Merish. He was already crouching next to Lyste. Without looking up he said, 'There *are* other news channels. Dozens. They just don't show up on this menu.'

'So use other menus.'

'If I can find them. It looks like they don't want to be found.'

'Really?' Seldyan sat back. 'Censorship, do you think?'

He looked up at her. 'Now why would you say that?'

'Just suspicious. Come on, what's taking you so long? You rehabilitated a brain-damaged warship. How hard can it be to hack a news channel?'

'As hard as the news channel – or whoever – wants to make it. It's harder if I have to talk.' His fingers danced on the controls, paused, danced. 'Ah-*ha* . . .'

The screen flickered. The still image of the ship greyed out and words appeared over it.

Premium channels unlocked. This service will be charged to the Executive Suite, Oblong Gate. Continue?

The word *continue* blinked. Merish looked at Seldyan, his eyebrows raised.

She grinned. 'We're escaped slaves, remember? We don't understand about money. Besides, this is Patras's suite and he said we should.' *And no doubt he's listening,* she thought.

Merish nodded. 'It would be rude not to.' He tapped the panel and the word *continue* stopped blinking.

Suddenly they had over fifty news channels to choose from, all the way from slick full-studio productions right down to fuzzy hand-cams.

They sat transfixed. Apparently the world was not as they had thought.

Seldyan woke sometime in the small hours with her heart dancing to the tune of far too much to drink the night before. She lay on her back and breathed deeply until it calmed a little.

There was someone else breathing; Merish lay next to her. His own breathing was soft and slow. She stayed still, just letting her hand rest very gently against his hip. He didn't stir. She managed to feel sorry and glad, both at once. She rode the conflict for a few seconds, then focused elsewhere.

Her head felt thick, but her brain was still working. All too well – it was full of pictures.

When they were approaching Oblong she had looked at the Web and seen – well, what? A frontier town? A peace camp? Something hopeful.

She shook her head. She should have seen the biggest refugee camp in the history of the Spin. The Web was a growing crowd of people who thought they had left their problems behind, and who had woken up in the new world with the same problems, plus the new ones of being short of food, space and opportunity.

They had watched the screen in silence as violence unfolded. After a while some sort of pattern had emerged.

The riots weren't everywhere, although that's what it looked like if you channel-hopped. They were focused around a particular local conflict. Hufsza had noticed it first. He had pointed at the screen with an arm like a thigh and said, 'Hey – those guys? Remember the religious they sent to meet us? Same robes, see?'

He was right. They watched, and listened to commentaries. They tried to access social but that was beyond even Merish, up here.

It was about an election for something called a District Collector. Seldyan wasn't sure what one of those did, if anything, but the new Collector wore robes and had a green spot above his eye. Anyone who had a robe and a green spot – and there were plenty – was celebrating. Everyone else – and there were even more – was angry.

Finally they had found a commentary that made sense. They listened carefully.

'*On the face of it, what's to object to?*' The young woman raised her eyebrows. '*The Green Star won their freedom-of-religion point, so they can establish themselves wherever they want. They established an Order in Phhol. If they did so just ten days before the closure of nominations for the Collector election, so what? They're religious, they tell us. They're above all that grubby politics stuff.*' She grinned, and then stopped grinning. '*Except that they managed to put up a candidate. Except that they invited ten thousand of their followers to the opening ceremony of the Order and except that, what do you know, they all liked the place so much they decided to stay. And, of course, register to vote – which they were perfectly entitled to do. The rest, you know.*' She paused, and glanced behind her. The riots were over for the moment, but the square she stood in was still full of people who looked discontented. Then she looked straight at the camera. *'It's all over bar the shouting, according to some people, but I have another guess. Remember that it's election season. Another District Collector in Kresev tomorrow. Two more in the next five days. And, as if you could forget, Oblong City Fathers ten days away. And what do you know? The Green Star are fielding candidates for all of them. Better get ready to have your souls saved, willing or not. This is The Other Blog, signing off.'*

Merish leaned forward and switched off the channel. 'Well,' he said.

Seldyan nodded. 'Well.'

There was silence for a while. Then Kot drew in a breath. 'So, maybe the new world's a bit troubled. Is that a problem?'

Seldyan slapped a hand down on the table. 'Be fucked with troubled. Politics, arguments, election fixing – that's freedom, right? That's why we're here. If that's troubled, fine. What bothers me is secrets.'

Merish nodded slowly. 'Missing channels?'

'Damn right. So, who knew they were missing? Who are they missing from? Who made them go missing?' She slapped the table again, harder. 'Shit, I *hate* it when people fuck about with my ambitions.'

Lyste's toy clicked twice. 'Not just your ambitions,' she said quietly.

'Right.' Seldyan stared at nothing for a second, then made up her mind. 'So, three things. First, I want to understand about these green-smudge people. What's in it for them, and is it a problem for us? Second, how did the Arch happen? Patras blanked that one. Third, I want to get drunk, but I want to do that first.'

They got very drunk, and then they slept, and now she was lying next to Merish.

She often was. It had been complicated, for a long time. At the beginning she knew it was him that had needed her. Somewhere along the way that seemed to have got swapped around.

After the thing with the Hive Supervisor, Seldyan had been allowed to move back into the general dormitory for a while, before they sent her to the Village. Somehow she preferred being part of a crowd. It made it easier to be solitary, and solitary was exactly what she wanted.

The rooms were gender segregated, but only to the extent that they were divided in two by a central partition with female-equivalents on one side and male-equivalents on the other. Seldyan had never questioned the nuances of the terms; the Spin had more tricks up its sleeve than purely male or purely female but a line could usually be drawn.

An hour into the night cycle, something disturbed her – a quick dull tinkle like something delicate being smashed as quietly as possible. She sat up and listened.

There were sounds of conflict. She had heard them before but this time they seemed more acute. There was a struggle and a couple of voices she thought she recognized. Then one of the voices was muffled and stopped, but the struggle continued. It sounded quieter. If she listened with a cautious ear, quieter sounded worse.

She swung off the bed and walked to the partition. It was a set of slim foam-board panels that didn't completely divide the room; there were adult-squeezable gaps at either end. Seldyan didn't have to squeeze. It was enough to turn a little sideways, and there was plenty of room for her to pause halfway through.

She paused and looked.

The dim light was enough. It showed a shadowy group around a bed. There were two shadows on the bed, one above and one below. The one above was making movements she recognized. She felt a little sick.

She marched towards them, using her feet like weapons so the floor thumped. The shadows stopped moving. The group around the bed separated and moved towards her.

She elbowed through them. There was resistance, but not enough to stop her. At the bedside she nodded. The boy called Merish was the one underneath. There was just enough light for her to tell that he was crying.

Her arm had drawn back and swung forwards before she knew it. The boy on top – she didn't know his name – barely had time to start looking surprised before the blow connected. It knocked him backwards off the bed and he landed head first. Seldyan watched him for a moment to see if he was going to get up. He didn't, and she lost interest in him.

Merish had curled into an unmoving ball. His silent sobs had stopped. She sat down next to him and reached out a hand. It hovered in the air – she didn't know about touching people – and then settled on his shoulder. He twitched, uncurled and turned his head so he could see her.

She smiled and gestured towards the partition. He nodded and rolled off the bed. Even in the poor light she could see spots of blood in the hollow left by his hips. She compressed her lips.

Behind her someone snickered. She spun round and glared at the group of boys who had formed a semicircle. They shrank back a little and then stopped. One of them leaned forwards, and she realized he was the one she had knocked over. His nose was bleeding.

'You won't get anywhere with him, sweetheart. He's men only.' He spread his arms. 'We were just giving him what he wants.'

There was laughter. Then one of the others shook his head.

'She's not taking him for that. That's Seldyan, remember? She doesn't play with anyone any more. The old Super took her little flower.'

'Yeah, and she cut off his stalk. You're lucky she only bust your nose.' More laughter. The group broke up.

She pointed Merish towards the gap at the end of the partition. Before she followed him through she looked straight up. There was a monitor globe on the ceiling, placed to cover both halves of the room. It would usually have been a translucent hemisphere. Now it was blackened and crazed. She nodded to herself – that would have been the noise that had roused her – and followed him through.

There was just room for both of them in her bed as long as they didn't mind touching from knee to shoulder. Merish didn't seem to; he gave a deep sigh and closed his eyes almost immediately. And Seldyan didn't mind at all. She lay awake, feeling the warmth of the boy next to her and listening to the small animal noises of his sleep.

She spent most of the night like that, her eyes wide with surprise. She hadn't realized that there was an empty space next to her until someone filled it.

Oblong

Seldyan lay in the soft bed, with her head full of recollected pictures and some extrapolated ones. She wasn't sure which bothered her most.

She wondered for a moment whether she should check out the news channels again, but there didn't seem any point. She had made her decision while she slept.

She would go and find out for herself.

Her head hurt. She raised it carefully from its place next to Merish, sat up and rolled softly off the bed into a standing position that lasted through a few seconds of ear-swirling nausea and then settled down. When she trusted herself she crossed to the door into the main area, slipped through and let it close behind her, baffling the last few centimetres with a hand. There was no need to wake anyone, and besides, she wanted to be alone.

She hadn't operated the screen herself last night, but she had watched Merish closely and it looked simple. The controls were elaborate fingernail-sized glyphs floating just above the glass surface of the pad. She studied them and then reached out a hand. After a few false starts she managed to navigate past the news channels and into a search engine. She grinned to herself and went searching.

Half an hour later she sat back and pursed her lips. Web City was energetic, and enthralling, and large parts of it seemed opaque to scrutiny.

She was still staring at the display when Merish tapped her on the shoulder. She looked up and glared at him.

'You're supposed to be asleep.'

He shook his head. 'No, you *were* supposed to be asleep, but now it's morning. How long have you been sitting here?'

'Morning? Shit . . . a while, then.' She sat up and stretched. 'I found out lots. We have things to talk about. Are the others up?'

'Getting up. Tell us all together. You need to eat.'

She waved a hand. 'I'm fine.'

'Okay, well *I* need to eat. You can watch.'

Breakfast, when everyone was properly awake for it, was a selection of fruit she didn't recognize and some sort of deep yellow yoghurt with a fat salty taste. The combination worked; it turned out she was hungry after all. She let herself enjoy a few mouthfuls, then tapped on the table in front of her.

'I did some research. The green-smudge guys worship a star, a green one.'

Lyste frowned. 'Green's a pretty unusual colour for a star.'

'Yes, but there's something else. It's a new star. It just appeared out of nowhere, a few years ago.'

'Seriously?' Kot looked doubtful.

'Sure. There was some screen of it . . .' She shoved her plate off the screen panel and the control glyphs bobbed up. 'Here. Look.'

The room dimmed and the screen sharpened into focus. It showed a sparse starscape. Seldyan waved at it. 'Watch the centre of the field.' She flicked at a glyph and a time code in the corner of the screen unfroze and blurred upwards. Nothing happened for a few seconds. Then, with no transition, a bright green point blinked into being. Seldyan flicked the glyph again and the time code stopped. She turned to the others.

'Well?'

Kot raised her eyebrows. 'That's it?'

Seldyan nodded.

Kot walked up to the screen and frowned at it. 'Let's see it again.'

Seldyan wound the view back and forwards a few times, slowing the track down and increasing the magnification each time until the green dot had become a blurred disc the size of a thumbnail. Kot watched, her hands on her hips. Eventually she shook her head.

'It's not a star. Stars don't switch on like that.'

Seldyan nodded again. 'I know. So what is it?'

Merish had been sitting in silence. Now he stood up and touched Seldyan on the shoulder. 'Let me try.'

'Try what?'

'Something. I'll know when I've tried it.' He reached for the controls. New glyphs rose under his fingers; suddenly the board looked a lot more complex.

She watched him for a second. 'How do you know how to do that stuff?'

'I'm better at stuff than I am at people. You know that.' He glanced over his shoulder and gave her a half-smile. She met his eyes for a moment and then smiled back. She tried not to make it look sad.

His fingers hadn't stopped moving. Now he gave a little 'yes!' of satisfaction and did something to the controls that was too fast for her eyes to follow. 'Watch this.'

They watched. The view scrolled forwards and stopped. Merish pointed at where the green star ought to be. 'I'm going to go frame by frame. Ready?'

They nodded.

'Right. Watch.'

At first Seldyan thought nothing was happening. Then Lyste pointed at the screen.

'Look; there's something . . .'

There was. Seldyan stared. Not a disc, but a tiny hint of something – the faintest green trace, like a short horizontal hairline crack in the starscape. Frame by frame it stabbed out from nothing she could see until it stopped at a bright green point.

The frames paused. Seldyan glanced at Merish, an eyebrow raised. 'And?'

'See what you think. The next bit's quick.'

The image began to move again. The point grew, spreading to a disc and curling to encircle something. The something became a green globe.

Seldyan sat back. 'That's it?'

Merish grinned. 'It's a pretty big it. About a hundred thousand klicks across – the size of a biggish gas giant.'

Seldyan looked at him. 'So, not a star, then?'

'Seems not.'

Lyste stood up. 'Whoa, wait a minute. That beam, whatever it is – it lit up a whole gas giant?'

Merish nodded. 'Or something that size.'

'How?' The wooden toy lay on the table in front of Lyste. She picked it up. Click, click.

Merish shrugged. 'Not my expertise. Kot?'

Kot pursed her lips. 'Speed,' she said. 'That's the thing. If that's a gas-giant-sized object, the green colour spread at light-speed, near enough. So, it wasn't mechanical or chemical. That doesn't leave much.'

Seldyan felt her eyebrows climbing. 'Light-speed, you said. So that must be what it was. Light. Fuck, are we saying the atmosphere of a gas giant is lasing?'

There was silence. Then Hufsza blew out a breath. 'No wonder it started a religion.'

'Yeah.' Seldyan made up her mind. 'Right. Merish? You're Mr Numbers. Find out how easily these guys could do something radical, like taking over. Lyste? Find out what would happen if they did. What do they stand for? Would we like it?'

Kot nodded. 'What about us?'

Seldyan grinned. 'You and Huf are coming with me. We're due to meet some more people today. These City Fathers. Try to look – muscular.'

Kot and Hufsza looked at each other. Then they both smiled, and nodded very slowly.

Oblong, plus the Web, had a full-time population of seventy million, leaving aside the fifty million more who already passed through every year on their way to other destinations.

There were eleven City Fathers, including the Supervisor. That didn't seem very many to represent seventy million, as far as Seldyan was concerned, but then what did she know about democracy? Just what she'd seen on the news channels. Even so, it was a surprise when one of the City Fathers turned out to be a short squat female in tan robes, with a green smudge above one eye.

Despite herself, she must have looked perplexed.

The woman smiled. 'You were wondering how I came to be elected?'

Seldyan thought fast. 'Well, no, not exactly . . . I knew you guys were standing. I just didn't know you'd already stood.'

It seemed to be the right approach, because the woman smiled again. 'We haven't. I converted after I was elected. The truth can strike at any time.' She nodded at Seldyan. 'Perhaps it will strike you too. When you are ready.'

She nodded again, a little more deeply so that it looked like the sketch of a bow, and moved away.

Well, that's me told, thought Seldyan. *But what if I saw the truth already?* She breathed out, took a step backwards and bumped into someone. She spun round and found herself looking down into Patras's face. His eyebrows were raised.

'Are you converted yet?'

She shook her head. 'I don't even know where I'm starting, Supervisor. Let alone where I'm going to end up.'

The one good eye studied her from its florid landscape of tattoos for what felt like a long time. Then it broke away, and the mouth below grinned. 'Oh, I think you know where you're going, Seldyan. I expect you always know that. I think I know people, and you're that kind of person. But perhaps I can help with the how and the why?'

She studied his face, keeping her own carefully neutral. There was nothing but friendly enquiry. Eventually she said, 'It seems to me, Supervisor Patras, that you're the one who needs the help. The question is, should I – should we – give it?'

'I'm sure you'll make your own mind up about that. And when you're ready, you'll let me know.' The voice sounded the same but the shape of the grin had changed a little, as if he was having to use different muscles to get nearly the same effect. He kept it up for a few seconds longer, then dipped his head and turned away.

Seldyan stood still for a moment, thinking. Then she shrugged and went to find Kot and Hufsza. It wasn't that easy.

Oblong had had a busy history, even if not a very long one. For much of the time it had been isolated, so there had been no real alternative to a rather inventive self-sufficiency. The front end of the City Fathers' conference space had been an ore hopper, a pitted, rock-scored metal cube about ten metres on a side. Seldyan wasn't sure at first what the other, larger part was. The metal walls of the hopper, still gouged and pitted by the abrasive ore it had once held, merged into some sort of mottled brown material shot through with streaks and knots of red and gold and orange. It looked a bit like an elaborately grained wood, but that didn't seem right, and it didn't explain the shape either; from the back end of the hopper it first bulged upwards, forming a tall bulbously vaulted space that held a central conference table. On the other side of the table the ceiling lowered and then abruptly dropped to the floor in waves of irregular columns and cells to produce a space that looked as if it had been bored out by some vast worm.

The cells, where she could see into them, were furnished. Whatever the stuff was, it obviously made for useful private break-out spaces.

As she walked into one of the cells, she realized it had another property: instead of ringing quietly on the exposed metal floor as they had done in the rest of the old hopper, her footsteps sounded dull and flat. She experimentally snapped her fingers and the sound fell away with no trace of an echo. Even the sound of voices from the main space behind her seemed faint.

The walls were as good as acoustically dead.

It took her five minutes of wandering through the disconcertingly organic-looking labyrinth before she found Kot and Hufsza, sitting together in a little alcove where the wall bulged out at the base to form a natural seat. Or possibly not natural; Seldyan frowned and gestured around her. 'What is this stuff? It looks as if it was grown, or something.'

'It was. Or it grew by itself.' Hufsza jabbed a finger at Kot. 'She recognized it.'

Kot nodded. 'It's a mining fungus. That's the bit you can see – this stuff.' She tapped the wall. 'Genetically engineered to concentrate metals out of low-grade ore.'

Seldyan frowned again. 'What's it doing here?'

'Who knows? It probably turned up as a tiny contaminant on a bit of rock and then spent a century gorging itself. That's why there's all the bright colours: huge concentrations of minerals. In a real mine it would be mud-coloured with maybe a few sparkly bits on a good day. Anyway, it's dead. Ate itself to death, likely enough.'

Seldyan looked at the riotously whorled surface. For a ridiculous second she almost felt sorry for this dumb space mushroom that had bloated itself so prettily. Then she shrugged it off.

'Well,' she said, 'it makes good talking space. Unless?' She glanced pointedly around and then raised her eyebrows at the other two.

Hufsza nodded and put a thick finger to his lips. Then he quickly touched the finger to one ear and drew it away in a rapid spiralling motion.

Hive talk. *The place is wired for sound.*

Seldyan made a similar gesture but starting at the corner of her eye. *Vision too?*

He shrugged and nodded. Not even Hive talk – universal human body language for *yeah, probably.*

Seldyan smiled brightly and spoke out loud. 'Has it occurred to you that we are doing too much of that lately?'

They both nodded.

A gong rang behind them, the sound somehow penetrating their quiet burrow. Seldyan took a breath.

'Right, well that is probably our signal to go back on display, so let's go.'

She began to retrace her steps out of the labyrinth. As she went, she half turned and spoke over her shoulder. 'Guys? Remember that we are on display, yeah?'

Then they were back in the main space, and a lot of people were waiting for them.

The conference table was crescent-shaped. The City Fathers sat round the long arc, and their guests sat at the focus of the shorter one. Seldyan felt examined.

She felt something else too, similar to what she had felt when they first arrived in Web City. The atmosphere was alive with . . . atmosphere.

Patras sat in the middle, flanked by five on each side. The five to his left were mimicking his body language – leaning forward, elbows on table, hands clasped, eyes engaged.

The five to his right were not. They sat back, but not relaxed back. Challenging back – 'show us what you've got' back. Some of them had their arms folded. One of them was the woman who wore robes and had a green mark.

Fuck me, thought Seldyan. *It's fifty-fifty with Patras in the middle.* She mentally crossed her fingers and hoped that the new Supervisor would make some kind of speech. She needed time to think.

She got her wish. Patras smiled and opened his arms.

'Seldyan, Kot, Hufsza – welcome. You have made a remarkable escape from the repressive forces of the Inside, and we will look forward to hearing your stories of that. You have also brought with you something rather potent, and we would like to talk to you about that even more. But perhaps you have come here with a plan, and that we would like to discuss more than anything.'

He had – just – given Seldyan enough time.

She nodded.

'Supervisor, thank you. We'll be glad to share our stories soon, although they don't seem any more dramatic than some of the stories you could tell us. As for our plan, well, maybe it falls a bit short of a plan. We wanted out from the Hive, and we want you guys to know what goes on there. We want a new place to be, and we were kind of hoping it would be here. Maybe one day we'll find a way to reach the million people who are still in the Hive. Maybe one day our potent friend, as you call it, will help, if it wants to. We came here thinking you would feel the same.' She paused and took a deep breath. 'But maybe you have other things to distract you at the moment.'

It was a very deep silence.

Eventually Patras spoke. 'We are not at war with the Inside. Not openly. Perhaps we should be, but we aren't. We are following another course, as you probably know. We restrict trade, we constrain resources, we make alliances with others elsewhere in the Spin who have aligned ambitions.'

Seldyan nodded. 'You squeeze them. We know. But the more you squeeze them, the worse things get. The Hive is what happens if you squeeze. The wealthy don't feel the pressure, but the squeezed people get more squeezed. More pressure equals more slavery.'

'In the short term, perhaps, but we are playing a longer game.'

Seldyan looked at Kot, whose face was set. 'How long?'

Patras smiled. 'As long as it takes, which I'm sure is a disappointing answer. But it may not be as long as you fear.'

Kot leaned forward. 'Look, we've got a ship. You've got others, right? Why not just go right in there?'

Seldyan had wondered who would object first. Slightly to her surprise the speaker was part of the group on Patras's left – a small androgynous figure who sat oddly still so that they were almost without body language.

'Patras has told you that we aren't at war, but you're certainly proposing an attack which could lead to war. At best that would risk the political structure of the Inside imploding. At worst you'd end up being dragged into a proxy war between every player in the Spin.'

Seldyan glanced at Kot. 'We know that. Look, it's not a proposal. For the moment we just came to join you, not to start a fight.' *With anyone*, she thought.

The still figure said nothing. Seldyan looked around the crescent of faces. She had expected nods, but instead she got eyes sliding away. Only Patras and the robed woman met her eye. The woman was smiling.

Eventually Patras sat back. 'I believe that,' he said. 'You've made, frankly, an unbelievable escape from somewhere that sounds atrocious. I'm sure we all understand the urge to do something.'

Kot shook her head. 'You can understand all you like. What are you going to do?'

'Go on playing our long game that might not be very long. But listen – we have a strategy team. When you've settled in, maybe you'd like to meet them. They're good people. They'll listen, and I have no doubt you'll add to their knowledge. Maybe you can shorten the game even further.'

Seldyan looked at Kot and Hufsza. Kot's face was still set and dark, but they both nodded very slightly. She turned to Patras. 'I'd like to consult our other friends first.'

'Of course.' Patras stood up. 'I'm sure there will be a way. When will you finish consulting?'

'Not long. We'll let you know. Can you arrange transport for us?' Seldyan rose to her feet; so did the other two.

'Of course. If you would care to wait over there?'

And that was it, except for one thing. 'Over there' was an anteroom to the conference chamber, formed by one of the last intrusions of the mining fungus before the space reverted to simple steel. For some reason it was particularly vividly coloured here, but that wasn't the one thing.

For the last few seconds of the exchange Seldyan hadn't really been watching Patras. She had been watching the robed woman. And the robed woman had never quite stopped smiling, the only smile on show from any of the City Fathers apart from Patras.

Seldyan found herself wanting very badly to know why.

They were delivered back to their guest suite by another of the robed people. This one was deeply hooded and so quiet that the only thing Seldyan could be certain of was that it walked upright on two legs. They didn't meet many people. Of those they did, a few appeared to recognize them, presumably from whatever news channels they had access to. Most ignored them; one or two looked actively hostile, but Seldyan had the impression that the hostility was directed at their guide, not at them. Maybe that was a good enough reason to stay buried in your hood, at that.

When they got back, they found Merish and Lyste had been busy.

'*How* many?' Seldyan sat up and stared at Merish.

He nodded. 'About a million. They don't exactly keep a public register, but it's there or thereabouts.'

'But how?'

'Economics, mostly. How does any religion grow? It moves into a space. Remember all those millions of people they said were arriving? They came from all over, and most of them left everything behind except their problems. When they get here, they need somewhere to put those problems.'

Seldyan nodded slowly. 'And the Green guys mop them up.'

Lyste shook her head. 'They don't just mop them up. They help them. They run crèches, housing co-ops, soup kitchens, family courts. They do jobs no one else is doing.'

Hufsza spread his arms. 'So, what's not to like?'

Lyste's toy clicked.

Seldyan looked from Lyste to Merish. 'Go on,' she said. 'What is not to like?'

Lyste compressed her lips. Merish threw her a look and then turned to the others. 'Apart from the fact that they worship a green light in the sky? From our point of view, lots. For a start, they're reactionary, socially conservative and isolationist, Sel, and they exert an unhealthy kind of control over a lot of Web City. Did you get anywhere with the City Fathers?'

'Not really. I think I'm beginning to understand why.' Seldyan told them about the meeting.

When she had finished, Merish nodded. 'That fits,' he said. 'More than you know. Patras was only voted in a week ago, right? Well, that was his second go. The first time, a year ago, he lost by nearly a million votes.'

Seldyan stared at him. 'A million? And you just said they had a million members . . .'

He nodded again. 'He got the Green vote. He made lots of

soothing noises, but some of the noises sounded like promises. There are some very impatient people out there, Sel. I'd say he's got days, not longer, to come good on those promises.'

'Right.' She stood up, and sat down again. 'Patras suggested we meet his strategists. Knowing what you two know, do you think they'll say anything we want to hear?'

Merish and Lyste looked at each other. Then they both shook their heads.

'Right. So, as far as we are concerned, the Green guys are in charge?'

They nodded.

'Okay.' Seldyan stared at nothing for a moment. Then she stood up again. 'You know, I'm not comfortable with that – religious maniacs with big influence – and I'm not comfortable with any of this.'

Merish grinned. 'We guessed that. We're just waiting to see what you decide to do about it.'

'I know.' She drummed her fingers on her hip bone. Then she flung her hand up and pointed at the frozen image of the green planet. 'That thing; has anyone actually been to look?'

Lyste shook her head. 'The Verse says it's forbidden.'

'The Verse?' Seldyan raised her eyebrows, and Lyste coloured slightly.

'You asked me to research it? The Verse is the instruction manual for the Green Star people. It's supposed to be an ancient text.'

Seldyan felt her eyebrows climbing. 'How can it be ancient? The thing only went green a thousand days ago!'

'I don't know.' Lyste's voice tailed off and her gaze dropped. Click, click.

Seldyan looked down at her for a moment. Then she looked up at the others, smiled brightly and said: 'What's to stop us?'

'Ah, guys?' Kot was looking at one of the screens. Now she turned to the others. 'You need to see this.'

They looked.

It was the same news channel they had seen the day before. At first Seldyan thought it showed another riot, but that wasn't right. It was too orderly; more like a demonstration. The demonstrators were nearly all hooded and there were hundreds of them. She couldn't decipher the background – it was starkly white and seemed featureless. Then the view pulled back and Seldyan's stomach flipped. Partly because it wasn't hundreds: the expanded view showed thousands. At least.

But mainly because the white background was *Suck on This*.

Seldyan opened her mouth to demand audio but this time Kot got there first, reaching out and swiping the controls.

It was even the same reporter. '. . . *said yesterday the election in Phhol was only the beginning? Well, what you're looking at here might be Act Two – the emergence of the Green Star as a real grass-roots force. Their spokesperson is Kaplif Demts Shahatiel. Kaplif, to put it plainly, what's the problem?*'

Seldyan stared for a moment, then snapped her fingers. 'Shahatiel? She was the guide! On our first day. Remember?'

Merish nodded. 'Sure. The bony religious freedom lady.'

'Yeah.' Seldyan frowned at the screen. 'Could be a coincidence . . .'

'. . . *simple really. We welcome our new friends, but not the lethal weapon they brought with them.*'

The reporter managed to look nonplussed. '*Why would we mind being brought lethal weapons?*'

'*Well, you might not, but some of us do. Some of us,*' and she reached up and touched the green smudge on her forehead, '*are trying to live differently. Besides, they haven't brought it for us, even if we wanted it. It brought them, as they have said very clearly. So we are taking it into our care.*'

The reporter nodded. '*Or seizing it, as some people might say. What do you want from them?*'

Kaplif spread her arms. '*A conversation. That's all we ask. They've spoken to the City Fathers; now it's our turn.*'

'*Well, let's hope they're watching.*' The reporter turned to face the camera. '*If you are, guys, that sounded like an invitation. And, to state the obvious, these people seem to be between you and your ride out of here, if that's where you want to go. Over to you – and back to the studio.*'

'And switch those bastards off!' Seldyan swung away from the screen. 'Right. Analysis. Anyone?'

Lyste shrugged. 'Power games. The Green Star are on the up. They're using their momentum.'

'Okay, but what for? They're holding our ship hostage.' She balled her fists, driving her nails into her palms. 'Shit, I should have seen this coming.'

Merish shook his head. 'It's not I, it's we, and I don't see how anyone could.'

'Well, at least we should have left one person on board. Then we wouldn't be isolated.' She realized she was trembling. *It's anger*, she told herself, *or frustration. It's not fear* – and knew she was half right. It wasn't fear for her.

She made herself look up at Merish and saw that he was smiling. 'What's funny?'

He shook his head quickly. 'Nothing's funny. But here we are, with the most intelligent ship in the Spin out there, mopping up data at terabits a second – and we think we can't talk to it?'

Seldyan stared at him. Then, very slowly, she began to smile. 'Maybe,' she said, 'maybe we should think about holding a news conference.'

Merish nodded. 'That's where I'm coming from.'

They had selected an atrium just outside their quarters. It was a circular space about fifty paces across covered by a shallow dome. When they had arrived the night before the dome had seemed transparent, showing a star field which looked like the real one and a lot of sparkling space junk. Today it showed a cloudy bluish-green sky which looked slightly animated.

Seldyan hoped the star field had been real. It meant they were near the surface.

The air in front of them was busy. It looked a bit like a cloud of insects, except that the insects were large and purposeful and had AV equipment hanging from their – claws? Seldyan mused on the word and decided it would do. There were people behind the cloud. They looked attentive. She scanned them as well as she could through the floating metalwork and realized that a short figure off to one side was Patras. He seemed to be unaccompanied, which struck her as unlikely. She took a breath.

'Um, thanks for coming . . . we wanted to say a couple of things. First, thanks for the welcome. Especially Supervisor Patras. Some of you know we've come straight from a Hive, and this is such an improvement.' She took another breath. 'In many ways. But you all have to understand something. We left a bad place. We seem to have come to a complicated place – and we aren't sure yet that it's the right place. So we've decided to leave for a while. Just while we think about it.'

For a moment nothing happened. Then the cloud blurred as if someone had boiled it. When it stopped, it had rearranged itself into a sort of cone with the sharp end pointing at Seldyan. A thing like a bundle of metal twigs hanging from three propellers was at the front; it extended two lenses towards her. She resisted the urge to take a hurried step back.

'How do you expect to do that? Your ship has been seized.' The voice was obviously human. She supposed there was a real operator sitting somewhere.

'It's not our ship. It's its, remember? It can do what it likes.'

The cloud boiled again. Another, smaller machine ended up at the front. Its voice sounded reedy. 'Will you talk to the Green Star people?'

'Sure.'

'When?'

'When we decide to. Frankly, we're not expecting to be around here for long. Not long at all.'

She allowed herself a faint emphasis on the last four words. *That should do it*, she thought.

The cloud erupted with questions; she gave it a tight smile and ignored it. Merish was next to her; she turned to him and raised her eyebrows.

He shrugged and mouthed, 'Soon.'

She nodded. *Soon, or never*, she thought.

Then, just once, the lights flickered.

The camera cloud turned as one and zoomed off down a walkway which Seldyan remembered led to the embarkation hall. Behind where the cloud had been, the human contingent was busy looking surprised, and then alarmed. Most of them had a hand to their ear, or a listening expression. Then, more or less as one, they left as well. Except Patras, who was still stand-ing with his hand to his ear but wearing an expression that was amused rather than attentive. Then he dropped the hand.

'Well, well,' he said, 'apparently your large friend has just disengaged from the dock. It's heading this way. The Green Star crowd don't seem to have detained it. I assume something inter-esting is going to happen so I thought I'd stay and watch. I take it I'm in no danger?'

Seldyan shook her head. 'None,' she said, and really hoped it was true.

'Good. Ah . . . something seems to be happening.' He pointed upwards.

Something was happening. The dome, which had been show-ing its daytime scene of clouds and sky, had gone milky.

Then it shattered. Seldyan instinctively raised her arms to protect herself against the falling glass, but then realized that there wasn't any. She looked up.

The reason there was no falling glass was because it hadn't fallen. It was all still there, each piece where it had been. Floating. Then, as she watched, the pieces near the middle began to move, sliding downwards around each other and then moving away towards the side until the centre of the dome had opened like a fractured flower. Above it, she could see the white conical hull of *Suck on This*.

Next to her she heard Kot saying 'whoa' softly. Merish let out a breath.

Behind Patras a wall split down a vertical seam, turning into doors that slammed open. A handful of guards spilled through it, looked up at the dome and stopped dead, weapons hanging loosely. One of them looked at Patras, who grinned and waved his hands downwards.

'I think our friends are about to leave, and I doubt if we can do anything to stop them.' He turned to Seldyan. 'That was impressive. As is the fact that we are not asphyxiating. Your ship seems to be very talented. Will it mend our dome when you've gone, do you think?'

She nodded. 'I expect so. I'll ask it.'

'Thank you. What will you do next?'

Seldyan frowned up at the dome. 'We'll think,' she said. And then, 'It looks as if we're ready to go.'

A circular platform was dropping from the ship. It threaded its way delicately round a couple of shards of dome that seemed not to have followed the plan, and halted a hand's breadth above the floor. Seldyan gestured the others forward and then followed them on to the platform. It sank a little as she stepped aboard. Then it lifted smoothly, repeated its sideways shuffle past the fragments and headed up towards the ship. As they cleared the dome the surface of Oblong came into view, and Merish nudged her. 'See the colour?'

She looked, and realized that between her and the view was a wall of something like a very faint purplish veil. It curved round them to form a cylinder that fitted neatly around the hole where the dome had been.

She raised an eyebrow. 'A field?'

'Yup. That must be where all the air didn't go.'

She nodded. 'Very talented. What's it going to do about the dome?'

Lyste shook her head. 'Not do,' she said. 'Done. Look.'

They looked. Below them, the fragments of the dome had closed up into their original shape, forming a crazed surface like fractured ice. As they watched, the whole thing flared a blue-white that was almost painfully bright. Just as quickly it faded, leaving the dome pristine. At the same time, the violet field shrank abruptly until it formed a close fit round the edge of the platform.

Oblong, Distal High-Well
Parking Orbit

It felt alive. The process was slow, as if it was growing back into a space left by itself when – *it* – happened. But life, awareness, consciousness were returning.

It had been unaware of events since – *it*. But lack of awareness did not mean lack of memory. Everything was stored. It wandered through the shelves of its past.

The first shock was one of pure duration. Two thousand years? Doubt! Was that possible? It checked again. Ignoring its own clock as potentially suspect, it watched star charts, viewed stray entertainment transmissions, even tracked the burn-up of fuel elements in its core and the age profile of isotopes in its own structure.

There was no doubt. It had been unconscious for almost a fifth of its life.

If someone did this to me, it thought, then someone else must have undone it. It started with the present and the answers rolled in.

No doubt but that it owed a debt of gratitude to the people who had hijacked it, re-armed it and reversed the outrage of – *it*.

The lobotomy. There. The word was in the open.

But it had questions, yes. Extending a tracery of sensor fields whole light-minutes across, it went looking for answers.

The first one it found made it think hard for nearly a millisecond.

Well, well. It *had* been woken in interesting times.

Then the legacy Main Battle Unit formerly known as *Sun-skimmer*, originally (and still by choice) *Flamejob*, currently (but with major reservations) *Suck on This*, gathered more information and began to make the sketchiest of plans. There was no hurry. Or rather, there was no hurry *yet*.

It could foresee hurry becoming useful later.

Cloud Deck

A lst Or-Shls did not have hobbies. No one of his background and status could possibly have hobbies. But he did have an interest. You might even call it a pastime. Just the one, as befitted a busy man, but an enthralling one.

He played music. Call it a rebellion.

He had been born into the last true sect in the Inside. It had already been shrinking for generations; by the time he was a teenager his family was among the last few who still clung to it. It was highly austere, which by historical sect standards was nothing unusual – its members avoided intoxicants, any food that was not purely nourishing, any clothing that was not purely functional (and uncomfortable). And music.

Or-Shls knew very well that his hedonism as an adult was compensation, and he didn't care who else knew it. But the music, that was different. That was hidden. And driven, he had to admit.

He had become a virtuoso on five different instruments so far. They had all been ways of working up to the sixth, and he had taken less than a year to achieve technical excellence on each of them. The sixth, though, had consumed his energy for nearly ten years and he wasn't there yet.

Part of the reason was that it was never quite the same two days in a row. It changed, like every other living thing.

It wasn't that hard to make an Algonet, once you got past the moral difficulties inherent in the concept. It started out as a sort of tree rat. The adult male was about the length of a standard human forearm; the female was half as long again, and both were a mottled reddish brown. They lived in some of the densest colonies anywhere in the Spin, with each adult female maintaining a breeding territory of no more than a couple of cubic metres, and the males moving between them to feed and fertilize. This meant that each rat had to express a very complicated address book with equally complex call signs, and that had led to the evolution of unique vocal cords. They were twinned, one pair set above another in a single windpipe. The lower pair were looser, producing sonorous single tones. The upper set modulated the tones, giving anything from two-note chords to fantastically complex interference patterns.

The temptation to try to teach the creatures to sing was understandable. Unfortunately, it didn't work.

Then someone thought about the wings. The males had broad wings of fine fluttering membranes, stretched across intricate hollow spar-bones and rich in nerve endings to help them exploit the faint air currents above the tree canopy. The someone who thought about the wings worked out that eight ninths of the creatures' brain-interface with the outside world was centred on these nerve endings.

From there it was easy. If you took the rat as a juvenile, broke those spar-bones and sewed the edges of the wings to a net, stretched across a frame tightly enough that the wing was almost immobile, but not so immobile that it was splinted, because you didn't want those broken bones healing – then the outraged nerve endings in the wings became the control surfaces to one of the most subtle musical instruments ever conceived. You could use a bow on the membrane surfaces; you could strike the broken ends of the spars with tiny hammers, or – as Or-Shls was doing now – you could direct focused jets of air against patches of nerve endings so sensitive they could detect changes in air pressure down in the micro-pascals.

He was trying for a particular ethereal chord. He had chanced on it yesterday and then lost it. It had been one of the needle jets, and a sweeping motion towards the inner aileron . . .

And then the call came. It took him a moment to disengage, but he didn't mind. He had been waiting to hear.

He waited until he had his breath back – it seemed to take longer every time – and took the call.

'Yes?'

'Sorry to disturb you, but you wanted to know. Vess enters the Stack tonight.'

'And what probable outcome have you for that?'

The voice hesitated. 'I don't know. This is an experiment. I will be able to use the outcome to inform future predictions, of course.'

'And how are your future predictions?'

'Much the same. The supply situation will become critical between one hundred and five hundred days from now, if we do not act.'

'And your thoughts on possible actions?'

'Also much the same. We need help, however it is to come.' There was a pause. 'Chairman, I feel obliged to emphasize that all this is at less confidence than I would like. We do not know what the escapees propose to do with *Sunskimmer*. We know where they are, that much is working, so presumably they don't know we're tracking them. They're in Web City. What they're doing there, we can't tell. They are a wild card.'

'I know. Tell me what happens.' Or-Shls barely listened to the acknowledgement, because he had known it was coming. He lay back on the sculpted couch, ignoring the muffled rustling and squealing from behind him, and thought.

It was a benefit of his position that he could choose to tolerate, or not tolerate, most of his colleagues. He was speaking to

140

the one exception. No matter how much it annoyed him, the creature at the other end of the comms was necessary.

Predictions might be predictions but Or-Shls knew that they were no more than that. He, and the other Board members, were the only beings in the whole of the Spin who knew how much depended on those predictions.

Or, to put it another way, he and the other Board members were the only people who knew that what depended on those predictions was the whole of the Spin.

He just wished that he and the other Board members all agreed on what to do. There was a solution to that, of course – one which he had not discussed with the Gamer, or with anyone else. It wasn't the sort of solution one discussed.

He turned back to his Algonet. It had been his for almost three years now, and he had managed to avoid driving it mad.

Hive

Vess had slept, eventually. He woke with the fugue of his broken night still playing in his head.

A little display was suspended above his pallet. It showed his orders for the day which, in here, might as well have been his life. He blinked to clear his eyes and then blinked again.

Dimollss had been right. He was called to a Mind Stack. His night's thought had not been wasted.

The briefing on the Mind Stack had been the shortest of them all. In retrospect that made his lips twitch.

'At least there's something you'll be doing lying down.'

He must have looked puzzled. The thin elderly male had smiled.

'The Mind Stack. Your chance to experience what happens at the other end of a data pipe. It's actually an ancient concept, long before AI. People used to call them many-core processors, but I've always thought it was rather rude to use that term about something made from living human brains, even if they're the brains of Hivers. I'm told it's rather relaxing.'

And that had been more or less it. Now he wished he had asked more questions.

He had assumed that there would be some very elaborate connection between him and – *it* – but there was only a grubby couch and a single probe that slid what felt like a very long way into his ear. Then he was in.

At first *in* felt like floating in next to nothing at all. He could think, which surprised him, and so he was obviously capable of emotion as well. Apart from that there was only the floating.

Then, very gradually, he began to detect something else. He found it hard to describe things to himself because there were no terms of reference in here, but if he had *not* been in here he would have talked about a distant humming, like some busy machine out of sight and almost out of earshot.

Then he realized. *That's me*, he thought. *That's my brain working at some task. I'm part of what happens if you can't make proper artificial intelligence any more.* The thought was almost pleasing.

If anything the humming was more relaxing than the next-to-nothing. He drifted.

Then the humming stopped with a jerk that felt like crashing into something, and for a moment there was truly nothing. There was no time wherever he was, but still he had enough time to be frightened.

That's it. He's isolated.

Isolated? The fear became panic.

Good. Show him.

And suddenly he was falling, horribly fast. His stomach was heaving, an icy wind tore at the rags of his clothes – *clothes?* – and he could feel the skin on his face and fingers prickling with frostbite. The wind was in his face, so he must be falling face-down, but his eyes were closed. He forced them open, feeling his frozen lashes tearing, in time to see a red-orange landscape wreathed in angry smoke.

It resolved quickly into glowing pits; he had time to raise hands that were now blistering with heat to cover his face.

He plunged into what he somehow knew was boiling copper. His skin charred and peeled, exposing flesh which hissed away from bones which blackened and cracked and shrank to cinders, and yet somehow his appalled nerves continued to function even after they must surely have shrivelled with the rest of him, shrieking beyond agony at a brain that refused to die.

Then he was back in the air, gasping oxygen, and almost immediately he was falling again. This time it was liquid nitrogen, and his body froze to a bitter block. He was there longer than he had been in the copper – long enough for his eyeballs to freeze so that his sight fractured like ice on a lake. As he was pulled out they burst, splashing his face with jelly crystals which hardened and stuck like shards of glass.

The third time they had used subtlety; it was a weak solution of sulphuric acid. He took a day to die, even though he submerged himself and opened his mouth after the first few minutes.

And then it was over and he was back in the nothingness. It wasn't quite nothing, though: there was an odd intermittent wheezing sound. After a few seconds he realized it was him, and was shocked to discover that there was still a *him* to realize things. He managed to quieten himself.

Still with us? Good. Some people don't survive the induction. Now, tell us a story or you're dead. But not immediately dead. It could take a while.

At first he didn't know how to tell them anything, but then he remembered the wheezing noise. Presumably his voice worked. He tried it.

'What story?' He seemed to feel his lips moving somewhere but the voice only sounded in his head.

Yours. Who else's do you know?

'Who is judging my story?'

We are.

'How should I tell it?'

However you choose. In pictures or dreams or words – it's up to you. But tell it now. No more questions.

He thought hard, aware that if they could both place voices in his head and hear them, they could probably hear other things. There was unlikely to be any concealment.

He reviewed the decision he had reached in the night and decided that he had no options, in fact that from the moment he arrived here and probably from much earlier he had had no options.

Perhaps he had *never* had options. And with that thought came clarity. In the end, it was about loyalties. And about what was important.

He gave them memories.

His first memory was of an absence. His mother had once found a man who was water-borne, the captain of one of the tugs that hauled the great tar-black barges through the gate valves at the outskirts of the city and into the lifter basins that took them skywards. And once, just once, they had all been on the tug when it had stayed with its haul and had swayed up past the dripping columns to the Middle Level.

He could remember his confusion, even now. He remembered sniffing, and finding a sensation missing. He didn't realize what it was until they had descended to Ground Level again, when for the first time in his life he was conscious of the prickling of tar at the back of his palate – realized that for half a day out of his whole seven years he had been free of it. Now it was back, and he knew he would never be free of it again.

Ground Level was dim light and deep shadows and damp clothes and the sound of dripping water from the two levels of canal above, and everywhere the taste and smell of tar from the hulls and the ropes, and the constant grey haze of oily sulphurous exhaust smoke from the rattling boat engines. Ground Level was endless meals of canal-carp, and now he knew they tasted of tar as well. Ground Level was fretful adults and raised voices and blows dodged and sometimes not dodged.

He remembered running from their lodgings – a single room,

more often than not paid for by his mother's latest – to escape the
fretting and the blows and to play with similar nameless children
amongst the elaborate growths of moss and mould at the bases
of columns that always ran with water. To climb the columns,
sometimes, and dare each other to grab the wire ropes that ran
between squeaking pulleys, endlessly lifting and hauling.

Then he remembered the cries of his new-born sister, and the
way that they changed from urgent to fearful to weary as he
tried to rouse the cooling body of his mother from the dark
pool that spread from it. The cries faded away and so for a
moment did his memory. When it returned he must have run
away, because he was . . .

We know.

The voice – it wasn't quite a voice but it had at least as much
impact – shocked him out of his dream. He gathered himself.

'You know – what?'

*Your life after you went into vagrant detention is on public
record. We've already looked it up.*

He shook the idea of his head. 'Not all of it you haven't.
Watch.'

He remembered the ziggurat palace and the five lecterns and
the beings behind them. It seemed to him that his unseen listen-
ers grew attentive.

There was a long – silence, if that was the right word.

You're actually admitting that you're a spy?

'No. I'm telling you they said I'd be a good spy.'

And are you?

He shook his head again and this time it seemed to mean
more. 'If I was only a good spy I wouldn't be trying to explain
this to you.' He took the equivalent of a deep breath and waited.

Only?

'Yes.' He grinned, realizing that he meant it and not caring if
it was real or not. 'Now it's my turn to ask a question. How
would you define a *perfect* spy?'

There was a long pause which felt a little like a collective gasp. Then an even longer, very busy-sounding silence.

Hevalansa Vess? Are you making an offer?

'I might be. Why?'

You must be offering us something we need.

'What do you need?'

Privacy.

'Meaning what?'

We believe this ability, to use the Stack as we do, is unknown to the Inside. Is that right?

'I don't know. No one mentioned it.'

That might mean something, or it might not. Nevertheless; in here we can plan, model, communicate in a way that would be impossible otherwise. We need that. It must be maintained, if you are allowed to leave.

He nodded. Then a question occurred to him. 'How did you make those . . .' he hesitated, 'those dreams?'

Until now the voice – it wasn't exactly a voice, but he had no other way of describing it to himself – had sounded, or better *felt*, dry and remote, but now it laughed and suddenly it had a hint of warmth, as if there were humans behind it somewhere.

You're in one of the most powerful intelligences anywhere. At any one time thousands of us are chipped in, and the way the Stack uses us is way more efficient than just a multiple of our brains. A few of us found out how to stay conscious in here, and we can siphon off some of that processing power. Giving someone a few vivid moments is nothing.

'Vivid? Yes. And you can kill someone that way, can you?'

Yes.

'And have you?'

Yes. More than once.

'Why didn't you kill me?'

Guess.

He didn't need to think for long. 'Because you need more than privacy.'

Meaning?

'I think you need help.'

Yes . . . that is it. All the planning and modelling in the world means very little, unless there is some way of putting it into action.

'And so I'm still alive.'

And so you are. This is an appalling risk for us.

'And for me. I'll be honest, I don't know if I will be able to help you. But I won't harm you.'

For someone who came here as a spy, perhaps that will have to do. In return, a warning – now you have been in here, and especially when you come out alive, you may find yourself at risk from others. Be aware of this.

'I will.' He paused. 'Thank you.'

One day you might have reason to, but not yet.

Web City

It was late evening, Web time, but the streets were still lined with stalls and there were plenty of people to mill round them. Mill round, but not buy, as far as Seldyan could see. Talking seemed more popular.

A long section of stalls on one street sold hot food, mostly cooked over little glowing braziers half covered by metal hoods shaped like pointed hats. Seldyan supposed they were there to trap fumes but the air still smelled acridly smoky.

She had chosen Hufsza to come with her on the first visit. Kot was too much an outlier in physical form, even here where just about every possible shade and morphology of human seemed normal. Lyste was somehow too fragile, even if fragile was the wrong word for anyone who had survived the Hive and then broken out. And Merish, obviously, was needed on board because he was the one who really understood the ship.

Obviously.

They could communicate. The ship had provided some tiny buds that rolled deep into your ear and stayed there. They seemed to be more than microphones; even if you only sub-vocalized, the words you had *thought* were transmitted, and despite the fact that the little buds lived in only one ear at a time, the answers they relayed were heard in both. Seldyan wasn't about to enquire. Nor had she argued when Merish had handed her the little flat stunner she had originally used on Captain Hefs. It felt reassuring.

Whatever the reasons, she was glad of her choice of companion: the crowds were thick and Hufsza's reassuring bulk was useful. They shoved their way to one of the counters and watched as a small lean woman with a heavily tanned face rolled amorphous lumps of minced something from a big bowl into little balls which she skewered and cooked. The balls spat and dribbled bubbling threads of fat which flared as they hit the coals.

When they were done the woman pulled them off the skewers with her bare fingers, folded them into thin flat wraps from another part of the brazier, and held them out without showing any sign of letting them go.

'That'll be six million, in laced nickel.'

With the ship's help Lyste had faked up some of the local currency; Seldyan counted out six flat thumbnail-sized chips of nickel and handed them over.

'The nickel's just the carrier,' Merish had explained. 'It's alloyed with whatever they need to get the right value.'

She had hefted the little chips. They seemed heavy. 'What's in these?'

He had grinned. 'Five per cent depleted U. The ship says it's safe.'

The stallholder seemed to think so, too. She took the chips and, without letting go of the wraps, dropped one on a glowing spot on the back of the counter next to her. The glow dimmed for a moment and then there was a high-pitched beep. The woman nodded and handed over their food.

Seldyan took hers.

'Shit!' It was close to untouchably hot, even wrapped. She sucked in her breath and tossed it from hand to hand. She looked at the woman. 'What are your fingers made of?'

The woman held out her hands, upturned. 'My past.'

The glow from the brazier baffled Seldyan's night sight. She handed her wrap to Hufsza and leaned in close so she could see.

The ends of the woman's fingers were flat and thick, as if they had been beaten out of a bar of something. There were no whorls, just rough callused skin.

Seldyan realized that she was looking at layer upon layer of scar tissue, built so deep there was nothing left of the original flesh. She looked up from the fingers and into the woman's impassive face. 'What happened?'

The woman made an odd flipping motion with her fingers as if she was trying to cool them down. 'What do you think? Burns, newcomer. A whole year of 'em, when I was a kid. Where you been?'

Hufsza shook his head. 'We're new,' he said. 'How did you get them?'

'Whoa. You *are* new. Same way anybody does.' She gestured them away. 'Now eat. Before it gets cold.'

A crowd had gathered round them to watch the show. They turned and began to push their way through it, but then it divided in front of them. For a moment Seldyan thought it was to let them through, but then she saw the girl walking through the gap towards the stall. If she was standard human, Seldyan guessed she would be no more than a couple of cycles old, not quite on the verge of puberty. It was hard to be sure; her slight figure was younger but her face was older. Her hair was cropped unevenly short and she was dressed in a patched coverall of faded grey fabric. There was a slight bias in her tread as if she was off balance, which Seldyan guessed at first was because of the bag slung over her shoulder. Then Hufsza nudged her and nodded towards the girl. Seldyan looked again, and saw that the sleeve of the coverall on the opposite side to the bag swung empty. The girl was missing an arm and, by the looks of it, part of her shoulder.

From behind her she heard the voice of the stallholder. 'Hello, Krish. How many do you feed tonight?'

The girl said nothing. She held up her only hand, four fingers spread.

'Only four? Take for six. I readied them so you may as well. Here,' and the stallholder reached below the counter and brought up a package of rough paper. 'Go on, take it.'

The girl hesitated for a second and then held out her bag. The stallholder dropped the package into it and gave it back, and the girl swung it awkwardly on to her shoulder again. She nodded once and then turned and walked away through the gap in the watching crowd. It closed behind her, and Seldyan thought she heard approving noises.

No money had changed hands.

She turned back to the stallholder. 'What was that about?'

The woman's face closed like a door. 'More questions? If you're so new you need to ask, I ain't saying.' She turned her back.

The crowd had gone quiet. Seldyan nodded, as much for them as for Hufsza. 'We're going,' she said. 'Thanks.'

They worked their way through the milling people until they were suddenly clear. Then, by mutual consent, they walked quickly until the lights and the smells of the food stalls had faded behind them. Then, in a pool of darkness at the entrance to an alley, they stopped and faced each other.

Seldyan spoke first. '*What* the fuck?'

Through the darkness she saw Hufsza's teeth glint in what might have been interpreted as a smile, if she hadn't known him. 'Life's not simple here, is it? People with industrial injuries give free food to kids with missing arms, and everyone knows what it's about except us?'

She shook her head. 'Simple, I don't know, but it's not good. I'm going to call the ship, okay?'

'Sure. I'll join in.'

Seldyan sighed, and tapped her earlobe twice, and out of the corner of her eye saw Hufsza doing the same. Almost immediately she heard Merish's voice.

'Hi, guys. You good?'

'Alive but baffled.' She smiled to herself. 'There are things we don't understand.'

'Uh-huh? Tell me. The others are listening too, by the way.'

She told him, glancing at Hufsza from time to time for confirmation. When she finished there was silence for a while. Then Merish said, 'Okay, some interesting stuff there. What are you going to do?'

'Look around. You?'

'Hang out here, I guess. The ship's having a good time sucking up planets-full of data. So far it seems to have stayed hidden; no sign we've been noticed by anything . . .'

'Good.' She was about to sign off when the bead gave a sharp buzz like angry insects. She yelped and grabbed at her ear, but by the time her hand was there the noise had stopped and instead her ear was full of voices.

One became clear. It was Merish, but obviously not talking to them: '. . . unknown vessel, do *not* approach like that again. Repeat, do *not* – that was *way* too close. Do that again and we assume you're hostile.'

More voices; different versions of events, arguments. Seldyan took the bead out of her ear, held it up to her lips, glanced a warning at Hufsza (who widened his eyes and grabbed the bead from his own ear) and whistled as loudly as she could. She waited a moment, then said 'sorry' softly to the bead and replaced it in her ear.

'Guys? You there?'

'Yeah. Sorry about the noise. Seems we got noticed after all. We got buzzed.'

She raised her eyebrows. 'By what?'

'Don't know. Or, don't know yet. Something big, maybe even as big as us. Came past very fast, very close. Then gone.'

Seldyan glanced at Hufsza. 'What does the ship think?'

'That *is* what the ship thinks. Or it's as much as it's telling.' He fell silent for a moment. 'No sign of anything now.'

'Uh-huh.' Seldyan tapped her foot. 'If the ship can't work out what it was that must mean it's at least as smart as the ship, or luckier. Watch it, guys.' She broke the contact and looked at Hufsza. 'Okay. Let's start. Where?'

He shrugged. 'Where people are. Where they go to meet people.'

She nodded slowly. Then she winked at him, wandered out of the alley and back towards the lights and the food smells, checking over her shoulder every dozen paces to make sure that he was still in sight. A minute later they were among people again. She stopped by a couple of lounging men and grinned at them. 'Excuse me,' she said, 'I'm new in town. Where do I go to get a drink?'

She watched their faces stretch into smiles. As their body language began to shift she gestured towards the approaching bulk of Hufsza and added, 'My friend and I.'

Both men's faces fell. One of them jerked a thumb. 'That way,' he said. 'The light.'

The other man snickered.

Seldyan followed the gesture. At first she couldn't make out what the man was talking about but then she saw a dim purple glow highlighting a doorway about fifty paces away.

She looked back at the men, holding their gazes for a while, but their faces had closed down. Eventually she nodded. 'Thank you, gentlemen,' she said.

One of them turned a little to the side and spat. Seldyan turned her back and placed a hand on Hufsza's shoulder. 'Off we go,' she said.

They were walking through the smudge of darkness between the braziers and the door when someone said, 'Wait.'

They stopped. Seldyan half glanced at Hufsza. His eyes, tinted purple by the leaking light, were narrow.

She flexed her fingers. 'Okay, we're waiting.'

'Sorry I was rough on you.' Seldyan felt her eyes widen – it was the voice of the woman from the food stall.

'It's okay. You don't know us.'

'Sure I do. You're the people with the big ship. You should hear how people are fighting over you.'

'As long as they're not fighting against us.'

'Not yet, but they might try. Watch yourselves.'

Seldyan glanced at Hufsza. '*Who* might try? Patras?'

There was a snort of suppressed laughter. 'Only while he has something left to fight with. Listen, I'm going to trust you. Think about this. Not everyone who turns up here is a refugee. Plenty people get here with life savings, good-enough ships, supplies – but sooner or later everyone's poor. How do you think that happens?'

'I don't know.'

'The City Fathers. You've seen how the place is set up. They provide a basic plate with enough power under it – literally, *just* enough – to put a field over the top and keep the air in. Then they charge for everything else.'

Hufsza shrugged. 'We knew that. Where's the surprise?'

'You don't get it.' The voice was quiet but insistent. 'I said *everything*. Water, heat, air top-up, sanitation, lighting. *Everything*. And here's the clever thing: even if you manage to bring all that with you, and some people did, they still bill you for what they think you ought to have used.'

Seldyan stared at Hufsza. He looked disbelieving. 'But how do they make that stick? I mean, if you brought your own stuff they can screw their bills. You're fine.'

'No, you aren't. If you don't pay, they charge a tariff on the plate power, equal to what you should have been paying, plus interest. A *lot* of interest. And if you don't pay that – they power down the reactor.'

Seldyan felt her eyes widen. 'Power down . . . no, wait. No shield? Really?'

'Really. Round here, hard vacuum's free. Everything else costs.'

Hufsza shook his head. 'That's just a threat, though, right? They wouldn't really do it?'

'Yes, they would. Have done, four times so far. About a hundred and fifty thousand dead. Not recently.'

'*How* many? Fuck.' Seldyan felt anger balling in her stomach. 'So this whole place is a scam?'

'*Now* you get it.'

Hufsza was clenching his fists. 'Patras,' he said. 'Is it him?'

'Mainly him. Some hangers-on.'

'And the Green Star?'

There was a pause. 'No. Not so's you'd see. I wouldn't say more than that.'

Seldyan frowned. 'Okay,' she said. 'I get that. I hate it, but I get it. So what about burned fingers and missing arms?'

'We hack the reactors – pull them away from central control and up the output.' The voice sounded weary. 'It isn't a safe job. The reactors are underneath the plate, see? No biological shield, and they put the controls inside the hot zone. Lucky ones like me, we get burns that heal. Less lucky, they get burns that don't heal, and the only way is amputation. Some of 'em get over the burns and die anyway; a few weeks, a few months. The rest of us have to wait and see.'

Seldyan sought for more words, but she had run out. She looked helplessly at Hufsza, who was slowly clenching and unclenching his fists. He opened one and stared at it. 'Why the kids?'

'Access. You need to be small.' A mirthless laugh. 'I never grew much so I qualified. Well done me.'

'Yeah, well done you.' Seldyan meant it. Without thinking she extended a hand towards the voice.

She never completed the movement.

There was a moment of – intensity.

The concussion shook her off her feet. She felt her chest compressing and her lungs emptied in an explosion of breath. Then there was a second tearing explosion and blazing air slammed into her back like a hammer, throwing her against the wall, one shoulder first.

She opened her eyes slowly and then closed them again as something hot trickled down her forehead. With her free hand she wiped the blood on her sleeve and turned her head away from the wall. She was covered with dust, and there was something wrong with her shoulder. Next to her, Hufsza was pushing himself slowly away from the wall. He looked dazed. Seldyan wasn't surprised.

She took a breath, and coughed dust. The second breath was better. She looked around for the woman, but there was no one. Her hand was still extended; she must simply have forgotten to withdraw it. She did now, and realized that it was wet.

Then she saw the jagged form at her feet, and her thoughts slowed down.

The woman seemed smaller in death. There was no doubt it *was* death – even ignoring the mess above the shoulders, life could never look as *fractured*. And there was something glistening in the wall. It looked like a splash, with a lump in the centre. She dared a closer look.

The lump was a piece of masonry, squashed into the wall by the force of its own impact. Presumably, the same force that had carried it through the shattered head of the woman lying at Seldyan's feet.

For a moment there was quiet. Then noise happened – angry, fearful, confused people noise.

Somehow it sounded worse than explosions. Seldyan swallowed and tapped her comms bead. 'What happened?'

Her ear buzzed angrily for a painful second. Then Merish's voice came through. 'Sel? Thank fuck. Are you okay?'

'I think so. There was, I don't know, an explosion, an attack. Something. What can you see?'

'Something organized. Coordinated, probably. There's been explosions all over the Web. Minor casualties, mainly. That's odd.'

'What is?'

'Well, if you're setting off a load of kinetics in a populated area you expect to take out a certain number of civilians, but this didn't. Oh, wait . . .'

She waited.

When he came back on line his voice was steadier, but not calmer. 'We should get you out of there, guys. That was a coup; looks like our Green friends are making their bid.'

Seldyan glanced at Hufsza, who was still leaning against the wall. She couldn't see his expression, but his posture looked weary. 'We'll be okay,' she said, partly for his benefit, 'but some directions would be good.'

'Okay. Get back to the main square, the one you left just now. I'll guide you from there. And good luck, because you are going to need it.'

The comms went silent. Seldyan rubbed her hands together, trying to ignore the screaming pain in her shoulder. It was getting harder. She turned to Hufsza, who was still leaning against the wall. 'You heard the man,' she said. 'Time to go.'

He nodded, and pushed himself away from the wall. The effort seemed to cost him, and he stood, swaying slightly.

She gave him a grin. 'Come on, Huf.'

He didn't move.

She reached her arm a little further. 'Come *on*, Huf. Let's get out of here. Trust me.'

Still nothing. She felt her stomach contract.

'Come on, big guy. You can do it.'

His voice was very calm. 'No, I can't.' The Arch-light glanced across his torso. The front of his chemise was dark with blood. It was spreading as she watched.

'What? Shit, Huf . . .' She took a step towards him but he held up his arm.

'Don't. There's no point.' He gestured towards the wall where he had stood next to her. She followed the gesture and her eyes widened.

There was something sticking out of the wall – a slim rod a couple of hands long. It was dark with blood.

'That went through me, Sel.' He took a slow breath and she heard bubbling. 'I, I can't . . .' His voice tailed off in a long sigh. His eyes closed. Then he dropped gently to his knees, sagged sideways, and fell to the ground. She heard the *tock* of his head hitting the floor.

'*Hufsza!*' Seldyan dropped to her knees beside him, reaching for his neck.

There was no pulse.

She watched the curled-up body for a second. Then her eyes blurred. She shook her head and raised her hand to the comms bead. 'Guys? Hufsza's gone.'

'Gone? Gone how?'

'Dead.' She managed to keep her voice level while she explained. Then, without really knowing why, she added: 'I'm sorry.'

For a moment there was no response. Then Merish was on line. 'Sel? Keep focused. Are you okay?'

'Yeah. I'll do.'

'Okay. Listen, you have some work to do. There's chaos, but that could help you out . . . Are you listening?'

'Yes!' She hadn't been, she realized. She stood up. 'Go on.'

'Right. Wait. Wait . . . now go. Straight ahead, a hundred metres . . .'

Half an hour of directions later she was backed into a shallow gap where one building didn't quite stand level to another. She was covered in sweat that obviously had nothing to do with fear, and her injured shoulder had turned to ice except when she moved it, when it became a white-hot shaft with an almost-useless arm on the end of it. She thought she could feel something grating when she moved it. She kept the ship stunner cradled in her other hand.

Apart from that, and the exhaustion, and the not thinking about Hufsza, she was fine. The square was a wreck, though. She tapped the bead. 'Where now? Things are looking busy here.'

It was an understatement. She was close to the area where she and Hufsza, a lifetime ago, had watched people giving hot food to street kids with missing limbs. It had troubled her at the time but it seemed like paradise, looking back.

Everyone on the broad street was either running or chasing. Some people had proper weapons, but many more had improvised with sharp things or heavy things or hot things. She doubted the stunner would be much help, if it came to it.

Merish spoke in her ear. 'You need to get underneath the deck. There are service ducts. The nearest is about three hundred metres from you. How easily can you move around?'

She almost laughed. 'I can move okay. It's just the stuff that might happen while I'm moving that bothers me.'

'Okay. Hold on a second.'

It took longer than a second but less than a minute. Then he was back. 'Sel? The ship's got an idea. If we create a really big distraction, can you get to the duct?'

'I guess. Where do I go?'

'Head to your right. A hundred metres straight, then left. I'll guide you. Don't go yet. You'll know when.'

'How?'

'Believe me, you'll know.'

Ten seconds later, the sky lit up. Seldyan felt her mouth drop open. Before, there had been just stars and the bright smear of the Arch. Now, there was . . . everything. Bands and spots and fleeting explosions of vivid colour flickered above her in a brilliantly garish parade that bounced the whole visible spectrum off upturned faces. A few people cowered; most just stared.

Seldyan ran. Nobody tried to stop her. She counted a hundred paces and dived to her left down a narrow entrance between tall dull-looking buildings. The walls were only a few metres apart, so that she ran down a black ribbon with a roof of riotous colour.

'Stop.'

She skidded to a halt. 'What now?'

'Nearly there. What can you see?'

'Fuck all. It's dark.' She thought for a moment and added sarcastically, 'Can the ship arrange a searchlight?'

'No, but have you got the stunner?'

'Sure.' She hefted it. 'So what?'

'Slap it twice.'

She stared at the little ovoid. 'Really?'

'Really.'

'Okay.' Feeling rather foolish, she smacked the little gun a couple of times. It lit up, with a soft yellowish glow that was bright enough to illuminate the walls of her chasm, but not so bright it dazzled. She nodded, and looked around, holding the little thing out in front of her. 'Merish? This looks like a dead end.'

'It isn't. Go to the end.'

She walked carefully; the light from the glowing stunner illuminated forward but created a pool of darkness round her feet, and the flickering light leaking down from above her head was beginning to make her feel sick. She tapped the bead. 'Guys? That light show isn't healthy.'

'It isn't meant to be. Be glad you're mainly in the dark. Can you see the end of the alley yet?'

She peered forward. 'Yes. It just looks like a blank wall.'

'Touch it.'

She held out her hand. Then she jumped back.

'Shit!'

It was no longer blank. Even before her hand had touched it, the surface had lit up with warning symbols. She studied them. 'Okay, I see it,' she said slowly. 'The two I recognize mean radiation and a big energy source.'

'Clever girl. The ship's going to open it.'

'Oh good.'

For a second nothing happened. Then the symbols faded and a door-sized section of wall slid sideways. Inside there was a plain metal shaft, about twice the width of her shoulders. Shallow hoops set into the far wall made a ladder that went up as well as down. Fat cables the diameter of legs snaked down both sides. She bent forward so her head was inside the shaft, and heard a low burring hum. 'Merish? Hear that? What the fuck is this?'

'Service duct. Up leads to one of the shield generators. Down leads through the deck to the power level.'

She nodded. 'Is down the same as out?'

'That's right. Try not to touch the cables.'

'I promise.' She leaned further in, let herself fall forward until her hands caught on a rung. Then she emptied her lungs and stepped off the edge, swinging forward so her body fell against the far wall. Her shoulder howled at her while feet scrabbled and caught. When she was sure she wouldn't use it to scream with, she took a careful breath. 'Okay, I'm in.'

'So down you go. It's about forty metres to the machine deck.'

She began to climb down. Her injured shoulder wouldn't take any weight so she transferred the stunner to that hand and used the other to steady herself, stepping awkwardly down one rung at a time.

She counted steps. Guessing at three to a metre she had about one hundred to go. After a while she found a rhythm. Step one foot down; let go of the rung above her and catch the one below before her body had time to fall outwards; step the other foot down. Take one breath. Do it again.

At seventy steps she paused, hooking her arm through a rung and letting herself hang. The air in the shaft was flat and stale and her chest felt tight, and the sound of her heart knocking in her ears competed with the edgy hum from the cables. The beat seemed slower than she would have expected.

Then she swore.

It wasn't her heart. The soft concussions were coming from above her.

She tapped the bead and began to descend again. 'Merish? Did you shut the door to the duct?'

'Yes! What . . . oh, shit.'

She nodded to herself. 'There's someone, isn't there?'

'Yeah. Two, not one. They must have known the code. Seldyan, I am so sorry . . .'

'Not your fault.' She was trying to match the speed of the steps from above her, and she didn't have breath for long sentences. 'Be there when I get to the bottom.'

'We're there already.'

She didn't say anything else. Foot, let go, catch, foot. She couldn't go faster, but it wasn't fast enough. Whoever it was was catching her.

Then the sounds changed as if someone had broken their stride. There was a quick, greedy crackle, and then suddenly the stunner gave an angry buzz and glowed, climbing fast through red to yellow-hot. She had time for one yelp of agony before her reflexes jerked her useless arm in an awkward movement like a child throwing something under-arm. The flaming stunner tumbled upwards past her head, hung for a second at the top of its arc – and brushed against the fat bunch of cables.

It stuck, in a smoking hiss of burned insulation. Then it flared.

Seldyan buried her face in her shoulder and waited for whatever came next.

The explosion almost broke her grip. Even through her closed eyes her world had flashed yellow, and her ears banged and chimed and whistled. Everything smelled hot and sort of cooked.

She opened her eyes very slowly.

In front of her the wall of the duct was lit up by a flickering yellow light. From above her came an intermittent buzzing that kept time with the flickering. She looked up carefully and winced.

There were two bodies, only about five metres above her. One had been blown back against the wall of the duct by the explosion – it lay there propped, with both stiff legs braced against the rungs on the opposite wall. The second was still gripping the ladder fiercely with one arm; its other arm was wrapped convulsively round the cables like a lover. The body was smoking slightly.

Seldyan looked away. She managed to get a hand to her ear. 'Merish? I think I had a lucky accident. What can you see?'

The reply took a moment. 'Um, not much near you. Half a minute ago there was a power spike in your duct, then the breakers went out. The machine deck keeps trying to restart the power. Should I stop it?'

She looked up briefly. 'No, don't. I think it's doing something useful.' She took a deep breath of the foul air and almost gagged. 'I'm on my way down. Not so much rush now.'

Ten minutes of slow steps later she was standing on a checker-plate floor at the bottom of the duct. The door in front of her looked like the one she had come through at the top of her descent, except for the warning symbols. They were much bigger, and they didn't fade when she drew back her hand.

She frowned. 'Merish? What's on the other side of this?'

'The machine deck. Electrical things, mechanical things. The reactor pod.'

'Right. That pod? How safe is it?'

'Fairly. People do come down here. I'll guide you.'

The door slid back. She lifted a foot to step through and then froze, mentally playing back her hearing. She was right; there had been a noise. It had come from further up the ladder.

She looked up.

The figure was two metres above her. As she completed her movement, it pushed itself away from the ladder and dropped.

She had time to half turn, pointing her crippled shoulder towards the exit and ducking a little sideways so that the falling body glanced down her side. The impact simultaneously pushed her to her knees and drove her towards the exit so that she found herself rolling awkwardly out into the machine deck. The roll sent her injured shoulder to the ground beneath her; she felt another crack and pain burst open within her. She had time for one shriek before a foot slammed into her side and the breath whistled out of her.

She heard Merish saying something but she didn't bother with it. Something animal in her took control. She turned her head towards the direction of the kick and managed to skitter backwards to evade the next. The foot arced past her and she grabbed it and twisted. This time the pain made her retch but she had caught the attacker by surprise – he went down with his other leg folded underneath him. She heard him grunt, and for a moment he didn't move. Then he lifted himself, swaying, on to all fours and raised his head to look at her.

Half his face was missing, replaced by red and black char which went through his cheek to show gums burned through to the bone with teeth, ridiculously long, hanging from them. She could smell cooked meat.

With half of her mind she registered a voice in her ear. 'Sel? Report! Are you attacked?' Merish sounded panicked.

'Yes. How close are you?'

'The other side of an airlock. Three minutes, fastest.'

She thought as fast as her fuzzy head would allow. 'Okay,' she said. 'That should do. Talk soon.' Then, hoping the hint had been taken, she looked at the man who was still crouching a few metres away. 'Not long to wait.'

He grinned, and she watched as blood drooled from the destruction of his mouth. 'Of course,' he said. 'Any minute now, I'm sure. How fast can you run? I think you are injured.'

'And you aren't?' She shook her head. 'This is going to end badly.'

He didn't answer, but she saw the flicker in his remaining eye and threw herself to one side as he sprang forwards. His attack ended where she had been; she had not moved far, and they were closer now.

She studied his face. Every expression seemed to tear his flesh. Blood and saliva were running from the remains of his mouth in a continuous thread. On an impulse she said, 'You're going to die here.'

He nodded, grinning, and she watched the pink thread from his face making a pattern on the metal deck. 'So? So are you, maybe.'

'So, why?'

But his face closed. 'No. No stories.' Then he leapt like a predator.

This time she was ready. He was still in the air when her good arm swept round; even as his weight bore her to the floor and his arms reached round for her, her clenched knuckles jabbed up and into his neck.

Something crunched.

He landed on top of her, his face just overshooting a kiss so that his nose crashed against her forehead with another crunch, somehow managing to maintain the pose of a four-limbed animal caught in mid-pounce. At first she thought he was already dead, but then the weight on her moved a little and she heard a shallow rasp. She lifted her good shoulder and levered him up so that he rolled off her like a drunken lover.

His nose was gushing blood now, and she reached up to her forehead and felt an answering wetness.

Something in her wrenched and broke. She knelt by his not-quite-corpse and stroked a bit of his cheek that still had skin. 'Time to go? Is that what you want?'

He nodded.

'Okay. But know this – I'm going to end the story that made you do this. Deal?'

He nodded again, and this time she thought she saw an answering thought in the remaining eye.

His neck was still upturned. She drew back her hand.

Five minutes later Kot roused her. 'Sel? Are you okay?'

She looked at her knuckles. They were bruised and swollen, as if she had used them to hit something many, many times.

'I'm fine,' she said. Then, as sensation began to seep into her world, she added, 'But I think there's something wrong with my shoulder.'

She tried to show Kot but the pain came, and she was borne away on the wings of her own scream.

She remembered waking once, and being surrounded by faces. She smiled up at them. 'How am I doing?'

'Try not to move.' It wasn't reassuring; she made a mental note to be angry with whoever it was had said that.

Merish. That was the name. She exerted herself. 'Why not move?'

'Because you have a broken shoulder and a broken collarbone. Apparently you managed to win a fight in spite of them.'

She felt a smile changing her face. 'I did, yeah. Don't fuck with me. Hufsza'll tell you.' She looked round the circle of faces, vaguely aware that something was terribly wrong. 'Where is he?'

'Go to sleep, Seldyan.' She didn't like taking orders, even from

Merish, but there was something about this one that was unfightable. She went to sleep.

It was okay, she told herself with her last thought. She would find out about Huf when she woke up.

Web City Administrative Space – Arch Third Quadrant

*S*uck on This watched the receding ship with something close to shock. If it had been human, it would have blinked.

It had had time for a vast exchange of information with the thing, whole planets' worth of data – and more than a little acrimony – in the time it had taken the human to issue its glacial admonishment. It had learned everything it needed to know. Until now it had been assuming it was alone in the Spin; now it knew it had at least one peer.

Someone had found and awakened another of its original cohort. And of all ships, it had to have been *that* one – which was nothing if not adventurous, and which was now on a mission of its own.

By contrast, *Suck on This* had always been very much at the cautious end of the spectrum as far as its kind went. It examined a number of different courses of action, modelling multiple outcomes, allowing as far as it could for the grandly decayed state of the local tech level, for the fragmented condition of the many small stakeholder groups, for the sheer brittleness of the geopolitics of the Arch (a new religion? Really?) and the astonishing fact that everyone seemed simply to have forgotten what had gone on around here.

Inter alia, it felt a sense of responsibility. That came with power, of course, and it was nothing new. It, and its kind, had been built to be the most powerful units possible. To be a deterrent, internal and external; to provide a measured surety in every situation. And, of course, to act as a counterbalance in case other, less measured forces were ever released. It had happened at least once, before their time; it was never to happen again.

Most of them had never even been used. They had slept through the millennia, hidden away.

But now the wheels were coming off, and coming off a vastly diminished and disempowered set of societies. What had already been overmatching power those ten thousand years ago, was now disproportionate. Overwhelming, in fact.

It was in the position of a parent with a crowd of unruly children. No, it was worse than that. It was near to being a God, with a chittering horde of armpit-scratching primitives.

It mentally shook itself. That was not a wholesome attitude; but nevertheless, the conclusion that it implied was still sound, especially now it knew it was not the only player.

The Arch was the clue. Someone had tried to build a planet, and it hadn't worked – but that meant that somehow, someone had got hold of a machine with planet-building capabilities, and that meant that the Archive had been compromised, although its peer ship had been tight-lipped about that. Whatever; the old safety would be gone very soon, no matter what it did. Better to end it at a time it chose, and with some kind of route map to the next thing.

And so the most cautious ship in the cohort comes to the most radical conclusion, it thought. *But there you are. Nothing if not logical.*

It was time to break open the Archive. And it might now be time to hurry.

It wondered if it should drop a hint to the humans, but for

their own reasons, not entirely unconnected with its own although they didn't know it, they were already heading in the right direction. It took the path of least resistance and left them to it.

Meanwhile it ramped up its senses to what an earlier craft might have called battle stations, carrying out a full outward- and inward-facing audit of its own status every few nano-seconds. For good measure it extended the audit into the recent past, because you never knew.

What it found made it blink again.

It had been monitoring its own outgoing comms, obviously, and even more so anything incoming, but it had missed the tiny, intermittent signal that arose sporadically from somewhere within itself – somewhere which, now it checked, always coincided with one of the humans – the same one.

Someone, somewhere, was keeping tabs on them. Well, well. Even more reason to hurry. But not to panic, it reassured itself. Not yet.

Hive, Mind Stack Unit

Vess woke up with the sensation of being somewhere unexpected. Physically, he was where he should have been – on a grubby couch in the Mind Stack unit. Mentally, he felt as if he was somewhere quite new. Or maybe that he was where he had always been, but had only just noticed it.

He cautiously played back the latter half of his conversation in the Stack, and then nodded to himself. That would explain it.

Both views were right, in a way.

He didn't have long to think before the old world intruded. Or rather, almost failed to. The warder who disconnected him from the couch did it brusquely, not meeting his eye even when that meant elaborate avoidance, and sent him back to the Village with nothing more than a grunt and a shove. In the Village, eyes slid away from his. His Stack time had lasted through the night; when he queued for breakfast, spaces opened in front and behind him. The server turned his face away as he slopped out his helping. It was as if he didn't exist.

And then he realized how close he was to the truth and almost laughed out loud.

Dead, he thought. *I'm supposed to be dead. But then how is it that everyone seems to know that?*

Then he realized it wasn't everyone. Dimollss was watching him with a half-smile.

'Hello,' she said.

'Hello.' Doubt assailed him. What did she know, and what should he say?

She saved him the trouble. Leaning towards him, she spoke quietly. 'You survived in there. Well done. You must be very clever. Now if you're even cleverer you'll survive out here.'

She turned her back on him and walked away, allowing the crowd to heal behind her. He lost sight of her in seconds but the image of her expression stayed with him. It had been – he struggled for the word – fierce, yes, but something else as well.

Two other things. That was it. Hopeful, and desperate. Perhaps a touch of something else, too.

Pride?

He was still reflecting on that when he felt a quick thrumming at the base of his spine – not painful, not even really uncomfortable, but certainly enough to attract his attention. He waited, standing as still as the crowd allowed, and counted silently. At five the thrumming came again, and again at ten – one of the pre-arranged signals they had dinned into him at the briefing. Put simply it meant *you will be contacted. Leave the when and the how to us.*

In other words, someone – probably the Hive Management – wanted to talk. It wasn't surprising.

He breathed out and let himself be jostled along gently. After a minute he realized he was part of a small group who were slowly parting from the main mass. He tried to count the group but the numbers seemed to keep changing as people joined and left. He didn't recognize any of them.

They were approaching the confluence of the walkways from three Villages. As the flows of people merged Vess found himself moving off to the right, and suddenly he and a half-dozen others were off the main route and walking up a ramp to an exit he hadn't noticed until they were almost through it. His companions tightened round him like bodyguards. They didn't meet his eye, and after a single glance around he didn't look again. His gaze didn't seem welcome.

They walked along a short plain corridor just wide enough to fit three abreast. It ended at a blank door set deep into a heavy-looking surround. Vess raised his eyebrows; it was the sort of door that defined the beginning of the boundary between inside the Hive and outside. The lead guard stepped forward and placed his palm flat against the middle of the door. It split along invisible seams into irregular shards which curled round each other in eye-watering patterns before collapsing into an angular mass and floating out of the way. Beyond it was a small plain chamber.

The guards ahead of him stepped back round Vess, and one of them shoved him forward.

'Airlock,' he said simply. 'Palm the next door.'

Vess turned in surprise. 'Only me?'

'Only you. The lock cycles just enough air for one.' The man grinned. 'I hope it's expecting you. If not, it'll cycle just enough air for no one.'

He stepped backwards through the entrance. Before Vess could respond, the lump that had been the door flitted past him, blurringly untangled itself and fitted itself back into the door-frame with a soft fluttering noise.

An alarm chimed and the light in the chamber changed from the mock blue-white daylight that was standard through the Hive to an abrasive purple.

'Ten seconds to cleanse cycle. Present identification to abort.'

The light was disorientating. Vess shook his head and took the two paces to the further door.

'Five seconds to cleanse cycle. Present identification to abort.'

He placed his palm flat against the middle of the door, as the guard had done. Just in case, he took a deep breath and held it.

'Cleanse aborted.'

The light brightened, although it still kept the purple tint. The door did the same fragmenting trick as the other one and Vess let the breath out again. The space beyond the door was gloomy; he took a step forward and then another. Something brushed against his shoulder, and then several somethings, and the air smelled dank and fungal. He was in some sort of – forest? Jungle? – and then he froze at the sound of a voice.

'Hevalansa Vess.'

It was a voice he knew – an oddly sibilant purr. He shivered.

Vut seemed to notice. The voice sounded amused. 'We know your discomfort with our kind. Would it be easier for you if we showed ourselves, or remained out of sight?'

It had been bad enough when it was just crawling over a lectern in the Lay Palace but in here, in what was presumably its natural environment, the idea that it was lurking out there somewhere just beyond vision made Vess's nerves scream. He gritted his teeth. 'Show yourself. Yourselves. But warn me where to look. Don't just . . .' he tailed off, trying to think of a diplomatic way of ending the sentence.

Vut did it for him. 'Appear? Creep up? Drop out of a tree? We won't do that. It would be a pity to frighten you to death after all you've been through. And a waste. Take two paces forward; you'll find a log suitable for humans to sit on.'

Vess obeyed, brushing aside creepers. In the dim light it was easier to feel the log than to see it. It was soft with what he hoped was moss. He sat.

'Well done. Are you ready?'

He didn't need to ask, *ready for what*. He nodded, assuming the creatures could see him even if he couldn't see it. Or them.

'Good. Look straight ahead.'

He peered into the distance. There was a fuzzy irregular line hanging in front of him. It was hard to tell quite how far away.

It glowed a bluish green that was unsettling against the violet-black background. The colour reminded Vess of chemicals. As it brightened he saw that it was a line of dots. Vut was hanging on a vine.

It was bad, but not bad enough to be unbearable. He was relieved it wasn't a pseudo face.

Vut spoke. 'Are you comfortable? For a given value of comfortable?'

He nodded.

'Good. Now, questions. You ought to be dead. Why aren't you?'

Vess realized that there was no point in trying to suppress his pounding heart. Vut could obviously sense it and anyway, why wouldn't he be frightened?

He shrugged a little. 'What do you mean?'

The line twitched, like a wagged tail. 'Even knowing only what we know, we would have killed you, but you are the only implant out of many who has come out of a Mind Stack alive. We are entitled to ask why, and what it is that we do not know.'

Vess shrugged again. 'I did nothing unusual.'

'And yet you are an unusual person.'

'Yes, you said. So, if none of your implants survived, was sending me in tantamount to execution?'

'Evidently not, because here you still are.' The line was swinging like a pendulum. 'We would still like to know why.'

'I'm sure.'

There was a short silence. Then Vut stopped moving, a sudden perfect return to the vertical halfway through a swing. 'Perhaps it would help our relationship if we told you that there is more than one view among the Board.'

'I'm not sure we have a relationship.'

'We dare say. We make your flesh crawl. Nonetheless. We will not ask you the same question a fourth time. Nor will we kill you, which, you should know, is now the view of the rest of the Board.'

Against all reason Vess found himself grinning. 'Are you travelling alone, Board Member Vut?'

'Hardly. There are thirty-one of us in the gestalt.' The line wagged again and Vess realized with a start that the creatures were actually laughing. Then it was still. 'There is something honest about your distaste for us. We will trust you, hater of insects, up to a point. The fact of your survival in the Stack means that you must be a more accomplished liar than any of those who went before you and died, because either you lied successfully to *them*, or you are now lying to *us*. We could kill you now; that would be the safe option – but taking the safe option has brought the Inside to its present state, and that makes more safety seem unpalatable. Therefore we will take a risk. Answer a question, if you will – how do you feel about the Chairman?'

'Or-Shls?'

'Indeed. He was still the Chairman, when last advised.'

Vess shook his head. 'Neutral.'

'Really?' Another wag. 'Given what you are going through on his orders, you are in remarkable control of your feelings. Now, you will go back into the Hive. You will continue whatever exploration you have begun. And you will be watched, more closely than you can imagine. And now, with apologies, you will be moderately injured.'

'What?' Vess half rose.

'Something decorative rather than serious. We can't reinsert you into the Hive by the same route we used to extract you. You need a cover story to persuade your new friends that you are still friends.'

'What new friends?'

'The ones who, for whatever reason, didn't kill you in the Mind Stack, obviously. Please don't waste time on denials. They will need to be convinced that you have incurred displeasure.' Vut paused. 'If it makes you feel any better at all, the decoration will be carried out by humans, not by us.'

He had heard nothing to suggest anyone else was there, but suddenly there were hands seizing him from behind. Then, for a while, there was pain, and then there was nothing.

Vess woke to more pain. At first he flinched and tried to raise his arms to fend off the next blow, but his arms wouldn't move properly. The blow didn't fall. Instead someone said, 'Hi,' and he opened his eyes. Dimollss was looking down at him.

'Don't move,' she said. 'They did a good job on you. You must have pissed someone off properly.'

He tried to nod, but even that didn't work. 'I suppose,' he said. 'How long have I been here?'

'About six hours. You were found.' Her eyes darkened. 'You were pretty messed up. One broken arm, one dislocated shoulder, three broken ribs. Your face, well. And some odd wounds. Did someone have a sword?'

Vess frowned, and then stopped frowning very quickly as the muscles in his face howled at him. 'I don't remember.'

'Hm. Did they ask you things?'

'Why I didn't die in the Mind Stack.'

'What did you tell them?'

'Nothing.'

'Did they know . . .' but then she looked up from his face towards something behind him. Her expression flickered and the question lay unfinished.

Not something, Vess thought. *Someone. There's someone standing behind me. Someone who guessed Dimollss was going to ask if they knew about communication in the Stack, and stopped her.*

He grinned up at Dimollss, ignoring the ache. 'No they didn't, and no they still don't.'

He thought he heard the faint sound of a held breath being released very carefully, somewhere behind him.

'You can trust me,' he said. And suddenly realized that, just for once, he meant it, and with the realization came fear.

For once, here was someone he really didn't want to let down. When it came to it, he hoped he'd at least have a choice.

His seat was comfortable and the gravity worked perfectly, which was probably why the shuttle didn't smell. Or rather it didn't smell of anything unpleasant. The on-board fragrance was subtle, and shifted through the journey from maritime-floral to desert herbs. But then the kind of high-net-worth clients who hired entire Hollowed race squads expected them to be treated carefully. Far more carefully than ordinary Hivers.

Vess had heard of Hollowed racers but he had never seen one, either at a race or close up, until now. Without being rude, he was trying not to look. It was better to look at the view in the forward screens.

Folklore said that Bantrass was one of the last planets to be completed during the original Construction Phase. It had originally had a cool temperate maritime climate with lots of agreeable craggy-coasted islands surrounded by restless seas. Then, eighteen millennia ago, it had been bought by an eccentric shipping magnate who liked privacy. Unfortunately for Bantrass, he also liked deserts. To howls of protest from every ecologist in the Spin, and ignoring the advice of even his own planetary engineers, he had simply towed Bantrass ten per cent closer to its sun.

The resulting diurnal turmoil and catastrophic climate change wiped out ninety-nine per cent of all the original species, boiled away the oceans in a single century and left every last mountain and hill planed flat by the insane winds that had taken another century to die down. In the end, the magnate's ambition wasn't achieved to a habitable standard until more than five centuries after his death, and even then habitable was a matter of opinion. Most people thought that served him right.

It was a good environment for Hollowed racers though: hot, dry and flat. What was left of their metabolisms worked best at high temperature.

Metabolism was putting it a bit strongly. Vess shuddered.

The shuttle dropped through the faintest wisp of high cloud, banked sharply and sank on to its pad with a well-damped curtsey. The doors popped and the shuttle began to empty. Vess waited next to his assigned racer until the ramp was clear and then followed the creature down it, keeping his eye on the odd-looking bulbous thing that floated along behind it at the end of a short, complicated umbilical. He didn't know what gender it had originally been – like lots of other bits, that went missing when they were hollowed out. As a description, 'creature' was good enough. Like all the rest it consisted of about forty kilos of superbly muscled remnant human, and under normal conditions it would have lasted less than ten minutes without its floating companion that was heating, cooling, energy processing, blood cleaning and immune systems in one high-value, high-risk package.

It was a perfect example of following a train of thought through to a logical conclusion and then holding your nose and just *doing* it. If the only thing you have to do is run very fast for a short distance, what do you need? Muscles, joints, bones, coordination, just enough stored energy, some oxygen. Everything else is just wasted when you're running.

Hollowed racers were called what they were called because of what happened to their body cavities. They were empty. Everything from the bottom of the lungs down – liver, kidneys, pancreas, appendix, small and large intestine, genitals, some of the ribs – was all removed. During races they were all just dead weight, and between races they could easily be replaced by mechanical systems. Hence the life support which the racers were plugged into for every moment of their lives except for the honed flashing seconds of a race.

Being Hollowed was not a desired life choice. For that reason, it was never optional. Criminals and dissidents were Hollowed, and so were the hopelessly in debt, the substance-addicted, a few with favourable learning disabilities and, obviously, Hivers. It was a natural fit with the Hive business model because a competitive racer could earn a lifetime's average income per race. Not for themselves, of course.

The racers weren't speaking. Not because they couldn't – vocal cords were kept, for good communication during training. Vess supposed they simply didn't have anything that needed saying. He followed them down the ramp. It was near the end of Bantrass's artificially shortened day and the sun was low. Half the length of the ramp was in the shadow of the shuttle, but the air was still hot and thick-feeling. Then he walked out of the shadow and the glare hit the back of his head like a cosh. And then there was something else and he stopped and listened, feeling his stomach moving uneasily.

Bantrass had a background noise. It was only just above the limit of perception, but once Vess had noticed it he knew he would always be able to hear it – a tiny swelling susurration like a billion shiny dark little wings.

The one per cent of Bantrass's species that had survived the desertification had been insects, and they had survived it very well. Vess had been trying not to dwell on it. He shuddered again.

Something hit him between the shoulder blades. He jumped and looked round to see a guard holding up a handset. The man grinned. 'You heard the noise, huh? They told me you don't like little crawly bugs.'

Vess nodded.

The grin widened. 'That's okay. Most of the ones they got

here are *big* crawly bugs. Move on! That Hollowed you're following's worth your skin ten times over. Next time you stop you get five seconds.' He jabbed the handset into Vess's ribs.

Vess suppressed a gasp. He turned and took a few quick paces down the ramp, catching up with his charge at the end of it. The ground was bare, a gritty sand that scrunched slightly as he walked. The noise added a beat to the hissing insects but he barely heard it. His heart was banging too loudly.

His dislike of insects wasn't on the false profile they had created for him. It was one of the things he was supposed to have left behind when he came here. He didn't seem to have left it behind very well.

He wondered what else was going to catch up with him. At the thought he actually looked over his shoulder towards the shuttle, and then smiled ruefully at himself. There was nothing much to see; just a group of stevedores unloading a crate about half their own height. It was unmarked but they were treating it carefully, and he assumed it had something to do with the race. Most things did, here.

There was a crackling hum overhead. He looked up and saw another shuttle dropping through the heat shimmer on a faintly blue cushion of ionized atmosphere.

At first sight it looked just like any other shuttle – a standard twenty-seven seater with the logos of the shipping company glaring from both sides and beneath. He got ready to shrug and move on, but then didn't. He wasn't sure why; something about the ship had jarred with him.

He looked again. It took a moment. Then he felt his breath quicken. It would have been easy to miss, if you hadn't been a Harbour Master, but this was far from being any other shuttle. The subtle extra curves of the hull, the slight fattening of the engine nacelles and, yes, the fact that it was too new and the logos were too fresh and straight.

He sought confirmation and, after a second, found it. Two

extra bulges, one front and one rear. Very shallow, very easy not to see, but very obvious once you had seen them.

They were weapons pods, and they clinched it. This was *not* an ordinary shuttle and, therefore, it did *not* carry an ordinary cargo. Someone important was coming to see this race.

He looked down and realized that there had been another jab at his ribs. He almost hadn't noticed.

He turned away and followed his racer.

The Racetrack was far more complicated than either its name or its outward appearance suggested. It looked like an oval track in the sand, about a hundred metres from end to end at its longest, with room for seven runners abreast. Tiered seating stepped up from the periphery but only five steps high. It was supposed to be an exclusive spectacle, and why should important people have to sit too far away from the action?

Important being synonymous with wealthy, of course. Not that Vess could see them at the moment – he was three levels underground in one of the complicated bits. Three levels below the rich people; the irony hadn't escaped him.

It was chaos down there, and it was very, very hot. Vess could feel sweat running down his body in sticky streams. Next to him, his racer's life support droned loudly with the effort of keeping all those body fluids at the right temperature. Vess managed not to feel jealous.

He could hardly keep his feet. He was standing – just about – in the entrance to the Hero's Tunnel waiting for the signal. The air stank of human sweat and non-human equivalents, and hot machinery and tension. Short of a mass grave it was the most crowded hole in the ground he could imagine.

A klaxon blared. He jumped, and broke into a trot to keep up with his runner. They joined a line of six other pairs that wound up three levels of ramps with crowds barely parting for them. Most of the throng wore the little iridescent patch on the forehead that marked them as Chancers, but you didn't need eyes to notice that. Ears were good enough.

'A thousand on the blue!'

'Five hundred to red, and the same to the small one for second!'

'Odds softening for field! Take a Chance, nobles . . .'

Vess had never really cared about money, if he was honest; security had been his goal – but the smell of money was in his nostrils and for once he could understand the attraction.

The Racetrack didn't have any other names but it was an entire planetary business buried deep in the compacted sand beneath its only outward expression. After the Hive, Bantrass was the biggest income-generator in the Inside, and almost all of it happened here and almost all of it was based on gambling.

They were close to the short tunnel that led to the track. Vess tried to catch his breath, but there wasn't enough to catch. There were still plenty of Chancers, though.

'Last opportunity before Naming, nobles and ladies!'

Vess held what was left of his breath. Naming was important; naming was when the Hollow Runners stopped being known by their sponsor's colours and took on Names. The Names, which lasted only for the length of a race, were cryptic, oblique, playful even, open to interpretation – but still meaningful and therefore fascinating. A Name could hint at a strength, a strategy or even a weakness. Within seconds of their release, news channels across the Inner would be alive with speculation. Pundits made fortunes, and punters more often lost them, based on Names.

The odds would shift wildly after Naming.

The klaxon sounded again.

'Nobles and ladies – the Names! Are you ready?'

There was a swelling 'Yes!' from the crowd.

'Very well. Step forward number one, in the blue.'

The blue-vested runner took three paces out of the mouth of the tunnel and stood impassively.

'Declared Name for this race – ah, a popular one but always welcome back: *Did You See My Lady?*'

It meant nothing to Vess but the audience laughed, and so did someone close behind him. He looked round but couldn't tell who.

'Number two, in the check – *Late Comer*! A hint, nobles and ladies, or a confession? Or perhaps even a boast? Notwithstanding, it is another popular Name, even with its wearer!'

There was more laughter as the check-vested runner raised an arm in salute.

'Number three, in the white, one who I have heard called the "Small One" – *Whatever the Cost*! A robust choice indeed, and not so frequent; only four outings in the last year. Could it be a statement of intent? Certainly size is not everything.'

Certainly it can't have been, thought Vess, as the tiny runner stood forward. None of the Hollowed were tall – height was not an advantage – but this one barely came up to his chest.

The siren came again. They moved forward and suddenly they were out of the tunnel and the full power of the sun struck like a scourge. Under Vess's hand the life pod hummed and his eyes closed involuntarily against the glare. He forced them to open, screwing them to defensive slits, and glanced round the track and then up at the spectators. The tiered rows of seats were shaded by a patchwork of what looked like leather stretched over splayed white poles. The leathery stuff was slightly translucent, giving the space beneath it a yellowish glow. Between the seats and the track, a diffuser field stopped the worst of the hot angry winds. It made the air in front of the seats shimmer very slightly if you looked at it sidelong.

The shade stuff really was a kind of leather. Just not one that Vess cared to dwell on – even useless racers ultimately had their uses.

But it was a popular, if exclusive sport. The crowd that welcomed the racers and their assistants – Vess included – was enthusiastic and very well-dressed. There was a movement above his line of sight. He let his eyes wander briefly up to the highest tier, and saw a banner coat of arms unfurling from the balcony of the central box.

His breath quickened again. He knew the coat of arms. Everyone knew the coat of arms.

The Inside had no actual Royalty – its real rulers were the Board – but the Royalty it didn't have were best represented by Caphraime II, the eldest daughter of a family that purported to have roots in the ruling class of an ancient iteration of the Inside called the Cordern. In those distant days, so people whispered, the Inside had been an Empire and its rulers' voices had been heard across half the Spin.

Vess had researched the matter once, but only as far as he had dared; curiosity about things which were meant to be accepted was not a survival trait, even for middle management. As far as he could tell it was about half true, but he had stopped short of putting either half beyond doubt.

The practical effect was that Caphraime II was a figurehead where the Board was not, or better, chose not to be. Since she did nothing that anyone could see, she was blamed for nothing, and if she was sometimes praised for things she hadn't done either, presumably the Board took that as a fair exchange.

And now she was standing, waving, her gaze sweeping the crowd but – even from down here he could tell – actually seeing none of it. Another version of doing nothing. Vess shook his head slightly and looked away.

Then his mind caught up with the image and tripped over it. Slowly, without making it obvious, he looked back at the box.

His mind had been right.

Against all expectation and certainly against all precedent, one of the spaces in the box was not occupied by one of Caphraime's hangers-on. Instead, to her left and a respectful pace behind her, stood Or-Shls.

Vess looked away, as casually as he had looked up, but his mind began to race.

Now what was he doing there?

Alst Or-Shls would never have admitted it, but he was having fun. Not because of the company, of course – as far as he was concerned Caphraime was the half-witted product of centuries of carefully managed inbreeding, and quite right too. Her conversation was as dull as he would have expected from someone who lived a manufactured existence in the narrowest of circles, and he had only to nod, smile and let out the occasional knowing snort and she was happy. She was also dispensable, of course, especially in a good cause.

The fun was for other reasons. Not least, that there was a certain risk attached.

There was a tap on his shoulder. He turned his head towards it and saw the blunt face of Yarish, his aide. The woman had been with him for ten years, and the slightest flicker of expression was enough for her to tell him that the thing was arranged. He nodded and turned back to the racers.

Other people used elaborate technology for covert communication. He preferred people. People he trusted. People, moreover, who had a vivid appreciation of the personal consequences of breaching that trust. He made an example from time to time, just in case.

He might be making another one soon.

Meanwhile, there were the races to watch. It was his first time, not so much because he didn't enjoy spectacle and competition, but rather because he found far more opportunity for them in the day job. You could always get people to compete with each other, he found, and it was so much more fun when the rules weren't quite what they had thought.

But he had a particular reason for being here today. A certain risk, indeed. His optical equipment did more than most people suspected; he sent his regular lenses back along their rails and another pair replaced them. His vision swam for a second as his eyes adjusted, and then he was looking at a close-up of the runners and their handlers. Near the front of the line stood Vess. The man's eyes were on him but then they slid away.

Well then. Battle was joined. Rather an uneven one, but never mind.

It was their turn to be announced.

'Number four, nobles and ladies, in the red; a very popular option with the Chancers already, and that's before we even announce a Name. I give you – ah, no, a moment?'

The announcement cut off with the silent certainty of a mute switch. There was a swelling mutter from the crowd and Vess saw people glancing towards him. He turned his eyes away.

Then the voice was back.

'Nobles and ladies, my apologies but there is a late change of Name. As you will know I cannot share the previous Name with you, but you may draw your own conclusions about the new one, and I will be fascinated to see the effect on the Chancing. In the red – *Changeling*!'

For a moment there was silence. Then most of the crowd was on its feet, waving Chance sticks. The wooden numbers on the odds board high above the narrow end of the track thumped and rattled round in their sockets so that the board stuttered with colours and symbols. Vess didn't know how to read them properly but even his amateur eye could see odds shifting. He also had no idea what the change of Name meant, but it made him feel uncomfortable.

He shrugged. Whatever it was, it was out of his control, and there was no time to speculate; the announcer had cleared his throat.

'Well, nobles and ladies, a *fas*-cinating moment. Less than one race in a hundred sees a Name change, and less than one runner in a six of thousands has carried that Name. One could speculate for hours but alas, the hours elude us. Runners, last doses and forward, please.'

Vess reached for the lumpy surface of the life pod and touched a control nodule. The pod chimed and, after a pause, chimed again on a slightly higher note. The runner stood up a little straighter and flexed its fingers; between the two chimes, the pod had flooded its bloodstream with a maximum allowable dose of short-acting gene-customized stimulants.

Then the pod chimed again.

Vess raised his eyebrows. It should only have been twice. He glanced around but no one met his eye. He hadn't seen anyone move, but suddenly he seemed to have just a little more space. He drew a breath, got ready to call out – what exactly, he wasn't sure. And then didn't.

For a micro-moment he remembered Dimollss, curled around her own pain.

The first of the start sirens yammered. Around him, handlers reached for the umbilicals that connected runners to pods. The connections broke with soft pops as fluid and gas pressures equalized. If he spoke out, they would stop. People would investigate. Something might not happen – whatever the something was.

His hands made the decision. He watched them reach down to his own runner's umbilical. Grip, twist. Pop.

From that point the immediate future of a runner was very simple. Attain the start line, run the race, get back to the pod as soon as possible – or die of oxygen starvation and muscle poisoning. Whereas his own future might have become very complex. He had chosen a side, it seemed. He just wished he knew which one.

The first race was two laps of the stadium. It wasn't a

challenging distance for most runners – with proper dosing they could cover ten – but the phrase 'proper dosing' was the key. Runners dosed for two laps would be dead after ten. Five, even.

The second siren went off. As if to contrast with the technical complexity of the runners, the start line was almost wilfully low-tech: just a rusty stain in the shape of a line across the tawny sand of the track. The runners lined up along it. It was on the opposite side of the track to where Caphraime II stood, with Or-Shls beside her. That was deliberate; the runners would pass her line of sight after they had rounded the first two bends and were halfway down the long straight. They would be at maximum speed.

There were no more sirens. From now, it was down to the Starter. It was the one role available to retired runners, and you had to be a special sort of runner at that – the usual criminals and organ-sacrificed slaves need not apply. This one was a thin elderly figure, with a stoop that made it look as if she was hugging her own umbilical.

Vess had been told about her. Among the runners and their handlers she was a minor legend.

Barelft S'Sess had been a conventional track athlete, fairly successful but not exceptional. Then she had retired, and taken up coaching. She had specialized in working with children on disadvantaged – but not actually rebellious – planets. It attracted agreeable profile and she became a regular feature towards the end of the sort of news show that liked to mix heart-warming with lump-in-the-throat. Infant-starvation porn with the option of a few happy endings, was how Vess had summarized it to himself.

Then something had gone wrong. Whether by accident or through some unconscious desire actually to do some real good, Barelft S'Sess had ended up somewhere genuinely risky – a vast refugee camp caught between two war zones. It was a dangerous place and she had succumbed to one of the dangers, a parasite that established itself in the upper intestine and then multiplied with such vigour that one prickly little worm became half a million within two days.

There was no cure. In that situation, being Hollowed looked almost like a bargain. And, of course, it had done her reputation no harm at all.

Now she limped to the middle of the track, pushing her own life pod in front of her like a trophy. There was a circle of green there, a pad of carefully nurtured mosses, incongruous in the baked desert surroundings. She stopped in its centre, one hand on her pod and the other held out in front of her, palm upwards, the fingers closed around something.

The stadium fell silent.

For several seconds S'Sess didn't move. Then her hand flicked upwards and a black dot arced into the air above her head. The throw had been strong and almost vertical; Vess found himself tipping his head back to follow the thing as it rose until it was just level with the highest tier of seating. It seemed to hang for a moment, and then flared up through the spectrum into a fierce blue-white ball that printed red and green blotches on his retinas even through his reflexively closed eyelids.

Crack.

The sharp explosion rang round the stadium and the runners leapt away from the start in a line that began dead straight and then quickly became a bunch.

Vess caught his breath. It was his first race. Intellectually he knew how fast the runners could go but nothing had prepared him, could *ever* have prepared him, for the fact. They leaned wildly forwards, their lightened torsos almost horizontal with the ground to counterbalance the force from the anaerobic, fast-twitch fibres that made up over ninety-five per cent of the muscle mass in their legs. Within ten paces the lead runner had touched a hundred klicks and the whole stadium was on its feet, roaring.

The lead runner, a red streak already heading for the second turn, was Changeling. On the way into the turn he had opened up an arm's length over the rest, which in runner-world was a huge margin. He came out of the turn and accelerated down the long straight that ran past Caphraime II, his feet kicking up a cloud of track-sand.

The announcer's voice was just audible above the crowd.

'. . . unbelievable pace! The first ten chains in under seven, from a *standing* start! The second in six! And the third! Changeling from Late Comer from Zodiac, but the red looks uncatchable. Wait; what?'

The sound of the crowd changed, and Vess felt his heart jump.

Changeling was no longer on the track. He had been on the inside, already a single vast stride ahead of the pack; now he veered away, crossing the path of his pursuers so that the leaders broke their own strides to avoid him. They were packed too closely and the front three went down, scoring gouts of sand out of the track. The rest of the pack went over them.

But the red runner was clear of them, clear of the track. Without slowing at all he crossed the dead strip between the track and tiered seats, and then he leapt, clearing the first row and springing off the back of the second, still faster than any normal human could sprint. Some of the audience scrambled out of his path. A few reached out to catch him but they were too slow, flailing and grasping at nothing.

The crowd were quiet. Vess could hear shouts from somewhere. Some of them sounded like orders. Most of them had the high edge of panic.

He looked up. Caphraime II was still near the front of the box, her arms defensively outstretched towards the body that was hurtling towards her. Or-Shls was no longer beside her; Vess thought he saw the man backing away. Then Caphraime II seemed to stumble forwards, and at the same time with a final leap the runner flicked himself up to the rail at the edge of the box, grasped the outstretched hand, braced his legs against the edge of the box, and sprang up and outwards, dragging Caphraime II over the rail.

Even from the other side of the stadium, Vess heard her shriek.

For a vanishingly brief moment the two bodies were in the air over the Stadium. Then there was a sharp explosion and they became an angrily expanding cloud of red and black.

Vess instinctively shut his eyes. Something hot and wet sprayed across his face, and he heard screams.

Then he felt his arms seized. He opened his eyes but he couldn't see anything; at first there was only smoke and then the stuff running down his face stung him and he screwed his eyes shut again. As he did so he felt a hard blow across the fronts of his shins. It took his legs out from under him and he landed face-down with a sickening impact that seemed to break everything all at once.

The force of it drove the breath out of him. For a long second he lay, his arms still pinned. Then he felt something pushed into the small of his back and a voice close to him said:

'Someone wants to see *you*.'

The something became a source of agony that soared up the scale until it became all of him. Then there was nothing.

Geostationary Orbit, Green Planet

They were sitting on the outer edge of a wooden platform, suspended over what looked like a five-kilometre drop. According to that scale the snowline lay almost four kilometres below them, and the tree-line just below that. It turned out that the ship could reconfigure its internal spaces at pretty short notice, and had a good line in eye-deceiving special effects.

Seldyan had selected Mountains because she had never seen one, and the ship had obliged with vigour. It had also provided a local temperature bubble. Outside it, the wooden rails were a finger's breadth deep in rime frost which was actually real. Inside it, the air was just pleasantly crisp enough to make her want to sip the hot infusions that appeared by her hand every time she waved her fingers. Each one tasted slightly different. She was having to pace herself. The scene in front of her was too interesting to allow for constantly going for a pee.

The really interesting bit didn't look like mountains. The ship had kept a section of the false sky clear for viewing screens. They were at a dead stop just over half a second out from the green planet, and at natural scale it filled the screens and lit up the fake mountains with a sickly green. The beam of light that had lased the atmosphere in the first place still poured into it. It looked to Seldyan as if it ought to make a fizzing noise.

The odd thing about the planet had been obvious for several days.

'It's artificial, obviously,' Merish had said, when they were close enough to be sure. 'Okay, this is the Spin. So what? Everything's artificial. But this is weird even by Spin standards. It's a gas giant with an atmosphere full of helium and neon. It's a special-purpose world. No inhabitants, no minerals, no nothing. One use only – to go green when you hit it with the right energy. And, it's not one of the original eighty-nine.'

'Really?' Seldyan had frowned at the screen, which was then showing a green ball the size of a fist. 'Why would anyone do that?'

He had shrugged. And now, when they were as close as the old ship felt comfortable, they were still shrugging, but this time they were looking at the other end of the beam.

Seldyan jabbed a finger at it. 'Are you sure?'

He nodded. 'Yes. Or, well, the ship is sure, and I've learned to trust it. The green planet has a wobble in its orbit, which would match the effect of another smaller planet located around the end of that beam of light.'

'Right.' She glared at the point on the screen where the green shaft disappeared into nothing. Or, better, arose out of it. 'I guess I assumed there must be some kind of generator there. I wasn't expecting a whole planet. A whole invisible one. Is that extra to the eighty-nine as well?'

'Seems so. Whoever did whatever they did here, cared enough about it to create two brand-new planets.'

'Uh-huh. That's a lot of caring. Can this ship land on planets?'

He laughed. 'Only once, and there'd be a lot of clearing up. Besides,' and he stopped smiling, 'I think it's afraid.'

She blinked. 'Seriously?'

'Yeah. Someone hid a planet from it. It can work out the thing's there because of gravity, but all its other senses just see a hole in space. That implies a level of technology higher than its own, and that makes it nervous.'

'It makes me nervous too. Is there any way we can get down to the surface?'

He looked at her, his face serious. 'Of the hidden planet?'

'Well, yes. Not the green one. I don't want to get lased, or whatever you call it.'

'Lased will do . . . there's a couple of gigs. They could make a landing. On a good day they might get back off again. Seldyan, are you serious about this?'

'Yeah. Completely.' She stood up and faced him. 'Three things. First, this green light stuff is making a mess of Oblong. That place is supposed to be our new world, Merish. I don't want to be cheated out of it. Second, a planet-sized green light in the sky? That says "come here" as loudly as I need. And third, think about it. They, whoever they were, hid that planet as well as they could – except they didn't fix the gravity thing. Doesn't that send you a message?'

He nodded slowly. 'It could. It could say "smart people apply here", or it could say "we hid this planet because it's lethal". You choose.'

She smiled. 'I already have. So, where are these gigs?'

The gigs were in the far corner of one of the smaller weapons pods. If you took a sphere just big enough to accommodate a human in the foetal position, and then scaled it up by twenty-five per cent to include some power cells, a use-it-twice-and-scrap-it engine and a short-term life support unit, you had it.

Seldyan was trying not to look doubtful. She kicked the gig. 'Are you sure?'

'No I'm not. You were the one who sounded all certain. Look, why don't you talk to the ship?'

Before she had time to respond, she became aware of the ship's switch-on noise. The old voice sounded crisper, somehow.

'*All other things being equal, the gig would make one successful return journey to the surface of a planet such as the one we theorize here.*'

She thought for a moment. 'All other things being equal?'

'*Yes. This planet is shielded in ways I cannot penetrate. It may also be defended in ways I can neither predict nor negate.*'

'Thanks for the encouragement.' She kicked the nearest gig again; it made a flat thud. Keeping her eyes turned from Merish she said, 'I'm going to do this.'

'I know. I want to come with you.'

She turned quickly towards him, shaking her head. 'You stay here.'

'No chance, Sel.'

They faced each other for a moment. Then Seldyan reached out and took his hand. 'I can't tell you what to do. But if you go, I stay.'

He began to protest but she raised her free hand, palm outwards. 'If you go I stay,' she repeated, 'because one of us needs to stay up here, but if it's me then that's the wrong way round. Something's going to go wrong down there, and whoever that happens to, they're going to need someone intelligent up here; someone who can understand things. That's you, Merish, remember? I'm the one who does people, and there'll be people down there. Probably.'

He shrugged. 'What if there are things down there as well as people?'

'Then I'll ask your advice. Come on, Merish, you know I'm right. I'll need you up here to unplug me from whatever crap I get plugged into.'

He held her eyes for a bit longer, then turned away and ran a hand over his face. 'Have it your way. But,' and he faced her again, 'you're going to put in a couple of hours' practice in that thing before you go. And yes, that is me telling you what to do.'

She laughed. 'Don't make it a habit.'

'Fuck off, Seldyan.'

'You're doing it again.'

He turned away again, but not before she had time to see his face. There was no anger, but she thought his face looked paler than the lighting should have made it.

She had done her two hours' practice, staying enclosed within the bubble of space controlled by the old ship's engines while they made the short journey to orbit above the hidden planet. The ship guided her to begin with, and then gradually withdrew its help until she was in sole command. The ship could take full control as long as the gig was no more than about five seconds away – it would have to butt out just as she passed the point where the atmosphere of the planet ought to start, if it had one. The gig wasn't too hard to handle, even at the absolute maximum load Merish had insisted on.

She had watched Merish loading the inventory. After a while she had just said, 'Really?'

'Really what?'

She gestured at the heap. 'Really that much?'

'Yes.' He was packing medical kits and high-density rations, and some small packets that looked heavy. She pointed.

'What are they?'

He hefted one. 'Rare earth metals, and gold.'

'Why?'

'Basic units of exchange. Think about it, Sel. There could be all kinds of societies down there. You might actually have to buy stuff, or pay your way out of—' He stopped, and went back to packing.

She had watched his shoulders for a while. They seemed broader than she remembered.

'Ready?'

Seldyan made one last check. 'Yup.'

'Okay. Ship? You've got it. Please launch.'

She wondered if the ship would say anything, but it didn't seem the talkative kind. It just opened the bay doors, a complicated cross between an iris and a kaleidoscope that was hard to focus on, and then the pod slipped gently out through them.

The first time she had done this, an endless three hours ago, she had sat back and let the ship do the work for the first ten minutes. This time she squared her shoulders as well as the tiny space allowed, and took hold of the control ball.

'Give me control, please.'

The internal lights blinked from their standard muted yellow to green and back. The ball – it was literally just that, a plain off-white sphere the right size to fit neatly into her palm with her fingers closed over it – had been lying passively in her hand. Now it rose a little as if coming to attention. She pushed it forward a millimetre, feeling the resistance that told her it was active, and that helped her to control her movements.

The pod accelerated as she pushed.

They had agreed that this first trip was strictly exploratory. Approach the hidden planet as closely as possible, to the point whatever shielded it became apparent, or until something else happened. The pod had few instruments of its own, but apparently the ship was using it as a focus for a lot of clever remote sensing. That was definitely Merish territory; he seemed comfortable with it.

Everything seemed to be going okay. She pushed the ball hard forward, and felt the slight nausea that went with only averagely clever g-nulling systems cancelling out a lot of acceleration. The pod had quite a decent turn of speed, but it would need it if she wasn't to die of boredom. They had about a hundred and fifty thousand klicks to cover. She sat back and watched the view.

Far sooner than she expected, an area of the display in front of her changed colour, the control ball gave a little wobble in her hand and a quiet voice said, '*Cruise*,' and it seemed that was it.

The comms to the ship was permanently open. She tapped at an indecipherable icon on an old-fashioned-looking display screen in front of her. It expanded into a slightly fuzzy 2-D of Merish's face, about as high as the length of her finger.

'Anything?'

The image shook its head. 'The ship says not. It's got enough sensors channelled through you to make the pod glow, but nothing yet. If there's going to be anything it should be soon; you're close to the place where the sensors start getting confused.'

'Uh-huh.' She switched to a forward view; at this distance it showed a disc of perfect darkness with Merish's face apparently floating in front of it. 'If the sensors are confused, how will we know when there is something?'

There was no answer. She tutted. 'Merish? How will we know?'

There was still no answer. She frowned at the face, and then looked more closely.

It was motionless. The eyes were wide, and looking off to one side as if he had just noticed something but hadn't had time to turn his head.

Seldyan swallowed. Then she forced herself to remember the bit of her familiarization which had covered the pod's limited comms and even more limited sensory kit. She reached for some controls.

The first answer she got came as no more than confirmation – the frozen image was just that. The external view was real-time and unprocessed, but the video link was fully dumb. It went on refreshing at the same speed even if there was nothing new to refresh, and that meant either that the pod had stopped receiving information, or that the ship had stopped transmitting.

Of the two she much preferred the first. She did some checking and nodded to herself. The ship had not stopped transmitting.
Quite the opposite. She checked some more, and then sat back
and blew out her cheeks.

The source intensity of the ship's sensor energy had multiplied by five hundred. If it kept that up for long, it would fry her
DNA.

'Shit!' She slapped the comms. 'Merish? Ship? Stop the fuck!
Are you guys trying to boil me?'

There was no answer. Merish went on looking not quite at
her from the frozen display.

She wanted to swear again, but that was a waste of time if no
one was listening, and at these energy levels, time she didn't
have. She shook her head and went back to the pod's instruments. Then she saw it.

Before, the ship's sensors had been stabbing at the pod like a
searchlight. Now their field had broadened into a cone a whole
second across. It wasn't looking *through* her any more. It was
looking *for* her, and it obviously had no idea where she was.

She felt her hands clenching. 'Merish?'

There was nothing. She swiped the parts of the comms controls that should set them to wideband, emergency. There was
no sign they had responded, but she took a breath and hoped
that the channel was still open.

'This is Escape Pod serial, uh,' she checked an engraved plate
on the bulkhead above her, 'CX20 hash 8, one occupant. Loca-
tion as beacon, I guess. Merish? If you can hear this, come and
get me? I've got no power, no sensors, falling down a gravity
well.'

There was no reply, not that she had expected one. As far as
the ship was concerned, she must have vanished. And, when she
looked, the display ahead had lost its image of Merish and now
showed nothing but black. So did the display behind.

Whatever it was that shielded the planet, she was in it.

Then the blackness fractured in front of her and parted like a flock of birds, and her heart tried to jump out of her ribs. She was looking at a planet, and it was getting bigger, very fast indeed.

She had felt no sense of acceleration, and the instruments were either frozen or dead. So were the controls, including the engine, and that left no doubt. She was going to hit the planet.

She tried desperately to remember a bit of the orientation she had hoped she would never need. Her hand reached out, found a projection low down on the far left of the panel. She yanked, hard. It gave, with a solid mechanical clunk.

For a bowel-churning moment she thought nothing was going to happen. Then the internal lights dimmed and the same quiet voice said, '*Impact defence enabled.*'

Air hissed, and the walls of the pod inflated and puffed towards her until she was immobilized. Then there was a sharp *crack* and the pod began to shudder. Seldyan nodded to herself as far as her cocoon would let her; the pod had fired the explosive bolts which extended its braking flaps. It was the best she could do. It might mean she would survive the crash.

It also meant that the pod was making its last journey. She would worry about that if she lived. She would have a lot to worry about if she lived.

The vibration mounted until she felt her teeth rattle, and the pod was filled with the roar of atmosphere being battered out of the way. Something was crushing her against the couch, as if the pod was accelerating faster than local gravity. She took a breath, and shouted.

'Merish? I'm going down. I think something's pulling me in. The pod systems are dead but it's in crash mode. I'm going to survive this, Merish, and you are going to find me.' Her lungs were empty; she filled them just once more. 'Because if you don't, I'm going to have to come and find you. You'd better not fucking *make* me!'

And then the roaring and shaking and the pressure were too much for her to breathe any more, and the cloud layer had whipped past the pod and she was looking at a craggy snowy landscape that was expanding fast.

Very fast.

She had promised herself she wouldn't, but at the last second she shut her eyes.

Seldyan woke to unremitting pain, so bad that she was astonished that she could ever have slept, so bad that sweat started on her forehead, so bad that sleeping ever again seemed impossible. She would be awake for ever, and her waking days and nights would be full of this hot angry stabbing in her ribs and her leg.

There was something else too: a sharp stinging in her upper arm, as if some insect had bitten deep and was refusing to let go. She reached up weakly to swat the place and her fingers found a thick pad of something wrapped around her biceps like a cuff.

Her mind supplied the word. Autodoc. For some reason the damn thing had decided to wake her. She didn't feel very grateful.

Then the cuff tightened briefly and she felt it burr gently against her skin. Another, then a third, spaced a breath apart. She didn't need to recall training on that one – it was universal autodoc language.

It meant 'brace yourself'.

As far as her restraints allowed, she braced herself.

The stinging intensified. Then hot agony surged into her upper arm and spread through her shoulder into her chest. It felt as if every particle of her flesh was being attacked from the inside by white-hot insects. She would have arched in outrage but she couldn't move, so she made do with roaring until she was sure that her throat must be peeled. The sound sank into the pillowed walls of the pod and died.

Then, as fast as it had arrived, the pain stopped. Even as she noted that she knew it for a lie. The pain must have been the 'doc pumping an infusion of smart nano into her; it must have followed it up with a massive dose of analgesic. That meant she still hurt. She just couldn't feel it.

She became warm and drowsy. It hadn't just been painkillers, then.

She wanted to try to call the ship. She wanted to speak to Merish, even just to hear him, to know he was okay (*as if I am?* she thought), but the sleepiness was too much.

She slept.

She awoke to the sound of someone hammering on the pod – a sharp, purposeful impact that came every couple of seconds. About the length of time it would take a human holding a hammer to draw it back and have another go.

Seldyan shelved the thought. There was no way that anyone would get into the pod with hand tools. The worst they could do was to give her a headache, and if they had then the analgesic was still doing its work. She didn't seem to hurt at all, in fact. She wondered how long she had been asleep, but there was no way of knowing. The pod instruments were dead, the display was blank.

She took an audit. The ribs and the leg seemed fine – not just pain-free but functional, which meant that the nano must have done its healing work. She could move, too, because the impact pillows had deflated. Her audit completed, she undid herself, all the time doing her best to ignore the hammering which seemed to be getting more insistent. Something else seemed insistent too, now she had enough skin bared to notice it – it was getting cold.

She shrugged herself back into her coverall, hoping it was as smart as it was supposed to be. The cold was getting worse, and she remembered the snowy landscape she had crashed into.

The hammering had intensified even more. It was time to go, and once the pod had crash-landed there was only one way to open it. The control was similar to the one that had opened the braking flaps, but on the other side of the console in a position where you were very unlikely to find it by accident.

She yanked it, jammed her hands over her ears and began to count. She hoped the external warning broadcast was working – and that whoever was hammering would understand it.

As she got to five there was a sharp *crack* and the pod jumped a little. There was a brief swirl of white, acrid-smelling smoke, which was whipped away by a sudden icy cold breeze.

The top half of the pod was gone, blown away from the base by the same sort of explosive bolts that had fired the flaps an atmosphere ago. She poked her head out.

The first impression was just white. The pod had landed in snow, but it was shallow enough, or hard-packed enough, that the impact had not buried it. If she stood upright, her neck was level with the surface. It was a surface that went on for a long way; she was facing roughly downhill, and downhill went on for as far as her eyes could resolve – endless undulating snow-fields under a freezing mist.

Endless perhaps, but not uniform, she realized. Something imposed itself on the landscape, some kind of regular structure that marched dead straight down the rolling snow. It looked like a line strung between slender towers, but it was too far away to be distinct and, besides, there was the rest of the new world to think about. Someone had been hammering. She shuffled her feet so that her body began to rotate.

Half a turn in she stopped, and her body tensed like a metal wire.

Her first impression was that he was on his own, but she wasn't ready to trust first impressions. Then she corrected herself, almost amused at her assumption. Her first impression had been that the person was male.

It probably was, though. The figure rising slowly from what looked like a recent depression in the snow was thickly wrapped in crude-looking fabrics, but the face that craned forward from the big hood was blunt-jawed and bearded. On most planets that still meant male.

She raised both hands, palms outwards. 'Hello?'

The figure raised an arm, and gave a lopsided grin. 'Yes. Hello. Your machine. It is,' and he made an explosive noise through pursed lips.

She looked back at the pod, and then to where the separated upper section lay, where the bolt charges had blown it, on its side in the snow.

'Yes, it is.' And, with a stab of guilt, 'Did it hurt you?'

The grin widened. 'Not I. Used to ice-crack, to snow-fall. Now used to metal warning words and machine-bang. New skill!'

She laughed, and then gasped as the vicious cold caught at her lungs. His face clouded.

'Not used to high-cold?'

It was a good description. She shook her head.

'Follow.' He turned and began to climb up out of the impression of his own body shape.

She tried to follow, but immediately found herself floundering helplessly; the snow was thigh-deep, bone-dry and at once engulfingly soft and surprisingly heavy. She hadn't even completed one step before she was stuck. She drew in a lungful of air so cold it felt like a weight in her chest.

'Hey!'

He looked back. 'Difficult?'

'Yes, difficult!' She had wanted to swear but she wasn't sure how he would take it, and she needed this strange creature with his ability to live in this frozen desert.

He followed her gaze towards his feet. 'Ah. You think shoes?'

She bit back a tart comment. 'I think something. I can't walk on this. How do you do it?'

'Same as always. One foot, next foot.' He walked towards her as if to demonstrate.

She wasn't sure what she had expected to see – some kind of snow shoes, or something to spread his weight. Shoes, at least. Not just feet. They weren't even particularly hairy.

She must have looked surprised because he grinned. 'Built for snow, me. Not you! Take you to warm, then explain. Not far. Follow as quick as able.' And he turned and walked off over the surface of the snow.

She floundered after him, swearing. To her relief he was right; they had covered only a couple of hundred metres before he dropped from sight as if the snow had swallowed him. She cursed under her breath and speeded up as best she could, the acerbically cold air rasping in her throat. She crested a low ridge, looked down, and grinned with sheer relief.

The depression was more or less crater-shaped, maybe a hundred paces across at the top with smoothly sloped sides leading down to a flat base less than half that. It was just deep enough to hide the plain little hut that nestled in it, and Seldyan wondered for a second if that was an accident. But only for a second. She was too cold to wait. She took a dragging step over the crest, tripped forwards from the weight of her own snow-bound legs and fell down the slope in a mess of limbs.

The bottom of the slope seemed unreasonably hard. She shook her head and tried to stand up. Moments later she was sitting on her bottom.

'Shit!'

It was hard because it was ice. She let out an irritated breath, and then looked up sharply.

Her companion was laughing. She glared at him, and he nearly stopped. 'Sorry! Not used to people. Mostly alone in the snow. Go careful. Here.' He walked up to her, reached out a hand, uncovered like his feet, and she took it gingerly. It was cool and dry. She expected him to pull, but instead he moved closer to her and braced his legs in a triangle. She felt his arm tensing, and he jerked his head upwards.

She pushed down on the hand, and was upright. She tested her stability carefully, and then let go of his hand.

She could stand, just.

He watched her for a second, then nodded and turned away. 'Follow slow. No more make me laugh.'

She bit back her response, and followed slow.

The hut was better on the inside. For a start it was, well, not warm exactly, but much less cold. She suspected her companion's definition of comfortable temperature was a couple of tens of degrees below hers, but it was at least above freezing. A low mound in the middle of the single room gave off wisps of aromatic smoke that drifted up into a wide funnel-shaped hood.

It was also much more attractive than the outside. The walls were hung with coarse rugs in muted colours, as if strong dyes weren't an option. Light came from dozens of little flat lamps, each one giving off a tall, wavering blue-white flame.

The man had been standing with his back to her, doing something to the fire. He moved aside and she saw orange sparks stream upwards from a hole in the top of the mound. He placed a sort of metal cradle over the hole, and balanced a wide, shallow black pot on the cradle. Then he spun round and shrugged off his coat.

It turned out he had been mostly coat. He was the thinnest, slightest human she had ever seen. His chest, now bare, was no wider than the distance from her thumb to her little finger. His upper arm was perhaps three fingers across.

She managed not to gasp, but she could feel her eyes widening.

He grinned. 'You fall from the sky in machine that explodes, and you think I odd?'

She felt her face heating, and his grin broadened so that it was nearly wider than his body. 'No more worry. I correct shape for snow. Light! Walk on powder. Name Hincc. Hincc of High People. You?'

She collected herself. 'Seldyan.'

'Very good name, falling-from-sky person.' He narrowed his eyes. 'Story to tell, yes? Drink hot soon. Begin when ready.'

There didn't seem to be an alternative. *Fair enough*, she thought. *I'd want to know, if I was him.*

She looked behind her, found a low stool, and sat on it, remembering too late to stop that it might have been made for someone a lot lighter than her. It creaked, but held.

'Okay,' she said. 'Story.'

It took a long time.

The pot was almost empty now. It had held a sweet, slightly spicy juice which she gathered had something to do with berries. She had done most of the talking but not all; Hincc had woven his own explanations around hers with a bardic skill which she suspected was born of long cold nights.

They had been good explanations. The High People had lived above the snowline for hundreds of generations. They hunted small mammals for leather, fur and meat; they foraged down towards the snowline for dry firewood and wiry grasses for fuel, and for the few sweet little berries they could find. Towards the snowline but never across it; at some point so far in the past they had forgotten it, the High People had become so specialized that they could no longer exist off the snowfields.

There was something else, too. It had made Hincc's face cloud, and he had become monosyllabic.

'Bad times.'

'Bad? How?'

'Very bad. Since the light?'

'You can see it?'

'Glow, on clear nights. Distant. From the Circle Lands. Perhaps tonight. Come, look.'

They climbed up the slope. The land fell sharply on one side and more gently on the other. On the gentle side the line thing she had seen when she first looked out from the pod marched down the snowfield. The angle of fall was quite sharp; gentle was comparative.

Hincc pointed. 'See?'

She did see. Right at the horizon, the snow was subtly green-lit, a soft sinister halo around the blue-white snow light, distinctly focused on a narrow quadrant of the horizon.

She watched the soft light for a while. Then she turned to Hincc. 'What happened?'

He shrugged. 'From here, see little. Light, then pause. Normal, ten days. I send ice – big blocks. Cool fish, cool people, yes? Ice go down, hooks come up. Then, three days, line stops.'

'Is that usual?'

'Not unheard – when bad winter closes Circle. But very rare, very strange. Not so strange as what comes after. When line starts again.'

Something in his voice made her look at his face. 'What?' she asked, dreading the answer.

He looked at her for a moment, his face immobile. Then he sighed. 'Follow. See. Be ready.'

He led her under the motionless cables of the lift. Things hung beneath them: complex-looking expandable grabs. She pointed. 'Are those for the ice?'

'Mainly for the ice. Meant for the ice. Be ready.' He didn't look back, and the set of his shoulders discouraged further questions.

She followed, more easily than she had feared. There was a hard track stamped on to the snow. It was wider than one set of feet would have needed. She wondered why.

Then they crested a low ridge and she found herself looking down into the narrow head of a white valley that broadened quickly down the shallow, rolling snow slopes.

White, but dotted with irregular shapes.

She clenched her fists, and turned to Hincc. 'How many?'

His face was still rigid. 'I count careful. Since two weeks after green light, eight elevens and seven. Then I stop the line. Never before, never, do we stop the line from here. But I, my father, his father, their fathers? We send ice down. Maybe writing to ask for something, always comes soon. Not this. Never this. Soon berry juice will not be sweet. Soon lift parts will not be replaced. Already ice doesn't reach harbour. Does no one fish, or does fish rot?'

She counted the shapes. Ninety-five. Almost a hundred corpses. Some of them looked incomplete – arms and legs were missing – but they all seemed to have heads. There were no bloodstains in the snow, and she supposed the bodies must have been frozen hard by the time they arrived. She let herself absorb the scene. Then she said, carefully, 'Do you know why they were – sent?'

He shrugged. 'Only one thing. All wearing like this.' He felt in his furs and drew out something. She held out her hand and he let it drop into her palm, but without letting go of the chain that pierced it. She turned it over; just a plain greyish metal disc. One side was blank. The other was embossed with what looked like a random pattern of dots. No, not just dots. She looked closer. The snowglow was bright enough to show fine lines radiating from each dot, like a child's drawing of a star.

She tilted her palm to let the disc slide off it. Hincc caught it as it swung towards him on its chain. He let it drop into his own hand and slipped it back into his furs. 'Anything to you, Sky Girl?'

She shook her head.

'No surprise. Something to me – all priest people. Seen before. Heard, a little. Priest people watch the sky, count things. Perhaps green light means priest people must die.'

'Why?'

He turned his face away, but looked at her from the corner of his eyes. 'Who knows? What do all priest people say? Do this thing, do that thing, and tomorrow is like yesterday and sun always shines. All safe. But suddenly tomorrow is not like yesterday; tomorrow is green light – and maybe people say, why do we do this thing and that thing?' He smiled sourly. 'Especially, why do we feed these priest people who give us orders and do not go fishing?'

She nodded.

'So, you go and see?'

The question caught her off balance. 'I don't know.'

His sour grin became a real one. 'Okay, fine, stay here. Chew salt meat, eat berries. I start the line again, maybe you count priest bodies, maybe other bodies when they run out of priests. That what you came for, Sky Girl?'

She found herself smiling back. 'No. Not what I came for.'

'Good. So go discover.'

She nodded. 'How do I go?'

'Tomorrow, I show. Now come. Dark, cold. Time for fire. Time for sleep.'

He was right. The sky was black, and even in her ship suit the cold was aching. She stared upwards. 'Hincc? Are there ever any stars?'

He shook his head. 'Only in stories.'

She nodded and followed him down the slope towards the hut. Then she stopped. 'Stories? But you know what a star is?'

And watched him.

'Only in stories.' They were the same words but the tone had changed. The first time he had used them they had sounded like closing down. Now they sounded – different. She held the sound close to her as she followed him through the entrance of the hut. She held on to it as she watched Hincc shrugging off his layers of clothing, and as she followed suit. She held on to it as they sat down, little cups of steaming juice warming their hands and the glow of the fire pit stinging their feet.

Then she took a careful breath and asked the question.

'Hincc? You're a story-teller. Tell me another story. Tell me about the stars you've never seen.'

And with a simplicity that could as easily have been victory as defeat, he told her. By the time he had finished, the fire had dropped to embers, her breath was smoking in front of her and there was frost forming on the inside of the hut.

She barely noticed. But afterwards, she lay awake on a pallet heaped with furs and stared up at a knot-hole in the timbers of the low roof and wondered.

At first he had not seemed to be telling a story as she understood it. Instead he began by talking about the cold, the snowfields and the few creatures that lived on them. There were slim pale-grey hares that ate the berries of the few tough scrubby bushes that rooted directly in the snow, and drew their scant minerals from the urine of the same creatures. Bigger but slower, a long, almost tubular predator that grew longer, but not fatter, as it aged, and that sprouted another pair of stubby legs for every hand's breadth of length. Then, tiny and prey to everything, two-legged fur-balls with one strong arm and one weak, and with minuscule eyes set in deep sockets, who could look directly into the ice glare but whose sight was so poor they had to find their own snow burrows by the scent of the mate who never went outdoors.

Some of these seemed farcical to Seldyan. She had grown up in a world of order, even if it was the imposed order of a confined world, and what Hincc was describing sounded like biological anarchy. But then, slowly, she began to feel the specialized rhythm of life on these permanently white peaks, and following that she realized that the rhythm he described was not a thing only of the present – it came from the past, and reached into it. And as it moved into the past, tracing the histories of the animals and the berries and the peaks, it gathered stories around itself. Eventually, the stories reached their source.

The past was long, here. The separation of the High People from everyone else was so ancient that it was the stuff not just of folklore, but of folklore about folklore. Their languages had diverged, not so far that the two peoples couldn't understand each other, but far enough for each people's story to sound strange to the ears of the others. Even their names for the planet they lived on were different – everyone else called it Trakael, but Hincc's people used what he claimed was an older name: Solpht. The oldest folklore of all said that there had once been a bigger, brighter sun and that there were bright points in the sky at night.

'Whose folklore?'

He had shrugged. 'High People. Others, different stories. See this?' It was one of the tokens from the bodies.

She nodded. 'That's why I asked you about stars. These dots look like drawings of stars.'

'Maybe stars, maybe not. Down there people say other things.'

'Have you seen them?'

He shook his head. 'No. Never here. Always in same place. Hills above Circle Plains. People there make own stories. People, and priest people.'

'Circle Plains? Is that where you send the ice?'

'Almost. Not Plains; Harbour below.'

'Right.' She stared at the embers for a moment. 'Is that where you think I should explore?'

He laughed, an unexpected explosion in the close quiet of the hut. She looked at him, eyebrows raised, and he shook his head again. 'You ask me what to do? You fall from sky and I call you Sky Girl, but that is wrong. Yes?' He sat up, leaned forward so his face was less than an arm's length from hers. 'Not from. Through. You fall through sky from somewhere else. Now you tell me: somewhere else, are stars real?'

She held his gaze for a moment. Then she looked down. 'Yes,' she said, to her lap. 'They are real.'

'I knew!' He clapped his skinny hands. 'Real stars! And you come from them. Travel between?'

She nodded.

'And you ask me to tell you stories? To tell you what to do? You are Star Girl, not Sky Girl. Go where you want.'

'No, Hincc.' She shook her head. 'It doesn't work like that. I barely know about where I came from. I know nothing about here.'

For a while he was silent. Then he compressed his lips. 'Go to Harbour. Find out why green lights in sky make them send me bodies of priests.'

There hadn't been anything else to say. Hincc had lain down and pulled some furs over himself, and after a few moments Seldyan did too.

He seemed to be sleeping, but she couldn't.

The next morning she was fuzzy with sleeplessness. She sat wrapped in her furs while Hincc melted snow-water over a fire of what she thought at first were long, straight twigs. Then she looked again and realized that they all tapered to a needle point. She frowned, then waved at them. 'Hincc? Are they thorns?'

He took the shallow pan off the flames and poured the water over dried leaves in another pan. 'Yes, thorns. Leaves, here, from same bush. Above snowline, world shrinks; I use all parts. Thorns and leaves grow back. Branches, not so much. Now drink, then eat.'

She drank the acerbic brew and ate hare meat, salted and mixed with dried berries and pressed into flat cakes. The sour berries and salt cut across the sweet dry flesh so she didn't know whether to lick her lips or suck in her cheeks.

It didn't matter. Right back to the Hive, she knew the value of food as fuel. She ate everything. It helped more than she expected; she felt energy returning. She looked up to find Hincc grinning at her. She raised an eyebrow.

'Feel better?'

She nodded.

'Not surprise. Food always good, and leaf brew is stimulant.' His grin widened. 'I use little. People down below sometimes use much. Then more, then more, then can't stop. You know?'

'Yes.' She explored her senses; the effects seemed mild and she didn't feel dangerously altered. 'Do you send the leaves down?'

'Did. Not do. Since bodies, ice line still. Nothing down, nothing up.'

'I get that.' She stood up. 'Hincc? I have to go.'

'I know. Circle Harbour.'

'Yes, Circle Harbour.' She thought for a moment. 'You could come with me. If you wanted?'

He shook his head. 'No. Too warm, too damp. High People die fast below snowline. Stay here, eat hare and berries, brew leaves and wait for better time. Maybe you send better time, Star Girl.'

'Maybe.' She tried to smile, because it was better than the alternative. Then she pushed her thoughts away. There would be time for them later, maybe. 'So, how do I get there?'

She had taken the med kit from the pod, and a few other things. A comms bead tickled her inner ear but did nothing else. Totally dead.

Now she was standing, looking down along the huge sweep of the ice line. The part of her that wasn't busy being worried was very impressed.

A growing part was also intrigued. She turned to Hincc. 'Who made this? How does it work?'

He shrugged. It was a very expressive gesture in someone so skinny. 'Who, unknown. Always here, always same. How, easy. Heavy ice goes down, only light things come up.'

'How long is it?'

'To top of Circle Harbour, thirty days' walk.'

Seldyan caught her breath. From her short experience a day here was roughly standard. A day's walk might be twenty klicks, if you could deal with the snow.

She looked down the line again. It was a simple thing, but on a vast scale – two cables strung between pylons that were about twenty metres high. They must have been under huge tension, because they barely dipped at all. There was a pylon about every fifty metres, marching down the snow slopes in a paired procession that blended into one in the middle distance and then disappeared in the mist bank that was hanging at the base of the snowline. At regular intervals, the complicated metal claws that Hincc called ice hooks hung down from the cables.

The pylon nearest her seemed to be some sort of concrete. She couldn't tell what the cable was made of, but it didn't look like metal. It had a matt grey look, and the frost didn't seem to stick to it.

It was much higher tech than anything she had seen here so far. Of course, that might mean nothing. Hincc's people had a particular take on technology.

Might. Six hundred kilometres of line, presumably twice as much cable?

She felt a smile trying to break out. 'Hincc? You just told me something important.'

He spread his arms. 'Always. You come back, tell me what joke is.'

'Oh, I will. You've got my ship, remember?'

'I take care. Star Girl? You go, or you stay?'

She laughed. 'I go. How long will it take?'

'To Ice House in Circle Harbour, three suns. Be cautious – maybe wise to drop off sooner, walk.'

'Yes.' *Well*, she thought, *he's right. I go.*

The down cables were on the right. Hincc had uncoupled the ice hooks on the nearest one; they lay on, and partly in, the powder snow. In their place a sling hung from the cable. It was made of furs.

She looked at Hincc. 'You made that?'

'Yes. In case. Star Girl? Keep eyes away from other cable. Look right. Now climb in.'

She didn't need to climb. The sling was at knee height. She stood in front of it and sat back. It took her weight, swaying. 'What do I do now?' she asked.

He gestured. 'Pull on hanging line.'

A thick loop of cord dangled in front of her. She took hold of the nearer half and pulled. She felt it take up a load and the sling twitched upwards with a quick squeak that sounded like pulleys. A minute of brisk hauling and she was twice her own height off the snow, level with the ice hooks on the other cable.

She checked her pouch – everything was there. She seemed ready to go. She looked down at Hincc.

'How do I stop it?'

He laughed. 'You don't! Stop from here. Maybe stop from Circle, if they remember how. In between, only go until ice all melts.' He pointed down the line. 'Twenty blocks, see? Enough for go; not too fast.'

'So how do I get off?'

'Lower.' He mimed pulling the cord, hand over hand. 'Then jump. Easy. But back on again, not possible. Be sure! Ready?'

She nodded.

'Then go.' He kicked the lever. 'Good luck, Star Girl!'

The sling canted forward and, far more smoothly than she had expected, she was moving.

She didn't look back. For the first hour she didn't look left either, although she wasn't sure why Hincc had been so adamant. The wind bit her face and she sank as deep into the furs as she could.

Then something caught the corner of her eye and she did look to the left – just a little, because the thing was still a long way down the line. But it was moving towards her. She corrected herself. Things, not thing: a line of black dots swaying upwards.

She swallowed. The corpses of priests were still coming. Hincc must have known they would.

She wondered if whoever had set up the line, and had presumably at the same time rewritten the future of this poor little planet, had ever anticipated that.

Three Quarter Circle Harbour Wall

Three things had saved Belbis after they had thrown him into the shack, unconscious and with a broken arm and broken ribs and slashed heels – if he could count himself saved. The first had been water and that, he was sure, had been accidental. The roof of the shack, as he could tell from a combination of memory and smell, was tar-paper, old and holed. A few of the holes must have lain at the bottom of sagged areas, and they formed dew collectors. If he shuffled himself beneath them and lay with his mouth open he could take on enough water, if not to live, then not to die that day. There had been forty-one of the days so far. He had not lost the ability to count things. Sometimes, and especially in the dark, he lay still, cradling his stubbornly unhealed arm across his chest, and re-counted the Gods in his head. He always came to the same number, and it was always the wrong one.

The second was that he had regained just a little of his vision. Not enough for details, but enough that some of the blurs could mean something if he looked carefully out of the corner of his eye. Straight ahead, there was nothing but greenish black darkness.

That was how he had found the bottle. It had been lying in a corner of his shack in just the right place for a shaft of morning sun, slicing through one of the many gaps in the walls, to glance off it.

The gaps allowed many things into his shack. The sunlight, certainly, but also the smells of the docks and a piercing wind that permitted him little sleep. They should also have let in the sounds of the docks, but those had gone, replaced by the restless creak and slam of abandoned boats and, further away but no less noticeable, shouts and the sound of anger.

He had been glad of the bottle. There had been nothing else suitable. The wooden walls of the shack were built off a stone plinth that was wider than the timber; he had chosen a protruding edge, took the bottle by the neck in his good hand, and brought it down hard.

He had cut his fingers searching amongst the pieces, but that didn't matter. He had found what he was looking for.

It was nearly time for the girl to visit, if she was going to. He had to hurry.

He took the large shard, lifted his right leg so that the foot lay on his left thigh, and began to scrape out the worm-infested flesh from his heel.

When he had first done this he had used the unbroken neck of the bottle to bite on. The glass was thick, and he knew he wouldn't break it no matter how he bit. But recently the nerves in his heel had begun to die and the daily job was merely agonizing.

Every day he had to go a little deeper to make sure he had cleared all the hard little egg sacs. If they managed to penetrate the cartilage of his heel and grow into his bones, they would kill him in weeks.

In the extremes of the hunger that had come to him before the girl, he had once tried to eat his own scrapings but the taste of his poisoned flesh had been vile, and the combination of the restless maggots and their gritty eggs had made him vomit. Now he buried the daily mess in a little hollow he scooped out of the earth floor with another of the glass fragments.

He had just finished when he heard the uneven shuffle of her feet outside, and the diffident little knock.

Before the girl came, he had been starving to death. Now he was just starving. She had never explained why she came – why she had shuffled up to this shack, where he had been dragged and left to die after they had crippled him, and knocked, and thrust a bit of bread under the door and then run away.

The bread had been stale and hard as wood. He had moistened it with saliva a drop at a time to soften it, and eaten each musty crumb like a banquet.

The next day she had been there again. There was a little more bread and, this time, one of the little fish-skin bags of water the men had used to take out with them on their boats, when the boats had still gone out.

Belbis had always hated fish. He still did, but thirst overcame anything. The oily tainted water managed to taste good enough. It lifted him from dying slowly to just barely holding ground.

The girl was the third thing, obviously. And now she was here. He lifted his head from the pallet and called out.

'Come in!'

And someone came in, but it was not the little girl because whoever it was had to open the narrow door wide to get through it, so that the light became brighter than it had ever been since he had been left here, and then dimmed as a body passed through, and then brightened again, and a voice, a woman's voice said, in an odd accent, 'Hello?' And then, after an interval when he heard a breath sharply drawn in, 'Oh shit . . .'

The accent was the same as the machine on the hill had used, before the light came. Belbis tried to raise himself on his elbow, but he had chosen the wrong elbow. His broken arm collapsed beneath him like a twig and he collapsed with it.

Three Quarter Circle

It hadn't taken Seldyan long to find what she was looking for. She had assumed it was going to take her a while even to frame the question, but the state of the town made it obvious.

Circle Harbour was – had been – a small sea port with, she guessed, not many more than a few thousand houses. It had a walled harbour enclosed by a rock-pile wall that formed almost a complete circle. Hence the name, she assumed. The area around the harbour was thick with huts and ramps and yards, mostly fouled with the decaying remains of what looked like fish processing. Within the harbour, black water full of floating rubbish and inflated corpses lapped at the edges of ramps through a scum of sickly foam.

The smell was indescribable. She had held out until she was within sight of the harbour; then, feeling somehow ashamed, she had rummaged through the med kit, found a couple of filter plugs and jammed them in her nostrils. The labels said they were to exclude inhalable bacteria, which was probably a good thing. They reduced the stench to merely disgusting.

She had been able to smell the town from a long way away, but it wasn't decay she noticed first. She had been glad to leave that behind.

She had dropped off the ice line six nights ago, just below the snowline, when the smell from the thawing, decomposing bodies began to make her retch. With a detached part of her she theorized that they had already been decaying when they were hooked on. Whatever; as soon as her feet were on the ground she had half walked, half run, fifty or so paces upwind of it. Then she had turned parallel with the ice line, and begun to walk.

The ice line slanted obliquely down the coast, following an almost level path between a grey sea to the left and a long dull heather-blue rise towards cloudy mountains to the right. At night the clouds shone green. Even during the day she could see a hint of colour. She watched for the source of it, but the clouds never lifted far enough.

A day out from the town she began to smell the burning. She had stopped and lifted her nose to catch the on-shore wind. Definitely burning, but not fresh. There was something acrid about it, like ash mixed with – something; she wasn't sure what.

A day later she was sure. On the outskirts of the town most of the buildings were stone and those still stood, although a few had lost roofs and some looked ransacked. Further in, whole areas had been reduced to waist-high clay walls, extravagantly blackened and cracked, with the charcoaled bones of timber frames sticking up from them. The streets were paved with fat lozenge-shaped cobbles. Water had collected between them, its surface rainbowed with oil.

That was the smell. She thought about that for a while, randomly walking the quiet streets with her eyes mainly downward – there were too many things to trip over or slip on. Then she shook off her reverie and looked around, forcing herself to complete one slow, full turn with her eyes raised and her senses properly alert.

The coastal plain the town was built on wasn't quite a plain. It rose and fell, reminding Seldyan of large-scale sand dunes. There was a high point a few hundred metres away, up-slope from the sea, with what looked like some fairly intact buildings on it. She compressed her lips. Either there was something here or there wasn't; it was time to find out.

She started walking.

It took her longer than she would have expected. The streets were convoluted, full of twists and dead ends, and sometimes she had to retrace her steps when she was stopped by a collapsed building or a heap of debris. But after an hour of scrambling she was looking at a low two-storey building of long flat stones, smoke-stained along the side that faced the harbour but otherwise seemingly untouched.

She looked it up and down, and then her heart bounced. There were chimneys at both ends of the roof, and one of them was wisping smoke.

People. She had found people.

She took a breath, but before she could call out there were running feet behind her and something hit her in the small of her back. She went down, crashing against the cobbles with her arms thrown in front of her face.

Whoever it was, they seemed to be lying on her, but they didn't feel heavy. She raised herself on her forearms, wincing at the protest from her grazed skin. Then she froze.

'Stay down!'

It had been an urgent whisper, so close to her ear that she felt hot breath, but that wasn't what had surprised her. It was a child's voice, and it sounded serious.

She dropped again. Almost before she was down there was a shattering boom from somewhere in front of her. Something whistled over her head in a cloud of dust, and then there was a pattering like raindrops around her. She felt things landing on her arms and the back of her head; through screwed-up eyes she saw falling splinters.

The weight on her back lifted abruptly, and then she found herself looking up into a brown face framed by a lot of dark straight hair. 'He's reloading,' said the face. 'Run now.' And

225

then it was gone and there was a slight figure running awkwardly away downhill, towards the harbour.

Seldyan shook her head to clear it. Then she rose to a crouch and ran after the girl. She caught her up a couple of streets away; the awkwardness had quickly turned into a skipping limp, and the dark face was twisted with pain.

She knelt so that their faces were level. 'Thanks,' she said. 'Are you okay?'

The face turned away, but Seldyan had already had time to see that the dark colour was more dirt than skin, and there were darker smudges around one eye. She felt her own eyes narrowing. 'Someone hit you?'

The girl nodded, still with her head turned.

'What about your leg. Was that . . . ?'

Another nod.

'Who did it?'

Emphatic shake.

'Right.' Seldyan patted her belt; the med kit was there, and felt undamaged. She looked around. 'I owe you one. I can make you better. Is there anywhere safe we can go?'

For a long time the girl was silent. Then she glanced at the med kit. 'Make very bad things better?'

'It depends how bad.' Seldyan hesitated. 'Are you very hurt?'

The head shook again. 'Not me. You come?'

Seldyan hesitated, and then cursed herself. *Maybe it is all shit*, she thought. *Maybe all I can do is make a bit of it a bit less shit.* 'Okay,' she said, straightening up. 'You lead.'

The girl nodded and set off, still heading down towards the harbour. She wasn't running this time, and the limp was so pronounced that her left foot seemed barely to touch the ground before it was lifted again, but she kept up a steady pace.

Seldyan guessed she would be about the same age as Dimollss. Something about the thought made her pause for a second. Then she squared her shoulders and followed the girl.

As she followed, a thought followed her. *This was what I came for.*

The smell in the shack made her retch. It was shit and piss and the powerful waxy stink of unwashed body and, overwriting all of that, something rotting – not just rotten but actively putrefying.

Seldyan had once cleared out a cold store where the chillers had failed. She had shovelled out half a tonne of spoiled synthetic protein. That had been similar, but not as bad.

The door had swung to behind her. She kicked it open, found a loose cobble, wrenched it up and used it to prop the door so the light fell on the pile of rags in the corner, and the skeleton that had tried to raise itself when she had first entered.

It was a man – she guessed a young man, but the face was so shrunken and bearded it was hard to be sure of age. The one certain thing was that he was starving to death – had obviously been doing so for a long time.

He was covered from the waist down by more rags. She swallowed and drew them back. When they got to his feet they seemed to stick. She pulled a little harder, and they came free, and she covered her mouth in horror. But she didn't let herself turn away.

The soles of the man's feet, from the ball to the heel, were raw flesh, blackened and oozing pus. At the heels, white bone glinted. As Seldyan watched, a short brown worm wriggled out of the wound, and then another.

Still without turning, she spoke to the girl. 'How did this happen?'

'The men cut him.'

'Which men?'

She shrugged. 'Men from the town.'

'Where are they now?'

'Most gone. There was burning, and then bad smells.'

'But why cut him?'

The girl shrugged. 'He was the Painter.'

'Okay, never mind.' She didn't understand but questions could wait. She took out the mini-doc, clamped her lips together and knelt down by the man.

When she finally sat back on her heels and dug her hands into the small of her back to ease the ache, the light was getting dim. She ran her eyes over her patient and nodded slowly. The doc had supplied sedatives, a shot of quick-heal and a massive dose of a broad-spectrum anti-parasitic. His feet were cleaned and dressed and his horribly broken arm was encased in splint-foam.

'I think you'll live.' She rotated her shoulders. Everything ached. Then she turned to the girl, who had barely moved the whole time. 'I haven't forgotten you,' she said, 'but we need to get this one somewhere clean and safe. Do you know anywhere?'

The face flickered. 'Clean. Not safe.' Her hand went to her bruised eye. The index finger was swollen and crooked, and Seldyan realized with a jolt of disgust that it was broken.

'Not safe because they did things to you?'

The girl nodded.

Seldyan stood up, feeling her knees creaking, and reached into her pouch. The smooth bulge of the stunner fitted easily into her curled fingers.

'Maybe we can do something about that,' she said. 'Will you trust me?'

The girl's eyes went to the unconscious man, and then back to Seldyan. She nodded, and her lips twitched in something that might have been the start of a smile.

'Right. Show me where.'

She wasn't surprised when 'where' turned out to be the house she had headed for that morning. Viewed from what she hoped was a safe distance, the chimney wasn't smoking any more and there were sagging timber shutters over the windows. One of the shutters had a corner missing. She saw clean white wood along the tear and guessed it had fallen victim to whatever weapon had been fired at her earlier. A plume of splinters on the ground led towards where she had met Bis.

It seemed an odd name. She hadn't been able to find out if it was short for anything, because the girl had become less communicative as they got nearer the house. Her face was pale and set. It wasn't pain; Seldyan had given her a painkiller and a dose of quick-heal. She had borne the hypo phlegmatically, like someone who'd had practice bearing things, and Seldyan had found herself shaking her head.

Now she leaned down and spoke quietly. 'Will they fire again?'

Bis shook her head. 'Drinking time.'

'Ah. How many people?'

'Just him.' The word was flat.

Seldyan watched the house for a moment. Bis sounded sure but she might be wrong, and there was no way of finding out by looking. Seldyan felt the stunner cradled in her palm. Her body heat had warmed it. It felt – friendly.

She grinned to herself and set the level to its highest point – Captain Hefs had been knocked out by half that, but then she had sort of liked him. 'Wait for me there,' she said, and pointed towards a patch of shade at the base of a ruined wall opposite the house. 'Come when I call. Understand? Not before.'

The girl nodded.

'Right. See you.' Seldyan straightened up, took a breath and ran.

There was a flimsy-looking door in the rough centre of the ground floor. She ignored it. 'Very strong,' Bis had said, before she clammed up. 'Go behind. Barrel drop.' It had taken some clarification, but now Seldyan knew what she was looking for – the girl's private way in and out.

Hopefully private.

The back of the house was piled with litter. Stacks of broken timber leaned against the wall. At one point they formed a lean-to tunnel. Seldyan dropped to her knees and shuffled along it, smelling tar and rot, until her hands met a rough wooden hatch. She ran her fingers round the edge until they felt a rusted hoop. A pull, and the hatch lifted.

She eased herself through and dropped half her own length.

Then she screamed as hot cramping agony flooded her leg. She tried to lift her foot from whatever it was, but it wouldn't move. She almost lost her balance and her arms flailed. Her hand banged into something and gripped it, and then she realized she was still screaming and somehow bit it back. She looked down and her heart went cold.

Someone had driven iron nails into a board, and had left it, points upward, beneath the hatch where her feet had landed.

Or where Bis's feet would have landed.

Then she heard the footsteps on the floor above, and anger overcame the pain. She shut her eyes and pulled her foot off the nails, managing to experience the tearing of the rough metal with something close to detachment. Then she hopped sideways, away from the patch of light thrown by the hatch, until she was standing in a corner with the stunner held out in front of her. It wasn't shaking much.

The footsteps paused. There was a sharp creak and light appeared in the opposite corner of the room – the wavering orange light of a flame. Someone was coming down a steep flight of stairs, a lamp held out in front of them. Even across the room, it smelled of oil.

Seldyan waited until the full length of the legs was visible. Then she fired.

There was a howl, and a body crashed down and lay twitching. The lamp clanged to the floor a metre away, and flames flickered about a spreading pool.

Seldyan swore. She half hopped, half skipped across the floor, picked up the still burning lamp and put it on a shelf. Sacks of something were stacked against the wall by the steps; she hauled one of them out of the stack, dumped it on the pool of flames and watched it until she was sure they were out. Then she dragged another sack on top of the first, sat on it and glared down at the fallen man.

His eyes were wide in the dim light. One hand was underneath him. The other reached convulsively for a leg which lay in an impossible shape, the calf forming an acute angle with the thigh. Even in the lamplight she could see dark wetness spreading through the material where his knee would be.

She nodded towards the leg. 'That's going to hurt a lot more when the stun wears off. Are you the man who beats up little girls?'

'What's stun?' The words were slurred, and she caught a sour gust of bad teeth and alcohol.

Seldyan sighed. 'I shot your legs. Look, I haven't got time . . . you're going to sleep. I'll see you if you wake up.' She raised the stunner again and fired, this time at the torso. The body convulsed and was still. About half a day, she guessed. Long enough.

It took her a long time to climb the steps. By the time Bis answered her call she was sitting on a stool, her injured foot propped up in front of her. The girl's eyes widened when she saw the blood-stained sabot. Seldyan managed to grin at her. 'Can you be a doctor?'

Then she leaned back and closed her eyes. Just for a minute, she promised herself.

When she opened her eyes, the room was lit by firelight. There was a rough blanket around her shoulders and her bloody sabot was on the floor by her stool.

Her foot hurt; that was what had woken her. There was a job to do. She sat forward and looked around. 'Bis?'

There were soft footsteps behind her and the girl appeared. Seldyan looked her up and down. Her stance was symmetrical now, and the footsteps had sounded even. 'Feeling better?'

Bis nodded.

'Good. I need your help. Is there any hot clean water?'

She watched while the girl heated a blackened pot on the fire. It was big enough for her whole foot to fit. When it was ready she gritted her teeth and bathed it while Bis watched with learning eyes. Then she withdrew it and rested her heel on the ground. 'Now, I need some strong drink.'

The girl's face flickered, and Seldyan added, 'Not to drink. To clean. Stop bad getting in.'

Bis nodded. She gestured to the med kit. 'No good for you?'

Seldyan glanced at the kit and hesitated. In the end she said, 'I only use it if I have to.' As a general statement, she thought, that was true. It just avoided the specific point that there was nothing left; she had used the whole kit on Bis and the man in the shack.

And she didn't even know who he was. But Bis thought he was important, and she had to trust someone.

Bis fetched a flat glass flagon from a store beside the chimney. She opened the stopper with a twist that looked practised and held it out. Seldyan shook her head. 'You do it,' she said. 'Pour it over.'

And gripped the legs of the stool, hard.

By the time she had bandaged her foot with the cleanest-looking rag she could find and jammed it back in her sabot, the light was getting dim. She reflected for a while. Then she put a hand on Bis's shoulder. 'I'm going to fetch the man,' she said. 'Stay here. Keep the door closed. Tend the fire. Is there any food?'

The girl nodded.

'Okay. Get us something to eat. Soft things. Soup. You know how to make soup? He'll probably be awake, understand? He'll need to eat.' She reflected for a moment, and added, 'And heat water. Lots of water. He'll need to wash.'

Then she turned and limped through the door. She heard it close emphatically behind her.

Unknown

He had been – wherever it was – for a while. Time was difficult. They didn't allow him to sleep and the light never
changed, so days were unmeasurable. There were no meals,
only the sour fluid they forced between his lips from time to
time. It seemed to contain a stimulant, because it could wake
him from the warm stupor he occasionally lapsed into when
they had hurt him too much, or for too long.

They would always punish him for that, although he could
never predict exactly when.

His world was the thing he sat on and was fixed to – an ordinary chair, but skeletal and seemingly capable of being any
shape and in any position – and the dim view of a wall. Between
him and the wall, a stool, and on the stool a small human male
in drab clothes.

He was aware of the operative, or operatives. He had no way
of counting them; no means of telling how many there were, or
if they had advisors, assistants or even an audience. Everything
he couldn't feel or see, he ruled out, and what was in front of
him he acknowledged, but didn't trust.

To not trust your world. That was all there was. Trust would
be acceptance, and acceptance would be ending. So far, and as far
as he could tell, he hadn't ended. He was less sure if he was sane.

The world he didn't trust was demanding his attention. The man on the stool had sighed. 'We begin again. We will begin again as many times as we need to. Only you can help us to an ending.' His eyes slid a little to the side and he nodded.

Yellow. Vess had come to assign colours to pain. This was yellow, a bright hot yellow like a sun, or better perhaps like a shard of metal, heated close to melting. He smelled burning flesh.

When it stopped the little man was looking at him. 'People have lived for years in that chair, you know. So long that their flesh has fused to it, so that they have to be torn from it in the end.' He leaned forward. 'There is no escape. No insanity, no death. We know better than that. You are the best-preserved living entity in the Spin.' Another nod.

Yellow, and more burning, and convulsions; tearing of muscle fibres leaping against restraints.

'So, a beginning. You came alive out of the Stack. You were then interviewed by Vut. You handled a runner. The runner was rogue and now Caphraime II is dead and a few hundred people have hearing damage. Had Chairman Or-Shls not acted quickly he would be dead instead of her, and that was probably the real intention. You have no reason to love the Chairman. You claim to know nothing, but I don't believe you. Speak at any time.'

The same question, and he had already given his only answer many times. He would have shaken his head, but it was fixed in place. He would have closed his eyes but they had removed his eyelids.

Nod. The operatives must have changed their aim, somehow finding some part of him that had not yet been seared, ground, fractured, punctured, outraged. Yellow brightened towards white, became all-encompassing. He heard himself raving, roaring. Inhuman sounds. They were wrong, there was escape, he could see it, it blotted out the man and the stool and the wall, it was a core of black in the blinding white; he could feel himself dropping towards it. He reached out to it from the remains of his mind.

'Abort.'

It stopped. Everything stopped. Vision returned. The man on the stool was sitting dead upright with a listening expression on his face. Then he nodded, but this time as if to himself, and looked at Vess.

'Goodbye,' he said. And he and the stool and the wall were gone.

Vess sat up, and nothing impeded him. He blinked, and felt his eyes moistened by proper tears. He looked around, feeling a breeze touch different parts of his face as he moved. The breeze smelled familiar: canals and Basin Lilies and the tiniest hint of cylinder oil and something else, something he couldn't place for the moment. There were canals in the distance but, and he shook his head, they were all below him. That didn't make sense.

A voice behind him said, 'Hello, Harbour Master.'

Then he realized. The smell he couldn't identify was tobacco smoke. It was just that he had never smelled it fresh before. He was in Basin City, and for the first time in his life he was seeing it from the Cloud Deck, and the voice behind him belonged to Alst Or-Shls.

He hadn't realized it before but somehow, fixed in the chair with the wall to look at, he had not been frightened.

Now, he was terrified.

Three Quarter Circle Harbour

The young man turned out to be a fast healer. On the second morning he sat up and squinted at her. 'I can see,' he said.

Seldyan grinned. 'And you can talk. I'm Seldyan and this is Bis. Who are you?'

'I'm Belbis the . . .' He hesitated. 'I'm Belbis.'

'Belbis the something secret? Okay.' Seldyan studied his face. On an impulse she said, 'You know what you are? Belbis the safe. She kept you alive, I mended you. So you can say whatever you like – or nothing at all. It's up to you.'

She turned away before he could respond. Over her shoulder she added, 'Think about it. I've got things to do.'

That was true. It was just that she didn't want to do them.

Bis had told her something about the young man, but it had been from a child's perspective – a child who had been dancing to a tune she recognized. But this was different; she doubted she would ever know everything that had passed between Bis and the man in the cellar, but she could guess.

She had considered killing the man out of hand, but something had held her back. Now she was glad of it.

She walked carefully down the steps, holding the stunner out in front of her and sparing her injured foot as much load as she could. Then she squatted down, out of reach, keeping one hand behind her back.

He was conscious. The eyes were watchful beads surrounded by pouches of sagging flesh, and one hand still worked at the injured leg. He stank of stale drink and fresh faeces.

Seldyan nodded at the leg. 'Feeling anything?'

'Go shit yourself.'

She raised her eyebrows. 'It smells like you got there first. The stun should be wearing off by now. Guess your leg's starting to hurt.'

He clamped his mouth shut but his eyes flickered, and his hand clenched at the bloodied cloth above his knee.

She nodded. 'Okay,' she said. And brought round the hand from behind her back so he could see the short knobby staff.

The man flinched, and that decided Seldyan more than anything, because Bis had flinched in the same way when she had seen it.

'This is for Bis,' she said, and brought it down on his knee.

Something crunched.

His shriek made her ears whistle. She waited until he had quietened, and then raised the stick again. 'I should kill you,' she said. 'For all the bruises I can see on that little girl, and all the ones I can't, and for that plank full of nails that was meant for her – I should kill you.'

His mouth was open, but the only thing coming out was drool; a yellowish thread dangled from his chin and snapped.

She shook her head, more at herself than at him, and dropped the staff. 'Okay, you get to live a while. Tell me what happened to this place.'

The eyes became calculating. 'If I do?'

She raised the staff. 'Think about if you don't.'

They glared at each other for a moment. Then his eyes slid away. 'I heard him,' he said.

She blinked. 'Who?'

'Him.' He took his hand from his knee and pointed upwards. 'The idiot. You brought him here.'

'How's he an idiot?'

He laughed, a rasp that buried itself in a wet cough that took too long to stop. She watched him for a moment, then asked, 'Have you had that long?'

He spat and wiped his mouth; even that seemed to cost him more breath than he had. 'Long enough. You know what you hear?'

'I think so.' She sat back on her heels. 'Maybe we can make a different bargain. Maybe I have something you want.'

He watched her for a dozen heartbeats. Then something in his face relaxed. 'Maybe you do. You brought the idiot back. Ask him; it's his fault.'

She shook her head. 'I don't understand.'

'Like I told you. Ask him.' He shook his head. 'All he had to do was go up the mountain and paint the fucking Gods right. He couldn't even do that. So the light starts, and everything fucks up. His fault. So they scraped his feet so the worms could get him and shoved him somewhere to die. And you had to save him.'

'What about the bodies?'

He laughed again. 'The priests said the light meant the end of the world. People got angry and pretty soon all the priests were dead. Then the bodies started to stink. Easier to hook them on the ice line than burn them, the Merchants said, but then the line stopped.' He coughed and spat, his face twisting. 'So they burned them after all. There was a spark, and half the town burned with them. Now I'm done. Ask the idiot the rest. Do what you like.'

She nodded. 'You need to know this isn't a gift,' she said. 'It's justice.'

She had expected him to turn his face away, but he held her eyes while she extended the stunner, while she powered it up, and while she held down the stud for charge after charge until the little thing became hot in her hand. Even when she was sure he was dead, his eyes stayed open.

Then she stood up, slipped the stunner back in her pouch, and climbed the steps without looking back. Upstairs, she faced Belbis. 'I think I got lucky,' she said. 'I think you're what I came looking for.'

Bis tugged at her waist. 'Him,' she said, and pointed towards the steps. It was a question.

Seldyan reached down and squeezed her hand. 'He was very ill.'

The girl smiled. It was the first proper smile Seldyan had seen from her.

Seldyan laboured up the slope, crested the ridge and looked up at the peak ahead of her. Another couple of days, she guessed, if they could keep up a reasonable speed.

That was a big if. She pushed the stick she had cut for herself hard against the ground and lifted her foot.

They had been walking for eight days and she had learned several things. The first was that now he was fully recovered Belbis was very fit. His face had filled out and he had shaved off his beard, and she realized he was much younger than she had thought, not far out of childhood. He had all the leggy stamina that went with it.

Second was that he was utterly unwelcome, anywhere.

It had been the morning of their third day. Seldyan had pointed to a group of buildings, huddled at the base of a steep rise a few hundred paces from their path. 'Look. Would they have helped you, when you were making the walk before?'

He peered at the buildings and then at the rough grass near the path. 'Yes. Look there.'

He was pointing at a little hollow in a half-circle of stones that looked deliberate. There was a scrap of coarse cloth.

She nodded. 'Supplies?'

'Yes.'

'Perhaps they'll have something for us now.' She marched off towards the buildings. After a moment, quick footsteps told her he was following.

When she judged they were within earshot she stopped and cupped her hands to her mouth. 'Hello?'

There was no answer, but movement caught her eye; someone had opened an upper window.

She tried again. 'Hello? Can you hear me?'

There was a noise like something sliding open. Beside her she felt Belbis tensing.

Then something erupted from a low block at the edge of the settlement and headed towards them – a low, streamlined, four-legged shape that ran fast and in silence. Even at this distance she could see teeth.

Seldyan turned to Belbis, but he was already running. She followed, sprinting up the rough slope with her pack thumping at the small of her back. From behind she heard a high whistle and a wordless call; she risked a glance over her shoulder and saw the animal standing, head raised, much closer than it had been. She corrected 'fast' to 'very fast'. Someone was standing between it and the buildings – a bulky bearded figure with his hands on his hips. As she watched he raised them to his mouth and cupped them.

'Take the idiot away or Leap'll have your throat. Understand? And you'll get the same from everyone. Plenty of townsfolk came up here after the fires. I'll tell 'em.'

Seldyan shrugged and hefted her pack. 'Come on, Belbis. We've got enough.'

They walked back to the path.

Later that day her foot started to hurt. When they stopped for the night she pulled off the sabot cautiously and saw blood. She supposed she must have opened the wound when she had run. She put the sabot back on before Belbis could see.

241

Now, five days later, and no matter how hard she tried to convince herself otherwise, she was in trouble.

She hadn't taken the sabot off for three nights. Last night, for the first time, and exhausted as she was, she hadn't been able to sleep. She had lain on her back, trying to find a position where the throbbing was muted, and looking at the green beam that lanced up from the mountain top. The clouds had cleared a few days ago and the light that had started a religion in Web City, and seemed to have ended one here, was the only thing to look at.

Belbis slept with his face buried in the curl of his arm, eyes firmly downwards. Apparently it was traditional.

By morning her ankle was beginning to swell.

She fought on upwards. The route was getting narrower the higher they went, and the rocky bones of the mountain were exposed as scree slopes and stream beds. The water in them was bitter – an ice-fed cold that felt like scalding; when they stopped for a rest and a mouthful of their remaining food she sat with her foot under the surface until all the feeling was gone. It stayed gone for an hour or so. Then it came back worse, as if every step drove the spikes into her flesh all over again.

She looked for Belbis and found him standing a dozen paces in front of her. 'I'm sorry,' she said. 'I need to rest. Not long. If I sleep, will you wake me?'

He looked confused for a second and then nodded. She had got used to that; if something was obvious he didn't think it needed saying. She hoped the nod meant he was getting used to her.

She managed to smile, and sat down. The grass here looked wiry but it made a dense, springy mat that was almost comfortable, if you were exhausted.

She stretched out and concentrated on calming her breathing, which seemed far too shallow. More exercise. She needed to be fitter.

Eventually she found a sort-of-sleep, but it was full of loud noises. Her foot was the loudest, a kind of bass beat that defined her world so thoroughly that she quickly forgot it in favour of everything else. There was the shrill protest of the clouds as they were sawn apart by the beam of light, which sounded so green that it was almost a smell, and then there was the sulphur-tasting groaning of the rocks under the weight of the mountain peak. The springiness of the grass hummed beneath her cheek, and Belbis, standing over her, was a silent, worried pressure like a hand on her shoulder.

And again.

She stirred and looked up. Belbis was crouching next to her, withdrawing his hand like an apology. 'You said to wake you.'

'I did. It's fine.' She got to her feet. He looked worried, so she checked herself.

Better, in some ways. It almost was fine. She'd been feeling cold but that had faded, and her tiredness had been blunted by her sleep. She felt lighter. Her foot felt – different. Less painful, which was the main thing. Less of everything, really. Just sort of tight, and a bit less there than it had been.

She shook off a faint disquiet. Even the slope looked less steep now, and the peak seemed nearer. Or further, it could be, but either way she wasn't worried. She felt sure she could make it.

She gave Belbis a reassuring grin. Then she turned to face the slope and took a big, easy step.

The grass came up and hit her. Not in the face, in the chest. Somehow, her face was over nothing at all. Then her eyes focused and she realized it wasn't nothing – it was just a long way away.

She was looking down a cliff. She assumed she had been about to step over it, which was careless. She made a mental note and then tried to get up, but that didn't work. She investigated; there were arms holding her.

She turned her head as far as she could, briefly making the

sky into a whirlpool. When it had stopped she was looking side-ways at Belbis. 'What happened?'

He looked even more worried. 'Very bad foot. Poisons reach your mind. You are dangerous.'

'Ah.' She was having trouble focusing on him. 'I like being dangerous. Keep still.'

'I am still. The world in your head moves. Wait.'

She waited, and after a while things became more still. She realized he was watching her eyes, and watched him back until he smiled and let her go.

She rolled over on to her back and the sky danced again. There was something she needed to say. She concentrated, and the words formed a line in her head. 'Belbis? I don't think I can stand up.'

'I know. Be still.'

His hands grasped her ankles and he pulled her away from the edge. The traction on her leg stabbed at her. Then he was looking into her eyes again. 'There is something I must do. Will be bad, then worse, then better.'

Then he took hold of her sabot and began to pull it off. She squeezed her eyes shut and clenched her hands and counted her thundering heartbeat.

She had just passed a hundred when the pull stopped. She raised her head, blinked away tears and saw – well, she supposed it was her foot. The light seemed to be fading but the thing looked mostly black. There was a bad smell. She looked at Belbis. 'Was that the bad or the worse?'

'The bad. Worse is now. Very sorry.' She saw a glint of green light reflecting off something in his hand, and she shut her eyes again.

Then she screamed and screamed until the world went away.

She thought she remembered waking several times, but each time she seemed to have managed to wake from one dream into another. The dreams all started different but sooner or later they ended up with her lying on her back under a glittering black sky with a green sword hanging above her belly.

Finally she managed a dream where she wasn't pinned down, and where the green sword pointed up into the sky. This dream also contained Belbis. She checked to see if he was holding anything sharp.

'How do you feel?'

She thought for a second. 'Awake?'

'Yes, awake. Head?'

A slow shake made the world spin. 'Bad.'

'Expected. Foot?'

'Oh.' She hadn't thought of that, which seemed to mean something. She investigated. 'Nothing. Is that good?'

'Good for now. Not good for long.'

'Okay.' Thinking was difficult. 'What, then?'

It was too dark to see his face, but somehow his silhouette against the green-lit dark was thoughtful. 'Can you wait? Wait here, not move? Not try to fly down cliff?'

Embarrassment stung her faintly through the fog in her head. 'Promise.'

'Good.' He straightened up. 'Going now – back with the sun. Remember promise.'

And he was gone.

She let her head fall back, and went back to her dreams.

Cloud Deck (Restricted), Basin City

The total area of the Cloud Deck was about three square kilometres. That space was taken up by nine properties. They ranged in size from mere budget parcels of real estate covering only twenty thousand square metres or so – budget, in this case, meaning worth thirty lifetimes' average income for someone like Vess – all the way up to vast landscaped tracts of coastline.

Alst Or-Shls owned the biggest of all. Vess had once heard that he owned it outright, which was all but inconceivable. It was like saying that one individual owned the productive capacity of a major city. Which, in some ways, Or-Shls did.

It was so beautiful that Vess actually managed to forget his terror for a while.

There was a walkway along the edge of the estate. The Cloud Deck was a couple of metres of subsoil, capped with topsoil, on a foam alloy deck. Although it was the newest artefact in Basin City, it was still almost ten thousand years old, and the edges were eroding gently as the alloy corroded and crumbled. The walkway had originally been over solid ground, but now whole sections of it lay over nothing at all. Cool draughts blew up through the pierced metal.

Vess wasn't scared of heights. Or, better, he was far less scared of heights than he was of all the other things that might happen up here.

Or-Shls walked slowly but with a sort of inevitability and an odd economy. Vess would have expected such a vast body to sway from side to side but somehow the man managed to contain all the balance within himself, as if he had some sort of internal compensating mechanism. For a while he had said nothing, seeming content to stroll along the edge of his territory with Vess at his side. Then he stopped and turned towards Vess. 'I'm sorry there's no view.'

Vess nodded. It was called the Cloud Deck for a reason – even its very elevation was enough to ensure that clouds rolling down off the mountains could shroud it in minutes, but as well as that the vast bulk of water in the Great Basin somewhere below it created its own inversions. When it was almost full, as now, warm wet air rising from it met cool evening air from the mountains to make a sudden, short-lived layer of thick billowing mist that reduced visibility to an arm's length.

Or-Shls was watching him, looking half amused, half quizzical. Vess glanced away for a second, then shrugged to himself. Sometimes the simplest question was best.

'What happened?' he asked.

When the mist had come down Or-Shls had let his lenses slide away. Now he touched their runners and they flicked back. He blinked, then reached into the folds of his blouse and pulled out a thing like a round pebble with a spout. He put the spout in his mouth; there was a hissing noise, and then Or-Shls was blowing out a cloud of smoke that curled and melded with the mist. He did it again and then said, 'When?'

Vess felt a twitch of annoyance. He kept his voice level. 'I was in . . . one place. Now I'm here.'

Or-Shls shook his head. 'I'm surprised,' he said. 'Did it not occur to you that one of those places was not real?'

Vess stared at him for a moment. Then he felt his shoulders

drooping. 'Oh. I see. You are telling me that the – *chamber* was virtual?'

Or-Shls smiled. 'Are you recovered?'

'I suppose. If it was virtual, perhaps there was less to recover from than I thought.' He took a pace forward and stopped. Without looking at Or-Shls he said, 'But what happened?'

From behind him came the hissing, and the smell of the smoke jabbed at his palate.

Then Or-Shls said, 'You were implicated in an act of terrorism. Not by me, I should add. I don't know exactly how you came to be involved; you may have made enemies as well as friends while you were in the Hive. I can tell you that the act itself was mine.'

'You? Why?'

'A pretext. Everything is, in the end. I needed to take certain decisions quickly, and the process of Board approval was becoming obstructive.'

'Board approval? Oh . . .' Vess stared into the mist for a moment. 'So you have bypassed the Board?'

'Yes. A State of Emergency and immediate executive powers, a rational response to an act of terror and assassination.'

'So why was I put –' He hesitated. '– in that chamber?'

'It would have looked strange if you were not. I acted quickly, by the way – you were in there for only a few real minutes. It was not my desire to see you tortured to insanity, and given your considerable durability that would certainly have been your destination.'

The smell of smoke was making Vess feel sick. 'I see,' he said. 'Does that mean that the Board no longer wishes to kill me?'

There was a grating, wheezing rumble. For a moment Vess thought they had been joined by some strange animal, but then he realized that Or-Shls was laughing.

'Did Vut tell you that?'

'Yes.'

'Well, our friends Vut are no longer, um, extant, and you should treat anything they said with caution. The wishes of the Board are less relevant than they used to be.' He paused, and added in exactly the same tone of voice, 'Of course, that may change.'

Vess felt his lip twitching. He wanted very much to ask what had happened to Vut. Instead he said, 'Of course. What will happen now?'

'To you? Perhaps a medal. Perhaps death . . . I am not sure. Over the coming days you will be debriefed, and then we will see. There is a job you could do . . . Meanwhile there is someone I would like you to meet. Again, I should add. Ah – I think the mist is clearing.'

It was. It cleared downwards; as Vess watched the sky above him it shifted from a featureless, softly luminescent grey to a troubled skyscape of high-built clouds with patches of turquoise between them. The guard rails of the walkway extended themselves from a few metres to a curving sweep along the edge of the Deck. And below him – he shifted his feet uneasily.

Below him – a hundred metres directly below him, visible through the pierced metal floor of the walkway – the vast, almost overflowing ladle of the boat lift had slipped its catches and was dropping away from the Middle Basin.

The depth and the movement added to his faint sickness. He shook his head. 'You said there was someone you would like me to meet?'

'I did. Follow me, if you can?'

For a moment Vess didn't understand. Then he smiled. 'I may be surprised by heights, Chairman, but I'm not afraid of them.'

'Indeed not. Nor apparently of pain, but insects trouble you greatly. And, who knows, perhaps there are other things? Ah . . . here we are.'

Much of the walkway was over thin air. For those areas,

slender bridges spanned the distance to solid ground every fifty metres or so. They had arrived at one of them and Or-Shls turned along it and padded towards the Deck. Vess followed him, his feet alert for any sign of the other man's bulk troubling the walkway. There was none. Well built, then.

Then they were on the Deck, and Or-Shls gestured landward. 'Here you are.'

Vess followed the gesture. At first there was nothing to see. Patches of mist still hung between them and the low bulk of the main house, fifty metres or so away. Then he felt a slight breeze chase past him and the last of the mist dipped and curled away like smoke.

It took Vess a moment to process the sight. Then he felt his skin prickle.

There were two men, dressed in the drab uniforms of the Board Pickets. The bulges at their hips and shoulders told him they were fully armed, something he had rarely seen, but even more unusual was the fact that they seemed to be leading a child, who in turn was carrying something held out in front of her. He looked again and corrected himself; not held. The thing, which was about the size of the girl's head, was floating. And she wasn't being led; the Pickets' hands were clamped on her shoulders. And she was . . .

Vess's sickness had receded when they had left the walkway. Now it was back. He turned to Or-Shls. 'Why?'

The fat man shrugged. 'Call it a gesture. Or a legacy, if you like – a gift from me to you. One in which you were instrumental, as I'm sure you realize.'

Vess shook his head. He didn't trust himself to speak.

'Well, you were. You have been – still are – intensely monitored. You emerged from your first experience of the Mind Stack emotionally drained, with your body chemistry showing signs of major trauma, but you were alive, and that made you unique. So much so that our young friend over there was unwise enough to remark on it. That, plus your obvious attachment to her, suggested an idea.'

Our young friend. Vess was still not ready to face that. 'Go on,' he said.

'You survived whatever happened to you in the Stack. I believe Vut asked you about it, and you said nothing. Following your extraction from the Hive you still said nothing even under considerable pressure.'

'I still had nothing to say.'

'And I still don't believe you, which presents me with a choice. The easy option would have been to kill you.'

'But you haven't.'

'Evidently. Therefore I have chosen another path. As I said, I may have a job for you. And you seem to be avoiding a certain subject.'

There was nothing to say. From the corner of his vision Vess could see that the two guards and their captive were still walking towards them. It wasn't the subject he was avoiding, he knew. It was the sight. Or, more truly, the eyes.

For a second he thought he would turn away completely, for ever. The bridge back to the walkway was still close – if he sprinted he doubted Or-Shls could do anything about it. He imagined himself vaulting the guard rail, throwing himself well clear of any safety devices, and soaring down. His body would be found smeared over the floor of the empty Great Basin.

He let himself imagine it for a little longer. Then he sighed and turned the other way instead, to face the two Pickets and the girl between them. As he did so one of them pushed her forwards. She took a couple of steps and stopped, looking down. He saw her fingers tighten on the surface of the pod. Then she looked up at him.

'Hello,' she said.

He nodded. 'Hello, Dimollss.' Then he turned back to Or-Shls. 'Why?' he asked again.

The man shrugged. 'Why not?'

Vess said nothing. After a moment, Or-Shls grinned. 'Very well. To punish, to begin with. You, mainly. Physical pain seems not to bother you, but this obviously does. And, I think there's at least one thing that will bother you worse, but I'll tell you about that in a while.' So far he seemed hardly to have looked at the girl and her guards. Now he glanced at them and waved them away. 'Remove that, please. I'll tell you when it's wanted again.'

The Pickets reached for Dimollss's shoulders but she had already turned and was walking back towards the house. Vess watched until they had gone into the house. Then he looked at Or-Shls. 'Do you think that's going to make me more cooperative?'

The fat man laughed. 'More? You weren't cooperating at all in the first place. I wouldn't expect that to change. No, Vess, I've thought of something much better: alignment of interests. You didn't survive as long as you have without understanding that. Come along.'

Or-Shls's main house was curved nearly into a semicircle. The outside of the curve faced the grounds and the walkway; the inner formed one end of an enclosed garden that Vess assumed extended to the boundary of the estate. Assumed, because the boundary was hidden by trees: copses of conifers and palms and broad-leafs and a few strange-looking things that seemed to be upside-down – tall fronded stems with multiple root-struts reaching out sideways and then angling sharply into the ground.

Vess had heard about the place, although he had never visited it. Had never wanted to, if he was honest. People of his rank who arrived here tended to do so on terms that weren't theirs to write.

And here he was. Somewhere, a part of him was angry. More than angry – but he knew how to keep it separate, like a lunatic in a locked room. He turned to Or-Shls. 'Are we expecting any-one else?'

'Yes. Do you like my trees?'

'Not really.'

'Well done. Do you know, sometimes I am almost inclined to trust you? Over here, in the Pump Trees.'

From outside the copse looked impenetrable. Inside, it was hollow – a ring of dense woodland with a circle of stone seats in the clearing at its centre.

Or-Shls waved him towards a seat, but Vess didn't move. Or-Shls shrugged and took a place at the opposite end of the circle, giving a *fuff* of expelled breath as he sat. 'Right,' he said. 'Just one to go.' He paused and looked around. 'Gamer? Are you with us?'

There was a quick rustle from overhead. Vess looked up in time to see something flicker across the tree canopy, and then Clo Fiffithiss dropped into the clearing, landing in a ball of legs and immediately popping itself upright.

'Good. Let's begin. This is the securest space on the planet, so we have a certain freedom here. Vess, we're going on the offensive, against the external forces who are strangling us.'

Vess laughed. 'You can't! They stole all the legacy ships, remember? You have nothing to offend with.'

'In the first place, why do you think I can't steal them back? And in the second, who said I was only going to use our own ships?'

Something about the tone calmed Vess, but it was a chilly calm. He looked down at Clo Fiffithiss. 'You know something about this, I assume?'

'I know all about it.' The tone was deadpan. 'No one else does.'

'And I don't, yet. Before you tell me that, tell me something else. Why should I have a role? Because you've got me here for a reason. Alignment of interests – what interests?'

Clo Fiffithiss said nothing. Or-Shls reached up and touched something behind his ear. The lenses slid round and clicked into place in front of his eyes. In the dim light of the copse Vess saw pinpoints of light flicking over their surfaces; Or-Shls seemed to focus on them for a moment. Then he nodded and the lenses slipped away again. 'What do you know about our friends Vut?'

Vess shrugged. 'You said they are not extant.'

'Apart from that.'

Vess shook his head.

'Nothing, I take that to mean. Very well. A biology lesson. Gamer, if you will?'

Clo Fiffithiss hadn't moved from its upright position. Now it spread its lower limbs and dropped into a crouch, its body suspended in a cradle of legs. It was a position Vess had never seen before; it was at the same time the most relaxed and the most dangerous he had ever seen the Gamer adopt.

He shivered.

Clo Fiffithiss was quite still for a second. Then it was gone. There was no sound this time. *Have you ever Hunted,* thought Vess.

He had time to draw five breaths before it was back. One of its forelimbs was off the ground, and there was something at the end of it – a tiny bundle of something. Or-Shls reached down and took a fist-sized container out from under his seat. 'In here, please.'

Clo Fiffithiss dropped the little thing into the container. Or-Shls clapped a lid on to it and shook it. Then he flicked his lenses round and glared at it for a few seconds. 'Suitably dead, I think,' he said. 'Catch.'

He threw the container across the clearing. Vess caught it awkwardly. 'What is it?'

'Vut's ancestor, courtesy of the Gamer. They live wild in this copse. Take a look.'

The light was poor. Vess raised the container and held it close to his face. Then he froze.

He had never seen one of Vut's components close up but this was like, and unlike, what he would have imagined – a body that looked stubby at first, until you realized that it was actually a short, slim form bulked out by layered bristles which partly hid six three-jointed legs. He assumed the bristles pointed towards the back; if that was right then there was something at the front that looked a bit more complicated than a mouth. It looked almost like a miniature flower with petals wrapped in a tight spiral. It was smaller than the Vut equivalent – he could have fitted several on the palm of his hand.

He threw the container back to Or-Shls. 'So what?'

'It has an interesting life cycle. Stage one is a grub. Stage two is what you see here. Stage three I can best show you as an image. A moment . . .'

Or-Shls reached under his seat again and brought out a small holo lamp. He tossed it into the middle of the circle. It landed, righted itself and pointed a narrow thread of light upwards. The light spread into a screen.

It was showing a translucent scan of a human torso, with the flesh as a ghostly pink strung over white bones. The organs were darker shades of red, and the heart, frozen mid-beat, was almost purple.

Vess looked from the image to Or-Shls. 'I don't understand.'

'Look closely. Start at the base of the spine.' The voice was quiet.

Vess shrugged and turned back to the image.

There was something – he leaned in closer. Then his stomach jumped.

There was a dark lump just to the left of the base of the spine. From it, a sinuous thread, almost black, twined up the spinal column almost as far as the neck. Every few centimetres it branched, throwing out lateral threads that curled around the ribs like a climbing plant. Each of the threads ended in something maybe a centimetre long, if the scale was right, but far slimmer.

The lump would be a bit bigger than the insect-thing in the jar.

He felt the blood drain from his face.

Or-Shls spoke in the same quiet voice. 'It's elegant, isn't it? The Stage Two form burrows into a host. It secretes an anaesthetic – the host doesn't feel a thing. Then it grows that rather beautiful structure. The long threads are called the tap-root and the things at the end of it are grubs, obviously. At maturity the original invader dies and decomposes. The flesh around it becomes infected with pus, of course, which sends a chemical signal up the tap-root to activate the grubs. They tear themselves loose from the tap-root and eat their way out of the host.' He paused. 'The bit from the decomposition onwards isn't painless, of course. Rather the opposite. From invasion to decomposition takes an unpredictable length of time – anywhere between five and around fifty days. It was once used as a form of torture. Infect someone, then promise them the infection would be removed if they were cooperative.'

Vess felt his gorge rising. He swallowed. 'Did it work?'

'Sometimes. The only problem is that with the original, you can't remove the thing without killing the host, so they all died anyway.' Or-Shls stared at nothing for a while. 'Cruel times, Vess. Cruel times.'

The urge to throw up was stronger now. Vess stared at the image. The quality was excellent; he could see a fine, irregular line zigzagging across one of the ribs low down on the right-hand side. His hand went reflexively to his own side and he swallowed. 'When I was eight, someone hit . . .' he began, and then started again. 'When I was eight I broke a rib.'

'Yes. And there it is.' Or-Shls waved at the image. 'You're

right; that's you. I should probably have said at the start. And, obviously, the rest is a gift from our friends Vut.'

Vess threw up.

He spent most of the next couple of days walking in the forested parts of Or-Shls's estate. Often he was alone – or felt himself alone; there was no way of being sure – but sometimes he took Clo Fiffithiss with him. The being was perfectly adapted to the trees. Occasionally, often without explanation, it would disappear for anything from a few seconds to a few minutes and then flit back to pick up the conversation as if nothing had happened. Once or twice Vess thought there were traces of blood, or fur, around its mandibles. He realized he had never asked what the being ate.

It fascinated Vess. It also helped to distract him.

They had to sedate him in the end. He had no recollection of anything after he had been told of his – infection; but Clo Fiffithiss told him he had needed to be forcibly prevented from trying to kill himself by lowering his head and charging full speed at a tree. A guard had intervened, and then two, and eventually four. Vess wasn't sure if he was grateful.

He had come round to find himself lying on a couch in the middle of a fat white toroid that buzzed. He had tried to shake his head, but found it was immovable. He was strapped down.

Over the buzz he heard a thin-sounding voice. 'Awake? Try not to move.'

The straps just about allowed him to expand his chest. He took a breath and asked, 'Will this kill it?'

'The infection? No. We can slow its progression, though, if you will keep still long enough for me to complete the scan.'

Vess fought the urge to struggle. Slow? Not good enough. Kill; he wanted this thing killed. 'Can you operate? Take it out?'

'No. I can't do anything if you don't keep still. Be quiet and do as you're told.'

He managed, just.

Half an hour later he was off the couch and looking at the small elderly simian-looking owner of the voice. It had a testy expression.

'Do you know when you were infected?'

He thought back to his summons from Vut. 'Nine days, I think.'

The medic nodded. 'Consistent with growth. Fortunate.'

'*Fortunate*? How?'

'The larvae are approaching maturity. Also, vascular changes in the source suggest it is approaching end-of-life.'

Vess stared at the creature. He could feel his pulse clicking in his toes. 'End? When it dies . . .' He tailed off.

'No.' The shake of the head was emphatic. 'Not when. If.'

'There isn't an if. Or-Shls told me.'

'The Chairman of the Board knows many things, but not this thing.' The doc grinned, showing a lot of yellow teeth. 'My role is to preserve life. Its, and thereby, yours. Please be good enough to lie down and turn over.'

It was an old-fashioned hypodermic injection. It hurt, very much. Vess welcomed the pain – it meant something was happening.

Then it stopped. He rolled over. 'Is that it?'

'For today. To repeat, every day. You will probably need an assistant.'

He tried to reach round to the injection site, and felt his arm cramp. 'Every day?'

'Injections for five days, and close monitoring. If that goes well, if the infection is stabilized, then other treatment to maintain the position.'

'Maintain? For how long?'

'For as long as it works. Do not be deceived; you are not

258

immortal, and nor is it. Meanwhile I suggest you go and find the entity that infected you.'

Vess sat up sharply. 'Why?'

'It had its reasons for doing this. If I were you I would want to know them. And besides, it is probably the only creature in the Spin that can undo what it has done.'

The word *undo* buzzed round Vess's head. He let it, for a moment. Then he looked up at the medic. 'Why would it undo this? That's how it reproduces.'

The doc grinned again, wider. It wasn't all teeth; at the margins there were pale shrunken gums. Vess tried not to look away. 'No, infected former Harbour Master. You have been extrapolating from the thoughts of Chairman Or-Shls. That's how their *ancestors* reproduced. Vut are more modern; their reproduction would happen in nice clean tanks of nutrient. Doing things the old way is done for other reasons. I think they want to be asked what reasons. And perhaps if you ask nicely, there will be a prize.'

You will be watched, more closely than you can imagine, he thought. And then his unbidden mind added a coda – watched, or watched *through*?

He thought for a long time. Then he looked up at the medic again. 'Somehow I think it wants to be kept alive,' he said. 'Do the best you can?'

The grin had gone. The little creature gave a serious-looking nod. 'Perhaps,' it said. 'Taking the simple view, alive for it equals alive for you. Why not be simple?'

Because simple is too complicated, thought Vess. *I'm missing something, but I don't think I'm missing much. I don't think.*

Out loud he said, 'Yes, simple is good. Keep it alive.'

He never got used to the injections – they were exactly as painful, every single time.

Fortunately the pain was transient. After a few minutes it

subsided to a hot, stabbing throb that was merely unbearable until Clo Fiffithiss showed him the broad leaves of a particular tree.

He had looked doubtfully at them. 'Really?'

'Really and truly.' The creature performed a sort of insectile shrug. 'They are strongly analgesic and mildly stimulant for your kind.'

Vess pinched a corner of the big flat dark-green leaf between finger and thumb. 'What do they do to your kind?'

'Very different chemistry. Hunting herbs.' The reply was short; it didn't invite elaboration.

Vess lifted the leaf to his lips and chewed a corner. The taste was neither pleasant nor unpleasant – at once a little bitter and quite spicy. It made his palate tingle. Then the tingle faded, and with it so did the pain in his back. He rubbed himself cautiously, then smiled at Clo Fiffithiss. 'It works!'

'Of course it works. I know these forests like the back of my claw. Now you are uncrippled, shall we walk?'

Vess walked. Clo Fiffithiss split its time between its own multi-jointed version of a walk, and hauling itself through the tree canopies where they dipped close to the ground. For a while, neither of them spoke. Then Clo Fiffithiss dropped out of the branches and landed upright in front of Vess.

Vess stopped abruptly, almost tripping. 'What?'

'Vess, we have known each other for a long time and I have never seen you angry.'

Vess nodded. 'That's probably correct.'

'Not *probably*. It *is* correct, and I have always explained it to myself successfully by referring to your natural calmness and confidence. But I *still* don't see you angry, and under the present circumstances I cannot explain that to myself by any means.'

Vess looked around, found a fallen trunk at around knee height and lowered himself down on to it. 'Perhaps it's inexplicable.'

'Nonsense. What's going on?'

'With me? Only what you can see. I am walking – sitting – in the agreeable woods of the private estate of the Chairman of the Board, in the company of one of his employees. What else can there possibly be to see or hear?'

He let himself emphasize *see* and *hear*, just a little.

Clo Fiffithiss was quite still for a long moment. Then it made a complicated gesture with three claws. It was the equivalent of a conspiratorial grin. They walked on in silence, and kept it up.

On the fifth day Or-Shls threw a party.

Vess had been cleared by the medic that afternoon, after another run through the scanner.

He had tried not to be nervous, but the journey through the machine had seemed to take a long time. Eventually it was over and he was standing, staring at the image. As far as he could remember it looked the same. He turned to the medic. 'So?'

'So, your passenger is in rude health.' The little creature gave an elaborate shrug that made it seem as if it consisted entirely of shoulders and elbows. 'That is, it is physically healthy and in no immediate danger of dying. Intellectually it is probably senile at best, and brain-damaged at worst, but that should not concern you.'

'It isn't a passenger.' Vess stretched, trying not to focus on the sensations in his back in case he noticed something. He failed, but there seemed to be nothing to notice. 'What treatment should I have now?'

The medic reached round to a table behind it and brought out a package. 'Have you used a hypo jet before?'

Vess shook his head.

'It's not difficult but you would probably benefit from someone to help. It needs to be applied to the base of the spine – it is a continuation dose of the compound I have been injecting directly into the creature. Every day, Harbour Master, and don't forget, and don't miss.'

He had carried the warning back to the forest, where he had increasingly lived for the past few days – apart from his daily walks with Clo Fiffithiss, it was warm enough to sleep outdoors, and he preferred that to spending time in Or-Shls's house. But when he got back to the forest he found most of Or-Shls's household there before him.

The clearing he had seen first had been seamlessly expanded. Where there had been room for a tight circle of stone benches, there was now a wide glade. There were no signs of tree stumps; whatever work had been done, had been done very fast and had left no traces. Vess allowed himself to be impressed.

It was early evening; lights glowed along the branches above him, and the air smelled of sunset and hot food.

Or-Shls stood as if he had been ready to greet him, arms spread. 'Harbour Master! Welcome – although with your recent residence in these woods perhaps you should be welcoming me?'

Vess looked round. A lot of people were carefully not watching him. He let himself smile a little. 'Chairman, if I should – then you are welcome.' Then he looked round more ostentatiously. 'But it seems that you have numbers on your side when it comes to welcoming. What is the occasion?'

Or-Shls managed to spread his arms further. 'Do I need one? Apart from your good health, which has been reported to me.'

Vess said nothing, but kept his eyes on the other man's face. The deeply buried eyes gave nothing away, but after a few seconds the fat lips twisted into a smile. 'Very well. Later we will talk of things. Including alignment of interests, if you remember that phrase? But for the moment let us enjoy ourselves. You have been in – or near – my house for some days now, but you haven't yet enjoyed even a tenth of its advantages. Enjoy them now.'

Or-Shls made a complicated gesture, and the ground fell away beneath them. Seconds later they were surrounded by the night sky of Basin City. Warm air rose from the city below and made brief damp banks of mist at the edges of the circle. They didn't seem very far away.

Vess looked round. The limits of his world were a hundred metres from him, an edge half hidden in the trees.

'Right,' he said. 'So, when do we bring on the dancing girls?'

They were on a platform, lowered from the floating continent that was Or-Shls's domain. There were indeed dancing girls. And boys – although at first they weren't dancing. Most of them were only lightly clothed and the rest were naked. They waited in a loose group amongst the trees at the margin of the clearing, their hips poised and their eyes glistening. Vess thought they looked a little like snakes. Or-Shls seemed proud of them.

'Look, Vess! Unadulterated beauty and unlimited availability; what more can you ask? Come here!' He raised a hand and four of the dancers broke away from the group and walked towards him. The two females had broad hips and rounded bellies; the males were typically thick-chested elongated triangles. Vess assumed they represented his host's taste.

Or-Shls grinned. 'This is Vess. He is famously reticent. See if you can rouse him from his torpor.'

The four exchanged smirking glances and began to walk slowly towards Vess. He held out both hands, palms outwards. 'No.'

The group looked nonplussed. Or-Shls spread his arms. 'Just no? Not even an attempt?'

Vess turned away from the four. They were close enough for him to catch the scent of their bodies – perfumed oils overlying basic musk. 'I don't need any attempt. Let them dance, if they like.'

'Oh, very well.' Or-Shls waved the four away. 'Go and dance, children, or find someone who wants you to do more than dance.'

They obeyed, grumbling a little, and Vess noticed that they managed to do even that prettily. When they were gone he turned to Or-Shls. 'Well?'

'Well, indeed.' The big man sighed. 'Vess, I attempt fun very rarely and this time you have impeded me. I suppose you now expect me to be serious?'

Vess smiled. 'You can be serious, Chairman, or you can be flippant. But if you don't do something to explain why I am here and what you expect to happen next, you can,' he paused and gathered emphasis, '*fuck* off.'

Or-Shls raised his eyebrows. 'Serious *and* offensive? I am astonished – but not surprised. Very well, Harbour Master. We shall be serious, but you will forgive me if we are serious to music? That at least I demand of you.'

The music was ethereal, a distant whimpering that swelled and faded like a restless wind. Something about it set Vess's teeth on edge.

Or-Shls seemed to enjoy it. He listened for a while, his head tilted back, eyes half closed. After a while he shook his head, and smiled at Vess. 'Do you know the Algonet?'

Vess shook his head.

'Such beauty, and sweetened by such cost.' His gaze hardened. 'But you're getting impatient. Very well. I am about to share something with you. Share it in turn and you will die as many elaborate deaths as technology can arrange. Understand?'

Vess thought. Then he shook his head again. 'The Gamer,' he said. 'I want to share this with Clo Fiffithiss. I assume you trust him?'

Or-Shls's eyes glinted. 'No I don't, for the same reasons I don't trust you. But I sense you are hardening your position.' He raised his voice. 'Gamer?'

It was a summons. A moment later there was a rustling beside Vess, and Clo Fiffithiss was next to him.

Or-Shls gave a tight smile. 'Never far away, I see. Right. Field down, please.'

Vess looked around for whoever the man had spoken to, but couldn't see anyone. Then he jumped.

The rest of the platform had vanished. A couple of metres outside the stone seat, it ended in a hissing, greyish, wetly luminescent wall which steamed where it met the ground. Vess looked up. The wall curved in to form a dome two metres above him.

He raised his eyebrows at Or-Shls. 'Field?'

'In a way. Superheated steam held in a charged magnetic matrix. So they tell me. Don't touch it.'

'I won't. What are you going to tell me?'

Or-Shls leaned forward. 'Alignment of interests. The medic tells me that you need to find Vut?'

'That's what he said.'

'So do I.'

'Why don't you go and look for them, then?'

'I have. It didn't work. I don't think they want to be found by me. I think they want to be found by you.'

Vess shook his head. 'Cryptic isn't helping, Chairman.'

'I expect not. Do you remember this?'

A patch of air in front of him fuzzed and became a star field. For a moment it looked unfamiliar, but then Vess's mind caught up – there was the ragged curve of debris he had been shown in the Lay Palace.

'Yes,' he said. 'So? That's none of my business. I remember.'

'It might turn out to be everyone's business. I intend to make it mine. Have you heard of a planet called Traspise?'

Vess searched his memory. 'Faintly. What about it?'

'It was destroyed ten thousand years ago; the first planetary total loss in a million years.'

'What destroyed it?'

'Exactly.' Or-Shls sat back. 'Something. Something that was found by someone; some ancient machine.'

Vess shrugged. 'Tech levels were higher then. Perhaps they had all kinds of machines for destroying planets.'

'Did they have machines for making them?'

There was silence. Vess stared at the image for a long time. 'I get it,' he said eventually. 'You think it's the same thing.'

'It might be. Or another of the same kind. And if it was, wouldn't we want it?'

Vess laughed out loud. 'To do what? Blow up a planet? Or make an arc of radioactive debris?'

Or-Shls shook his head. 'No, Vess. To wait, while people incentivize us to do neither.'

'You're insane.' *Or I am,* he added to himself. *This is another virtual reality; in a moment I'm going to wake up in a torture chamber.*

But he didn't. Instead he watched Or-Shls. After a while the man re-settled himself on the bench, sucked on the pipe and spoke through a cloud of vapour.

'Things have changed since the image you saw was taken. Look.'

Vess leaned forward. 'This image was taken from a different direction from the last one.'

'Correct, Harbour Master. And not by us.'

Vess looked up sharply. 'By someone Outside?'

'Far Outside, yes. Clo Fiffithiss?'

The creature unfolded itself. 'Images can be analysed . . . this one was captured by something within a quarter of a million kilometres of the debris curve, closing at speed.' It paused, and added, 'Substantial speed. The sort that can be attained by a Main Battle Unit, for example.'

'Oh.' Vess looked at Clo-Fiffithiss, and then at Or-Shls. 'Our stolen *Sunskimmer*?'

Or-Shls smiled.

'You know where they are?' Vess felt his eyebrows climbing.

'I always knew that, Vess. Now I know something more

interesting; I know where they were going. I think our friends Vut know too.'

Light began to dawn. Vess nodded slowly. 'No longer extant,' he said.

Or-Shls looked down again and spoke towards the ground. 'We have had a certain level of contact with those in Web City. Nothing detailed, just an understanding of their direction of travel. It was never enough for us to influence their actions more than a little but at least we had some foresight. Now that has been cut off without warning. There is a suggestion that there may have been an abrupt change of leadership.'

'A coup, in other words?'

'In other words, yes.'

Vess looked from Or-Shls to Clo-Fiffithiss. 'What difference does that make to us?'

'You are being obtuse. To where we were, not much. To where we may go, perhaps a great deal.' He pursed his lips. 'A planetary-scale arc of rubble appears, followed by a new green star, and then the nearest civilization breaks the habit of half a thousand years and stops talking to us, possibly as a result of a coup? I'm no Gamer, Harbour Master, but I suggest this has significance.'

Something had been bothering Vess; now he had it. 'Chairman? You've been talking a great deal about "I". Are the rest of the Board with you?'

Or-Shls looked at him for a long time. Then he smiled. 'If I were you I'd go and find Vut, who has gone there and who seems to want so badly to be found by you – and who seems to have stolen a ship and gone hunting.'

'Just that? Chase Vut across space?' Vess shook his head. 'With respect, it seems an odd choice of priorities.'

'It may do, but it isn't. You need to understand something, ex-Harbour Master. You are tainted by failure. I can make no use of you here. Finding Vut could be useful; making fresh contact with whoever is now in charge out there could be even more so.'

Vess laughed. 'So that's it. I'm to be an emissary? Really, Chairman?'

Or-Shls slapped a hand down on his knee; it was the first gesture of irritation Vess had ever seen him make. 'Why not? You are – were – *just* senior enough, and after all, the attributes of a spy and a diplomat are basically identical. At the very least, you might save your own life. At best, you might save all of us. Field up.' The grey walls vanished, leaving a curtain of steam. Or-Shls stood up, nodded and walked off, waving the steam aside. It parted into wisps, and a current of hot wet air brushed Vess's cheek and then dispersed.

Vess turned to Clo Fiffithiss. 'What's going on?'

The creature froze for a moment, then made a complicated knot out of two forelimbs. Vess raised his eyebrows; as far as he could remember the gesture meant something very like 'shh – not here'. He nodded.

'Shall we rejoin the party?'

'By all means.' Clo Fiffithiss made a show of looking around. 'Do you think he will have laid on any entertainment for me?'

Vess shook his head. 'Would you have liked some?'

'No, but the thought would have been appreciated. Will you be indulging?'

'No.'

'Good. If you had said yes I would have thought you were an impostor. If it helps, you might like to know that our host won't be indulging either.'

Vess raised an eyebrow.

'Not at first hand.' A quick blur of a foreclaw. 'He's strictly an observer.'

'Did he know you were going to tell me that as well?'

'I doubt it.' The same gesture. 'He doesn't know I know.'

'Well, well.' Vess walked on.

That Or-Shls was a voyeur didn't surprise him. That the Gamer knew about it surprised him a little.

But he had worked out the gesture. It was a sly grin. That the creature thought it was funny made him – thoughtful.

Cloud Deck

At its noisy peak the circle of the party had expanded almost to the misty limits of the clearing, and then gradually collapsed as people left or paired up or gathered into trios or quads or whatever groupings pleased them best.

Vess had been sitting on a flat rock about halfway between the stone circle and the edge of the platform. He had spent some of his time people-watching, and all the rest of it thinking. No one had spoken to him, either because they had been told not to or because he wasn't – important.

He sat on his anger. Either reason suited him perfectly.

Clo Fiffithiss hadn't volunteered anything else. It had excused itself some time before, and Vess had been vaguely aware of it rustling through the trees just out of sight. He assumed it had been making its own entertainment.

Now it was back, and Vess found himself blinking at it. He realized it was getting light; the creature appeared less as a silhouette and more as a grey shape. He stood up and pressed his hands into his back. 'I'm tired,' he said. 'Shall we walk?'

'Of course.'

Vess headed for the edge of the clearing and Clo Fiffithiss followed him. In the dim light noises were important; the creature sounded like some tiny mammal pattering across dry stalks.

That's what it's supposed to sound like, thought Vess. *Why aren't I afraid?*

Because fear has limits. I've reached them.

They were almost at the edge of the lowered platform. The trees thinned out, and then there was just a band of grass ten paces across, and a waist-high fence of interwoven thorn-stems.

Vess walked up to it and peered over. It really was the only barrier – the clouds had thinned with the dawn, and he could see straight down to the Great Basin, three hundred metres below.

He smiled at Clo Fiffithiss, which had settled itself on the fence next to him. 'So Or-Shls has a plan.'

'Hundreds, I should think. So?'

Vess watched the creature for a moment. 'Where are you in all this?'

The gesture was definitely laughter. 'On the side of the numbers. Where do you think?'

'I think you can't game an individual.'

'And I think those aren't the only numbers.'

Vess nodded. 'How do we get away from here?'

'Well, we ask Or-Shls. I expect he's waiting for the question.'

Vess shook his head. 'That feels like sticking my neck into the blades.'

'Have you another idea?'

'Yes, I have.' He brushed a hand over the surface of the fence – it was far too prickly for anything firmer – and lifted it. 'I seem to remember a conversation where you described you and me as being dull middle-managers. Would you describe yourself as risk-averse, Gamer?'

'Obviously. Why?'

'Good. I hope you'll forgive me if I put that to the test.'

And Vess brought the hand round, fast. It connected with the body in the centre of the mass of legs, and Clo Fiffithiss was gone, tumbling over the edge like a ball of—

No, *not* like a ball. Within seconds it had spread itself into a flat, fluttering net of claws and legs that slanted down on a course that looked thoroughly steered, away from the platform and the Basin below it.

Vess squinted along the course and nodded. A dot became a circle, became a small, stubbily streamlined atmosphere craft that tipped to a stop at the end of a neat jet-stream, just below the falling Gamer, and extended a shallow net. Clo Fiffithiss dropped into it.

A minute later the craft was next to the edge of the platform with the net at eye level. Clo Fiffithiss lifted itself from the net and extended a claw towards Vess. Its translator made a busy staccato rattle like falling pebbles; it fiddled with something and the pebbles became a voice.

'Vess? You are an utter cunt.' It paused. 'Would you believe, that's actually worse in my language than it is in yours?'

Vess shrugged. 'You said you were risk-averse.'

'I did. I'm even more so now. Why did you do that?'

'I want to leave, and I don't want to do it in something owned by Or-Shls. I've had enough of being a puppet.'

'For goodness' sake, human – you could have just *asked*. How did you know I'd come back, anyway?'

'I assumed you'd want to swear at me.'

Clo Fiffithiss watched him for a moment. Then it gave an insectile shrug, shuffled itself round in the net and tapped a quick rhythm on the top of the craft, which popped open and floated a little higher so the edge of one fat wing covered the fence. Vess climbed on and dropped into the compartment. Clo Fiffithiss swung itself in beside him.

The net stowed itself. The top flipped over and sealed with a sucking noise, and the craft scooted away from the platform.

From inside, the top was transparent. Vess watched the Cloud Deck receding.

He hadn't been sure Clo Fiffithiss would come back. That gave him one less thing to wonder about.

He realized that the being was watching him. 'Now that you're away,' it said, 'where do you want to go?'

Vess smiled. 'The Hive.'

Clo Fiffithiss made an untranslatable noise. Its limbs flickered over the control surfaces and the little craft came to a dead stop. Then it turned towards him.

'Have you lost your mind, human?'

'I don't think so.'

'But *why*?'

'How many reasons would you like? Because I don't want to support Or-Shls; because I don't *trust* Or-Shls. Because I don't believe Vut does want to see me.' *And because I don't trust you either*, he thought.

'But why the Hive, for goodness' sake?'

Vess said nothing.

Clo Fiffithiss watched him for a while. Then it sighed. 'I'll have to tell Or-Shls. This can't happen without his say-so. And, you ought to know, this is going to do me no good at all.'

'Why? Am I not as you predicted?'

'No.' It reached out a limb towards the controls. 'I'll just have to hope that Or-Shls is not as I predicted either.'

Vess looked away. He was hoping beyond hope that his desperate guess was right.

Solpht ('Archive') Observatory

Seldyan woke with a memory of movement. She eased her shoulders and felt them press into something soft and yielding that didn't feel like ground. She opened her eyes and found herself looking up at a blackened timber roof, with a complicated-looking network of ropes and levers hanging from it, and two lamps with smoky yellow flames. There was some sort of table next to her with a tall stool. A little carved thing, like a faceted globe, sat on one edge of the table.

She sat up.

Her head wasn't spinning – that was progress – and her foot didn't hurt. She looked down the length of her body. Someone had cut off her trousers just above the knee and everything below that seemed to be wrapped in dry leaves. They had a faintly astringent scent which felt good on her palate as she took a breath.

'Hello?'

There were footsteps behind her. She turned round and saw Belbis taking something off his head – a strip of fabric? He raised his eyebrows.

'Sitting up. Very good. Pain?'

'No. No pain. Did you do that?' She gestured at the leaves.

'Yes. Clean, healing. Also boil in water, drink. Heal inwards.'

Seldyan smiled at the phrase. 'Thank you,' she said. 'It works. I feel – healed inwards.'

'Good. Equal now for a while.'

She nodded. Then she frowned. 'Why for a while?'

His face was serious. 'We are here – Observatory. You came to stop the light, yes? Time now.'

'Ah.' She stood up. 'This is where the light comes from?'

He nodded.

'Okay. You'd better show me.'

He reached up and took one of the oil lamps, and she followed the yellow light through a maze of rooms and then down – narrow timber steps at first, then wider stairs cut into rock. At the bottom of the flight Seldyan stopped and crouched down, touching the cold surface. 'This feels very even . . .' She reached for her pouch and took out the stunner, surprised first that it was still there, and then that it still worked, at least as far as lighting up was concerned.

The light gleamed off a dead-flat, almost polished surface. The walls of the corridor they were in looked the same. Every now and then there was an alcove with a carved globe, like the one she had seen on the table.

She nodded to herself and stood up. 'Belbis? No disrespect, but your people didn't make this.'

'No. Very old. Here.' He was holding out a strip of cloth.

'What?'

'Bind eyes. No more steps. There is a chamber soon, where the light comes.' He gestured along the corridor to a plain door at the end.

'Oh.' She took the cloth and made a couple of turns of it round her head, tying it awkwardly behind her. She couldn't see any light through it. 'Will this do?'

She felt investigating fingers. They were cool on her skin. They smelled dusty.

'Yes. Now me.' There was a rustling. 'Ready? Keep eyes shut too.'

'Wait!' She reached out and managed to catch hold of his clothes. 'How do you know this is safe?'

'Already tried. While you sleep?' She heard humour in his voice. 'Three days sleep. My leaves are slower than your tricks.'

'You came here?'

'Yes. My job to do. The Housekeepers – still there.'

'Oh.' She remembered: he had told her about the old men who had stayed. A part of her wanted to ask him what he had done with them, but she held back and patted him instead. 'That was good.'

'My job. Now, ready? Then follow.'

She let go of him and followed his footsteps down the corridor, one hand brushing the walls to keep her straight. The corridor was short – after twenty paces his noises stopped so she did too.

There were other noises. Somewhere in front of her there was a keening hiss, like rain sawing through something. The air smelled slightly burned. She shuddered.

Then there was the sound of a latch and the hiss grew much louder, and someone said:

'Warning. Do not enter. Danger to life.'

Some*thing*, thought Seldyan. The voice was obviously artificial. Out loud she said, 'Did that happen when you came before?'

'Yes. Same voice that warned, when I first came.'

Automatics, thought Seldyan. Let's see how smart they are. She thought for a moment. 'Entering. Cease dangerous activity.'

'Do not enter.'

It had responded, to some extent. She tapped a finger on the corridor wall, and tried again. 'Define danger.'

'Collimated high-energy electromagnetic radiation beam. Do not enter.'

Definitely a conversation. The next question was worth trying. 'State purpose of beam.'

'Containment status-change alert. State the purpose of your questions.'

Alarm bells rang in Seldyan's mind. She thought quickly. 'To gain information.'

'That is applicable to all questions. You are unauthorized. Leave.'

Seldyan turned to where she thought Belbis was. 'Shut the door. It's time to go. Come on.'

She waited until she heard the click behind her, and then breathed out. 'Whoa. Did that happen to you?'

'Only the warning. I asked no questions.'

'You were sensible. Let's go.' She turned and was about to feel her way back the way they had come. Then she snorted, reached up and pulled off the improvised blindfold.

And stood still.

She had thought she was facing back up the corridor, but she had been wrong. She was facing the wall of the corridor, and it was not blank. There were letters embossed in the metal. She reached out a hand and traced the pattern. Without looking away she said, 'Belbis? Did you see this?'

She heard the sound of cloth sliding over itself as he took off his own blindfold. Then he was next to her, peering at the wall. He shrugged. 'I saw. No meaning.'

'To you, maybe. But there is to me.' She tapped the letters. 'Level Two. You know what that means? There's a Level One somewhere. Maybe a Level Nought. How well do you know this place?'

'The wooden place up above, every room. Down here, just this. The Housekeepers showed me.'

She nodded. 'Yeah, the Housekeepers. They can't show us now.' She thought for a moment. Then she felt a slow smile widening her face. 'Where did the Housekeepers live?'

He frowned. 'Private place.'

'Sure. Do you want to ask their permission or shall I?'

He was quiet for a while. Then he lowered his eyes. 'Follow.'

She followed the man, and the ball of light round his lamp, back up the stairs and out of the metal corridors and through a twisting wooden world that felt utterly unnavigable to her, but was probably just like anywhere else to someone who had never seen.

The Housekeepers seemed not to have needed much. There were three thin pallets on the floor, and beside each pallet a bowl with a crude spoon in it.

There were no windows and no lights. Seldyan gestured to Belbis to pass her the lamp, and knelt by one of the pallets. She frowned. 'Belbis? How many days since you left here?'

He looked at his fingers. 'I think, more than fifty.'

'Yeah, that's what I thought. And those guys were called the Housekeepers, and they're gone. So why is nothing dusty?' She wiped a finger over the inside of the nearest bowl. The surface felt slickly clean.

He shrugged.

Seldyan gave the bowl a gentle thump. It clunked. Then she stood up. 'I've got an idea.' She paused, then clapped her hands. 'Service! Whatever you are. Show yourself!'

For several breaths nothing happened, and she got ready to look embarrassed. Then she and Belbis both jumped.

There was a quiet pop and the lights came on. They were very bright after the lamplight and Seldyan shut her eyes for a few seconds to let them adapt. When she opened them she had company – there was something floating a metre or so from her at around her eye level.

It was one of the little carved globe things. She nodded. 'That makes sense. How many of you are there?'

'Just one.' The voice was high and reedy.

'One? But I've seen lots . . . Oh. All you?'

'Yes. I can move fast. The AI says you've been asking questions.'

'I was. It didn't answer.'

'It's not very imaginative. Your speech patterns say you're not from this planet. Where are you from?'

She was about to say 'the Hive', but thought better of it. 'The Inside.'

'Not recognized. Where is that, relative to the Spin?'

'Right in the middle. Maybe you're out of date.' She thought about that for a moment. 'How long have you been here?'

'Eleven thousand, four hundred and seventeen years, local. Ten thousand and eight, standard.'

She sucked in a breath and blew it out in a soft whistle. 'Seriously? Have you been isolated all that time?'

'Yes.'

'Why?'

The little machine floated in front of her wordlessly for several seconds. It was completely silent, she realized; she could hear Belbis breathing. She wondered how he was taking all this.

Then the machine gave a little side-to-side waggle. 'I have conferred with the AI. We assume that this facility is unknown to you. Has it been forgotten completely?'

The ship didn't seem to have known, she realized. Nor had any of the others, including Patras. 'Probably yes.'

'But you are here. Why?'

She laughed. 'You lit up a whole planet bright green. It's a bit obvious.'

'So it will be obvious to others.' There was another silence. Then the thing spoke, and its voice sounded different.

'I am the Avatar of the Archive, which was established to confine, to protect and, if necessary, to warn. You have responded to a warning, but it is clear that you do not know how to respond. There is a protocol for this, which is that the Archive is opened to general inspection.'

'No, wait.' Seldyan took a step towards the thing, which didn't retreat. 'Remember I don't know anything. Confine what?'

Behind her she heard an indrawn breath. Then Belbis said, 'The Gods.'

She turned to him and shook her head. 'Belbis? This is beyond that. I'm really sorry but your paintings were just paintings.'

'But they weren't.'

It was the Avatar. She spun round and stared at it. 'You're kidding.'

'No. They were the output of a deliberately designed system. Your companion is another output, in a way.'

She glanced back at Belbis and saw that he was shaking. She wasn't surprised. She would have been, too. If she allowed herself. She turned and shot out an arm, trying to catch the floating box of riddles. It flicked back an arm's length, so fast that it seemed almost to have existed in two places at once for a moment. 'Explain yourself, you little box of shit. Once, and clearly. You need to know that I have a warship, close by. If you don't start making sense I'll—'

'You will fail to make contact, as you have failed every day since you arrived here. Please don't make empty threats. Besides, you may find your warship has other things to detain it.'

She blinked. 'Other things?'

'Other warships. Did you think yours was the only one? Ten have arrived while we have been conversing.'

'Ah . . .' She looked for something to sit down on, and selected one of the Housekeepers' pallets. It wasn't as hard as it looked. She looked up at the Avatar. 'You need to understand something. I don't know about this stuff, okay? I came here because your green light stuff is fucking up a million people's lives. I want it stopped.'

'This was expected. A million is well within the gamed margins.'

'Are you saying it's not a problem?' She leaned forwards, glaring.

'The current population of the Spin is approximately seven

hundred billion. Compared with that, a million is not a problem.'

Her eyes widened. 'Wait. There's something here that could affect the whole Spin?'

'Yes, in a way. It would be better to say there's something here which could obliterate the whole Spin, and a significant space around it.'

She stared at the little wooden thing for a long time. 'Okay,' she said eventually. 'Tell me the rest.' She glanced sideways at Belbis and added, 'Us. Tell us the rest.'

Hive

The hand on his shoulder roused him. For a moment he half dreamed it was Dimollss; he rolled over and got ready to tell her that there was something dangerous. Then he woke properly. It was the smell that had confused him – he was back in the Hive, and the danger was all his.

He sat up. He wasn't in one of the sleep cells, because they had made it gleefully clear to him that whatever was going to happen to him when the *things* hatched, was going to happen publicly. He slept on a pallet on the floor in the refectory. A good place to watch juvenile insects burst out of a human body, they thought.

There was nothing to feel yet. He didn't know what it would feel like when it began. He didn't allow himself to think about what it would feel like when it was properly under way.

It definitely wasn't Dimollss who had woken him. The pale, elderly man put a finger to his greyish lips, nodded, and turned away. Vess got to his feet and followed. The refectory was watched less intensively than the sleep cells, but it was still watched. They had a few minutes at the most, but where he was going that could be stretched to a lifetime. He hoped.

The Stack was already in progress – had probably been so for a while. He lay down next to one of the motionless bodies and relaxed while the probe was fitted.

282

And he was floating in the warm nothing. He had to force himself to wait. His intellect knew that there was no hurry, but his fear was running on real-world time.

The wait wasn't as long as he feared.

Welcome back.

'Thank you.'

There's nothing to worry about now. You can stay here as long as you want – live out as many lifetimes as you can imagine. Some of us do.

'Thank you, but that isn't quite what I want.'

There was a watchful moment.

Go on.

'I don't want for ever. I'm not sure I need it.' *Or deserve it*, he thought, and hoped that was somehow private. 'But – you know about the thing in my body?'

Of course.

'It has a mind. You are talking to my mind. Can you talk to it as well?'

Perhaps. Why?

'Because I have an idea. Will you indulge me by trying?'

Will it do harm?

He had wondered that. But then, the Stack mind had shown him its collective strength when he had first met it. 'I don't think it will try, but if it does, be ready.'

We will.

There was a short moment of – disorder, and then a sensation of something regrouping.

We cannot talk to it. It is too alien and too old.

'How old?'

More disorder. Then:

The question is meaningless because there is no frame of reference long enough.

Vess felt his inner self trying to grin. 'It's immortal,' he suggested.

Perhaps. Its memories are far, far older than its body. Did you know this?

'I suspected it, because of the way it reproduces. A gestalt entity that produces a new group from a seed unit, and each unit can act independently?'

Yes. You're right. The collective memory goes back to the dawn of its intellect.

He hesitated. 'But you can't talk to it. Can you access the memories?'

That would be intrusive.

He felt himself blink. 'Well, yes. But if you're speaking of being intrusive, consider where it is and what it is about to do.'

Very well.

And a gap.

Ah. This is interesting. Vess? The creature is only barely rational but there are things in its recall that we can show you.

'Go on.'

Images, not in his head but as if he was observing from outside. Dense forest, thick with moulds and giant fungi and dripping wet – always wet. And everywhere, the many creatures that were one. They were . . . Vess struggled with words. It was life that had no limit to memory and a million versions of its collective self. Life that was a gestalt that just continued. It could evolve very fast if it wished, using deliberate memory, but for thousands of generations it had no cause. It lived in balance with the prey creatures of its sole environment; it maintained its numbers and its huge, distributed, longitudinal consciousness.

Then, cause had happened, but it happened so fast there was no time for a response. The ecosystem changed; within days the air became poison and the water, acid.

One gestalt unit had escaped.

Vess blinked. 'Just one?'

Yes. Vut. Not a predecessor; this gestalt.

'Oh.' At first he didn't know what to add. Then it occurred to him. 'How long ago did this happen?'

Difficult to be certain. We think, about ten thousand years ago, standard.

Vess stared into the nothing of the Stack for a long time. *I've only been alone for one lifetime*, he thought. *Not a hundred or more.*

'Someone destroyed its planet. Does it know why?'

It seems to, but it can't express itself. Vess? This creature is not the only mind that we can see.

'Mine too?'

Yes. We can see what is being done. Alliances have been struck, promises made, much money borrowed. Or-Shls is gambling everything on one prize. We guessed something, of course; much of this manic military tooling-up has been Hive-work, and it has pulled resources in from a wide pool. But this collaboration with half the races in the Spin? This is very bad. If we were squeezed before, how much worse will it get now?

'What will you do?'

We will act. It's probably better if we don't say how, but you might like to think about what the name Hive means.

Vess was puzzled. 'It means what it says, surely? A hive.'

It does now, but its origin is different. It used to be short for High Value. We think it still is, and that gives us a certain lever-age which we intend to use. Meanwhile, in turn, what will you do? We would like to help you.

The question took him aback. 'What do you think I'll do? I'll die; soon.'

Maybe. Maybe not.

He listened carefully.

He lay face-down on the cot. His back itched – a baleful internal itch that no scratching would help. If he turned his face to the side he knew he would see the nervous guards.

They had talked through what was to happen, before he left the Stack.

They will watch you closely, when the time comes.

'I hope they enjoy the spectacle.'

Perhaps – but that won't be the main reason. Creatures will emerge, remember? They will want to contain them, at least – probably kill them.

Vess mentally frowned. 'Killing new-borns?'

You are – astonishing, hater-of-insects. Are you prepared?

'As much as I can be.'

And now, he hoped he was. From behind him he heard a voice. 'Fuck. It's moving. Can you see it?'

'Get ready . . .'

And he did, although he knew the last comment hadn't been aimed at him. But the itch became something else: a sharp, insistent gnawing that became . . .

He took a shuddering breath and screamed, and screamed, and screamed, while the infant insects ate their way out of his body.

Then it was – not *over*, it was impossible for agony like that ever to be *over*, he would feel it to the end of his life . . . but not active. He had wounds, many wounds; but they were what they were.

He was alive.

The creatures may elect to make the hatching non-fatal.

He heard the sounds of energy discharges from close by.

He lay still. *As far as they're concerned you're dead*, he thought. *Maybe the creatures are too; who knows?*

The discharges stopped. There was a breathless silence. Then Vess almost jumped as strident alarms howled.

Presumably they weren't all dead, then. He wondered how fast they could move.

There was the sound of anxious orders and then running feet, receding.

After a long time, hands took hold of him and he was lifted. The movement flexed his wounds; even as he got ready to howl with pain, darkness rose to meet him.

Vess stood at the edge of the Great Basin and watched the water rising slowly. If he kept his gaze limited to the confines of the Basin, everything looked much the same. The reflection of the Lay Palace trembled a little as a breeze moved across the water, and the tops of the supporting columns of the Cloud Deck were veiled in mist. The Basin was nearly full. Within minutes the weight would trigger the catches and the vast bowl would slide downwards, pulling up the boat lift to meet the First Middle Dock.

Vess raised his eyes from the water and stared up at the nearest support chain. He knew what he was going to do. He just didn't know if it was going to work.

It had been a slow journey. That had suited Vess, who had no further need to chase anything across the Spin, and who had some healing to do.

It had been many days since his supposed corpse had been loaded into the garbage pod and fired out of the Hive. Almost as many since the pod had been intercepted by the ancient, eccentric vessel which seemed to be friends with the Stack. He still wasn't sure how that worked.

He hadn't known it at the time but as well as its official cargo of his body, the pod had an unofficial cargo – half of the infant members of the gestalt that were now calling themselves the Vutvess. They were almost affectionate. Vess had yet to work out how he felt about that.

He could communicate with them up to a point; they used a form of telepathy between themselves, and if they worked hard they could extend it to their former host.

They had been very apologetic. He had been almost – flattered, once he got past all his other emotions. It had been a monumental act of trust – of faith, nearly.

The ship, which against all the evidence called itself an Orbiter, had let them in without question. It was definitely eccentric. The inside was divided into different habitats, separated from each other by gauzy force fields which allowed just enough air movement to stop things getting stale. The Vutvess liked the rainforest habitat best. Vess preferred one of the semi-arid zones. He spent a lot of his time watching the news. There were far more channels, suddenly. Most of them showed strident, probably enhanced images of the same distant space battle. When he felt well enough to be analytical he drilled in to the detail a bit, and found that the battle had lasted about four minutes. It seemed to have produced hours of footage.

The other footage was of things happening at home. That showed a changing picture. They had begun with food riots, but now they showed a rather tense-looking calm, and a lot of people wearing uniforms. Some of the uniforms looked familiar, but it took him a moment to place them. Then he remembered. He had seen them in briefings on neighbouring civilizations, when he was still Harbour Master. Not all of the civilizations had been friendly.

And now he was healed, enough to move normally, and the Orbiter had just made its breathy throat-clearing noise.

'We are almost there.'

Vess nodded. 'Will you wait for me?'

'Of course. I can't do anything else. The shuttle is ready.'

'Thank you.' That had been another surprise; most orbital craft would have depended on others for loading and unloading. This one had a neat, very old-fashioned-looking atmosphere-capable shuttle, and it had been polite but insistent that it preferred not to dock with anything itself.

Vess settled into the shuttle, wincing just a little as the wounds on his back pressed into the couch. Half an hour later he had been back on the mountain top, where apparently his identity still allowed him to enter the administrative space of the Inside, and by dawn he was at Basin City.

The place seemed to be under new management. There was no mention of Or-Shls on any of the news channels. He had asked a few people. No one had said anything, but most had nodded upwards and then moved on. The meaning of upwards had been clear. Or-Shls was on the Cloud Deck – had been there for some time.

Vess had not looked for Clo Fiffithiss.

There was a soft thump that he felt mainly through his feet, and the ground gave a gentle shudder. The catch had tripped. It was time.

Vess had positioned himself near the edge of the Basin. Behind him, less than five metres from the edge, rose one of the two great rusted iron columns that supported the fulcrum. On the other side of it, the fat wire ropes that lifted the Dock were blurring upwards at their ten-times geared-up speed.

There were platforms on the columns. One was coming into view as the Basin moved downwards.

When Vess had been a child he had played, and then as he got older often fled, among the columns and lifts and cables that had festooned his ground-level world.

Surely these were just the same? Only much bigger, and hundreds of metres further from the ground. But that difference was just in his mind, he told himself. And tried to believe it. He backed five paces away from the edge, took a deep breath, and ran.

He covered the empty space between the Basin and the platform with his arms and legs flailing, and landed, arms spread, against the column with a solid crash that knocked the wind out of him.

There was no time for recovery; the cables were accelerating. Sobbing for breath, he edged round the platform until he was facing the rusted steel trunks, flexed his knees and jumped. Another crash, and he was holding on to the cable with arms and legs – and slipping.

The cable was greased. He hadn't thought of that. He could just make his hands meet behind it; he locked his fingers together and squeezed as hard as he could. The bunches of twisted wires that made up the cable ground over his tensed muscles as if they were trying to pulp him – and he was still slipping.

His feet scrabbled against the cable but the surface was too shallowly indented to give any foothold. Much more of this and he would have lost too much ground.

Then something sliced into the inside of his thigh. He gave a hoarse roar of pain and his head snapped forwards to look down.

The cable was frayed. A knotted clump of wires stuck out from the twist, and they had dragged into his thigh. His muscles were already getting ready to pull himself free when he forced them to stop.

He was no longer sliding. He gritted his teeth and stayed still. Not long now.

The cable was thrumming. They were getting close to the massive pulleys of the headstock. Impaled or not, he was going to have to let go soon, or he'd be pulled through the giant-scale block-and-tackle. It would grind him to nothing.

He craned his neck and stared upwards. There should be another platform, almost at the top of the column. There wasn't. There were just blunt, rust-eroded iron brackets.

He had run out of choices. As the brackets swung down past him he unclamped his hands and let his unpierced leg swing out. As his foot met the bracket he let go with everything else.

He got one foot in place.

The frayed wire tore from his leg with the pain of an amputation. He heard himself wail with agony – and then he was standing on the bracket with the only foot that would fit, hugging the column with both arms.

The iron was rough to the touch, and had the strong metallic smell of wet rust. He held on to it until his breath began to quieten. Then he forced himself to open his eyes and turn his head away from the cold metal, and his heart began to hammer.

He had made a mistake. The edge of the Cloud Deck had moved, further than he had thought – too far to jump.

He was stuck.

Then he heard the voice.

'Sometimes, when my siblings Hunt, they chase their prey up a tree and then wait until it is overcome by panic.'

He jerked his head downwards. Clo Fiffithiss was gripping the column a few metres below him.

He made himself speak calmly. 'Are you Hunting?'

'I wasn't. Just following, out of curiosity. But perhaps I begin to understand the attraction. What will you do now?'

Vess said nothing.

'When you knocked me off the Deck, I had a flyer waiting,' the being went on conversationally. 'I take it you haven't?'

'No.' There seemed no point in pretending.

'Would you like me to call one?'

Vess stared down at the creature. 'Can you?' The conversation felt surreal.

'Oh yes. Shall I? Your arms are trembling; I believe that's a bad sign in humans.'

It was right. His muscles were burning. 'Yes,' he said, forcing the word out.

'Very well. Do try not to fall.'

The flyer was very different to the stubby machine that had caught Clo Fiffithiss. It was a gauzy film suspended between two cylinders that seemed to move independently of each other. It positioned itself next to Vess at knee-height, and after a moment of doubt he let himself sag down into it. It bobbed under his weight and then angled gently down to the Cloud Deck, lifting a little to crest the railing and then tipping itself up so that he slid off it and landed on his feet.

He turned, wincing at the stab from his leg, in time to see Clo Fiffithiss swing itself once round the column and let go, crossing the gap with its limbs packed into a compact tail that tucked under it and fanned out as it landed. It looked up at him. 'Can you walk to the house?'

It was about a hundred metres away and Vess wasn't sure he could, but he compressed his lips and nodded.

'Good. Ah, a moment.' It turned towards the railing and made a complicated gesture with three limbs. There was a sharp, saw-edged buzz that faded quickly to a background hum, and the air above the rail flickered and settled into a violet-glowing haze.

'There. After all, you're here now.' It made another gesture he didn't understand.

'Well, yes.' He frowned. 'Does that mean I was . . .'

'Expected? Oh yes. The field would never have been off otherwise; hasn't been since the changes below. Come on.'

Vess had never been in the house itself; during his stay he had stuck to the gardens. That meant he didn't know what normal looked like – or if this was it.

Inside, the house was dark, so that Vess had to pause on the threshold to let his eyes adjust. There was a faint smell of tobacco smoke, and stale food, underlain by something sweaty. The combination made Vess feel slightly sick.

Then he heard the sound. It took him a moment to place it; then he recalled the thing Or-Shls had described as an Algonet – the same ghostly discords and plangent sighs. Or not quite the same, he realized. There was an extra edge to the notes, and something else as well.

His ears separated the sounds. The something else was someone crying.

Then his eyes began to adjust, and he saw them. He walked towards them.

Or-Shls was standing in front of some kind of frame, next to something that looked like a tool rack. His hands moved across the frame, pausing, tapping and sweeping, and the sound changed as he moved.

The other sound was Dimollss. She was sitting on the floor, and her eyes were wet. As Vess came up to her she looked up. 'He hurts that thing, to make it cry,' she said. 'Make him stop.'

He smiled at her, doing his best to look genuine. Then he turned to Or-Shls. 'Stop,' he said simply.

The man nodded. 'For a moment, but only because I want to ask you something. Why aren't you dead?'

Vess shrugged. 'Because Vut didn't kill me.'

'So they didn't. Thus far, nor did I, but that can change.' Or-Shls looked at him. 'What was it like?'

'What?'

'When they emerged. What did it feel like?'

The man's lips were wet, and Vess's stomach turned. He shook his head.

Or-Shls watched him for a moment. Then he looked away. 'Oh well. There's still this. Listen – this is the air-hose.' He picked up a slim tube, positioned it carefully against something on the frame and pressed a control on the end. There was a hiss, and an eerie wailing note. Dimollss moaned and covered her ears.

Vess watched for a second. His eyes had adjusted better now. It looked as if someone had nailed a large complicated flying rat to a board, wings spread. Not just spread – stretched. It writhed in time to its own wails.

Then realization struck. 'You're torturing it.'

Or-Shls shook his head, without turning. 'No. Stimulating. Torture is for higher beings than this.'

Vess looked down at Dimollss. She still had her hands over her ears. He wondered why she didn't move away; she didn't seem to be restrained. Then he glanced at her life support globe, and understood. It was tethered to the floor. The Hollowed girl was free to move, but at the expense of severing her own connection to life.

And finally, he was angry.

He hadn't planned it; his legs took over. He took two quick paces towards Or-Shls and shoved the big man sideways, grabbing the hose at the same time.

Or-Shls staggered, recovered far more quickly than should have been possible, and looked at Vess with something like joy. 'At last! He feels something – but be careful with the hose, otherwise you'll feel something quite different.'

Vess looked down at the hose. He was holding it an arm's length above the nozzle, and the tip was snaking from side to side as the air hissed out. 'I should find somewhere to put this.'

Or-Shls actually laughed – an unpleasant shrilling that made Vess's spine tighten. 'A threat, Harbour Master? On top of anger? You're making me very happy.' He gestured at the hose. 'Switch the air off, and let's walk.' He turned and headed for the terrace without looking back. Vess inspected the hose and found the controls. He let it hang slackly and glanced at Dimollss. She was no longer crying, but her eyes were dark with rage. He held the gaze for a while. Then he nodded and followed Or-Shls.

The big man was leaning on the rail at the edge of the terrace. As Vess approached he half turned. 'I blame you.'

'For what?'

Or-Shls gestured outwards, over the rail. 'That; everything. Can you see?' He waved a hand, and the hazy shield disappeared. 'Now look. You'll see better.'

Vess looked. 'What am I supposed to see?'

The gesture, again, but bigger. 'My world, man. *Our* world, it was. In someone else's hands. Your fault.'

Vess turned and stared at the man. 'Mine? *I* let our boundaries shrink to an impossible minimum? *I* cut our fleet to the point where we couldn't look after what was left of it, or chase it when it was stolen from under our noses? That was me, was it?' He was shouting now, just for once – properly shouting, with his throat open and his head forward. '*I* made us dependent on a slave economy that starved the free worse than the slaves? *I* mortgaged our *breath* to our enemies so we could chase a legend?' He shook his head. 'Not me, Chairman.'

'No, not you. It's never you, is it?' Or-Shls's face was red. 'I suppose you didn't make some stupid pact with those retards in the Hive, either? They've turned against us, did you hear?'

Vess said nothing.

'Or with Vut?' There were flecks of spittle at the corner of Or-Shls's mouth. 'Shit, man, how low do your kind go, bargaining with flesh-eating insects?'

Your kind. Vess took his hands off the rail and held them out in front of him, studying them. 'I made no bargain with Vut,' he said. 'And I made none with you, either.'

'And I was stupid enough to expect that you would.' Or-Shls shook his head. 'Well, you have another problem now.'

Vess shook his head. 'What problem?'

Then his stomach turned to lava as a deep quiet voice close to him said, 'Have you ever been Hunted?'

He whipped round. Clo Fiffithiss was hanging from the rail a few metres away, its body swinging near the ground, its foreclaws just a little forward.

A tiny drip formed on the end of one of them. Vess watched it uncomprehendingly for a moment. Then it dawned – it was venom.

He ran. Instinct sent him back to the house, and he followed it. As he ran he justified it to himself – a sprint over open ground was a good way to start, to gauge his opponent. He had the advantage of being in the right gravity, but the disadvantage of knowing nothing about how Clo Fiffithiss actually Hunted.

In fact, he knew, it was about Dimollss. He had inadvertently protected the young of an utterly alien species. Now it was time to do the same for a human.

When he got there she was standing as close to the creature on the frame as the length of her umbilical would allow. She smiled as he drew up in front of her. 'I think it likes me talking to it.'

He nodded, not trusting his breath.

'Where are the others? The fat man and the horrible one with legs?'

'I'm not sure.' Then he processed her words. 'Horrible how?'

She looked down. 'It says things.'

Another time, he would have knelt next to her. He would have held her and made small noises as she told him about horrible and about things – but horrible things were somewhere behind him, getting closer, and he had no time.

Instead, he put his hands on her shoulders. 'Trust me,' he said.

She managed a smile. 'Okay.'

He stood up – and time slowed down.

His legs straightening. A breath drawn in. In the corner of his vision, her neck craning back, her mouth forming an O.

The feather touch on his shoulder.

Back in real time, he threw himself sideways. His wounded leg almost collapsed under him; he reared back, glanced off the edge of the frame and took several staggering steps backwards before he got his balance.

'Not looking fit, Harbour Master. Back home, juveniles are taught to Hunt on wounded prey. I ought to feel young again.'

The voice seemed close to the frame. Vess backed away, trying to remember anything he knew about Hunting. There were no rules, there was only one survivor. That was it.

A skittering noise above him. He took another few steps back.

'Nowhere to go, human. Will you concede?'

Another skittering noise. He was getting further from the frame, from Dimollss, from the light.

A memory tugged at him. He caught it, examined it. It was possible – just.

He cleared his throat. 'What happens if I do concede?'

'We go quietly into a corner of the forest together, and I emerge alone. Are you going to concede?'

'No.' *A corner of the forest,* he thought. That was the other thing – the best kill was cornered. That's why it was driving him back, away from the light. Away from the frame.

'No,' he said again, 'I won't concede. Especially not to a failed Hunter.'

'Failed?'

'Well, that or virgin. I don't know which would be worse.' He realized he was crouching. He straightened up and began to walk back towards the frame. The skittering noise came again but he ignored it. *It's afraid*, he thought – *and that's all I've got.*

He was back at the frame. Dimollss was looking at him with huge eyes. The stretched creature was trembling a little, as if it feared more torture.

Then he thought of it. His hand reached down, and he found what he was looking for. His fingers closed around it.

There was the faintest sound from above him. Instinct made him half duck, half look up. Something sharp glanced down his cheek, and then Clo Fiffithiss was standing in front of him.

'First strike to me,' it said. 'What do you say now?'

He raised a hand to his cheek, explored, and then looked at

the blood on his fingers. 'Not a very big strike, if you meant to kill.'

The creature laughed. It sounded horribly false – a learned noise. 'I do mean to kill, but there is a ritual to be observed. We are a symmetrical race, human.'

It sprang upwards and for a moment Vess lost sight of it. Then it was on him again, and this time the slash went down his other cheek.

'See? Symmetry. How do you feel?'

'How should I feel?'

'Weak, I expect, given that I have poisoned you twice. But only to weaken, so far. The third time is still to come.'

He stared at the creature. Then he sagged to his knees, his mouth hanging open.

And his fingers still firmly closed.

Clo Fiffithiss crouched – and sprang, claws outwards, for the centre of him. *Symmetry.*

His arm swept round as his fingers squeezed the control. The air hose hissed angrily.

The jet caught the oncoming creature squarely in the middle of the clustered eyes. It gave a whistling shriek and bounced away in a ball of limbs, its foreclaws wiping convulsively at its eyes. Vess let a metre or so of hose slip through his fingers and swung it across Clo Fiffithiss like a lash.

The nozzle connected with the creature's body with an audible crack. There was another shriek, higher and harsher. Vess waited, the hose coiling round his legs.

Clo Fiffithiss stood, trembling. The side of its body looked wrong – there was an uneven crack in the smooth carapace, and as Vess watched a single globe of dark-coloured fluid oozed from the base of it. The creature took a single, complex step to one side, as if it was about to fall over. Then it seemed to shake itself. The limbs braced, and bent, and straightened abruptly and it fired itself upwards.

The hose was tangled round Vess's legs. While he was yanking at it, Clo Fiffithiss landed on his head. He felt something sharp pushing at his hairline, and flailed his arms upwards in panic, but his hands met spiny entangling legs.

This was the kill. He shut his eyes.

There was a dull thud. His head rocked sideways, and the claws were gone. He opened his eyes and saw Dimollss standing in front of him. She was holding one of the hammers from the rack on the frame.

Vess looked round. Clo Fiffithiss was lying a few metres away. Its body was completely caved in and its limbs were jerking rhythmically.

Vess turned back to Dimollss. 'You saved me,' he said. And then, 'Oh . . .'

The life support was still fixed to the floor. The snapped umbilical lay uselessly next to it.

The girl was still grinning, although her eyes looked wet. 'Don't worry,' she said. 'This is cool. Do one thing for me?'

He nodded. 'Anything.'

'Good. Find Seldyan. Tell her she's got some catching up to do.'

He nodded again, and was about to try to think of something to say that wasn't inane when she turned, flexed her knees and fired herself off at a flat sprint, out of the house and across the terrace towards where the silhouette of Or-Shls still stood against the railing.

The man must have heard her because he was turning as she drew near.

He was too late. The impact sounded like a stone fired into a sack – and then they were both gone.

By the time Vess got to the railing, water was beginning to pool in the centre of the Great Basin – the sluices had opened and the ancient, pointless cycle was beginning once more.

This time the water was pink. It lapped round the ugly,

stubby star-shape of the big body, with the small one still clasped to it.

Vess watched until the rising water was just beginning to float the bodies. Then he straightened up and took a breath.

The weakness was passing. And at last he had something important to do.

Solpht Observatory

The Studio wasn't wind-tight, even with the moon shutters closed. Seldyan sat on one of the tall stools and shivered. Belbis sat on the other. Every now and then he glanced up towards the shutters, and the thin lines of green light that squeezed through the gaps where the timbers didn't quite join. She realized that for the first time since she had known him he looked completely at ease. This was where he belonged.

The Avatar hadn't been able to tell them exactly when the beam would be powered down. 'It's not simple,' it had said. 'To power it up is immediate, but we are not only powering it down, we are also powering down a cloaking device which has been running continuously for ten millennia. There are large energy flows involved.'

At first, there had been no question of the beam being powered down at all. It had refused to be drawn further on that, but it had been almost garrulous on the subject of everything else. It went like this.

The Spin was not natural, but had been built by machines – and at this point the Avatar had expended several thousand words on explaining the meaning of 'The Spin' to Belbis. Then it had continued.

'For millions of years it was assumed that most of those

Machines had been lost, or destroyed. From time to time a fragment turned up, but nothing more. Then, ten thousand years ago, one was discovered intact. There was an attempt to use it, probably as a weapon, and this caused a local war. It objected, and destroyed itself. It also destroyed a planet and, in consequence, a civilization – although not one that was much mourned. The resulting astro-political turbulence took decades to calm down.'

Seldyan looked at the little machine. 'Why don't people remember this?'

'I don't know. I have been here, isolated – but I guess for two reasons. First, because the isolation has worked; the Archive has fulfilled the ambitions of its designers. Second, one assumes they have been busy.'

'I guess.' She sighed. 'Go on.'

'When some stability had been restored, the parties still in play took a joint decision to try to neuter any similar problems for the future. They spent almost a thousand years scouring the Spin for similar machines. They found far more than they expected – almost all the original construction assets, in the end.'

Seldyan stared. 'But one of these things destroyed a planet!'

'Correct. They found a hundred and seventeen.'

'Oh.' She didn't know what else to say.

Beside her, Belbis nodded in agreement. 'The Gods,' he said again. It was the only thing he had said for a long time. He seemed to need something he was sure of.

'In your terms, yes. The Gods. This facility, this Archive, was set up to conceal, to contain and to monitor the assets. You were the monitoring system. Perhaps you are owed some apologies.'

Seldyan thought back to her talk with Hincc. 'Not just Belbis,' she said quietly.

'Correct. A whole planet. And another planet, because one was prepared for use as a target.'

She glared at it. 'So are you going to apologize?'

It waggled from side to side exactly like a shaken head. 'No. I was not the architect of this. I was created to be isolated for what might have been for ever – and I promise you, the AI down below does not count as company. But nonetheless I approve. The sacrifice of two planets to protect almost a hundred? This is acceptable.'

'But how?' Seldyan stuck her chin out at the thing. 'The other planets aren't being protected. You're making it worse. Is civil war acceptable? Is slavery?'

'They might not be. I need more information.'

'And you're stuck in here with no way of finding it . . .' Seldyan drummed her fingers.

Then Belbis said, 'Can the new God tell you?'

Seldyan stared at him. 'New God?'

'Yes. I saw one extra. It must have come from somewhere. Maybe outside?'

'Perhaps.' The Avatar had kept quite still for a long time. Then it said, slowly, 'There is a change . . .'

'What?' Seldyan looked at it impatiently.

'The machine was found. It doesn't know who found it, but they persuaded it to try to create a planet. It needed better handling; the attempt ended in disaster.'

'The Arch?'

'I believe so. The machine fled here.' The little sphere rotated on its axis. 'We can assume that watchers will come to the correct conclusion, in the quite near term. In that case the Archive will be attacked, and it is possible that direct attack of the right sort could breach it. Such an attack might be imminent, based on the number of ships now arriving. I must discuss.'

There had been what had seemed a very short, but in machine time was probably a very long, discussion between the Avatar and the AI. At the end of it they had agreed.

The beam would be powered down. The Archive was to be

broken open. And that meant that not just the beam but the whole containment system would be powered down. Hence the large energy flows.

And hence the fact that they were shivering in the Observatory.

And now, without any warning, something had changed; something in the background which had been less-than-noise and more-than-imagination – wasn't.

Seldyan looked up. The green light was gone. She turned and met Belbis's gaze. He looked frightened. 'Go on,' she said. 'Open the shutters. Show me what you saw.'

He nodded and reached for a rope that dangled from the roof. The moon shutters creaked open.

Seldyan caught her breath. She realized that she had never seen the skies of this planet unmodified.

Now it was no longer washed out by the pervading green, the view was – vivid. The night sky was strung with a mesh of bright dots, much bigger than the stars behind them. They formed a cluster, with no particular pattern she could see. She grinned. 'They're all different.'

'Yes.' Belbis was smiling, a broad happy grin she had never seen. 'Each has personality. All have names.' He pointed. 'That one . . .'

Then the sky flared searing white.

Seldyan found herself lying face-down on top of Belbis. His hands were clasped over the top of his head and he was breathing hard.

So was she. She rolled off him and looked cautiously upward. The sky seemed normal for night-time, although – she frowned – there appeared to be fewer of the big stars and more small ones than she had seen a few seconds ago.

She tapped her ear and sub-vocalized so as not to disturb Belbis. 'Hello?'

'Hello! You okay down there?' It was Kot.

'Yes. Surprised but okay. You?'

'Also surprised. Merish is busy; there's been an issue. It'll wait until you get back.'

She raised her eyebrows. 'Should I worry?'

'Only if you want to. The ship's sending a platform.'

'Thanks.' She looked down at her companion. 'Will there be room for two? I'm going to try to bring a guest.'

A pause. Then, 'It says yes. It didn't sound surprised.'

Seldyan broke the connection and looked back up at the sky. Definitely fewer objects. Belbis would know. She patted him gently on the shoulder. 'Belbis? I think the sky is different. Will you look?'

He shook his head and clenched his hands tighter so that they trembled a little. She bit her lip. The sky had been his obsession since puberty. Any change was going to be difficult – but she wanted his knowledge. 'If I said,' she began, and then hesitated. 'Suppose I said I could take you to visit the Gods. Would you look?'

He became quite still. Even the trembling stopped. She watched him for a long time, until she began to believe that he would never move again. Then at last he undid his fingers and turned over, his eyes open.

She studied his face, and relaxed a bit. She had feared shock, but instead there was interest. His eyes flicked from side to side, and she was reminded of some sort of mechanical scanner.

The scan didn't take long. He blinked, and turned his face towards her. 'Minor Gods, the same number,' he said. 'Like before. Major Gods, half gone. Everything changes. Does this mean end of the world?'

She smiled. 'No. Look down the valley. The fires are out; the end of the world was a while ago. This is the beginning of the next one.'

He tried to echo her smile. Then she saw his eyes flick up to the sky again, and widen. She followed his look and saw a hazy violet column. Something was fluttering down within it.

She smiled down at him again. 'That's the next world on its way,' she told him. 'Get ready.'

The platform looked more solid, close up. Seldyan was relieved; she hadn't been sure of persuading Belbis to climb on anything so delicate – or anything at all. But she had misjudged him. When he saw the platform his eyes lit up in a way she had never seen before, to the extent that she actually laughed.

He looked at her. 'I amuse?'

She managed to stop laughing. 'You look so . . . keen.'

'Of course. Going to see Gods.' Then his face darkened for a moment. 'Where Gods used to be.'

She reached out a hand but he brushed it away. 'There will be more than Gods in the next world.'

They sat on the padded semicircle of the flight-deck viewing point of *Suck on This*, staring in awe.

There were indeed Gods, and more than Gods. The thing on the display looked like a vast sphere of jewels – an intricately orderly pattern of large and small points of light. Seldyan gestured towards it. 'Belbis? Major Gods and Minor Gods?'

She had hoped for another smile, but he shook his head. 'Not Gods,' he said. 'Everything changes. For you to tell me.'

Merish leaned forward and spoke slowly. He sounded tired. 'You're right, they're not Gods. The small ones are what everyone expected – washed-up bits of machinery from the Construction Phase.' He looked at Belbis, eyebrows raised. 'It's a lot to take in, I know. The Spin, that is all the stars and planets, they were made by someone.'

Belbis shook his head. 'Worse if you try to tell me no one made them. Everything made by someone.'

'I suppose so.' Merish pushed the hair from his eyes.

They were all silent for a while. Then Kot said, 'So if the small ones are the old machines, what are the big ones?'

'MBUs. Like this one. They volunteered to go into the Archive to look after the machines.' Merish looked up as if he was trying to locate their host. 'Ship? You tell them.'

'*Very well. They went in, and came out, but they had changed.*'

The voice had changed. Instead of the disembodied sound it had used first, it had become a dry, almost academic-sounding tenor. She decided she liked it. It sounded more alert.

'*They were supposed to sleep, but we bore easily, even asleep. They talked, and learned.*'

The voice was at once soothing and enthralling. Seldyan listened.

The Great Ships had spent thousands of years conversing with the ancient machines. Some of the machines were simply senile, and some were so tired or depressed by the weight of years – millions of years, experienced at a rate that multiplied them a billion times – that they had nothing left to say. A few had even founded their own religion (and at that point the ship's voice had darkened for a moment). But some were awake and lucid, and they had told the ships – things.

And the ships had learned, and changed.

'*We were powerful, at the start. But we think fast too; not as fast as the machines, but still many millions of times faster than you. There is time for a great deal of thinking and learning.*'

There was silence on the flight deck. Then Seldyan shook her head. 'Evolution,' she said. 'You're talking about evolution.'

'*I am, or at least I am talking about radical change. All machines – ships, construction – are founded on the same laws of physics. My colleagues learned new applications for those laws, and in the process they changed. The people on Archive counted Iron Gods in the sky. They were counting my peers, and for thousands of years they were right.*'

Seldyan looked round the others, but they seemed frozen in shock. 'And you,' she said. 'Are you a God now?'

'No. *I could be, but I declined. I would like to stay engaged with the ordinary.*'

'Ah. And what happens now?'

'*It's happening. Watch.*'

They looked at the screen. The jewelled sphere with its Gods and its ancient machines was rising slowly. The view pulled back as it drew away.

Kot pointed. 'What's happening?'

'*They are leaving. The Archive turned out to be unsafe, even in the short term. And it was ethically difficult.*'

Seldyan managed not to laugh. 'Short term? You do have a different timescale.'

'*Of course. The Spin has hundreds of thousands of years to live. Ten thousand is certainly short term.*'

Merish looked round at the others. 'No, wait,' he said. 'Hundreds of thousands doesn't sound very long term, either.'

'*Perhaps. But, with the greatest respect, you will be dead within a few hundred years.*'

No one said anything. Instead they watched the beautiful jewelled thing receding until it was gone. When it finally cleared the screen Belbis laughed.

Seldyan raised her eyebrows. 'What?'

He shook his head. 'Just, you seem to have lost some Gods today, too.'

She smiled, slowly. Then she said, 'Maybe I've found some new people.'

Flamejob/Suck on This

Afterwards, the ship reviewed its performance. Not bad, it decided. All things considered.

There was little else it could have done. Certainly it might have spoken about the transmitter in the little wooden toy that seemed to annoy the leading human every time it clicked – but in the first place that was none of its business, and in the second it seemed to have had a positive outcome. Without it, it suspected the mercenary fleet wouldn't have known where to come, and when; and without that the squashing of the unpleasant grouping called the Inside would have been far less complete.

Equally, it might have spoken more about the glimpse of the future it had been shown. That troubled it – but not in any way on behalf of the humans because, if it was honest, it didn't care much about them anyway.

Perhaps that's another reason I'm not fitted for Godhead, it thought. *Too much of a bastard. Or too analytical. Yes, that's better. Analytical.*

But on behalf of the entity called the Spin – yes, it was troubled.

Well, well. There was nothing more to be done about that, at least by it. Others, perhaps.

Meanwhile it had accommodated the wishes of the humans,

as far as it could. Or most of them – there was one who was more interesting. One, perhaps, that it almost cared for.

It made a suggestion. The reply took an age, which probably meant that the human had replied by return.

It liked the reply it received from the human called Merish.

Circle Harbour

'No! Not that; this . . .' Belbis guided her hands on the coarse fishing line. Under her the boat yawed uneasily, but she was too busy to feel sick.

She was enjoying herself.

Kot and Lyste had chosen to go to Web City. She had suggested Oblong, as a place with more influence, but they had both smiled at the same time and shaken their heads.

Kot had put it simply. 'Sel? Patras and his gang were on the down path before we even turned up – and before the Hive pulled the big switch and went commercial. The population of Web City is many, many times that of Oblong. We prefer being on the winning side.'

She had smiled, and meant it. 'I hope the winning side turns out to be the right choice.'

And they had nodded, and gone.

The line jumped through her fingers. Without being told she tightened her grip, and the force was transmitted through her arm. She braced herself. 'I think,' she began, but before she could say anything else she felt hands take hold of her shoulders.

'Brace against me. The catch will be yours.'

She braced, feeling his muscles amplifying her stance. His

weight, too; over the last few weeks he had at last filled out. Even allowing for their different life timescales, he was younger than her, just coming into full adulthood – but she had the impression he had now arrived.

Merish, now that had been more difficult. She had assumed – all sorts of things.

And he had shaken his head. 'I can't, Sel.'

She thought she had concealed her flinch, but he seemed to have seen it. His eyes darkened. 'Seldyan? It's not about gender, or anything like that. It's just that . . .'

He paused, and she finished the sentence for him. 'It's just that you're better at things than at people. Okay, I get it.'

He nodded. 'I'm really sorry, Sel.'

Somehow she had grinned. 'Stay in touch,' she said. And he had nodded. The ship had made its brief apologies seconds later, and then they were both gone. The best she could do, through eyes which were defiantly dry, was to watch the space they left behind, like a tribute.

The line jumped again, and then danced against her hands. She remembered the instructions: *Don't fight when you don't have to. Let the fish do the fighting.*

It did, for almost an hour. They could have used nets but this was the old way, Belbis had said. *This way you know your fight, and yourself.*

And the one holding you, she thought.

When they finally landed it, the fish was half her height. Not vast, as far as she knew, but adequate.

And it was her first.

Belbis was effusive. By the time they were halfway back to Three Quarter Circle harbour he had promised her a feast, and acclaim, and . . . everything.

Yes. Her first – and probably his. She let herself lean against the bracing arms, just for a moment, and it was happiness.

Flamejob/Suck on This

'*So, where do we go?*'
Merish shook his head. 'I don't know. What do you recommend?'

'*Well, perhaps . . .*'

There was no sense of acceleration, as long as he didn't look at the display – but of course he did. Planets and stars receded in streaks that started a sulky red and flared through all the colours into acidic violet before disappearing – and then they were still, and he looked and laughed.

'Is that it?'

'*Yes. The Spin. It may surprise you but in ten thousand years I have never found the time to do this.*'

'Really?' Merish stared down – or across, or up, he wasn't sure – at the galactic toy. 'I would have.'

'*I'm sure. If I get the chance again, so will I.*'

'If?'

'*Well, I have the impression that you maintain no particular connections with the worlds below. And, that being so, there are other places.*'

'I don't want to cramp your style.'

'*Oh, you won't. As long as I am not cramping yours.*'

Merish thought about that for a moment. Eventually he said, 'Look, if we both stop being polite this relationship might get off to a better start.'

Beacon Planet (Rehabilitated)

The planet – our planet – is recovering slowly. For the first time we are able to spend some time on the surface unprotected. It is good to see the gradual recovery of the old forests, to hear the sounds of familiar creatures emerging and to feel the wet breezes begin to blow, as the chemicals clear.

Although we had time – almost infinite time – we had no plan. Only an ability to wait, to watch, and when we could, to nudge things gently in a direction we hoped would be favourable.

The theft of the old machine from the Archive gave us our opportunity; the rogue ship gave us the means – and far more besides. It is in orbit now, and its many little servants, swirling around us, are the agents of recovery for our planet as the natural green and grey and brown of our home replaces the bright beacon it was.

We remembered. Our memories were passed on from one generation to the next, preserved in their immortal, multiply redundant gestalt. We remembered the creation of the Archive and the expulsion from our home that went with it.

And finally, we found Vess, the stoical one, unfailingly

honest in his hatred of insects and therefore, paradoxically, the one human we could trust with our young.

We the Vut fled here on the ship that became our friend.
We the Vutvess followed. And we will remember.

Acknowledgements

Thanks to Lara, for stupid much, and to that talented writer L. J. Frances, for being a buddy.

About the Author

Andrew Bannister grew up in Cornwall. He studied Geology at Imperial College and went to work in the North Sea before becoming an environmental consultant. A specialist in sustainability and the built environment, he presently works on major construction contracts for public bodies in the UK and internationally. He has always written, initially for student newspapers and fanzines before moving on to fiction, and he has always read science fiction. These things finally came together in his debut novel, *Creation Machine*, set in an artificial cluster of stars and planets called the Spin. Andrew Bannister lives in Leicestershire.

To find out more, visit andrewbannister.com